_Al..._

Alan Furst has lived for lon... Paris, and has travelled as a ... Russia. He has written exte... _Inter-national Herald Tribune._ _The Polish Officer_ is his third novel – with _Night Soldiers_ and _Dark Star_ – about espionage in the Europe of the 1930s and World War II.

'My discovery of the year.' William Boyd, _The Times_

'Nothing can be like watching _Casablanca_ for the first time, but Furst comes closer than anyone has in years.' _Time_

THE POLISH OFFICER

A compelling work. Furst's telling of one Polish intelligence officer's war, against the Nazis, against the Soviets, against inhumanity when he can, is remarkable. The tension becomes acute as the bleak, ghastly atmosphere in Nazi-occupied Europe closes in on de Milja and the reader. . . brilliant.'

John Sweeney, _Observer_

'The best spy novel I have read in years. Perhaps the reason is that it is so much more than a spy novel: it is a moving love story; it is full of carefully observed and utterly unromanticised tradecraft; and the reader will learn more about the actual business of intelligence from this novel than from nearly all other "spy novelists" combined. This is a riveting "pure" story, rich with character, wonderfully exact. _The Polish Officer_ transcends the spy novel while delivering everything any fan of le Carré could ask for.' _Boston Globe_

'_The Polish Officer_ portrays ordinary men and women caught out on the sharp edge of military intelligence operations in wartime: the partisans, saboteurs, resistance fighters and idealistic volunteers risking their lives in causes that seem lost. Brilliantly imagined, vividly drawn, rich with incident and detail. . . amongst the most exciting and satisfying adventure stories I know.' _Chicago Tribune_

DARK STAR

NIGHT SOLDIERS

BY ALAN FURST

Night Soldiers
Dark Star
The Polish Officer

ALAN FURST

THE POLISH
OFFICER

HarperCollins*Publishers*

HarperCollins*Publishers*
77-85 Fulham Palace Road,
Hammersmith, London W6 8JB

This paperback edition 1996

1 3 5 7 9 8 6 4 2

First published in Great Britain by
HarperCollins*Publishers* 1995

Copyright © Alan Furst 1995

The Author asserts the moral right to be
identified as the author of this work

ISBN 0 00 649356 4

Set in Perpetua

Printed in Great Britain by
HarperCollinsManufacturing Glasgow

THE
PILAVA
LOCAL

In Poland, on the night of 11 September 1939, Wehrmacht scout and commando units—elements of Kuechler's Third Army Corps—moved silently around the defenses of Novy Dvor, crossed the Vistula over the partly demolished Jablonka Bridge, and attempted to capture the Warsaw Telephone Exchange at the northern edge of the city. Meeting unexpected, and stubborn, resistance, they retreated along Sowacki Street and established positions on the roof and in the lobby of the Hotel Franconia, called for dive-bomber attacks on the exchange building, and settled in to wait for the light of dawn.

Mr. Felix Malek, proprietor of the Franconia, put on his best blue suit, and, accompanied by a room-service waiter, personally served cognac to the German soldiers at their mortar and machine-gun positions. He then descended to the wine cellar, opened the concealed door to an underground passage originally dug during the Prussian attack of 1795, hurried down Sowacki Street to the telephone exchange, and asked to see "the gentleman in charge."

He was taken up a marble staircase to the director's office on the fifth floor and there, beneath a somber portrait of the director—pince-nez and brushed whiskers—presented to the officer in command, a captain. The captain was an excellent listener, and the questions he asked inspired Mr. Malek to talk for a long time. Arms, unit size, insignia, the location of positions—he was surprised at how much he knew.

When he was done, they gave him tea. He asked if he might remain at the exchange, it would be an honor to fight the Germans. No, they said, perhaps another day. So Mr. Malek made his way through the night to his sister's apartment in the Ochota district. "And what," she asked, "were they like?"

Mr. Malek thought a moment. "Educated," he said. "Quite the better class of people."

Mr. Malek had not been thirty years an innkeeper for nothing: the defenders of the Warsaw Telephone Exchange, hastily recruited amidst the chaos of the German invasion, were officers of Polish Military Intelligence, known, in imitation of the French custom, as the Deuxième Bureau. The Breda machine gun at the casement window was served by a lieutenant from the cryptographic service, a pair of spectacles folded carefully in his breast pocket. The spidery fellow reloading ammunition belts was, in vocational life, a connoisseur of the senior civil service of the U.S.S.R., while the commander of the machine gun, feet propped on the tripod, was Lieutenant Karlinski, heavy and pink, who in normal times concerned himself with the analysis of Baltic shipping.

The officer in charge, Captain Alexander de Milja, was professionally a cartographer; first a mapmaker, later assistant director of the bureau's Geographical Section. But Poland was at war—no, Poland had lost her war, and it was clear to the captain that nobody was going to be assistant director of anything for a long time to come.

Still, you couldn't just stop fighting. Captain de Milja stood at the open window; the night air, cool and damp, felt especially good on his hands. *Idiot!* He'd grabbed the overheated barrel of the machine gun to change it during the attack, and now he had red stripes on his palms that hurt like hell.

4:20 A.M. He swept the façade of the hotel with his binoculars, tried—based on the proprietor's intelligence—counting up floors to focus on certain rooms, but the Germans had the windows shut and all he could see was black glass. In Sowacki Square, a burned-out trolley, and the body of a Wehrmacht trooper, like a bundle of rags accidentally left in a doorway, weapon and ammunition long gone. To somebody's attic. De Milja let the binoculars hang on their strap and stared out into the city.

A refinery had been set on fire; a tower of heavy smoke rolled majestically into the sky and the clouds glowed a faint orange. A machine gun tapped in the distance, a plane droned overhead, artillery rumbled across the river. War—fire and smoke—had made autumn come early, dead leaves rattled along the cobblestones and caught in the iron drain covers.

Captain de Milja was a soldier, he knew he didn't have long to live. And, in truth, he didn't care. He was not in love with life. One or two things had to be taken care of, then matters could run their course.

The director's telephone was, naturally, of the very latest style; black, shiny, Bakelite plastic. De Milja dialed the military operator he had installed in the basement.

"Sir?"

"Sergeant, have you tried Tarnopol again?"

"Can't get through, sir. I've been up to Wilno, and down to Zakopane, just about every routing there is, but the whole region's down. We're pretty sure the lines have been cut, sir."

"You'll keep trying."

"Yes, sir."

"Thank you, Sergeant."

He replaced the receiver carefully on its cradle. He had wanted to say good-bye to his wife.

The Wehrmacht assault team got its air support at dawn; three Focke-Wulf 189s diving out of the clouds, engines screaming, cannon firing. But there was more drama than destruction; the 189 carried only one bomb. On the fifth floor of the telephone exchange, Lieutenant Karlinski swept the Breda across the sky and hammered off belt after belt of 7.35 ammunition. Grand streams of tracer, pale in the early light, showered up into the clouds, while hot casings ejected onto the director's Persian carpet and the office smelled like smoldering wool— until a bullet fired from the ballroom of the Hotel Franconia hit Karlinski in the collarbone and he collapsed back onto the floor and died of shock.

The lieutenant from the cryptographic service took over, while Captain de Milja steadied the tripod with his burning hands and the Russian bureaucracy expert fed belts into the gun. But by then the Focke-Wulfs had run dry of ammunition and headed back to Germany. At which point the telephone rang and somebody on the first floor, voice flat and controlled, informed de Milja that the building was on fire.

For a moment he went blank, the solution much too obvious. Then he said, "Call the fire department." Which they did and which, on 12 September, worked quite well because the city's water mains hadn't yet been destroyed. The firemen ran their hoses into the building on the side away from the fighting and pumped high-pressure streams on the flames, putting out the fire and, as water sluiced down into the switching stations, shutting down every telephone in Warsaw.

The Wehrmacht attack, from doorway to doorway up Sowacki Street, faltered, then collapsed. The support fire, machine-gun and mortar, from the roof of the hotel lasted less than a minute, then the positions were abandoned. Just before dawn de Milja had sent sniper teams to the roofs of adjacent buildings, and when the fighting started they'd knocked down first a mortar man, then an officer. It was improvised—the snipers were armed with hunting weapons and policemen's automatic pistols—but it worked.

De Milja watched through binoculars as an analyst from the economic intelligence section—the captain thought he specialized in feed grains—a man in his fifties wearing suspenders and a shirt turned up at the sleeves, suddenly appeared at a parapet on the roof of an apartment building and fired both barrels of an old shotgun, the sort of thing one found in the back halls of country houses, along with leather game bags and warped tennis rackets.

The sniper broke the shotgun and withdrew the empty cartridges. Smoke seeped from the barrels as he thrust new shells into the breech. *Get down,* the captain thought. He saw two German troopers at an upper window, bringing their rifles to bear. *Down.* The sniper lurched backward, his face showed a moment of pain. But he kept his balance, braced one foot against the parapet and fired both barrels. His shoulder jerked with the recoil, then he fell to his knees, shaking his head grimly at whatever was going on inside him.

The Wehrmacht units retreated minutes later, trying to break through to German lines after dark. Most never made it, victims of small bands of soldiers, farmers, teenagers—Poles. And those who got as far as the Jablonka Bridge found that, on the second try, demolition had been complete. The ones who couldn't swim were found on the bank the following morning.

16 September, 5:40 P.M. Military Intelligence headquarters, Savka barracks. Order 3135-c: *With exception of special documents identified by department directors, all files to be destroyed by 1800 hours.*

Captain de Milja watched, motionless, one foot on a chair, as this work was done, as the department clerks burned eight thousand maps. Watched, apparently, without feeling. Perhaps he didn't care, or cared too much, or had gone off wherever he went when life was too cruel or too stupid. Whatever the truth, his eyes were cold, he could not be read.

The clerks had built a pinewood fire in the great hall, in a fireplace of heroic proportions with the date 1736 carved in the capstone, a fireplace built to roast spitted boar for a cavalry squadron. But this was a clerks' fire, it smoked and sputtered,

. and the maps, printed on linen and mounted on wooden rollers, did not burn well.

The office wit had always claimed that the department's chief clerk suffered from Talpidia, mole-face, a condition encountered in particularly subterranean bureaucracies. The man had been, certainly, a fierce obstructionist—everything had to be signed, and signed, and signed some more. Now, as his clerks ran by him with armloads of maps, he just seemed lost, poked dispiritedly at the ashes with a broom handle, the flames' reflections flickering on his eyeglasses.

Drawer 4088: Istanbul by street. Istanbul harbor with wharf and warehouse numbers. Surveyor's elevations of Üsküdar with shore batteries in scale. Bosphorus with depths indicated. Black Sea coast: coves, inlets, bridges, roads. Sea of Marmara coast: coves, inlets, bridges, roads.

In the fire.

Drawer 4098: Timber company surveys, 1935–1938; streams, logging paths, old and new growth trees, drainage, road access, river access. For forests in Poland, Byelorussia, and the Ukraine.

"That series aside, please," de Milja said.

The clerk, startled, whirled and stared, then did as he was ordered. The timber surveys were stacked neatly atop maps, drawn in fine detail, of the Polish railway system.

16 September, 7:15 P.M. A message was brought by a young ensign, who saluted and stood stiffly at attention while the captain read it. Colonel Anton Vyborg requested his presence, in fifteen minutes, at the guardhouse by the east gate; another officer had been sent to supervise the destruction of the files. The captain initialed the message carefully, then made sure he was on time.

They walked in the stables of the cavalry barracks, added to the Savka fortress when the Tenth Polish Hussars rode with Bonaparte in the Napoleonic Wars. The indoor riding ring—a floor of raked dirt below ax-hewn beams—was by tradition the regimental *champ d'honneur;* not just pistols at thirty paces, but duels on horseback with cavalry sabers. Beyond the riding ring, the horse barns. The horses stamped their hooves and whickered softly as the officers approached. The air smelled good to de Milja; manure and straw, autumn evening and Vyborg's cigar. Not the smell of burning buildings, not the smell of burning paper. A cloud of gnats hung in the still air, the light fading slowly from dusk into darkness.

There was something of the Baltic knight in Colonel Vyborg In his forties, he was tall and lean and thin-lipped, with webbed lines at the corners of eyes made to squint into blizzards, and stiff, colorless hair cut short in the cavalry-officer fashion. He wore high leather boots, supple and dark, well-rubbed with saddle soap. His job was to direct the work of intelligence officers—usually but not always military attachés in foreign postings—who operated secret agents.

"Have one of these," Vyborg said.

Vyborg lit the captain's small cigar, then spoke quietly as they walked. "As of tonight, our situation is this: there are fifty-two German divisions in Poland, about a million and a half soldiers, led by thousands of tanks. Our air force was blown up on the ground the first morning. Our allies, France and England, have declared war, and made gestures—of course, we had hoped for more. America is neutral, and disinterested. So, as usual, we find ourselves alone. Worse, Stalin has forty divisions on the eastern border and all our intelligence indicates an attack within hours. Meanwhile, we have half a million men in uniform—or, rather, had. Our communications have broken down, but we know of a hundred thousand casualties and a hundred thousand taken prisoner. Probably it's worse than that. I suppose our view of the immediate future is implicit in the fact that we are burning the files. But it's not the first time, and this *is* Poland, and, for us at least, all is not necessarily lost. You agree?"

"I do, sir."

"Good. We want to offer you a job, but I'm to emphasize that you have a choice. You can go out to one of the regular combat divisions—we're going to make a stand at the Bzura River, and, in addition, some units are going to try and hold out in the Pripet Marshes in the eastern provinces. The nation is defeated, but the *idea* of the nation mustn't be. So, if that's what you want to do, to die on the battlefield, I won't stop you."

"Or?"

"Or come to work for us. Over on the west side of the building—at least that's where we used to be. It's no small decision, but time's the one thing we don't have. The city's almost completely cut off, and by tomorrow there'll be no getting out. The Germans won't try to break in, they know they'll pay in blood for that and they aren't quite so brave as their reputation makes them out. They'll continue to send the bomber flights, unopposed, and they'll sit out there where we can't get at them and shell the city. We'll take it as long as we can, then we'll sign something to get it stopped."

"And then?"

"And then the war will begin."

A horse leaned over the gate of its stall and the colonel stopped to run his hand through its mane. "Wish I had an apple for you," Vyborg said. "What about it, Captain, shall we shoot these beasts? Or let the Germans have them?"

"Can they be hidden? In stables with cart horses, perhaps?"

"It's hard to hide valuable things from Germans, Captain. Very hard."

They walked in silence for a time. A flight of Heinkel bombers passed overhead; both officers looked up, then waited. The bombs fell on the southern part of the city, a noise like rapid peals of thunder, then the planes turned away, a few antiaircraft rounds burst well below and behind them, and the silence returned as the sound of engines faded.

"Well?" Vyborg said.

"The west side of the building, Colonel."

"You know the sorts of things that go on if the Germans get hold of people like us, Captain."

"Yes, sir."

"A dossier has been prepared for you—we assumed that you would accept the offer. It will be delivered to your office when you return. It assigns a nom de guerre—we don't want anyone to know who you are. It has also some memoranda written over the last forty-eight hours, you will want to review that for a nine-fifteen meeting in my office. Questions?"

"No questions, sir."

"There's a great deal of improvisation at the moment, but we're not going into the chaos business anytime soon. We're going to lose a war, not our minds. And not our souls."

"Understood, sir."

"Anything you want to say?"

"With regard to my wife—"

"Yes?"

"She's in a private clinic. In the countryside, near Tarnopol."

"An illness?"

"She is—the doctor puts it that she has entered a private world."

Vyborg shook his head in sympathy and scowled at the idea of illness attacking people he knew.

"Can she be rescued?"

Vyborg thought it over. Senior intelligence officers became almost intuitive about possibility—some miracles could be done, some couldn't. Once initiated, above a certain rank, you knew.

"I'm sorry," the colonel said.

The captain inclined his head; he understood, it need not be further discussed. They walked in silence for a time, then the colonel said, "We'll see you at nine-fifteen, then."

"Yes, sir."

"Officially, we're glad to have you with us." They shook hands. The captain saluted, the colonel returned the salute.

A quarter moon, red with fire, over the Vilna station railyards.

The yard supervisor wore a bandage over one eye, his suit and shirt had not been changed for days, days of crawling under freight cars, of floating soot and oily smoke, and his hands were trembling. He was ashamed of that, so had wedged them in his pockets as though he were a street-corner tough who whistled at girls.

"This was our best," he said sadly. Captain de Milja flicked the beam of his flashlight over a passenger car with its roof peeled back. A woman's scarf, light enough to float in the wind, was snagged on a shard of iron. "Bolen Coachworks," the supervisor said. "Leaded-glass lamps in the first-class compartments. Now look."

"What's back there?" de Milja asked.

"Nothing much. Just some old stock we pulled in from the local runs—the Pruszkow line, Wolomin."

Cinders crunched under their feet as they walked. Yard workers with iron bars and acetylene torches were trying to repair the track. There were showers of blue sparks and the smell of scorched metal as they cut through the twisted rail.

"And this?"

The supervisor shrugged. "We run little trains to the villages, on market days. This is what's left of the Solchow local. It was caught by a bombing raid on Thursday, just past the power station. The engineer panicked, he had his fireman uncouple the engine and they made a run for Vilna station. Maybe he thought he'd be safe under the roof, though I can't imagine why, because it's a glass roof, or it used to be. When the all clear sounded, the engine had been blown to pieces but the rest of the train was just left sitting out there on the track, full of angry old farm ladies and crates of chickens.''

De Milja and the supervisor climbed the steps into the coach. The captain's flashlight lit up the aisle; wooden floorboards, buckled and gray with age, frayed wicker seats—once yellow, now brown—chicken feathers, a forgotten basket. From the other end of the car came a deep, heavy growl. *What are you doing here?* de Milja thought. ''Come,'' he said.

There was a moment of silence, then another growl. This time it didn't mean *prepare to die*—more like *not yet*.

''Come here.'' *You know you have to.*

A huge head appeared in the aisle, thrust cautiously from a hiding place behind a collapsed seat. De Milja masked the flashlight beam and the dog came reluctantly, head down, to accept its punishment. To have deserved what had happened to it the last few days, it reasoned, it must have been very, very bad. De Milja went down on one knee and said, ''Yes, it's all right, it's all right.''

It was a male Tatra, a sheepdog related to the Great Pyrenees. De Milja sank his hands into the deep hair around the neck, gripped it hard and tugged the head toward him. The dog knew this game and twisted back against de Milja, but the man's hands were too strong. Finally the dog butted his head against the captain's chest, took a huge breath and sighed so deeply it was almost a growl.

''Perhaps you could find some water,'' de Milja said to the supervisor.

His family had always had dogs, kept at the manor house of the estate in the Volhynia, in eastern Poland. They hunted with them, taking a wild boar every autumn in the great forest, a scene from a medieval tapestry. The Tatra was an off-white, like most mountain breeds, a preferred color that kept the shepherd from clubbing his own dog when they fought night-raiding wolves. De Milja put his face into the animal's fur and inhaled the sweet smell.

The yard supervisor returned, a bowl filled to the brim with milk held carefully in his hands. This was a small miracle, but "he must be hungry" was all he had to say about it.

"What's your name?" de Milja asked.

"Koski."

"Can you keep a big dog, Mr. Koski?"

The yard supervisor thought a moment, then shrugged and said, "I guess so."

"It will take some feeding."

"We'll manage."

"And this kind of coach?" The captain nodded at it. "Have you got six or so?"

"All you want."

"Same color. Yellow, with red around the windows."

Koski tried to conceal his reaction. The middle of a war, Germans at the outskirts of the city, and this man wanted "the same color." Well, you did what you had to do. "If you can wait for daylight, we'll freshen up the paint."

"No, it's good just like that. We'll need a coal tender, of course, and a locomotive. A freight locomotive."

Koski stared at his shoes. They had improvised, borrowed parts, kept running all sorts of stock that had no business running—but freight locomotives were a sore subject. Nobody had those. Well, he had *one*. Well and truly hidden. Was this the moment? "Six red-and-yellow coaches," he said at last. "Tender, freight locomotive. That it?"

De Milja nodded. "In about, say, an hour."

Koski started to shout, something like *can't you see I'm doing the best I can?* But a covert glance at de Milja changed his mind— he wasn't someone you would say that to, much less shout it.

De Milja looked to be in his late thirties, but there was something about him, some air of authority, that was much older than that. He had dark hair, cut short and cut very well, and a pale forehead that people noticed. Eyes the color—according to his wife—of a February sea, shifting somewhere between gray and green. His face was delicate, arrogant, hard; people said different things. In any event, he was a very serious man, that was obvious, with hands bigger than they ought to have been, and blunt fingers. He wore no insignia, just a brown raincoat over a gray wool sweater. There was a gun, somewhere. He stood, relaxed but faintly military, waiting for the yard supervisor to agree to make up his train in an hour. This man came, Koski thought, from the war, and when the war went away, if it ever did, so would he and all the others like him.

The supervisor nodded yes, of course he could have his train. The dog stopped lapping at the bowl, looked up and whined, a drop of milk falling from his beard. A yellow flame burst from the hillside above the yards and the flat crump of an explosion followed. The brush burned for a few seconds, then the fire died out as smoke and dust drifted down the hill.

Koski had flinched at the explosion, now he jammed his shaking hands deeper into his pockets. "Not much left to bomb here," he said.

"That wasn't a bomb," de Milja said. "It was a shell."

17 September, 3:50 A.M. Freight locomotive, coal tender, six passenger cars from a market-day local. The yard supervisor, the Tatra by his side, watched as it left the railyards. Then it crossed Praga, a workers' suburb across the Vistula from Warsaw, and headed for the city on the single remaining railroad bridge. Captain de Milja stood in the cab of the locomotive and stared down into the black water as the train clattered across the ties.

For a crew, Koski had done the best he could on short notice. A fireman, who would shovel coal into the steam engine's furnace, and a conductor would be joining the train in Warsaw. The engineer, standing next to de Milja, had been, until that night, retired. He was a sour man, with a double chin and a lumpy nose, wearing an engineer's cap, well oiled and grimed, and a pensioner's blue cardigan sweater with white buttons.

"Fucking *shkopy*," he said, using the Polish word for Germans equivalent to the French *boche*. He peered upriver at the blackened skeleton of the Poniatowski Bridge. "I had all I wanted of them in 'seventeen."

The Germans had marched into Warsaw in 1917, during the Great War. De Milja had been sixteen, about to enter university, and while his family had disliked the German entry into Poland, they'd seen one positive side to it: Russian occupiers driven back east where they belonged.

The firebox of the locomotive glowed faintly in the dark, just enough light to jot down a few figures on the iron wall. He had to haul a total of 88,000 pounds: 360 people—43,000 pounds of them if you figured young and old, fat and thin, around 120 pounds a person. Sharing the train with 44,530 pounds of freight.

So, 88,000 pounds equaled 44 tons. Figuring two tons to a normal freight car, a locomotive could easily pull twenty cars. His six passenger coaches would be heavy, but that didn't matter—they had no suspension to speak of, they'd roll along if the locomotive could pull them.

"What are you scribbling?" The irritation of an old man. To the engineer's way of thinking, a locomotive cab wasn't a place for writing.

De Milja didn't answer. He smeared the soft pencil jotting with his palm, put the stub of pencil back in his pocket. The sound of the wheels changed as the train came off the bridge and descended to a right-of-way cut below ground level and spanned by pedestrian and traffic bridges: a wasteland of tracks, signals, water towers, and switching stations. Was the 44,530 correct? He resisted the instinct to do the figures again. Seven hundred and twelve thousand ounces *always* made 44,530 pounds, which, divided into five-pound units, *always* made 8,906. It is mathematics, he told himself, it is always the same.

"You said Dimek Street bridge?"

"Yes."

The steam brake hissed and the train rolled to a stop. From a stairway that climbed the steep hillside to street level came a flashed signal. De Milja answered with his own flashlight. Then a long line of shadowy figures began to move down the stairs.

17 September, 4:30 A.M. While the train was being loaded, the conductor and the fireman arrived and shook hands with the engineer. Efficiently, they uncoupled the locomotive and coal tender and used a switching spur to move them to the other end of the train, so it now pointed east.

There were two people waiting for de Milja under the Dimek Street bridge: his former commander, a white-mustached major of impeccable manners and impeccable stupidity, serving out his time until retirement while his assistant did all the work, and de Milja's former aide, Sublieutenant Nowak, who would serve as his adjutant on the journey south.

The major shook de Milja's hand hard, his voice taut with emotion. "I know you'll do well," he said. "As for me, I am returning to my unit. They are holding a line at the Bzura River." It was a death sentence and they both knew it. "Good luck, sir," de Milja said, and saluted formally. The major returned the salute and disappeared into a crowd of people on the train.

Guards with machine guns had positioned themselves along the track, while a dozen carpenters pried up the floorboards of the railroad coaches and workers from the state treasury building installed the Polish National Bullion Reserve—$11,400,000 in five-pound gold ingots packed ten to a crate—in the ten-inch space below. Then, working quickly, the carpenters hammered the boards back into place.

At which point Nowak came running, his face red with anger. "You had better see this," he said. The carpenters were just finishing up. Nowak pointed at the shiny nailheads they'd hammered into the old gray wood.

"Couldn't you use the old nails?" de Milja said.

The head carpenter shrugged.

"Is there any lampblack?"

"Lampblack! No, of course not. We're carpenters, we don't have such things."

17 September, 6:48 A.M. Gdansk station. The platforms and waiting rooms were jammed with people, every age, every class, babbling in at least seven languages, only one thing in common: they were too late. Unlucky or unwise didn't matter, the trains had stopped. A stationmaster's voice crackled through the public-address system and tried to convince them of that, but nobody was willing to believe it. In Poland, things happened in mysterious ways—authority itself was often struck speechless at life's sudden turns.

For instance:

The stationmaster's voice, "Please, ladies and gentlemen, I entreat you, there will be no more service . . . ," was slowly drowned out by the rumble of an approaching train. People surged to the edges of the platforms, police struggled to hold them back.

Then the crowd fell silent, and stopped pushing.

A war train. It had started raining, and water glistened on the iron plates in the twilight of the high-roofed station. The voice of the engine was deep and rhythmic, like a drum, and machine-gun barrels thrust through firing ports traversed the platform. This was a Russian-style armored train, a Bolshevik weapon, a peasant killer—it meant burnt villages and weeping women and everybody in Gdansk station knew it. The train, too heavy for its engine, moved at a crawl, so the crowd could see the faces, cold and attentive, of the antiaircraft gunners in their sand-bagged nests on the roofs of the cars.

Then someone cheered. And then someone else. And then

everybody. Poland had been brutally stabbed in the back, and so she bled, bled fiercely, but here was proof that she lived, and could strike back at those who tormented her.

But that was only part of the miracle. Because, only a few minutes later, another train appeared. And if the armored train was an image of war, here was a phantom from the time of peace, a little six-car train headed south for—or so the signs on the sides of the coaches said—Pilava. The Pilava train! Only thirty miles south, but at least not in besieged Warsaw. Everybody had an aunt in Pilava, you went there on a Sunday afternoon and came home with half a ham wrapped in a cloth. Vladimir Herschensohn, pressed by the crowd against a marble column, felt his heart rise with joy. Somehow, from somewhere, a manifestation of normal existence: a train arrives in a station, passengers ascend, life goes on.

But Mr. Herschensohn would not be ascending. He needed to, the Germans would make quick work of him and he knew it. But God had made him small, and as the crowd surged hungrily toward the empty train he actually found himself moving— helped along by a curse here, an elbow there—away from the track. After a moment or two of this, all he wanted to do was stay near enough to watch the train leave, to send some part of his spirit away to safety.

Watching from the cab of the locomotive, de Milja felt his stomach turn. The crowd was now a mob: if they got on this train, they would live. Babies howled, suitcases sprang open, men and women clawed and fought, policemen swung their batons. De Milja could hear the thuds, but he willed his face not to show what he felt and it didn't. A huge, brawny peasant shoved an old woman out of his way and started to climb onto the coupling between the engine and the coal car. The fireman waited until his weight hung on his hands, then kicked him full force under the chin. His head flew up and he went tumbling backward into the crowd. "Pig," the fireman said quietly, as though to himself.

But, in the end, the ones who pushed to the front were the ones who got on.

When the train was good and full, people packed into the cars, when it looked like a refugee train should look, de Milja raised his hand. Then something stopped him. Out in the crowd, his eye found a little peanut of a man in a long black overcoat, with a black homburg hat knocked awry. He was holding some sort of a case and an old-fashioned valise in one hand, and pressing a handkerchief to his bloody nose with the other. The policeman standing next to de Milja was red in the face and breathing hard. "Get me that man," de Milja said, pointing.

The policeman whistled through his teeth, a couple of colleagues joined him, and the little man was quickly retrieved, virtually carried through the crowd by the elbows and hoisted up to de Milja in the locomotive cab.

"Better go," the policeman said.

De Milja signaled to the conductor, who swung himself up onto the train. The engineer worked his levers and blew a long blast on the whistle as the heavily laden train moved slowly out of Gdansk station.

"Thank you," said the little man. He was somewhere in his forties, de Milja thought, with the face of a Jewish imp. "I am Vladimir Herschensohn." He extended his hand, and de Milja shook it. Herschensohn saw that de Milja was staring at his battered violin case. "I am," he added, "the principal violinist of the Polish National Symphony Orchestra."

De Milja inclined his head in acknowledgment.

"So," Herschensohn said. "We are going to Pilava." He had to raise his voice above the chuff of the locomotive, but he managed a tone of great politeness.

"South of there," was all de Milja said.

. . .

At the 9:15 meeting with Colonel Vyborg, de Milja had brought up the issue: what to tell the passengers. "What you like, when you like, you decide," Vyborg had said.

Vyborg's room had been crowded—people sitting on desks, on the floor, everywhere. De Milja knew most of them, and what they had in common was a certain ruthless competence. Suddenly the days of office politics, family connections, the well-fed wink, were over. Now the issue was survival, and these officers, like de Milja, found themselves given command and assigned to emergency operations.

The agenda of the meeting was long and difficult and devoted to a single topic: the dispersion to safety of the national wealth. War cost money and Poland meant to keep fighting. And there wasn't that much. A country like Great Britain had a national wealth of two hundred million dollars, but Poland had only been alive as an independent nation since 1918—this time around—and owned barely a tenth of that.

Stocks and bonds and letters of deposit on foreign banks were going to leave the port of Gdynia on a Danish passenger liner. British pounds, French francs, and American dollars were to be flown out at night by one of the last remaining air-force transports, while millions of Polish zlotys and German reichsmarks were being buried in secret vaults in Warsaw—they would be needed there. Senior code and cipher experts, the cream of Polish intelligence, had already left the country. And it was de Milja's job to take out the gold reserve, carrying it by train to Romania, where another group would move it on to Paris, the time-honored host to Polish governments-in-exile.

From Gdansk station they traveled slowly through the central districts of the city, where crews were filling bomb craters and repairing rail by the light of fires in oil drums. They crossed the railroad bridge back into Praga, then turned south on the eastern bank of the Vistula. Soon the city was behind them, and the track left the river and curved gently southeast, toward the city of Lublin.

The conductor who'd gotten on the train at the Dimek Street bridge was a man of old-fashioned manners and grave demeanor, with a droopy mustache, a conductor's hat one size too large, and a limp from wounds received when his train was dive-bombed in the first hours of the war. When he'd reported to de Milja at the bridge, he had stood at attention and produced from his belt a 9 mm Parabellum pistol—a 1914 cannon—and informed de Milja that he'd fought the Bolsheviks in 1921, and was prepared to send a significant number of Germans straight to hell if he got the opportunity.

As the train chugged through the Polish countryside, the conductor went from car to car and made a little speech. "Ladies and gentlemen, your attention, please. Soon we will be stopping at Pilava; those who wish to get off the train are invited to do so. However, this train will not be returning to Warsaw, it is going all the way to Lvov, with brief stops at Lublin and Tomaszow. The military situation in the south is unclear, but the railroad will take you as far as you wish to travel. Passage is without charge. Thank you."

From the last car, de Milja watched the crowd carefully. But the reaction was subdued: a number of family conferences conducted in urgent whispers, an avalanche of questions that God himself, let alone a train conductor, couldn't have answered, and more than a little head shaking and grim smiling at the bizarre twists and turns that life now seemed to take. The Polish people, de Milja realized, had already absorbed the first shock of war and dislocation; now it was a question of survival; ingenuity, improvisation, and the will to live through catastrophe and see the other side of it. So when the train stopped at Pilava, only a few people got off. *The farther from Warsaw the better*—what consensus there was among the passengers seemed to follow that line of reasoning.

For a time, the countryside itself proved them right. South of

Pilava there was no war, only a rainy September morning, a strip of pale sky on the horizon, harvested fields, birch groves, and tiny streams. The air smelled of damp earth and the coming October. The leaves a little dry now, and rustling in the wind.

De Milja's mother was the Countess Ostrowa, and her brothers, known always as "the Ostrow uncles," had taken it upon themselves to teach him about life; about dogs and horses and guns, servants and mistresses. They were from another time—a vanished age, his father said—but his mother adored them and they lived hard, drunken, brutal, happy lives and never bothered to notice they were in the wrong century.

His father was an aristocrat of another sort: second son of a family occupied for generations with polite commerce, senior professor of economics at Jagiello university. He was an arid man, tall and spare, who had been old all his life and who, in his heart, didn't really think very much of the human mammal. The vaguely noble name de Milja, pronounced *de Milya,* he shooed away with his hand, admitting there was a village in Silesia, some forty miles from where the family originated, called Milja, but the aristocratic formation he ascribed to "some Austro-Hungarian nonsense my grandfather meddled with" and would never say any more about it. Exiled to the top floor of the family house in Warsaw, he lived by the light of a green-glass lamp amid piles of German periodicals and stacks of woody paper covered with algebraic equations rendered in fountain pen.

So de Milja's world, from its earliest days, had a cold north and a hot south, and he spent his time going back and forth; as a boy, as a young man, maybe, he thought, forever. The uncles laughing and roaring downstairs, throwing chicken bones in the fire, grabbing the maids' bottoms, and passing out on the sofas with their boots on the pillows. Up two flights, a family of storks nested among the chimneys on the opposite roof and his father explained spiders and thunder.

They'd married de Milja off when he was nineteen. The fami-

lies had known each other forever, he and Helena were introduced, left alone, and encouraged to fall in love. She probably
saw the wisdom of all this much more clearly than he did—
gazed at his belt buckle, kissed him with swollen lips and a hand
on his jaw, and he was hers. Two weeks before the wedding, his
favorite Ostrow uncle had taken him into a disused parlor, the
furniture covered with sheets, where they fortified themselves
with Armagnac, and his uncle—scarlet face, shaved head, glori-
ous cavalry mustaches—had given him a premarital lovemaking
lesson with the aid of a dressmaker's dummy. "You're not a
bull, dammit!" he'd bellowed. "You don't mount her when
she's at the kitchen stove."

In the event, the problem did not arise: she never bent over
to get the bread out of the oven because she never put it in—
that was done by a series of country girls charitably called maids,
more than one of whom had flipped the back of her skirt at him.

Over time, Helena changed. At first she would flirt, touch
him accidentally with her breasts, and hold him between the legs
with both hands. But something happened, she would only make
love in the dark, sometimes cried, sometimes stopped. He
learned to work his way through her defenses, but in the process
discovered what she was defending. He began to realize that the
membrane that separated her from the world was too thin, that
she could not tolerate life.

She'd gotten pregnant, then lost the baby during an influenza
epidemic in the winter of 1925. That was the end. In the deep-
est part of himself he'd known it, known it the day it happened.
For three years, everyone pretended that everything would be
all right, but when little fires were started in the house she had
to go to the doctors and they prescribed a stay at a private clinic
near Tarnopol "for a few weeks."

Absence from the world cured her. He didn't say that back in
Warsaw, but it was true. Visiting once a month, bouquet in
hand, he could feel the calm she'd found. In fact she pitied him,
having to live amid anger and meanness. In good weather they

walked in the forest. She, wrapped in a shawl, said little, lived in a self-evident world—there was nothing to explain. Once in a great while she would reach over and take his hand, her way of saying thank you.

He woke suddenly, snapping his head erect just as his chin grazed his chest. He stood braced against the doorway of the last coach, track falling away through rolling fields, wheels in a steady clatter. When had he slept? Not for a long time.

He cleared his throat. Sublieutenant Nowak was pointedly looking elsewhere—no commanding officer of his, de Milja realized, would ever be seen to drift off.

"Coming into Deblin, Captain."

De Milja nodded. Nowak was too young—fresh-faced and eager. Out of uniform, in his Sunday suit, he looked like a student. "Map?"

Nowak unfolded it. Deblin was a river town, where the Wieprz flowed east into the Vistula. The route south continued into Pulawy, Krasnystaw, Zamosc, Tomaszow. Crossed the river Tanew into the Ukrainian districts of Poland at Rava-Russkaya. Then the major city of Lvov, down to Stryj, a sweep around the eastern tip of German-occupied Czechoslovakia—known as Little Ukraine—into Uzhgorod, and finally across the border into the Romanian town of Sighet in the Carpathian Mountains.

Four hundred and fifty miles, more or less. With the locomotive making a steady thirty-five miles an hour, about fourteen hours. Nowak heard the airplanes at the same time as he did, and together they looked up into the clouds. A flight of Heinkel bombers, in *V* formation, headed a little east of due north. That meant they'd been working on one of the industrial cities in the south, maybe Radom or Kielce, and were on their way home, bomb bays hopefully empty, to an airfield in East Prussia, probably Rastenburg.

"Nothing for you down here," de Milja said quietly.

He'd done the best he could: it was just a little train, yellow coaches with red borders on the windows and a locomotive puffing through the wheat fields. Pastoral, harmless.

The Heinkels droned on. Below and behind them, a fighter escort of ME-109s. The pilots were bored. Sneak attacks on Polish airfields had blown up the opposition on the first day—and stolen their war. Now their job had little to do with skill or daring. They were nursemaids. From the wing position, a fighter plane sideslipped away from the formation, swooped down a sharp angle in a long, steep dive, flattened out in perfect strafing attitude, and fired its 20 mm cannon into the annoying little train chugging along below as though it hadn't a care in the world. The pilot had just broken off the attack, soaring up through the smoke of the locomotive's stack, when the radio crackled furiously and the flight leader gave a short, sharp order. The plane slipped back into formation, maintaining rigid spacing and perfect airspeed discipline all the way home to East Prussia.

The engineer remembered his orders and followed them: slowed down, rolled to a stop. Flight excites hunting dogs and fighter pilots, nothing standing still interests them for very long.

De Milja called out to Nowak as he swung off the platform: "Go through the cars, get the dead and wounded out, see if there's anybody who can help."

He ran along the track, then climbed into the cab of the locomotive. A column of steam was hissing from a hole in the firebox, the engineer was kneeling by the side of the fireman, who was lying on his back, his face the color of wood ash, a pale green shadow like a bruise already settled on his cheekbones. De Milja cursed to himself when he saw it.

The engineer was breathing hard; de Milja saw his chest rise and fall in the old cardigan. He went down on one knee and put a hand on the man's shoulder. "That was done well," he said. Then: "You're all right." More an order than a question, the *of course* unvoiced but clear.

The engineer pressed his lips together and shook his head—very close to tears. "My sister-in-law's husband," he said. "My wife said not to ask him."

De Milja nodded in sympathy. He understood, patted the man's shoulder twice, hard, before he took his hand away. The engineer said, "She—," but there was nothing more. It was quiet in the fields, the only sound the slow beat of the locomotive's pistons running with the engine at rest. A bird sang somewhere in the distance. The fireman raised his hands, palms up, like a shrug, then made a face. "Shit," he said. As de Milja leaned over him, he died.

Nowak had the casualties laid out in a beet field; a dark woman with hair braided and pinned worked over them. When de Milja arrived, she put him to work tearing cotton underdrawers into strips for bandages and sent Nowak running up to the locomotive for hot water.

"This man has been shot through the foot," she said, carefully removing the shoe. "Went in above the heel, came out the sole just here, behind the second toe." She put the bloody shoe aside. "Foot scares me, I'm unfamiliar with it."

"You're a nurse?"

"Veterinarian. A paw or a hoof, there I can help. Grab his hand." De Milja held the man's hand as the veterinarian swabbed on antiseptic from a big brown-glass bottle.

"A little girl is dead," she said. "She was about ten years old. And a man in his forties, over there. We looked and looked—there's not a mark on him. An old woman jumped out a window and broke her ankle. And a few others—cuts and bruises. But the angle of the gunfire was lucky for us—no glass, no fire. It's fire I hate." She worked in silence a moment. "It hurts?" she asked the patient.

"Go ahead, Miss. Do whatever you have to. Did I understand you to say that you were a veterinarian?"

"That's right."

"Hah! My friends will certainly get a laugh when they hear

that!'' De Milja's fingers throbbed from the pressure of the wounded man squeezing his hand.

A grave-digging crew was organized, which took turns using the fireman's shovel, and a priest said prayers as the earth was piled on. The little girl had been alone on the train, and nobody could find her papers. A woman who'd talked to her said her name was Tana, so that name was carved on the wooden board that served as a gravestone.

De Milja ordered the train stopped at a village station between Pulawy and Lublin, then used the phone in the stationmaster's office—he could barely hear through the static—to report the attack to Vyborg, and to revise the estimated time of arrival "in the southern city.''

"The Russian divisions have crossed the border,'' Vyborg said. "They may not reach your area for a day or so, but it's hard to predict. The Germans are headed west—giving up territory. We believe there's a line of demarcation between Hitler and Stalin, and the Russians will move up to occupy the new border.''

"Does that change anything for us?''

"No. But German aircraft have been attacking the line south of you. The railroad people say they can keep it open another twenty-four hours, but that's about it. Still, we think you ought to find cover, then continue after dark. Understood?''

"Yes, sir.''

"All the roads out of Warsaw are now cut. This office is closing down, so you're on your own from now on. Consider that to have the status of a written order.''

"Understood, sir.''

"So, best of luck to you. To all of us.''

The connection was broken.

A corporal in the Geographical Section had made a specialty of hiding trains. Using his hand-drawn map, de Milja directed the engineer to a branch line south of Pulawy that wound up into the hills above the Vistula. There, twenty miles west of Lublin, a gypsum mining operation had gone bankrupt and been shut down some time in the 1920s. But the railroad spur that ran to the site, though wildly overgrown, was still usable, and a roofed shed built for loading open railcars was still standing. Under the shed, with the engine turned off, they were very close to invisible.

17 September, 8:25 P.M. Over the years, the abandoned quarry had filled with water, and after dark de Milja could see the reflection of the rising moon on the still surface.

The engineer had patched the hole in the firebox, using tin snips, a tea tray, and wire. A big kid, about fifteen, from a farm village volunteered to work as the fireman—what he lacked in skill he'd make up with raw strength. Nowak took the opportunity to sight-in four rifles, which, with a few boxes of ammunition, had been hidden behind a panel in the last coach. He chose four men: a mechanic, a retired policeman, a student, and a man who didn't exactly want to say what he did, to be armed in case of emergency.

There wasn't much else they could do. The engine moved cautiously over the old track, heading east for the ancient city of Lublin, the countryside dark and deserted. The passengers were quiet, some doubtless having second thoughts about being cast adrift in a country at war. Maybe they would have been better off staying in Warsaw.

They reached Lublin a little after ten. Warehouses along the railroad line had been blazing since that afternoon, and the city's ruptured water mains meant that the fire department could do little more than watch. The train crawled through thick black coils of heavy smoke, the passengers had to wet handkerchiefs and put them over their noses and mouths in order to breathe. A brakeman flagged them down. De Milja went up to the locomotive.

"We've been ordered to get you people through," the brakeman said, "and the crews are doing the best they can. But they bombed us just before sunset, and it's very bad up ahead." The brakeman coughed and spat. "We had all the worst things down here; wool, creosote, tarred rope. Now it's just going to burn."

"Any sign of Russian troops?" de Milja asked.

"Not sure. We had a freight train disappear this morning. Vanished. What's your opinion about that?"

It took forever for them to work their way through Lublin. At one point, a shirtless work crew, bodies black with soot, laid twenty-five feet of track almost directly beneath their wheels. The passengers gagged on the smoke, tried to get away from it by taking turns lying flat in the aisle, rubbed at the oily film that clung to their hands and faces, but that only made it burn worse. Farther down the line an old wooden bridge had collapsed onto the track and the huge, charred timbers were being hauled away by blindfolded farm horses. A saboteur—identified as such by a sign hung around his neck—had been hanged from a signal stanchion above the track. A group of passengers came to the last coach and pleaded with de Milja to get off the train. Nowak got the engine stopped, and a small crowd of people scurried away down the firelit lanes of the old city.

And then, once again, the war was gone.

The train climbed gently into the uplands east of the Carpathians. Warsaw, a northern city, seemed a long way from here—this was the ragged edge of Europe, border land. They ran dark, the lamps turned off in the coaches, only the locomotive light sweeping along the rails where, as the night cooled, land mist drifted through the beam. Beyond that, the steppe. Treeless, empty, sometimes a few thatched huts around a well and a tiny dirt road that ran off into the endless distance, to

Russia, to the Urals. Now and then a village—a log station house with a Ukrainian name—but down here it was mostly the track and the wind.

De Milja stood beside the engineer and stared out into the darkness. The boy who'd taken the fireman's job fed coal to the firebox when the engineer told him to. His palms had blistered after an hour of shoveling, so he'd taken his shirt off and torn it in half and tied it around his hands. When he stepped away from the furnace he shivered in the night air, but he was a man that night and de Milja knew better than to say anything.

At some nameless settlement, the train stopped at a water tower, the engineer swung the spout into position and began to fill the tank. It was long after midnight, and deserted—only the sigh of the wind, moths fluttering in the engine light, and the splash of water. Then, suddenly, a girl was standing by the locomotive. She was perhaps sixteen, barefoot, wearing a soiled cotton shift, head scarf, and a thin shawl around her shoulders. She was the most beautiful girl that de Milja had ever seen. "Please, Your Excellency," she said—the dialect was ancient and de Milja barely understood her—"may I be permitted to ride on the train?"

She raised her hand, opened her fingers to reveal a pair of tiny gold earrings resting on her palm.

De Milja was speechless. The engineer, standing atop the front of the locomotive, stared down at her, and the boy stopped shoveling coal. The hem of the shift was spattered with mud, her ankles thin above dirty feet. She is pregnant, de Milja thought. She stood patiently, her eyes not quite meeting his, a sign of submission, her other hand clutching the shawl at her throat. But when de Milja did not speak, she looked directly at him and, just for an instant, her eyes lit up green fire as they caught the light, then she hid them away.

"Please, Excellency?" The earrings must not be worth what she thought; her voice faded in defeat.

"You do not have to pay," de Milja said.

Her face hid nothing, and it was plain how she had struggled, all her life, to understand things. She had never been on a train before, but she knew one or two people who had, and she had asked them about it, and one certainly had to pay. Atop the locomotive, the engineer swung the water spout away so that water splashed on the ground beside the tracks until he shut it off.

De Milja waited for her to ask where they were going, but she never did. "You may ride on the train," he said.

Still hesitant, she closed the earrings in her fist and held them to her throat. Then turned toward the passenger coaches. Did he mean what he said? Or was he just making fun of her? No, he meant it. Before he could change his mind she ran like a deer, climbed cautiously onto the iron step of the first coach, peered inside, then vanished.

Past Lvov, then Uzhgorod.

Sublieutenant Nowak took the watch for an hour, then a little after four in the morning de Milja returned. Now the train was climbing a grade that ran through a pine forest, then past Kulikov, then deeper into the mountains that marked the southern border of Poland.

Captain de Milja and the engineer saw the dim shape ahead at the same moment. De Milja wondered what it was, and squinted to bring it into focus. The old man swore and hauled on the brake with both hands. The wheels locked and screeched as they slid on the iron rails, and the train finally shuddered to a halt just short of the barrier, tree trunks piled across the track.

The light was strange at that hour—not night, not yet dawn—so the shapes coming toward them from the forest had no color, and seemed to glide on mist, like phantoms in a dream, with white plumes steaming from the horses' nostrils in the cold mountain air.

The bandit leader—or ataman, or headman, whatever he

called himself—was not to be hurried. Rifle at rest across his saddle, he walked his horse to the cab of the locomotive and stared at de Milja. "Get out," he said softly. This was Ukrainian, of which de Milja understood that much at least. The bandit was perhaps in his fifties, wore a peaked cap and a suit jacket. Two or three days' white bristle covered a stubborn jaw below the small, shrewd eyes of the farmer's most cherished pig.

De Milja jumped to the ground, the engineer followed, the boy did not. *Hiding,* de Milja thought. All along the train, passengers were filing out of the coaches, hands high above their heads, lining up at the direction of the bandits. The leader looked him over: where was the danger in him? Where the profit? De Milja met his gaze. Back by the coaches there was a rifle shot. The bandit watched to see what he would do, so he did not turn around to see what had happened.

"Who are you?" the leader asked.

"I work for the railroad."

The bandit did not quite believe that. "You ready to die up in a tree?" Ukrainian executions lasted all day. De Milja did not react.

"Hardheaded, you people," the leader said. "You're finished," he went on. "Now it's the Germans and us."

De Milja was silent.

"Carrying anything valuable on that train?"

"No. Just people heading for the border."

The bandit glanced back at the passenger coaches, de Milja followed his eyes. The passengers had their hands on the sides of the railcars, their baggage was laid out on the ground so that the bandits could pick and choose what they wanted.

A bandit on a gray pony rode up beside the leader. "Any good?" the leader asked.

"Not bad."

"Gold?"

"Some. Polish money. Jewelry."

"And the women?"

"Good. Four or five of them."

The bandit leader winked at de Milja. "You won't be seeing them again." He paused, something about de Milja fascinated him. "Come over here," he said. De Milja stepped forward, stood beside the bandit's boot in a stirrup. "Give me your watch. It would be a railroad watch, of course."

De Milja undid the strap, handed up his watch, long ago a present from his wife. The bandit glanced at it, then dropped it in his pocket. "Not a railroad watch, is it."

"No."

The leader was getting bored. With one hand he raised his rifle until de Milja was looking down the barrel. "What do you see in there?" De Milja took a deep breath, the bandit was going to ask him to look closer. One of the passengers screamed, de Milja couldn't tell if it was a man or a woman. The bandit on the gray pony trotted a little way toward the sound. A rifle fired, a flat, dull crack like the earlier shot; then another, deeper. The bandit leader puffed out his cheek so hard it burst in a red spray, his horse shied and whinnied. De Milja grabbed the harness and pulled himself close to the horse's body. The barrel of the rifle probed frantically, looking for him. Somewhere above, the bandit was wailing and cursing like a child. De Milja hung on to the reins with one hand and snatched the rifle barrel with the other. The weapon fired but he didn't let go. Then the boy came out from behind a locomotive wheel and hit the bandit on the head with the shovel, which rang like a bell as the rifle came free in de Milja's hand and the horse tore away from him.

The other bandit danced his pony around and shot the boy again and again, de Milja could hear the bullets hit, and the boy grunted each time. He fumbled the rifle around to firing position but the bandit galloped away, jumped his horse over the coupling between cars and disappeared. De Milja flinched as something hissed by his ear. Then Nowak called to him from the coal car and he ran up the ladder mounted on the wall as a bullet struck a silver chip out of the iron and the locomotive's light

went dark. Two horses thundered past, then a cluster of rapid
rifle shots, a yell of triumph.

Nowak was lying on the coal at one end of the car, firing a
rifle into the darkness. De Milja threw himself down beside him.
Between the train and the forest, dark shapes were sprawled
amid clothing and suitcases. A yellow spark from the trees—
both he and Nowak swung their weapons. Nowak fired, but de
Milja's clicked as the hammer fell on an empty chamber. He
threw it aside and worked the pistol free from beneath his
sweater. "Who has the other rifles?" de Milja asked, meaning
the weapons they had hidden behind a panel.

"Don't know, sir," Nowak said. "It's chaos."

He couldn't permit chaos. Rolled over the lip of the car, slid
down the ladder on the other side, stood between cars for a moment, then jumped to the ground and ran along the length of
the train. The conductor ran by him going the other way,
eyes white, teeth clenched, pistol held up in the safe position.
Combat-mad, he never even saw de Milja, who wondered who
he was chasing. Passengers were climbing through the coach
windows; some of them had gotten a horse off its feet and it
kicked and whinnied in terror as they tried to kill its rider, who
howled for mercy. De Milja stepped on a body, then through a
tangle of clothing that reeked of cloves—hair tonic from a shattered bottle. He tripped as he leaped for an open doorway, then
went sprawling into the last coach.

The smell of gunpowder and urine hit him like a wall. Someone moaned softly, but mostly it was very dark and very quiet—
the people packed together on the floor were breathing audibly,
as though winded. A bullet from the forest went through the car
and a triangle of glass fell on a seat without breaking. A silhouette rose suddenly in the middle of the car and returned the fire.

As de Milja crawled along the aisle, the train moved. Barely,
only just making way, but he thought he could feel the logs
being slowly forced off the track. The engineer is alive, he
thought, using the locomotive like a bulldozer. The rifleman

knelt quickly, moved on his knees to a neighboring window, straightened up, and fired. It was Herschensohn, the violinist. The homburg was jammed down on his head, a muscle ticked in his jaw, and he was muttering under his breath—"Stay still, you"—as he took aim.

De Milja reached the far end of the car—the back of the train—just as something seemed to give way and, with the sound of splintering wood, the train moved a little faster.

"Wait!"

A running shape burst from the forest—the peasant girl who'd begged to be let on the train at the water tower. "She got away!" Herschensohn had appeared beside him. The girl ran in panic, tripped, went sprawling on her face, struggled back up again, limping now and much slower. She waved her hands and screamed as the train gradually picked up speed.

De Milja was abruptly shoved aside. A man in a gray suit, with carefully brushed hair, leaped off the train and ran toward the girl, circled an arm around her waist and tried to help her. No longer young, he could barely run fast enough to keep up with the injured girl. "For God's sake don't leave us!" he yelled.

The bandits, on horseback and in the woods, saw what was happening. De Milja pinpointed the muzzle flashes in the half-light. The range was absurd but he aimed with both hands, changed the action to single-shot, and squeezed off round after round from his automatic. Herschensohn muttered angrily under his breath, talking to the target, as he fired his rifle. A young woman in a sweater and skirt jumped from a window, stumbled, came up running, took the girl around the waist from the other side. De Milja heard footsteps pounding above him as Nowak ran down the roof of the car, firing into the trees. Somebody yelled "Save her, save her, save her," like a chant, and others took up the cry. De Milja thrust his empty pistol into his pocket and stood on the lowest step as the three people gained on the car. Herschensohn was firing over his shoulder and

Nowak was shouting something from the roof. The three faces were distorted with exhaustion, with tears of effort, mouths gasping for breath, hands clawing frantically at the railings beside the door. But as the last log rolled away, the locomotive accelerated, the three runners flailing and staggering as the platform moved away from them.

Then the train quivered—the shock slammed de Milja against the wall—and suddenly the runners were close. He reached out and grabbed handfuls of shirt, coat, hair, whatever he could get, and hung on desperately. Someone caught the back of his coat just as he started to fall onto the tracks, other hands reached over his shoulders, people yelled, shoes scraped on the boards as somebody fought for traction, and the two rescuers and the girl were hauled aboard with a cry of triumph.

De Milja ended up on hands and knees as the train—something wrong with the way it ran now—slowly ground through a long, gentle curve. At the bottom of the embankment lay what was left of a truck: cab torn in half, gasoline flames flickering over the radiator, a tire spinning, a mounted machine gun aimed at the sky, and a man, arms flung wide, half-buried in a pile of broken brick.

When de Milja worked his way forward to the cab of the locomotive, he found bullet marks everywhere—the Ukrainian gunners had had their moment—and a very pale engineer. They'd mounted a machine gun on a brick truck and parked it on the tracks behind the log barrier. Just in case.

For the last hundred miles they were well up in the Carpathians, some of the passes at seven thousand feet, and the train switched back over ridges and granite outcrops, through sparse grass and forests of stunted pine where hawks floated on the mountain thermals. The train barely went now, maybe ten miles an hour, crawled along a trestle over a thousand-foot gorge as the passengers prayed silently and not-so-silently, oil trickling from beneath the engine. The sun didn't reach them until ten in the morning; they were cold, there was nothing to eat, and very little water.

They crossed the Tisza River; there'd been a fire on the bridge, but it still held. De Milja walked along in front of the engine, watching the track bow under the weight, trying not to hear the sounds the wooden girders made. They traveled for a time beside a deeply rutted dirt track, where stone mileposts gave the distance to Romania. A burned-out Polish army car had been shoved into a ditch, a wagon and a pair of horses hit by a dive bomber, a truck lay on its side in the middle of a mountain stream.

They worked at it all day, Nowak and de Milja taking turns standing with the engineer in the locomotive, sometimes running the train themselves since he was long past exhaustion. Slow as their progress was, there were no other trains. The stationmaster at Mukachevo told them the Germans had bombed the lines running south—the Polish railway system didn't really exist any longer.

They were what was left. De Milja and Nowak changed into officers' uniforms a few miles before they reached the frontier at Sighet. The train stopped at the Polish border station, but it had been abandoned: an empty hut, a bare flagpole. A mile farther on, at the Romanian customs post, a tank was parked with its cannon facing down the track. "So," said the engineer, "we are expected." De Milja took a set of papers, prepared in Warsaw, to the Romanian major who greeted him at the wooden barrier pole.

The two officers saluted, then shook hands. The major was dark, with a movie-hero mustache and excellent manners. Yes they were expected, yes everything was in order, yes they'd be processed through in a half-hour, yes, yes, yes. The sun dropped lower in the sky, the children cried because they were hungry, the truth was to be seen in the eyes of the passengers on the train: despair, boredom, fatigue—the refugee life had begun. Please be patient, the Romanian major said. Please.

Two Polish diplomats materialized; eyeglasses, Vandyke beards, and overcoats with velvet collars. Negotiations continued, they reported, but a diplomatic solution had been proposed: the Polish passengers could enter Romania—temporary immigrant status would be granted—the Polish train could not. A troublesome technicality, but . . . The hanging sentence meant *what can be done?* Poland could no longer insist on anything. It was a *former* nation now, a phantom of international law.

Meanwhile, de Milja used the diplomats to make contacts he'd been given in Warsaw, and with a few code words and secret signs, things started to happen, not the least of which was the delivery of hampers of bread and onions and wormy pears brought by Romanian soldiers.

And eventually, long after dark, another Polish Captain Nom de Guerre showed up. They recognized each other from the meeting in Vyborg's office: shared a cigarette, a walk by the tracks, and the news of the day. Then a phone call was made and, an hour later, a train appeared at the Romanian frontier post: a few freight cars, a small but serviceable locomotive, and Polish regular army soldiers with submachine guns. This train was moved up to the edge of the barrier on the Romanian side, and the Antonescu government, an uncertain mistress to several lovers—England, Germany, Russia—agreed that the passengers could bring whatever baggage they had onto Romanian soil.

It was very dark at the border, so pitch-pine torches were brought. And several volunteers among the passengers were given prybars. The floorboards in the coaches were prized up and, by flickering torchlight, the Polish National Gold Reserve, more than eleven million dollars, was carried into Romania.

Standing with Nowak by the train, Captain de Milja felt his heart stir with pride. From the Pilava local, with its shattered windows and bullet gashes, its locomotive reeking of singed bearings and burnt oil, the passengers handed out crates stamped NATIONAL BANK OF POLAND. Blood had been shed for this; by a locomotive fireman, a ten-year-old girl, a boy from a country village. By a conductor of the Polish National Railways who, teeth clenched, pistol in hand, had disappeared into the darkness. De Milja did not believe it had been shed in vain and stood very nearly to attention as his little army struggled past with the heavy boxes: Vladimir Herschensohn, his violin carried off by Ukrainian bandits, the veterinarian who had treated the wounded, the pensioned engineer, the peasant girl, the man and woman—from some comfortable professional class—who had run onto a battlefield to save a life, a few country people, a few workers, women and children. Poland had lost a war, this was what was left.

ROOM 9

20 October 1939. Bucharest, Romania.

Now the war was over, a pleasant autumn.

Hitler had what he wanted. Maybe he did, after all, have a right to it, a case could be made, you had to accept the reality of politics in central Europe. The days were cool and sunny, the harvest in, a little fog in the morning and geese overhead. Germany had Austria, Czechoslovakia, and Poland, and was, officially, *officially,* at war with England and France. But this was politics; eddies and swirls and tidal shifts in the affairs of diplomats. Slowly the sun warmed the squares and plazas, the boulevards and little winding streets and, by midmorning, all across Europe, it was just right for a coffee on the café terrace.

On the terrace of the Dragomir Niculescu restaurant, a man at leisure—or perhaps he simply has no place to go. A respectable gentleman, one would have to say. The suit not new, of course. The shirt a particular color, like wheat meal, that comes from washing in the sink and drying on a radiator. The posture proud, but maybe, if you looked carefully, just a little lost. Not defeated, nothing that drastic. Haven't we all had a moment of difficulty, a temporary reversal? Haven't we all, at some time or another, washed out a shirt in the sink?

Still, it must be said, the times are not so easy. The police are seen a good deal lately in the neighborhood of rooming houses that take in refugees, and the medical school does have all the, ah, *subjects* that its anatomy students might require, and the police launch on the nearby river almost always has a customer on the early-morning patrol, sometimes two. Difficult, these times. Discontent, dislocation, shifting power, uneasy alliance. The best way, nowadays, is to remain flexible, supple. Almost everybody would agree with that.

Speaking of the police: the gentleman on the terrace of the Niculescu is evidently of interest to at least three, one uniformed, two not, and they are in turn doubtless assisted by various barmen, drivers of horsedrawn trasuri cabs, and the rouge-cheeked girls left over from last night. Such a wealth of attention! But, frankly, whose fault is that? Poor Romania, the flood comes to its door—Jews and socialists and misfits and Poles and spies and just about any damn thing you care to name. It's gotten so bad they've had to put little cards on the tables at the Plaza-Athénée. BY ORDER OF THE GOVERNMENT, POLITICAL DISCUSSION IS FORBIDDEN.

The gentleman on the terrace of the Niculescu ordered a second coffee. When it came, he took a handful of leu coins out of his pocket, then hesitated a moment, uncertain what was worth what. The waiter, the natural curl of his lip tightening just a bit, deftly plucked out the right ones and dropped them in his waiter's saucer. Here was the land of "*saruta mina pe care nu o poti musca*"—kiss the hand you cannot bite—inhabited solely by the contemptuous and the contemptible, and those who had some doubt as to where they belonged could find instruction in the eyes of any café waiter.

If the gentleman on the terrace of the Niculescu didn't particularly care, it was, at least in part, because his head swam with hunger. Just behind him, lunchtime lobsters and crayfish were being set out on beds of shaved ice, the Niculescu's kitchen was preparing its famous hot-meat-and-fried-mushroom patties. Two peddlers with packs and long beards had stopped nearby to eat slices of white cheese and garlic on cold corn polenta, even the Gypsies, just across the square, were cooking a rabbit over a

pot of burning tar. The gentleman on the terrace took a measured sip of coffee. Discipline, he told himself. Make it last.

The woman was stylish, somewhere in middle age, wearing a
little hat with a half-veil. She arrived in a trasuri, bid it wait with
a wave of a gloved hand, and accepted the doorman's arm to descend from the carriage. The gentleman on the terrace was
pleased to see her. He stood politely while she settled herself on
a chair. The waiter pushed the lank hair back from his forehead
and said "Service" in French as he went for her coffee.

She drank only a sip. They spoke briefly, then she whispered
by his ear, and they held hands for a moment beneath the table.
He stood, she rose, he took her hand, she presented her veil for
a brush of his lips, said a parting word behind the back of her
hand, walked quickly to her trasuri and was gone, leaving a
cloud of lilac scent. "God go with you, Captain," was what
she'd said.

The gentleman on the terrace touched the pocket of his
jacket, making sure of the money she'd passed to him, then
strolled slowly across the square, past the policemen, uniformed
and not, and their helpers, past old women sweeping the cobblestones with twig brooms, past a flock of pigeons that rose
into the air with beating wings.

Captain de Milja left that night. He'd had enough of Bucharest: the rooming house, the police, and the assorted ghosts and
wolves who lived in the cafés. And more than enough of Romania. The country, under German diplomatic pressure, had
started to intern Polish army units crossing the border—as they
had interned most of the senior ministers of the Polish government. Time to go.

He traveled under a cover he'd created for himself, using a
blank identity card they'd left in his dossier the night he went to
work for Vyborg. Name: Jan Boden. That made him a Silesian
Pole—like his father—with a good knowledge of German and
likely some German blood. Profession: Buyer of wood for cof-

fins. That made it normal for him to travel, yet wasn't a profession that the Germans would want to draft—not, for example, like an expert machinist—for labor in Germany. He wore a leather coat so he wouldn't freeze, and carried a VIS, the Polish army automatic pistol, so he wouldn't be taken prisoner. If he had to drop it quickly somewhere, he could always get another. After six years of war, 1914–1918, then the 1920–1921 campaign against the Red Army, Poland was an armory. Every barn, every cellar, every attic had its weapons and ammunition. And the Poles were not Russian peasants; they cleaned and oiled and maintained, because they liked things that worked.

He had some time to spare—the message that the courier delivered along with the money was *Room 9 at Saint Stanislaus Hospital on Grodny Street by 23 October*—and that probably saved his life. He took a train from Bucharest up to Sighisoara in the Transylvanian Alps, then another, going west, that crossed into Hungary near Arad. Changed again, this time going north to Kisvarda, in the Carpathians. As it grew dark, he caught a ride on a truck into a border village by a stream that fed into the Tisza, close to one of several passes over the mountains.

He entered the local tavern, ordered beer and sausage, and was approached by the local *passeurs*—smugglers—within the hour. He said he wished to be guided into Poland, a price was set, everybody spit on their palms and shook hands.

But soon after they started out, he realized that, contractual spits notwithstanding, they meant to kill him and take his money. It was black dark. The two *passeurs,* reeking of taverns, goats, and rancid fat, squatted on either side of him. They whispered, and touched his arms. Too much, as though familiarizing themselves with his physical capacity, and dissipating his protective magic. One of them had a knife in his belt—a dull, rusty thing, the idea of being stabbed with it gave de Milja a chill.

"I have to go behind a tree," he said in Polish. Then he faded away in the darkness and just kept going. He found what he believed to be the south bank of the Tisza, then a dirt track that someone might have intended as a road, then a bridge, where he could hear the unmistakable sounds of Russian soldiers getting drunk: singing, then arguing, then fighting, then weeping, then snoring. As one of the Ostrow uncles used to say, "Here is something a man can depend on—never mind some silly ball rolling down an inclined plane."

De Milja crossed the bridge a little after two in the morning; he was then in Soviet-occupied Poland. He walked another hour, winter cold numbing his face at the high altitude, then came upon a deserted farm—no barking dogs—opened the milking shed, kicked together a straw bed for himself, and actually slept until dawn.

By midday on the twenty-first of October, he was in the town of Kosow, where the railroad went to Tarnopol. He bought a ticket and caught the next train; his night in the milk shed had left him rumpled, unshaven, a little smelly, and thoroughly acceptable—proletarian—to the Russian guards at the railroad station. He leaned his head against the cold glass of the window as the train crossed the Dniester: yes, he was under orders to go to Warsaw, but he meant to find his wife at the clinic, meant somehow to get her across the border into Romania. Let them intern her if they liked—it was better than being at the mercy of the Russians.

In Tarnopol, the taxis had disappeared from the railway station, so he walked through the winding streets in late afternoon, found the way out of town, and was soon headed for the clinic down a rutted dirt path. He knew this country, the Volhynia, it was home to his mother's family estates, more than three thousand acres of rolling hills, part forest, part farmland, with bountiful hunting and poor harvests and no way to earn a zloty, a lost paradise where one could gently starve to death with a contented heart beneath a pale, lovely moon.

The birch trees shimmered in the wind as night came on, butterflies hovered over a still pond in a meadow, the shadowy woods ran on forever—a fine place to write a poem or be murdered or whatever fate might have in mind for you just then. The little boy in de Milja's heart was every bit as scared of this forest as he'd always been, the VIS pistol in his pocket affording just about as much protection from the local spirits as the rock he used to carry.

It was near twilight when he reached the clinic. The wicker wheelchairs stood empty on the overgrown lawns, the white pebble paths were unraked; it was all slowly going back to nature.

He walked up a long path lined with Lombardy poplars, was not challenged as he entered the hundred-year-old gabled house, formerly the heart of a grand estate. There were no bearded doctors, no brisk nurses, no local girls in white aprons to bring tea and cake, and there seemed to be fewer patients about than he remembered. But, on some level, the clinic still functioned. He saw a few old village women making soup in the kitchen, the steam radiators were cold but a fire had been built in the main parlor and several patients, wrapped in mufflers and overcoats, were staring into it and talking quietly among themselves.

His wife was sitting a little apart from the group, hands held between her knees—something she did when she was cold—face hidden by long, sand-colored hair. When he touched her shoulder she looked startled, then recognized him and smiled for a moment. She had sharp features and generous, liquid eyes, the face of a person who could not hurt anything. Strange, he thought, how she doesn't seem to age.

"Helena," he said.

She searched for something, then looked down, hiding her eyes.

"Let's sit over here," he said. Often it was best just to go forward. He took her hand and led her to a sofa where they could be private. "Are you all right?" he asked.

A little shrug, a wry smile.

"Have you seen soldiers? Russian soldiers?"

That bore thinking about—she simply did not hear things the way others did, perhaps she heard much more, echos and echos of meaning until no question could have an answer. "Yes," she said, hesitantly.

"Was anyone . . . hurt?"

"No."

She was thinner, her eyes seemed bruised, but they always did. She disliked the Veronal they gave her to calm down and sleep, and so hid it somewhere and paced away the nights.

"Enough to eat?"

She nodded yes.

"So then?" he said, pretending to be gruff.

This never failed to please her. "So then?" she said, imitating him.

He reached for her, resting his hand lightly on the soft hair that fell to her shoulder, it was something she allowed. "Helena," he said.

Her eyes wandered. What did he want?

"The Russians," he continued, "are here now, perhaps you know, I—"

"Please," she said, eyes pleading. She would not stand for exegesis, could not bear it.

He sighed and took her hands. She took them back—gently, she didn't want to hurt his feelings, she simply wanted the hands—folded them in her lap and gave him a puzzled look. Usually he was so courteous.

"I have been thinking that I ought to take you away from here," he said.

She considered it—he could see a certain shadow touch her face as she reasoned. Then she shook her head no. The way she did it was not vague, or crazy, but sharp, completely in control. She'd thought through *everything:* soldiers, what they did, how bad it was, that she was not vulnerable to whatever he feared might happen to her.

He dropped his hands into his lap. He felt completely helpless. He considered taking her away by force, but he knew it wouldn't work.

"To go where?" she asked, not unkindly.

He shook his head, defeated.

"Will you walk me to the lake house?" she asked. She could be soft and shy to a point where he came near tears—the ache in the back of the throat. He stood and offered her his arm.

What she called "the lake house" had once been a pavilion, where guests were served cream cakes, and tea from a silver urn, and the doctors could speak frankly in peaceful surroundings. Now it was dark and abandoned and some bird out in the reed marsh beyond the lake repeated a low, evening call.

She stood facing him, almost touching, reluctant to speak at first, and, even for her, very troubled. "I want you to make love to me as you used to," she said. *One last time*—her unspoken words were clear as a musical note.

Looking around, he found a cane deckchair, gray with years of weather. He sat down, then invited her to sit on his lap with a flourish, as though it were a masterpiece of a bed, all silk and wool, in some grand hotel. She liked to play like this, raised her skirt just an inch, settled herself on his legs and laid her head against his shoulder. A little wind blew across the lake, the reeds bent, a few ducks flew over the marsh on the horizon. Idly, he stroked her dry lips with an index finger, she raised her face to it, and he saw that she had closed her eyes.

He took the hem of her sweater in his fingertips and lifted it to her shoulders, then lowered her slip, pulled her coat tight around her for warmth, wet his finger in her mouth and rubbed her breasts for a long time. They were heavier than he remembered but that had always been true of her, even when she was nineteen—her body full and round for a girl with a small face.

She sighed, sentimental, yes, this was what she'd meant. Then she hummed softly and where her weight rested on him he could feel the V of her legs widen. When he slid his hand beneath her skirt, she smiled. Covertly, he watched her face, wondered what sort of dream she was having. Her lips moved, drew back slowly, then parted; her breathing became louder, shallow and rhythmic, until her weight suddenly pressed into him.

"Stand up," he said. He stepped behind her, slid her coat down her arms and spread it on the broad, dry planks of the pavilion floor. She took her skirt off, then stepped out of her underpants. He knelt, embraced her hips, hard, as though something in the sky meant to sweep her away. She smoothed his hair—it didn't matter, it didn't matter. Then she settled herself on the coat, and swung her knees to one side, hands clasped beneath her head, a girl in a soap ad. He laughed.

They made love for a while; like strangers, like husband and wife, eventually like lovers. "I want to ask you," she said quietly, almost to herself, as they lay curled around each other to keep warm. "You didn't bring flowers, this time." The words trailed off into the evening sounds by the lake.

"And you think, do I love you? Yes, I do."

"But you always . . ."

"Left on the train," he said. "You have to forgive me."

She burrowed closer to him, he could feel the tears on her face.

On the train back to Warsaw he made a mistake.

He went north from Tarnopol, to Rovno. Stayed overnight in the railway station—technically illegal but tolerated, because people had to wait for trains, yet dangerous, because security police knew that railway stations attracted fugitives.

A uniformed NKVD guard looked through his documents, reading with a slow index finger on each word, then handed them back silently. He got out of Rovno on a dawn train to Brzesc, near the east bank of the river that formed the dividing line between German and Russian occupation forces. On this train, two men in overcoats; one of them stared at him, and, foolishly, he stared back. Then realized what he'd done and looked away. At the very last instant. He could see from the posture of the man—his age, his build—that he was *somebody*, likely civilian NKVD, and was about to make a point of it.

De Milja's heart hammered in his chest, he felt prickly sweat break out under his arms, he did not even dare a glance to see if the man had accepted his "surrender": breaking off eye contact. Could not put a hand on the VIS, just tried to shrink down into the seat without a single sign of bravado. He *was* strong. And unafraid. And the way he carried himself, people knew that, and it would bury him in a hurry if he didn't learn some other way to be in public.

The two men got off the train one station before Brzesc. From the platform, his enemy squinted at him through the window. De Milja stared at his shoes, a proud man subdued. The Russian didn't buy it; with a certain casual violence he turned to get back on the train and, de Milja was sure, haul him off. But his partner stopped him and grabbed the shoulder of his coat, pulling him, with a joke and a laugh, along the platform—they had more important things to do. From the corner of his eye, de Milja could see the Russian as he glanced back one last time. He was red in the face. The man, de Milja knew beyond a doubt, had intended to kill him.

In the German sector it was different. Much easier. The black-uniformed border police did not hate Poles as the Russians did. Poles to them were truly *untermenschen,* subhuman, beneath contempt. They were to be treated, like all Slavs, as beasts, controlled by "*zuckerbrot und peitsche*"—sweets and the whip. They checked his identity card, then waved him on. He was nothing, they never even saw him.

Of equal interest to de Milja was a siding some fifty miles

south of Warsaw: eight German tank cars, pointed east, clearly going to the Soviet ally, marked NAPTHALENE.

Yes, well, what couldn't one do with that.

23 October, Warsaw. Saint Stanislaus Hospital.

An excellent safe house: all sorts of people went in and out at all hours of the day and night. There were cots for sleeping, meals were served, yet it was far safer than any hotel ever could be.

Room 9 was in the basement, adjacent to the boilers that heated the hospital water. It had a bed, a steel sink, and plaster walls painted pale green in 1903. It had a military map of Poland, a street map—Baedeker—of Warsaw, two steel filing cabinets, a power-boosted radio receiver with an aerial disappearing through a drainpipe entry in an upper corner, three telephones, several tin ashtrays, a scarred wood table with three chairs on one side and one chair on the other. Illumination was provided by a fifteen-watt bulb in a socket in the middle of the ceiling.

Of the three people facing him, de Milja knew one by acquaintance: a Warsaw hellion called Grodewicz who was not, as far as he knew, in the military and who should have been, as far as most of his friends were concerned, in prison. One by reputation: Colonel Jozef Broza, the former military attaché to Belgium. And one not at all, a woman who introduced herself only as "Agata." She was in her late fifties, with a square jaw, a tip-tilted nose, and thick, dark-blond hair shot with gray, pulled back in a tortoiseshell clip. She had the fine skin of a nun, a filigreed gold wedding band, nicotine stains on the fingers of both hands, and unpolished but well-buffed fingernails. De Milja could easily see her in a country house or on horseback, obviously a member of the upper gentry.

She lit a cigarette, blew smoke through her nostrils, and gave him a good long stare before she started to speak. What she told him was brief but to the point: an underground organization had been formed to fight the Germans and the Russians—it would operate independently in each of the occupied zones. His job would be in the western half of the country, the German half.

The underground was to be called the ZWZ, Zwiazek Walki Zbrojnej—the Union for Armed Struggle. The highest level of command, known as the Sixth Bureau, was based in Paris, part of the Polish government-in-exile now led by General Sikorski. In German-occupied Poland, the ZWZ was headquartered in Warsaw, with regional stations in Cracow, Lodz, Poznan—all the major cities. Operational sections included sabotage, propaganda, communications—couriers and secret mail—and an intelligence service. "You," she said to de Milja, "are being considered for a senior position in the latter." She stubbed out her cigarette, lit a fresh one.

"Of course it is folly to say *anything* in this country in the singular form—we are God's most plural people and losing wars doesn't change that. There are, in fact, undergrounds, run by the entire spectrum of political parties: the Communists, the Nationalists, the Catholic Nationalists, the Peasant Party, and so on. The Jews are attempting to organize in their own communities, also subject to political division. Still, the ZWZ is more than ninety percent of the effort and will likely remain so.

"But, whatever name it's done under, we have several months of hard, dirty fighting ahead of us. We now estimate that the French, with England's help, are going to need six months to overrun Germany. It's our job to survive in the interim, and keep the national damage at the lowest possible level. When Germany's finished off, it will be up to the League of Nations to pry the U.S.S.R. out of Poland and push it back to the August '39 borders. This will require diplomacy, patience, and perhaps divine intervention—Stalin cares for nothing but brute force. There will be claims for Ukrainian, Byelorussian, and Lithuanian sovereignty, the Jews will want restrictive laws repealed—it won't ever be what it was before, but that's maybe not such a bad thing as far as the people in this room are concerned. Any questions?''

''No questions,'' de Milja said.

''Right now,'' she continued, ''we have two problems: the Polish people are in a state of mourning—how could the country be beaten so badly? And we lack explosives, incendiaries, and medicines for the partisan effort. We're waiting to be supplied by air from Paris, but nothing's happened yet. They make promises, then more promises. Meanwhile all we can do is insist, and not lose faith.''

Colonel Broza opened a dossier and glanced through it. He was barely five and a half feet tall, with massive shoulders, receding curly hair, and a pugnacious face. When he put on reading glasses, he looked like a peasant turned into a chess master which, the way de Milja heard it, wasn't so far from the truth.

''Aren't you something to Eugeniusz Ostrow?''

''Nephew, sir.''

''Which side?''

''My mother's family.''

''Ah. The countess.''

''Yes, sir.''

''Your uncle . . .'' The colonel tried not to laugh. ''You must forgive me, I shouldn't . . . Wasn't there a formal dinner? A trade minister's wife, something about a goat?''

''A sheep, I believe it was, sir.''

''In diplomatic sash.''

''Yes, sir.''

The colonel pinched the bridge of his nose. ''And then . . . a cook, wasn't she?''

''A laundress, sir.''

''My God, yes! He married her.''

''A large, formal wedding, sir.''

The woman called Agata cleared her throat.

"Yes, of course, you're right. You were at Jagiello university?"

"I was."

"In mathematics?"

"Yes, sir."

"How'd you do?"

"Very poorly. Tried to follow in my father's footsteps, but—"

"Tossed out?"

"Not quite. Almost."

"And then?"

"My uncles helped me get a commission in the army, and an assignment to the military intelligence service, and they sent me off to study cartography."

"Where was that?"

"First at staff college, then at the French military academy, Saint-Cyr."

"Three years, it says here."

"Yes, sir."

"So you speak the language."

"Yes, sir."

"And German?"

"My father's from Silesia, I spent time there when I was growing up. My German's not too bad, I would say."

Colonel Broza turned over a page, read for a moment. "Vyborg recommends you," he said. "I'm going to run the ZWZ intelligence service, I need somebody to handle special operations—to work with all the sections. You'll report directly to me, but not too often. You understand what I'm saying?"

"Yes, sir."

"Do you know Captain Grodewicz?"

"Yes, sir."

"Spend a little while with him. He's going to run the ZO unit."

"Sir?"

"Zwiazek Odwety. Reprisal. You understand?"

It snowed, early in November, and those who read signs and portents in the weather saw malevolence in it. The Germans had lost no time stealing Polish coal, the open railcars rattled ceaselessly across the Oder bridges into ancient, warlike Prussia. The men who ran the coal companies in ancient, warlike Prussia were astonished at how much money they made in this way— commercial logic had always been based on buying a little lower, selling a little higher. But buying for virtually nothing, well, perhaps the wife ought to have the diamond leaf-pin after all. Hitler was scary, he gave these huge, towering, patriotic speeches on the radio, that meant *war* for God's sake, and war ruined business, in the long run, and worse. But this, this wasn't exactly war—this was a form of mercantile heaven, and who got hurt? A few Poles?

The wind blew down from Russia, howled at the windows, piled snow against the door, found every crack, every chip and flaw, and came looking for you in your house. The old people started to die. "This is war!" they shouted in France, but no planes came. Perhaps next week.

Cautiously, from a distance, Captain de Milja tried to keep an eye on his family. He knew where one of the maids lived, and waited for her at night. "Your father is a saint," the woman said at her kitchen table. "Your mother and your sister are in Hungary, safe, away from the murderers. Your father managed it—I can guess how, there's barely a zloty in the house these days."

"What is he doing?"

"He will not leave, he will not go to the country, he will not admit that anything has changed," the woman said. "Will not." She shook her head, respect and apprehension mixed together. "He reads and writes, teaches his classes. He is a rock—" She called de Milja by a childhood pet name and the captain looked at his knees. He took a sheaf of zloty notes out of his pocket and laid it on the table. The maid gave him a wry look: *How do I explain this?*

"Don't talk about it. Just go to the black market, put something extra on the table, he won't notice."

He had the woman turn out her oil lamp, they sat in the dark for a time, listening to the wind whine against the old brick, then he whispered good-bye and slid out the door into the night. Because of the curfew he went doorway to doorway, alert for the sound of German patrol cars. It could be done—anything could be done—but you had to think it through, you had to concentrate. A life lived in flight from the police, a life of evasion, had the same given as always, it hadn't changed in centuries: they could make a thousand mistakes, you couldn't make one. Once upon a time, only criminals figured that out. By November 1939, every man, woman, and child in Poland knew it.

Something had to be done. De Milja met with his directorate in Room 9—he was living in a servant's garret in Mokotow that week and the sudden warmth of the hospital basement made him giddy. He sat in the chair and presented his case: the heart was going out of the people, he could sense it. Colonel Broza agreed, Agata wasn't sure, Grodewicz thought maybe it didn't, for the moment, matter. Broza prevailed. All sorts of actions were considered; some violent, some spectacular. Should they humiliate the Germans? What, for an underground army, constituted a resounding success? How would people find out about it? Cigarette smoke hung in the still air, the perpetual dusk in the room grew darker, one of the hospital nuns brought them tea. They made a decision, Agata suggested a name, the rest was up to him.

The name was a retired Warsaw detective called Chomak. De Milja went to see him; found a man with stiff posture, shirt buttoned at the throat but no tie, dark hair combed straight back. Young to be retired, de Milja thought, but the prewar politics of the Warsaw police department could hardly concern him now. Chomak accepted the assignment, a worried wife at his side, a dachshund with a white muzzle sitting alertly by his chair. "Everybody thinks it's easy to steal," Chomak said. "But that isn't true."

He seemed to take great pleasure in the daily repetitive grind of the work, and always had a certain gleam in his eye: *not so easy, is it, this kind of job?* They rode trains together, bicycled down snowy roads at the distant edges of Warsaw; following leads, checking stories, seeing for themselves. They needed to steal a plane. Not a warplane, that would have required a massive use of the ZWZ resources. Just a little plane. Working through a list of mechanics and fuel-truck drivers—these names coming from prewar tax records secreted by the intelligence services before the Germans took over—they discovered that the great majority of small aircraft, Fiesler-Storch reconnaissance planes for example, were well guarded by Luftwaffe security forces.

But the Germans did have a gentlemen's flying club.

Flying clubs had gained great popularity at the time of the record-setting flights of the 1920s and 1930s, and served as training grounds for future fighter pilots who had come to aviation as airplane-crazy teenagers. And so, a few days after German victory, the flying club had taken over a small airfield at Pruszkow, about ten miles west of Warsaw. De Milja and Chomak bicycled slowly along the little road past the field. There wasn't much to see; an expanse of brown grass, a nylon wind sock on a pole, a hut with a swastika flag, and six single-engine planes, of which two had had their engines taken down to small pieces in the lone hangar.

Part Two: The printer across the river in Praga had all the work he could handle. The Germans *loved* print; every sort of decree and form and official paper, signs and manuals and instruction sheets and directives, they couldn't get enough of it.

Especially that Gothic typeface. The Wehrmacht, as far as the printer could see, would rather publish than fight. Hell, he didn't mind. What with four kids and the wife pregnant and his old mother and her old mother and coal a hundred zlotys a sack on the black market, he had to do something. Don't misunderstand, he was a patriot, had served in the army, but there were mouths to feed.

This book? Yeah, he'd printed that. Where the hell had they ever found it? Look at that. Doesn't look too bad, does it? Quite a problem at first, didn't get a call for that sort of thing very often and he and his chief compositor—poor Wladek, killed in the war, rest in peace—had had to work it out together, combining different letters from a variety of fonts. Mostly it was just the usual thing but now and then you got a chance to be creative in this business and that made it all worthwhile did they know what he meant?

Do it again? Well, yes, shouldn't be a problem. He still had all, well almost all the letters he'd used for this book. He'd have to work at night, probably best to do the typesetting himself—if he remembered how. No, that was a joke. He remembered. What exactly did they need? Single sheet? A snap. Had to have it last week, he supposed. Wednesday soon enough? How many copies? *How* many? Jesus, the Germans kept him on a paper ration, there was no way he could—oh, well, if that was the way it was, no problem. As for the ink, he'd just add that into the German charges over the next few months, they'd never notice. Not that he habitually did that sort of thing, but, well . . .

It was December before all the other details could be sorted through and taken care of. Chomak spent two nights in the forest bordering the airfield, binoculars trained on the little hut. The light stayed on all night, a glow at the edges of the blackout curtain, and the watchman, a big, brawny fellow with white hair and a beer belly, was conscientious; made a tour of the field and the hangar twice a night.

They found a pilot—not so easy because Polish airmen who survived the war had gone to London and Paris to fight for the Allies. The man they located had flown mail and freight all around the Baltic, but poor eyesight had disqualified him for combat flying. When approached, he was anxious to take on the mission.

They picked up the printing in a taxi, storing the string-tied bundles in Chomak's apartment. The mission was then scheduled for the ninth of December, but that night turned out cold and crisp, with a sky full of twinkling stars. Likewise the tenth and eleventh. The night of the twelfth, the weather turned bad, and the mission was on until an icy snow closed down every road out of Warsaw.

December fourteenth dawned warm and still, the snow turned to slush, and the sky was all fog and thick cloud. A wagon full of turnips transported the leaflets to a forest clearing near the airfield, then de Milja and the pilot arrived by bicycle an hour later. By 5:20 P.M. the field manager and the mechanic had gone home, and the night watchman had arrived. De Milja and his crew knocked on the door around seven. At first the watchman—a German it turned out—struggled and swore when they grabbed him and pulled a pillowcase over his head. Then he decided to cooperate and Chomak started to tie him up, but he changed his mind and got one hand loose and they had to hit him a few times before he'd calm down. Chomak and de Milja then rolled a plane to the gas pump and filled the tank. The pilot clambered in and studied the controls with a flashlight, while de Milja and Chomak pushed the plane to the edge of the grass runway.

At 8:20, Captain de Milja cranked the engine to life, the pilot made the thumbs-up sign, the plane bumped over the rocky field, picked up speed, then staggered up into the sky—airborne and flying a mission for free Poland.

. . .

The trick for the pilot was to get the plane *down*—quickly.

There certainly was hell to pay in the Warsaw air-defense sector—the Germans could hear something buzzing around up there in the clouds but they couldn't see it, the searchlight beams swept back and forth but all they found was gray mist. The antiaircraft batteries let loose, the drone of the plane vanished to the west, the pilot headed around east on his compass until he picked up two gasoline-in-a-barrel fires lit off by de Milja and Chomak, then wasted no time getting down on the lumpy field, since Luftwaffe nightfighters were just that moment slicing through the sky over Warsaw looking for something to shoot at.

Down below, hundreds of people broke the curfew to run outside and snatch up a leaflet. These were, with the aid of friends and dictionaries, soon enough deciphered—the English-style printing, as opposed to the usual Polish letters, made it just a little more difficult to read—and by breakfast time everybody in Warsaw and much of occupied Poland felt good the way one did when a friend came around to say hello.

To the Brave People of Poland

> Greetings from your British allies. We are
> flying over your troubled land tonight to
> let you know that you are not forgotten.
> We'll be back soon, there will be lots more
> of us, and next time we won't be dropping
> leaflets. Until then, keep your chin up, and
> give the Germans hell any way you can.

> Long live Poland!

> Tenth Bomber Wing
> RAF

''. . . but he changed his mind and they had to hit him a few times before he'd calm down.'' Thus the night watchman at the

Pruszkow airfield. But nothing more. De Milja had carried a small 9 mm automatic—there wasn't any point in not having something, not for him. But Colonel Broza had said in their last meeting before the operation, "Don't kill him, Captain. Let's not start that yet."

Yet.

But then, it wasn't really up to them, of course it never had been, and the miracle was that fifty days or so of occupation had passed so—*peacefully.* Then it happened, out in Praga one Friday night, and that was that.

A workers' tavern in a workers' part of town. What was a Wehrmacht noncom even doing in such a place? Probably a worker himself, back in Dusseldorf or Essen or wherever it was. Not the classic Nazi—some fine-boned little blond shit quivering with rage and overbreeding, cursing Jews in a squeaky voice with saliva on his chin. The breed existed, but it didn't fight wars. Who fought wars was the guy in the Polish tavern: some big, blunt, slow-thinking German workingman, strong as an ox, common as dirt, and not such a bad type.

Here it was coming Christmas and he was stuck in Poland. He wasn't making out with the Polish girls, everything was a little grimier than he liked, there was garlic in his food, and people either wouldn't meet his eyes or glared with hatred. Hatred! Christ, he hadn't done anything. They put him in the army and they said go here, go there, and he went here and there. Who wouldn't? That was the way of the world; you did what the Wehrmacht told you to do, just like you did what Rheinmetall or Krupp told you to do.

And Friday night, like always, you went to a tavern, just to get out from underneath it a little. Ordered a beer, then another, and minded your own business.

But taverns were taverns, especially in working-class neighborhoods, and it was always the same: a word, a look, some little thing that just couldn't be ignored. And people who couldn't afford to lose their tempers brought them in here on Friday night in order to do exactly that. And then, some people didn't like Germans. Never had, never would. Maybe they thought that Hansi or Willi or whatever his name was was spoiling a good night's drinking. Just by being there. Maybe they told him to leave. Maybe Hansi or Willi had never been told to leave a tavern. Maybe he figured he was a conqueror. Maybe he re- fused.

Well, he wasn't a conqueror that night. Somebody took out a knife and put it just the right place and that was that. The Ge- stapo came running, hanged the tavern keeper over his own door and next day executed a hundred and twenty neighbor- hood men. So there. The Germans were famous for reprisal long before they forced the Polish frontier. In 1914, stomping into Belgium, they encountered *franc-tireurs*—snipers—and re- sponded with heavy reprisals, shooting hundreds of Belgians when they couldn't get at the *franc-tireurs*. They didn't invent it—revenge killing was right up at the front of the Bible—but they believed in it.

And it was just about that time when Hans Frank, named gov- ernor-general of the swath of Poland around Warsaw not di- rectly incorporated into Germany, wrote in his diary that "the Poles will be the slaves of the German Reich." Meanwhile they had the Jews sewing Stars of David on their breast pockets and hanging signs on the shops that said NICHT ARISCH, not Aryan.

The ZWZ was beseiged. Everybody wanted a piece of a Ger- man. De Milja didn't exactly recruit, but he did look over candi- dates before passing the name on to a committee, and the first two weeks of December he barely had time to do anything else.

Two days before Christmas, de Milja went to see the maid who was taking care of his father, a newspaper-wrapped parcel in hand: sausage, aspirin, and sewing needles, the latest items that had become impossible-to-get treasures. "He wants to see you," the woman said. "He told me to tell you that."

De Milja thought a moment; he was staying in the basement

of a large apartment house in central Warsaw, just off Jerozolimskie Avenue, one of the city's main thoroughfares. "There's
a bar called Zofia, just by Solski Park, with a public room above
it. Ten minutes after seven, tell him." The maid nodded that
she understood, but de Milja could see she disapproved of the
idea that the professor would set foot in a such a low place.

It *was* a low place, an after-curfew nightclub with a room upstairs that held three pool tables and an assortment of Warsaw
lowlife—mostly black-market operators and pimps and their
entourages. Tough guys; plenty of hair oil, overcoats with broad
shoulders and ankle-length hems, a little bit of a cigarette stuck
up in the corner of the mouth. They played pool, bet on the
games, practiced three-bank wizard shots, sold a tire, bought a
few pounds of sugar. De Milja liked it because someone was
paying off the Germans to stay away, and that made it useful to
people like him who'd had to learn one of the cardinal truths of
secret life: anything clandestine is temporary. So the room
above the Zofia was a welcome item on a list that could never be
long enough.

Watching his father walk through the smoky poolroom, de
Milja felt a pang in his heart. With hair combed faultlessly to one
side, and round tortoiseshell spectacles, he looked like photographs of T.S. Eliot, the English banker/poet. His face was thinner and brighter than de Milja remembered, and he wore a
raincoat, not his winter overcoat. Where was that? de Milja
wondered. Sold? Clutching his professorial briefcase tightly, he
excused his way through the crowd, ignoring the stares of the
poolroom toughs. Some of them would have liked to humiliate
him—he was an inviting target, a large ungainly bird who cried
out for insult—but he was moving faster than they realized and
before the right words could be said, he was gone. He paused
while a boy with a huge pompadour and a royal-blue suit
squinted down his cue to line up a shot, and winked suddenly at
his son: *there in a minute, must wait while Euclid here gets it all
worked out*. Thus had his father survived years of the Ostrow un-

cles: the more his sensibilities were offended, the more he twin-kled.

They shook hands, his father settled himself at the table, not-ing the rough wood with hearts and initials carved in it, the water glass of vodka, wilted beet slices on a plate, and a salt-shaker. "How've you been?" he asked.

De Milja smiled. "Not so bad. You?"

That was ignored. "Most thoughtful of you, that package. We ate the sausage, and sent the aspirin and the needles on to your mother and sister. They are in Hungary, I believe Sonya told you. Near Eger, in a sort of tumbledown castle—decrepit nobility wearing earmuffs at the dinner table, very Old World, I'm sure."

"I think you should join them."

"Me? What would I do for a library? Besides, I still have stu-dents, a few anyhow. As long as they show up, I will."

"But Hungary is safe, you think."

The professor hesitated. "Yes. They're just now Germany's great friends. Maybe later it will turn out they loved England all along. In their secret heart, you see."

"And the house?"

"Cold as a donkey's dick." A sly smile bloomed for a mo-ment—*shocked you, did I?* "I've got newspapers stuffed in every crack, but it doesn't seem to help."

"Look, why don't you let me find you an apartment—"

The professor cut him short. "Really, you needn't bother." Then he leaned closer and lowered his voice. "But there is something I want you to do." He paused, then said, "Am I cor-rect in assuming you've been recruited into the underground? That you remain under military orders?"

De Milja nodded yes.

"Are you anything important?"

No reaction, at first, then a slight shrug: *important?*

But the professor was not to be fended off. "Don't be coy. Either you can talk to the leadership or you can't."

"I can." De Milja felt his ears getting warm.

His father searched his face, then decided he was telling the truth—it really was some other boy who'd thrown the chalk—reached into his briefcase and surfaced with three pages of densely written pen-and-ink script. "For the right person, this would be of consequence," he said.

"What is it?"

"A study." His father stared at it a moment. "The research is thin. I merely talked to a few of my old students, had a coffee, a little gossip. But they're smart—that I know for a certainty because I made them prove it more than once—and well placed. Not at the very top of the civil service but just below it, where they actually read the paper and make the decisions and tell the boss what to say. Anyhow, it's the best that I could do, an outline, but useful to the right people."

He paused for effect. "The point is, I'd like to be asked to do more." He met de Milja's eyes. "Is that clear? Because what I have in mind is far more ambitious, an ongoing study that—"

A sudden commotion interrupted him; two of the local princes had reversed their pool cues and were snarling at each other while friends held them back. When de Milja looked back at his father he caught him with a particular expression on his face: irritation, disappointment, why did he have to see his son in places like this? Why wasn't it a faculty dining room or an intellectuals' café? The response was irrational—he would have admitted that—but it was the truth of his heart and for a moment he'd forgotten to hide it.

De Milja took the papers from his father's hand. "I can only promise that it will be read."

"Well, naturally. I don't expect more than that."

De Milja glanced at his watch. "I'd like to spend more time, but if you're going to get back home before curfew . . ."

His father stood quickly. "You'll be in touch?" he said.

"Through Sonya."

They said good-bye; it was awkward, as their time together

always was. They shook hands, both started to say something, shook hands again, then parted. At the door, his father turned and looked back; de Milja started to wave but he was too late. The raincoat and briefcase disappeared through the doorway, and de Milja never saw him again.

It was cold in Warsaw that night, there was ice in Captain de Milja's basement room; a rust-colored stalactite that hung from a connection in the water pipe that ran across his ceiling. A janitor had once lived here, his church calendar—little girls praying with folded hands—and his French movie star torn from a magazine, a Claudette Colbert look-alike, were still stuck on nails in the wall. Cold enough to die, the captain thought. Wondered how cold that actually had to be. He wore an army greatcoat, a scarf, and wool gloves as he sat on the edge of a cot and by the light of a candle read the report his father had written.

He read it twice, then again. The writing was plain enough, and the facts were not obscure—just a listing of things governments did on a daily basis; a few administrative procedures, some new policies and guidelines. Really, not very interesting. But look again, he told himself. *Principles of the German Occupation of Poland: 10 December 1939.* There wasn't anything in the report that Colonel Broza and the directorate didn't know—all his father and his informants had done was to gather up what was available and synthesize it. Three pages. Four principles:

1) Calculated devaluation of the currency. 2) Replacement of the judiciary. 3) Direction of labor. 4) Registration. That was all—the real, arid horror of the thing lay in its simplicity. The essential mechanics of slavery, it turned out, weren't at all complicated. With registration you knew who and what and where everyone was—a Jew or a metallurgical engineer, it was all filed for future reference. With the direction of labor they worked where you wanted, and had to meet production norms you set. With your own judiciary, you controlled their behavior with their own police. And with devaluation of the currency you

"bought" everything they owned or produced, and then you starved them to death.

De Milja passed the report to Colonel Broza in Room 9. The colonel put on his reading glasses and thumbed the pages over. "Yes," he said, and "mmm," and finally "thank you." That was all.

But there was something much more troubling on the agenda that day: the man who had printed the RAF leaflets had been arrested in his shop by the Gestapo. "Find out about it," Broza said. "Then see Grodewicz."

He went to visit the printer's wife. They lived in a quite good neighborhood—surprisingly good for a man with a small job shop—broad avenues with trees, solid apartment houses with fire-escape ladders on the alley side, toilets in the apartments instead of the usual privies in the courtyard, and a building superintendent, a heavy woman in a kerchief, polite and not a bit drunk. De Milja asked her about the family. She took notice of his warm coat, and heavy, well-made shoes and raised her palms to heaven: didn't know, didn't want to get involved.

The apartment was on the seventh floor, the top of the building. De Milja trudged up the endless staircase, the marble steps gray from years of scrubbing with Javel water. He stopped to get his breath at the door, then knocked. The wife was a small woman, tepid, harmless, in a faded apron. They sat at the kitchen table. "I don't know what he did," she said.

"What about the neighbors?"

"Mostly they only knew me. And I never made an enemy, Mister."

He believed her. "And him?"

"He was away, you know. Here and there. Some wives, they know when their husband breathes in, when he breathes out. Not me. You couldn't do that with him."

"What did you imagine?"

"Imagine? I only know we had a lot—a lot for who he was

and what he did. He was ambitious, my husband. And maybe rules weren't made for him, you know? But nothing serious. I swear it. Whoever you are, wherever you come from, go back and tell them he didn't do anything so wrong."

She started to cry but she didn't care, didn't touch her face where the tears ran and didn't seem to notice it; everybody cried these days, so what?

"Are you in touch with the Gestapo?"

She nodded that she was. "On Szucha Avenue."

That wasn't good—Szucha Avenue was the central Gestapo headquarters. "I go every week to get his laundry," she continued. "Do the wash and bring it back." Her eyes found his, just for an instant. "There's blood on his underwear," she said.

"We can stop the interrogation," he said.

Just for a moment she believed him, and her eyes widened, then she realized it was a lie.

"He did something for us," de Milja said. "For the underground. Will he tell them?"

She wiped the tears away from her face with her hand. "Not him," she said. "If only he would—but he won't."

"A last question," he said. "How did they catch him?"

She thought for a time, stared out the window at the gray sky over the winter city. "Betrayed," she said. "He never gave himself away."

She was right, de Milja thought. He sensed it wasn't the jealous neighbor, or the business partner with a grudge. It wasn't a denunciation in that sense. He went to see another detective, a man with a big stomach and white hair, who had a line into the Gestapo office on Szucha Avenue. A clerk, perhaps, or a janitor. Information was fragmentary, and uncertain—as though somebody saw an open register, or a list on a desk. Nonetheless, his question was answered: Chomak.

De Milja hadn't expected that. "Why?" he asked.

The detective shrugged. "A man reaches a certain time in

life, and a certain conclusion. He's alone. For himself. At war with the world. So he'll do this for that one, and that for this one—he's a spider, this is his web. *Everybody* is corrupt, he thinks. So he'd better be the same."

It wasn't much, de Milja thought. But there might never be any more, and they were at war, so it had to be enough. As Broza had directed, he went to see Grodewicz. They met at night in the office of a broom factory.

He had known Grodewicz for a long time, they belonged to the same social class, were not quite the same age but had overlapped for a year or two at university. While de Milja had labored desperately—and, it turned out, fruitlessly—to be a mathematician, Grodewicz had thrown himself into drinking and fighting and whoring to such a degree that it had become an issue with the police, and eventually with the university authorities, who finally had to expel him. What bothered de Milja was that Grodewicz not only didn't care, he didn't suffer. He walked away from university life, served as a merchant seaman, was said to have smuggled emeralds into the Balkans from South America, killed a shipmate in a knife fight, screwed a movie star in Vienna. Too many rumors about Grodewicz were true, he thought.

De Milja watched Grodewicz as he spoke quietly into the telephone—making him wait, naturally. He had long, lank, yellow hair that hung over his forehead, was handsome in some indefinably unhealthy way, and arrogant in every bone in his body. Now *Captain* Grodewicz—perhaps a post-invasion commission. De Milja sensed he'd gone to war not because Poland had been attacked, but because Grodewicz had been insulted.

"We'll paint the south wall first," Grodewicz said, obviously using code, from memory and with great facility. "And extend the line of the roof over that window, the south window. Is it clear?"

Grodewicz met de Milja's glance and winked at him. "Good," he said. "Just exactly. Plumb line, chisel, ripsaw and

so forth. Can you manage?" The answer evidently pleased Grodewicz, who smiled and made a galloping rhythm with three fingers on the desk. "I would think," he said. "Maybe we'll all
move in." He replaced the receiver on its cradle.

They talked for a few minutes. De Milja explained what he
needed, Grodewicz said there would be no problem—he had
people ready to do that sort of work. They smoked a cigarette,
said nothing very important, and went off into the night. The
following day de Milja went to a certain telephone booth,
opened the directory to a prearranged page, underlined a word
on the second line, which set the rendezvous two days in the future; circled a word on the eighteenth line: 6:00 P.M.; and
crossed through the twenty-second letter: 6:22 P.M. Very
quickly, and very painfully, the ZWZ had learned the vulnera-
bility of personal contact. Telephone books were safer.

It worked. The operative was on time, appearing suddenly in
a heavy snow of soft, wet flakes that muffled the streets and
made it hard to see. God, he was young, de Milja thought.
Moonfaced, which made him seem placid. Hands shoved in the
pockets of a baggy overcoat.

Chomak's dachshund knew right away who he was. It exploded in a fit of barking and skittered about at the detective's
feet until his wife gathered it up in her arms and went into another room.

They took the evening workers' train across the Vistula. The
snow was falling thickly now, and looking out the window, de
Milja could just see the iron-colored river curling slowly around
the piers of a bridge. Nobody talked on this train; it had been a
long day in the factories and they didn't have the strength for it.
De Milja and Chomak and the operative stood together in the
aisle, holding on to the tops of the seats as the train swayed
through the turns, the steamy windows white with snow blown
sideways by the wind. At the second stop, a neighborhood of
red-brick tenements, they got off the train and found a small bar

near the station. They sat at a table and drank home-brewed beer.

"We're trying to find out about the printer," de Milja said. "The Gestapo arrested him."

Chomak shrugged. "Inevitable," he said.

"Why do you say that?"

"He was a thief," Chomak said. "A Jew thief."

"Really? How do you know?"

"Everybody knew," Chomak said. "He was clever, very clever, just in the way he went around, in the way he did things. He was always up to something—you only had to look at him to see it."

"And the Gestapo, you think, acted on that?"

Chomak thought for a time, then shrugged and lit a cigarette. De Milja saw that his hand was shaking. "Types like that get into trouble," he said after the silence had gone on a little too long. "Sooner or later. Then they get caught. It's a flaw they have."

De Milja nodded slowly, the dark side of human nature making him pensive. "Well," he said, "we can't be late for our meeting."

"You don't think *I* did anything, do you?"

"No." Pause. "Did you? Maybe by accident?"

"Not me."

"Time to go," de Milja said. Then to Chomak: "You're armed?"

"You didn't tell me to bring anything, so I didn't. I have to tell you, I don't care for being suspected. That's not right."

De Milja stood up and left, Chomak following, the operative waving Chomak out the door ahead of him. "Don't worry about it," de Milja said.

Hunched over in the cold and the snow, they hurried along a narrow street that wound back toward the railroad. Chomak took a fast two steps and caught up with de Milja. "Why would you ask me a thing like that?" He had to raise his voice a little because of the wind and it made him sound querulous and in-

sulted. "I served fourteen years in the detectives." He was
angry now. "We knew who did what. That type, you're always
on the short end of the deal—just once turn your back and then
you'll see."

A Gestapo car, a black Grosser Mercedes with headlights
taped down to slits because of the blackout, honked at them to
get out of the way. They stood with their backs against the wall,
faces averted, as it bumped past, the red taillights disappearing
into the swirling snow.

"You see?" Chomak said, when they were walking again. "I
could have flagged them down. But I didn't, did I?"

At an arched railroad bridge, where the street dipped below
the track, de Milja signaled to stop, and the three men stood
by the curved wall and stamped their feet to keep warm. It
was dark under the bridge and the snow was blowing right
through it.

"Hell of a night for a meeting," Chomak said, a good-
natured laugh in his voice.

De Milja heard the sound of a train approaching in the distance. Bending over to protect the match from the wind, he lit a
cigarette, then cupped his palm to shield the glow. "Face the
wall," he said to Chomak.

"What did you say?"

"Face the wall."

Chomak turned slowly and faced the wall. The approaching
train was moving slowly because of the snowstorm. "It's not
right," Chomak said. "For a Jew thief. Some little sneak from
the gutter. Not right."

"Why would you do a thing like that?" de Milja said. "Were
you in trouble?"

De Milja could see that Chomak's legs were trembling, and
he thought he might collapse. He looked at the operative and
their eyes met for a moment as the train came closer. The sound
of the wheels thundered in the tunnel as it passed overhead,
Chomak bounced off the wall, then sagged back against it, his

hand groping for a hold on the smooth surface. Very slowly, he slid down to his knees, then toppled over on his side. The opera-tive straddled him and fired once into his temple.

January 1940. The French planes did not come. Perhaps, people thought, they are not going to come. Not ever. In the streets of Paris, the Communist party and its supporters marched and chanted for peace, for dignity, for an end to war. Especially this unjust war against Germany—Russia's ally. On the Maginot Line, quartered in a schoolhouse near Strasbourg, Private Jean-Paul Sartre of the artillery's meteorological intelli-gence service sent balloons aloft, reported on the speed and di-rection of the wind to gunners who never fired a shot, and wrote in his journal that "*Life* is the transcendent, psychic object constructed by human reality in search of its own foundation."

In Great Britain, German magnetic mines had taken a consid-erable toll of merchant shipping, and rationing had been estab-lished for butter, sugar, bacon, and ham. Winston Churchill spoke on the radio, and told the nations of Europe that "each one hopes that if he feeds the crocodile enough, the crocodile will eat him last. All of them hope that the storm will pass before their turn comes to be devoured."

As for the United States, it remained stern and unrelenting in the maintenance of a "moral embargo" it had declared against Germany.

Meanwhile, Warsaw lived in ice. The calendar froze—a win-ter of ten thousand days was at hand. And as the hope of help from friends slowly waned, it became the time of the prophe-cies. Sometimes typed, sometimes handwritten, they were ev-erywhere and, whether casually dismissed or secretly believed, were passionately followed. A battlefield of contending specters: rune-casters and biblical kings, the Black Madonna of Czes-tochowa and Nostradamus, the fire at the center of the earth, the cycles of the moon, the springs of magic water, the Apocry-pha—the fourteen known books and the fifteenth, only just now revealed. The day was coming, it couldn't quite be said exactly when, but blood would flow from stones, the dead would rise from their graves, the lame would walk, the blind would see, and the fucking *shkopy* would get out of Poland.

At a time when national consolation was almost nonexistent, the prophecies helped, strange as some of them were, and the intelligence service of the Polish underground certainly wrote their share. Meanwhile, hiding in their apartments from winter and the Gestapo, the people of Warsaw listened—on pain of death if caught—to the BBC on illicit radios. And they also studied English. That winter in Warsaw, an English grammar couldn't be had for love or money. Even so, the joke everybody was telling around town went like this: the pessimists are learning German, the optimists are learning English, while the realists, in January of 1940, were said to be learning Russian.

In Room 9, Agata leaned back from the committee table, ran long fingers through her chopped-off hair, blew savage plumes of smoke from her nostrils, and said, "Next. The eastern zone, and the need to do something about the Russians. As of yesterday, a courier reported six more arrests by the NKVD."

It had been a long meeting, not a good one, with too many problems tabled for future consideration. Colonel Broza did not respond—he stared absently at a map of Poland tacked to the green wall, but there was certainly little comfort for him there.

"The efficiency of the NKVD," Agata went on, "seems only to increase. They are everywhere, how to say, *inside our lines*. In the professions, the peasantry—there is no social class we can turn to. People in the Russian zone have simply stopped talking to their friends—and I can't imagine anything that hurts us more than that. The fear is on the streets, in the air. Of our top echelon, political and military, nothing remains; those who are alive are in the Lubianka, and out of contact. From the officer camps in the Katyn forest it's the same thing: no escapes, no letters, silence. So, since it is Poland's great privilege to play host to both the NKVD and the Gestapo, it's time to admit we are not doing all that badly with the Germans, but have not yet learned how to operate against the Russians.''

Broza thought about it for a time. "Why?" he said.

"Why are the Russians better at it?" Agata said.

"Yes."

"Oh, tradition. A thousand years of espionage, the secret police of Ivan the Terrible—is that what you want to hear?"

Broza's expression was grim, almost despairing—wasn't there perhaps a little more to it? No? Maybe?

Agata tapped a pencil eraser against the open page of a notebook. "There is a difference," she said slowly, "that interests me. Say that it is the difference between nationalism and, ah, what we might call social theory. For the Germans, nationalism is an issue of race, ethnicity. For example, they accept as their own the *Volksdeutsch*—descendents of German colonists, many of whom do not even speak German. But their blood is German blood—these Teutonic philosophers really believe in such things. Cut a vein, listen closely, you can hear the overture to *Lohengrin*—why, that's a *German* you've got there! The Bolsheviks are just the opposite—they recruit the mind, or so they like to pretend. And all the world is invited to join them; you can be a communist any time you like—'Good heavens! I just realized it's all in the dictatorship of the working class.'

"Now as a practical matter, that difference serves the purposes of the NKVD very nicely. We all accept that every society has its opportunists—criminals, misfits, unrecognized geniuses, the pathologically disappointed—and when the conqueror comes, that's the moment to even the score. But, here in western Poland, the only job open is collaborator—you can't just get up in the morning and decide to be German. On the Soviet side, however, you can experience insight, then conversion, and you'll be welcomed. Oh, you may have to tattle a little, tell the NKVD whatever you happen to know—and everybody knows *something*. You can invite your former friends to join you in conspiracies, you can inform on your enemies. And what are you then? A traitor? No, a friend of peace and the working class. And, if you turn out to have a bit of a flair for the work, you can be a commissar.''

Agata paused a moment, lit a new cigarette. ''And if that's not bad enough,'' she said, shaking out the match, ''the NKVD is very shrewd, and never in a hurry. They follow the spirit of resistance like a hidden current running through an ocean: they detain, interrogate, torture, turn a few to work for them, shoot the rest, and start over.''

Colonel Broza nodded slowly. ''Tyranny,'' he said, ''has become a science.'' He turned to de Milja. ''What do you think we can do, Captain.''

De Milja was in no hurry to answer. ''Perhaps, over time, we'll prove to be stronger than they are. But right now, I would say the important thing for us is to hammer at the links between the Germans and the Russians. For us, in this room, the worst would be if NKVD methods were to spread to the Gestapo.''

''We know they've been meeting in Cracow,'' Grodewicz said, ''but the Russians aren't sharing much. They cooperate by handing over German communists who fled to Moscow in the thirties, but they don't talk about methods.''

''That is because,'' Agata said, ''they are going to fight.''

''Yes. They must, eventually,'' Broza said. He thought a moment, then his eyes met de Milja's. ''Take some time and a few people, Captain. See if you can get a sense of when that might be.''

A week later, he left the freezing basement. Life immediately improved, was certainly warmer, better in a number of ways. He moved to a room in the Mokotow district, down a long hall-way in the apartment of a former customs official, now a clerk in a factory office and a great friend to the resistance. Since the oc-cupation authority had closed the schools—Poles, as a slave race, needed only to understand simple directions and to count to twenty—the official's wife taught at a secret school in a church basement while the children attended classes.

That left de Milja alone in the apartment for much of the day. Alone, except for Madame Kuester. Fortyish, probably a little older, a distant cousin of one side of the family or the other, she had met and married a Dutch engineer—Herr Kuester—who had gone off to work on a bridge in Kuala Lumpur in 1938, then vanished. Madame Kuester, childless, had then come to stay with the family. Not quite a servant, not quite an equal, she had worked in fashionable women's shops before the war, lived quietly in her room, proud of not being a burden to anyone. The title "madame" was a survival of the world of the shops, where she had been, evidently, a bad-tempered and difficult supervisor to a generation of young assistants.

Given the hours of proximity, a love affair seemed inevitable. But the captain resisted. A deep, almost haunted longing for the wife who wasn't there, a nominal—and sometimes not so nominal—Catholicism, and ZWZ security procedures: everything was against it. Including the attitude of Madame Kuester, haughty and cold, clearly meant to discourage familiarity between two people forced by war into the accidental intimacies of apartment life.

She was, de Milja came to understand, a snob to her very marrow. She set herself above the world, looking down on its unrefined excesses with small, angry eyes set in a great expanse of white brow. Her mouth was mean, down-curved, she wore her coarse hair elaborately pinned up, went about the apartment in gray blouse and long wool skirt—the prewar uniform of some of the better shops—that hung shapeless over a thick, heavy figure, and her walk, hard and definitive, told the world all it needed to know: *you have left me alone, now leave me alone.*

But it was cold, always cold.

The February snow hissed against the window, the afternoons were silent, and dark, and endless. Captain de Milja was now subject to increased ZWZ security constraints; stay out of the center of Warsaw, where police patrols were abundant, try not to be on the streets during working hours—use the morning and evening travel periods as cover for getting around the city. He had to hold agent meetings as he probed for German intentions toward the U.S.S.R., but he scheduled them early in the morning and late in the afternoon, always in public places—libraries, railway stations, the thicker the crowd the better he liked it. But for much of the day he was a prisoner in the Mokotow apartment.

Where he discovered that he was keeping track of Madame Kuester by the sound of her presence: the scrape of the match as she lit the stove for midmorning tea, the rhythm of a carpet sweeper rolled relentlessly back and forth, the polite slam of a firmly closed door as she retired to her room for a midday rest, the creak of the bedspring as she lay down to nap.

Every afternoon at about 2:35, that was. She rather believed, he sensed, in the idea of routine, consistency. It was the way *her sort of people*—never defined, yet always with her—chose to live. After lunch she would sit primly in the corner of the sofa, then, after forty-five minutes of reading, rise majestically and disappear into her room. On Sunday, with the family present, everything was different, but six days a week her habit never varied, never changed.

Well, perhaps just once it did. On an otherwise unremarkable day in the middle of the week, she forgot her book. Ha! What absurdly spiteful joy he felt at such a lapse. He was immediately ashamed of himself, but there it lay, open, facedown on the arm of the sofa, protected by the blue paper cover she fussily wrapped her books in. Curious, he had a look. French. Well, of course, he should have known. A French novel, the very thing *her sort of people* would amuse themselves with.

De Milja scanned the page to see what kept Madame so occupied that she hadn't a thought for the rest of the world. ". . . *dans une position en lequel ses places ombrées étaient, comme on dit, disponi-*

bles, mais c'était le sens de la caresse de l'aire sur elles, ces ouvertures, qui faisait battre fort son coeur . . ."

What?

In pure astonishment and disbelief he slipped the cover off the novel: *La Belle Dominique.* Written by that well-known and time-honored author, Vaguely Saucy Nom de Plume. The French novel was a French novel! He flipped the pages, and read some more, and flipped the pages, and read some more. It was the sheer contrast of the moment that struck his heart. The dying, ice-bound city, heavy with fear and misery and the exhaustion of daily life, set against these brittle pages of print, where gold passementerie was untied and heavy drapes flowed together, where pale skin flushed rose with excitement, where silk rustled to the floors of moonlit chambers.

De Milja's eyes sought the door to Madame Kuester's room, which, in defiance of her cherished routine, stood open a suggestive inch. He opened it the rest of the way and stepped inside. A small room in a Warsaw apartment, winter light yellow behind the drawn shade, an old steamer trunk used as a wardrobe, a shape curled up on a cot beneath a wool army blanket.

As in a dream, she drew her knees up, arched her back like a yawning cat, then rolled slowly onto her stomach and nestled against the bed. One hand snaked out of the covers and smoothed the loose hair off the side of her face. Now he could see that her eyes were closed, but she smiled a little smile for him; greedy and bittersweet and sure of itself all at once. And if, somehow, he still didn't get the point, she breathed a soft, interrogatory sigh. He stepped to the side of the bed and lowered the blanket to her bare heels. She moved a little, just the signature on an invitation, took the pillow in both hands, and slid it under her body until it rested beneath her hips. Which elevated her, he thought as he undid his belt, *"to such a position that her shadowed places were, as it is said, available, but it was the feeling of the touch of the air upon them, these openings, that made her heart beat hard."*

. . .

They never spoke of it, not ever. *One doesn't*—that was her unspoken law and he obeyed it. So she remained, in the daily life of the apartment, as remote and distant as she had always been. He spent the middle part of the day with his notes and papers, mostly numbers and coded place names, while she, nose in the air, dusted, and ran the carpet sweeper over the rugs. She read every day after lunch, sitting properly in the corner of the sofa. Then, at 2:35, she went to her room. He followed a few minutes later, and found each time a different woman. In this bed, for this hour, everything was possible. It was as though, he thought, they owned in common a theater under a blanket where, every afternoon, they rehearsed and performed for an audience of themselves. Only themselves. The city would not know of it—at the conclusion of each scene she stuffed the blanket into her down-curved mouth and screamed like a Fury.

Wizna, on the Narew River, 7 March 1940. Encampment of the Nineteenth Infantry Division, Grenadierregiment, Wehrkreis XIV, Kassel. 5:30 A.M. The floodlights were turned out and the dawn fog pooled at the bases of the barbed-wire stanchions. The Russian troops were camped on the other side of the river; when they ran the engines of their tanks, the Wehrmacht soldiers could hear them.

Each day at dawn the garbage cans were brought out to the regimental dump on hand trucks; the contents spilled out with a spirited banging, the garbage detail working in shirtsleeves despite the bitter cold, cigarettes stuck in their mouths to mask the smell. First the dogs came, trotting, heads down, silent—precedence had been established in the first days of occupation and there were no more fights. Next came the old Polish women in their black shawls and dresses, each holding a stick to beat the dogs if they got too insistent.

Oberschützen Kohler and Stentz, the two privates first-class on guard duty, stood and watched the Polish women, dark figures in the morning fog, as they picked through the mounds of garbage. This guard duty was permanent, and they did it every morning. They didn't like it, but they knew nobody cared about that, so they didn't, either.

At the age of nineteen, though, it was a sad lesson. These women, fated to spend this early hour picking through the garbage of a German garrison in order to have something to eat— could they be so different from their own mothers and grandmothers? Kohler and Stentz were not barbarians, they were Wehrmacht riflemen, not so different from generations of infantry, Swedish or Prussian or Corsican or Austrian—the list was just too long—who had stood guard at camps on these Polish rivers back into the time of the Roman legions.

Kohler looked around, made sure there were no officers in the vicinity, then he tapped Stentz on the shoulder. Stentz whistled a certain clever way, and the crone showed up a few moments later like she always did. Her face, all seamed and gullied beneath wisps of thin, white hair, never stopped nodding, *thank you, Excellency, thank you, Excellency,* as she moved to the edge of the barbed wire. She reached out trembling hands and took the crusts of bread that Stentz got from a friend in the camp kitchen. These vanished into her clothing, kept separate from whatever was in the burlap sack she carried over her shoulder. She mumbled something—she had no teeth and was hard to understand, but it was certainly thankful. It wished God's mercy on them. Heaven had seen, she was certain, this kindness to an old woman.

Later that morning she walked to the edge of her village to meet the man who bought rags. For him too she thanked God, because these were not very good rags, they were used, worn-out rags with very little rubbing and cleaning left in them. Still, he paid. She had gasoline-soaked rags from the motor pool, damp, foul rags that had been used to clean the kitchens, brown rags the soldiers used to polish their boots, a few shreds of yellow rag they used to shine brass with, and some of the oily little patches they used to clean their rifles.

The rag man bought everything, as he always did, and counted out a few coppers into her hand—just as he would for all the other old ladies who came to see him throughout the morning. Only a few coppers, but if you had enough of them they bought something. Everybody was in business now, she thought, it was always that way when the armies came. Too bad about the nice boys who gave her the bread. They would die, pretty soon, nice or not. Sad, she thought, how they never learned what waited for them in Poland.

7 March 1940, Budapest. The offices of Schlegel and Son, stock and commodity exchange brokers based in Zurich. Mr. Teleky, the brisk young transfer clerk, took the morning prices off the teletype just before noon and wrote them in chalk on a blackboard hung from the oak paneling in the customers' room. Behind a wooden railing a few old men sat and smoked, bored and desultory. War was bad for the brokerage business, as far as Mr. Teleky could see. People put their money into gold coins and buried them in the basement—nobody believed in the futures market when nobody believed in the future.

Still, you acted as though everything would come out for the best—where would you go in the morning if you didn't go to work? Mr. Teleky printed the morning numbers in a careful hand. A few customers were watching. Gottwald, the German Jew, trying to make the money he'd earned selling his wife's jewelry go a little further. Standing next to him was Schaumer, the Austrian Nazi party functionary, who came here to speculate with money stolen from Viennese Jews. Then there was Varski, the old Polish diplomat who walked with a cane, proud and poor, earning a few francs one day and losing them the next. Mr. Teleky privately wondered why he bothered, but you couldn't talk to the Poles, they were hardheaded and did what they wanted, you might as well argue with the sea.

So, what did he have for these august gentlemen? Cairo cotton was up a point, Brazilian coffee unchanged, London wool down a quarter and so was flax, iron ore had gained half a point, coal was off an eighth. Trading in manganese was suspended— the Germans meddling, no doubt. Mr. Teleky went on and on, rendering each symbol and number carefully, for whoever might want to come to the Schlegel offices and witness the fluctuations of world trade. Gottwald turned on his heel and left, then Schaumer. Varski the Pole stayed until the bitter end, then stood, nodded politely to Mr. Teleky, and went on about his daily business.

The chemist and the commodity analyst.

The chemist in Lodz—the traditional home of industrial chemistry in Poland, where dyes for the fabric mills had been produced since the nineteenth century—wrote the most careful, the most studied report of his professional life. If he'd been an indifferent patriot before September, '39, before dead friends and vanished family, before his house was taken and his salary halved, he wasn't one now.

Now he was a patriot of reports. He had tested, and retested, used infinite care, worked to the very limit of his technical abilities. And his conclusion was:

No change.

An analysis of seventy-five samples selected from a range of over five thousand cotton patches bearing traces of the oil used to clean and maintain weapons showed no meaningful variation in the viscosity of the oil. Samples were obtained from disposal areas abandoned by Wehrmacht units in September of 1939—in eastern, now Russian-occupied, Poland—and these were compared with samples from bases currently occupied in Silesia, East Prussia, and western Poland. The analyzed material, a lightly refined petroleum-based oil also used in machine shops for lubrication and protection of bored and rifled metal surfaces, had not been significantly altered during the seven-month period in question. The viscosity of the oil was consistent to a low temperature of $-5°$ Fahrenheit, but below that point effectiveness was rapidly degraded. For the maintenance and cleaning of rifled weapons below $-5°$ Fahrenheit, a lower viscosity, lighter-weight oil would be required.

The commodity analyst in Warsaw was a Jew, and suspected he hadn't long to live. A few people he knew of had managed to leave Poland, but most hadn't. The German Jews had been attacked by means of taxation and bureaucratic constraint since the ascension of the Nazi government in 1933—a six-year period. Two thirds of them, about four hundred thousand people, had gotten out of Germany before the borders closed. They had bribed South American consular officials, filled the British quotas in Palestine, deployed wealth and influence to evade immigration regulations in the United States and Great Britain. But in using those methods they had, in effect, worn out the administrative escape lines. For the three million Polish Jews, there was nothing.

So the commodity analyst, a yellow Star of David sewn to the breast pocket of a suit made by a London tailoring establishment in 1937, wrote what he believed to be his final report. Since the German occupation he had worked in a small factory that made needles and pins, sweeping up, running errands, whatever was needed, but even this little job was ending. And he had been told that he and his family would have to move into the old Polish ghetto just south of Gdansk station. The Germans meant to kill him, a forty-eight-year-old man with a wife and three children. If there was something he could do about that, some tactic of evasion, he had not been able to discover it. He had a good mind, trained in Talmud, trained in business, and recognized that some problems cannot be solved. What would happen next would happen next, it wasn't up to him.

He would have liked to be, in this analysis written at the request of an old friend, brilliant, at least ingenious. He had specialized in the behavior of the wool markets for twenty years, and he thought he knew them just about as well as anyone could. But facts were facts, numbers worked a certain way, and after an intensive study of twelve months of buying and selling activity in the commodity exchanges of London, Chicago, and Geneva, there was only one, rather dull but plainly evident, conclusion to be drawn:

No change.

Captain de Milja met privately with Colonel Broza in Room 9. Outside, the evening streets were awash with spring rain. "There is no preparation to attack," de Milja said.

"Hard to believe that," Broza said.

"Yes. But that is what we found. Germany will have to deploy three million men to attack Russia, led by tanks as they were in Poland. Supplied by horse and wagon, and freight train. Attacking on a line from the Baltic to the Black Sea. As for the time of the attack, that too can be deduced. Today is the sixteenth of March. Russia must be invaded in the late spring, after the rivers crest and the floods recede, and it must be defeated by the middle of autumn, before the winter freeze. Napoleon learned that in 1812, and very little has changed since then. The temperature in Russia in December goes down, habitually and unremarkably, to minus thirty degrees Fahrenheit. It can go lower, and when the wind blows—which it does, for weeks on end—the cold is acutely intensified. You can't send three million men into that kind of weather without preparation.

"So, we have the sixteenth of March and three million men. As of a week ago, not a drop of low-viscosity oil had been issued at any Wehrmacht base we know about. And there has been no change in the international wool markets—which means no warm coats for the Wehrmacht. The Germans have been clever all along about covert logistics—disguised orders for chemicals and rubber—but you can't slaughter millions of sheep or buy up that much wool production without a reaction from the markets. So if the Wehrmacht goes east in April, they'll go without wool coats, and by January they'll freeze to death with useless rifles in their hands."

Broza wasn't so sure. "Perhaps. But Hitler thinks he'll be in Moscow by late October—that's the point of the blitzkrieg. They'll take their wool coats from the cloakroom at the Kremlin. What's to stop them? The Red Army is sick as a dog; officers shot in the purges, all the tactics they tried in Finland failed miserably."

"The Russians *won't* stop them. They'll slow them down, bleed their strength—it will be some variation on defense-in-depth."

Broza paused to consider that. Defense-in-depth was the ancient, traditional military doctrine of Russia. For a thousand years, they'd protected their cities by use of the abatis: trees cut down at the three-foot level, the logs hung up on the stumps and pointing out toward the enemy. Among the felled trees were pits camouflaged with cut brush—intended to break the ankle of a horse or a man. These defenses were eighty miles deep. With raiding parties harassing their flanks, an invasion force would find itself exhausted when it finally reached the site the Russians had chosen as a battleground.

By 1938, building what was called the Stalin Line on the U.S.S.R.'s western boundary, various refinements had been added: artificial lakes—five feet deep, to tempt an invader to try a crossing—artificial marsh, cornfields cut to accommodate enfilading machine-gun fire, concrete bunkers three feet thick, with barbed wire now tangled in the trunks of the fallen trees.

"Defense-in-depth doesn't happen overnight," Broza said, thinking out loud. "And the Stalin Line is being dismantled now that the Russians have moved up to the middle of Poland. That advance may cost them more than they suspect.''

''They will sacrifice lives,'' de Milja said. ''And land. Burn the villages, blow up the bridges.''

Broza thumbed through a sheaf of papers in a dossier. ''Granted, they are not distributing light oil for the winter, and they are not buying sheepskins. But we know they are building large hospitals on the border. For who? Not for us, certainly. And we've seen important commanders and staff logistics peo ple flown in to border camps for conferences.''

Both officers thought about that for a time. ''It is coming,'' de Milja said. ''But not this spring. Perhaps in '41.''

''And this spring?''

''France.''

''Nobody believes such a thing can happen,'' Broza said. ''You mean a major attack—tanks, assault planes, infantry, Paris in flames?''

''Yes,'' de Milja said.

Broza shook his head. It wasn't possible.

The first winter of German occupation turned slowly to the rain and mud of a long, slow spring. Perhaps the Poles lost heart a little. The first rage was spent—a few SS officers assassinated, several hundred hostages shot. But when the smoke cleared the Germans weren't frightened and the Poles weren't intimidated. And so they settled down to fight.

The recommendation of the ZWZ intelligence service—to hammer at the links between Russia and Germany—was endorsed by the Sixth Bureau administration in Paris, and the logical area of attack turned out to be the Hitler/Stalin Pact trade agreements. German technology needed Russian raw materials; a million tons of animal fodder, a million tons of crude oil, tons of cotton, coal, phosphates, chromium, and iron ore. The Rus-

sians had the matériel—it was simply a matter of shipping it to
Germany. By rail. Across Poland.

From the first days of occupation it was clear that all labor
would be performed by Polish workers, under German supervision. So the Germans, when they decided to enlarge Prez-
mysl railroad station, just on the German side of the border,
hired ZWZ carpenters, ZWZ masons, and ZWZ helpers to
hand them the proper tool. Broza, de Milja and company knew
everything before it happened. The railroad line Prezmysl/
Cracow/Breslau, entirely under the view of Polish underground intelligence, was soon ready to carry the goods that
would keep Germany rich and powerful, while the Poles were
itching to blow it all to hell, a small first step on the road to
making Germany poor and weak.

The battle started with Polish Boy Scouts, adept at crawling
under freight cars, opposed by German sentries, who shot anything and justified nothing. But it did not remain on that level.
The initial Polish thrust—we can blow up whatever we want—
was answered by a German counterthrust—we can fix whatever
you blow up. The Poles soon realized the magnitude of the job
they had taken on: the Germans *were* good fixers, and the strate-
gic sector of the German/Polish economy was no small thing—
it was going to require one hell of an effort to blow it all up. Not
only that, the means to blow it up had to be stolen from these
very Germans; at least until the French and British Allies found a
way to fly in the explosives they needed. Not at all daunted, the
Poles created a special blowing-up–and–stealing organization to
do the job. They called it Komenda Dyversji—Sabotage and Di-
version—Kedyv for short.

Like any organization, Kedyv measured its success in numbers. In 1940, a disabled locomotive was out of service for fourteen hours. Later, the period would rise to fourteen days. The
increase in productivity was achieved by Polish chemists and engineers, opposed by German chemists and engineers. At which

point the conflict had reached the level on which it would be decided: national intelligentsia versus national intelligentsia.

The Polish scientists took the offensive and never let up: they built incendiary devices that were swiftly and easily attachable to tank cars loaded with Russian crude oil, they then timed the fuse by the rhythm of the rails: x number of thumps would set off the explosion, sometimes in Poland, sometimes in Germany. Unable to determine the venue of the sabotage, the Germans found it impossible to investigate. Petroleum storage tanks were set afire by the introduction of cylinders of compressed hydrogen with open valves. Locomotives were disabled by the addition of an abrasive to the lubricating system. Russian iron ore was seeded with bombs that exploded while the ore was traveling down chutes into German smelters. When railroad tracks were mined, the first mine blew up a train, the second a rescue train, the third a repair train.

The Germans didn't like it.

These *untermenschen* were not to be permitted to interfere with the harmonization of German Europe. A message was sent to the Poles: the faculty of Cracow University was called to a meeting, then arrested en masse. It was thought to be the first time an entire university had been arrested. But a few nights later, on the Silesian border, a blue flash, a fiery spray of tank-car metal, five vats of flame towed through the darkness by a terrified engineer. *Fuck you.*

28 March, 3:40 A.M. De Milja woke suddenly. He listened, concentrated. First the strange, whispery silence of a city under curfew. Then a board creaked in the hallway.

So, 9 mm from the nightstand, safety thumbed off. He sat up slowly, sighted on the crack where the door met the jamb. The knob turned delicately, a cautious hand on the other side. De Milja took a breath and held it.

Madame Kuester. In a silk robe, hair in a long braid. "Don't kill me, please," she said. He understood only by watching her mouth move, her voice barely made a sound. He lowered the gun. "Germans," she said. Gestured with her eyes. She walked down the hall to her room, he followed, in undershirt and shorts. He stood close to her in the small room, could smell the laundry soap she washed with. The shade moved slightly in the air, the window behind it open an inch. From the roof across the narrow street, a hushed *"Ocht-svansig, Ocht-svansig,"* then a brief hiss of radio static. *Eight-twenty, then,* he thought. Meaning I'm in place, or proceed to apartment, or they're all asleep, or whatever it meant. Now de Milja's decision had been made for him: orders were specific, the response detailed; and he was not to permit himself to be taken alive. "Get dressed, please," he said.

He walked down the hallway, tapped lightly at the door of the master bedroom. He heard the man and his wife breathing deeply inside, opened the door, had finally to lean over and touch the man on his bare shoulder. *They made love tonight,* he thought. The man was immediately awake, saw de Milja and the 9 mm and understood everything.

He went back to Madame Kuester's room. When he opened the door she was naked, standing in front of an open bureau drawer. He knew this profile—the curve of her abdomen, flat bottom, heavy thighs. Her head turned toward him. She didn't exactly pause, skipped a single beat perhaps, then took underwear from the drawer and stepped into it. He wanted to hold her against him, something he had never done before. There were family noises in the hall; the children, the parents, an angry word. "Best to say good-bye," she said.

"Good-bye," he said. He couldn't see her eyes in the darkened room.

He hurried back to his room, put on a sweater, wool pants, heavy shoes, and a raincoat. The gun fit in the raincoat pocket. From inside a book he selected an *ausweis*—German work pass—and other identification meant for emergencies, as well as a packet of zloty notes and some gold coins. The family and Madame Kuester were waiting for him at the front door.

The bolt and lock mechanisms were heavily oiled, just a soft click and de Milja was looking out at the landing. A current of chilly air from the staircase meant that the street door was standing open. This was not normal. De Milja turned, silently let the others know what had happened. The reaction was calm; the father held a large military revolver, his thirteen-year-old son had its twin. The man smiled and nodded gravely. *I understand.*

Three flights below, somebody tried to walk silently through the lobby. Others followed, one of them stifled a cough. They could have climbed the stairs quietly if they'd taken off their boots, but the SS didn't do things like that, so de Milja and the family could hear them coming. When they came around the curve of the staircase onto the second floor, de Milja took the 9 mm out of his pocket and climbed the iron rungs of a ladder that led to a hatch that opened onto the roof. He tested the hatch with his gun hand, moving it only enough to make sure it wasn't secured from the other side. He was reasonably sure there were German police on the roof.

They reached the floor below. They weren't very careful about noise now, de Milja could hear the heels of their boots and the sound of leather belts and holster grommets and breathing deepened by excitement and anticipation. Then they pounded their fists on a door and yelled for somebody to open up, the guttural German rolled and echoed up the open staircase and rang on the tile landings. The door was flung open, knob hammering the wall, then there were shouts and running footsteps and a wail of terror as the downstairs neighbor was arrested.

They had, de Milja calculated, at most an hour.

The middle-aged couple who lived below would be taken to Szucha Avenue headquarters, a sergeant would put down basic information and fill out forms, and when the interrogators finally got busy they would realize that this was not Captain Alexander de Milja or *the man in the brown raincoat* or whatever description they had. Then they would come back.

There was, of course, at least the mathematical possibility that the police had not made an error, but those who indulged themselves in that kind of thinking were no longer alive in Poland in the spring of 1940.

A few minutes after five in the morning, when the curfew ended, the wife, both children, and Madame Kuester left the apartment with false identity cards and a wicker basket on wheels they used for shopping. Moments later, they came to the side street and turned right. Which meant, to de Milja looking out the window, that German police remained on guard in the lobby, checking papers as the tenants left the building. Five minutes later, de Milja was alone—the former customs official had walked out the door of his apartment, probably never to see it again. He too turned right at the side street, which confirmed the earlier signal, and touched his hair, which meant the Germans were checking closely. At 5:15, de Milja climbed the ladder, cautiously raised the hatch, then hoisted himself out onto the roof.

The dawn was a shock after the close apartment—cold air, dark blue sky, shattered red cloud in streaks that curved to the horizon. He took a moment to get his bearings, smelled cigarette smoke nearby, then knelt behind a plaster wall at the foot of a chimney. Somebody was up here with him, possibly a German policeman. He held the 9 mm in his right hand, pressed the fingertips of his left hand against the tar surface of the roof. He could feel somebody pacing: one, two, three, four, five. Pause. Then back again. Everything de Milja knew suggested a police guard on the roof—the raid, the document control at the front door. Germans were thorough, this was the sort of thing they did. He wanted to see for himself, but resisted the temptation to rise up and look around—the roof was cluttered; sheets hung on clotheslines, chimneys, ventilation pipe outlets, two tarpaper-roofed housings that covered the entries to staircases.

A few feet away, across a low parapet and above a narrow alley, was a fire escape on the sixth floor of the building next door. From there, he had several choices: climb in an apartment window, descend to the alley, or go up to the roof, which abutted two neighboring buildings, one of them a factory with heavy truck traffic in and out. All he had to do was jump the space above the alley.

Down in the street, a tramcar arrived, ringing its bell, grinding to a stop, then starting up again. He heard the clop of hoofbeats—perhaps the wagon that delivered coal—and the high/low siren of German police wagons as they sped through the city streets. The air smelled of coal smoke and onions frying in fat, and he could see the morning star, still sharp, but fading in the gathering daylight. He heard the rasp of a window forced up, he heard a woman laugh—shrill, abandoned, it was so funny she didn't care how she sounded.

Turning his head, he saw a woman appear at an open window in an adjacent building. Her apartment was one story above the roof, so he found himself looking up at her. She wore an old print dress with the sleeves rolled up, an apron, and a kerchief with the knot tied in the middle of her forehead. Her face was determined—here it was just after dawn and she was cleaning her house. She poked a dustmop out the window and gave it a good bang against the sill, then another, just so it remembered who was boss.

When she saw de Milja, she stared as though he were an animal in a zoo. Of course, he thought. What she sees is a man with an automatic pistol in his hand, kneeling behind the base of a chimney. *Hiding* behind the base of a chimney. Hmm. Probably a criminal. But he's not alone on the roof. From where she stood—she gave the mop a desultory rap just to keep up appearances—she could see another man. This man was pacing, and smoking a cigarette. Perhaps, if God wills, de Milja thought, he's wearing a uniform, or if he's in civilian clothes maybe he has on one of those stupid little hats with alpine brushes the Germans liked.

De Milja watched the woman, she stared back shamelessly, then looked away, probably at the pacing man. Then back at him. He sensed a motion behind her, and she was briefly distracted. She almost, he felt, turned away from the window and went back to cleaning the apartment—somebody in the room had told her to do that. Yes, de Milja thought, that was it. She turned her head and said something, something dismissive and sharp, then returned to watching the men on the roof below her. She had broad shoulders and big red hands—nobody told *her* what to do. De Milja now faced her directly and spread his arms, palms up in the universal interrogatory gesture: *what's going on?*

She didn't react. She wasn't going to help a thief—her expression was suspicious and hostile. But then, a moment later, she changed her mind. She held out a hand, fingers stiff: *stop*. De Milja put his hand back on the surface of the roof, three, four, five. Pause. The woman held her signal. Then, just as a new sequence of footsteps began, she beckoned abruptly, excitedly: *yes, it's all right now, he can't see you.* Three, four, five. Pause. *No, stop, he's facing your way.* Three, four, five. Pause. *Yes, it's . . .*

De Milja leaped up and ran for his life.

He almost got away with it.

But if he could feel the policeman pacing on the roof, the man could feel it when he ran. "Halt!"

As de Milja reached the parapet he could see the woman's face with perfect clarity: her mouth rounded into an *O*, her hand came up and pressed the side of her face. She was horrified at what was about to happen. The first shot snapped the air next to his ear just as his foot hit the parapet. It was a long way across. Seven floors down, broken glass in the alley glittered up at him. And the parapet was capped with curved, slippery, ceramic tile. It was a bad jump, one foot slipped as he took off. He flailed at the empty air, and he almost cleared the railing, but then his left heel caught and that spilled him forward, his head hitting the iron floor of the fire escape as something pinged in the stairway above him and somebody shouted.

He had not felt the bullet, but he was on his knees, vision swimming, a rock in his chest that blocked his air. He went away. Came back. Looked down at a windowsill, worn and weathered gray. A big drop of blood fell on it, then another. His heart raced, he clawed at the iron fretwork, somehow stood up. The world spun around him; whistles, shouts — a brick exploded and he turned away from it. Saw the ladder to the floor below, made himself half slide, half tumble to the iron platform.

His escape—from everything, forever—was six stories down into the alley and he knew it, he just had to get one leg over the railing and then the other and then the terrors of Szucha Avenue no longer existed. Hide under the ground, they will never touch you. He was going to do it—then he didn't. Instead, the window on the fire escape exploded into somebody's kitchen— glass, blood, and de Milja all showing up for breakfast.

A family around a table; a still life, a spoon frozen in air between bowl and mouth, a woman at a stove, a man in suspenders. Then he was in a parlor; a canary tweeted, in a mirror above a buffet a man with bright blood spattered on his face. He fumbled at the family's locks, somehow worked the right bolt the right way, the door opened, then closed behind him.

He froze. Then the door on the other side of the landing flew open and a man beckoned fiercely from the darkness of his hall. "This way," he said, voice thick with excitement. De Milja couldn't see—objects doubled, then faded into ghosts of themselves—then a bald man with a heavy face and small, restless eyes emerged from the fog. He wore an undershirt, and held his pants up with his hand.

When de Milja didn't move, the man grabbed him—he had the strength of the mad, he may have been mad for all de Milja knew—and shoved him down a long, dark hallway. Once again de Milja started to fade out, he felt the wall sliding past on his right shoulder as the man half-carried him along. There was a sense of still air, the odor of closed rooms. A hallway made unlikely angles, sharp turns into blank walls, a wood panel swung wide, and he found himself in a box that smelled of freshly sawn planks. Then it was dark, with a heavy silence, and as he blacked out he realized that he had been entombed.

There was more. It went on from there, but he was less and less a part of it. Merely something of value. It was not so bad to be something of value, he discovered. He was fed into a Saving Machine—a mechanism that knew better than to expect anything of fugitives, the damaged and the hunted. It simply saved them. So all de Milja ever retained of the next few days were images, remnants, as he was moved here and there, an object in someone else's operation, hidden and rehidden, the treasure of an anxious miser.

He came to rest on a couch in a farmhouse, a place of palpable safety. It was drizzling, and he could smell wet earth and spring. It took him back to Tarnopol, to the Volhynia. There too they burned oak logs, wet dogs dried by the fire, somebody wore oilskins, and the smell of a stone house in the rain was cut by bay rum, which the Ostrow uncles always used after shaving.

His head ached, his mouth was dry as chalk. A young woman doctor sat on the edge of the couch, looked in his eyes with a penlight, then put a delicate finger on a place above his forehead. "Hurt?" she asked.

"Not much."

"I'm the one who sewed you up," she said. "In a few days we'll take them out."

He had six stitches in his hairline. He had not been hit by a bullet, but the fall on the fire escape had given him a concussion.

An hour later an adjutant took him upstairs, to an office in an old farm bedroom with a little fireplace. The man behind a long worktable had tousled gray hair and mustache and the pitted complexion of childhood smallpox. He wore a country jacket with narrow shoulders and a thick wool tie. When he stood to shake hands, de Milja saw that he was tall and thin. "Captain," he said quietly, indicating a chair.

He was called Major Olenik, and he was de Milja's new superior officer. "You might as well hear all the bad news at once," he said. "The basement of Saint Stanislaus Hospital was raided by an SS unit, what files were there were taken. Colonel Broza was wounded, and captured. The woman you knew as Agata swallowed a cyanide capsule. You and Captain Grodewicz survived."

For a moment, de Milja didn't say anything. Then, "How did that happen?"

Olenik's shrug was eloquent: let's not waste our time with theories, we don't know and it's likely we won't ever know. "Of course we are working on that," Olenik said. "Did you know who Agata was?" he asked.

"I didn't, no."

"Biochemist. One of the best in Europe."

Olenik cleared his throat. "The Sixth Bureau in Paris informed us, a few days ago, that our senior intelligence officer in France has been relieved of duty. We are going to send you as his replacement, Captain. You studied at Saint-Cyr for three years, is that correct?"

"Yes. 1923 to 1926."

"And your French is fluent?"

"It's acceptable. Good workable French spoken by a Pole. I've read in it, in order not to lose it, but conversation will take a few weeks."

"We're sending you out, with couriers. Up to Gdynia, then by freighter across the Baltic to Sweden. We've created an identity and a legend for you. Once in France, you'll report to the Sixth Bureau Director of Intelligence in Paris. It's your decision, of course, but I want to add, parenthetically, that you are known to the German security services in Poland." He paused, waiting for de Milja to respond.

"The answer is yes," de Milja said.

The major acknowledged his response with a polite nod.

Later they discussed de Milja's escape from the Germans. He learned that the customs official, his family and Madame Kuester, had gotten away successfully and been taken to safety in the countryside.

As for the man who had hidden him in his apartment. He was not in the underground, according to Olenik. "But he did have an acquaintance who he believed to be in the ZWZ, he confided in her, and she knew who to talk to. Word was passed to us, and the escape-and-evasion people picked you up, moved you around for a time, eventually brought you down here."

"I owe that man my life," de Milja said. "But he was—perhaps he was not entirely sane."

"A strange man," Olenik said. "Perhaps a casualty of war. But his hiding place, well, it's common now. People turning their homes into magicians' boxes, some of it is art, really. Double walls, false ceilings, secret stairways, sections of floorboard on hinges, drawer pulls that unlock hidden passageways to other buildings."

Olenik paused and thought about it. "Yes, I suppose he was a little crazy. What he built was bizarre, I went to see it, and it was, *byzantine*. Still, you were lucky—your mad carpenter was a good carpenter. Because the Gestapo did search that apartment, every apartment in that building, in fact. But to find you they would have had to rip out the walls, and that day they didn't bother. That's not always the case—they've turned Jewish apartments into sawdust—but all they did was break up some furniture, and so here you are."

Olenik smiled suddenly. "We must look at the bright side. At least the *Kulturtrager*"—it meant culture-bringer, a cherished German notion about themselves—"brought us 'subhumans' some new and adventurous ideas in architecture."

. . .

3 April 1940. The "subhumans" turned out to be adept pupils, gathered attentively at the feet of the *Kulturtrager*. The Germans had, for example, a great passion for important paper. It was, all prettily stamped and signed and franked and checked, order and discipline made manifest. Such impressive German habits, the Poles thought, were worthy of imitation.

So they imitated them, scrupulously and to the letter. As de Milja was moved north through occupied Poland, he was provided with a splendid collection of official paper. *Passierscheine, Durchlasscheine, Urlaubsscheine,* and *Dienstauswelse*—general passes, transit permits, furlough passes, and work permits. The Poles had them all—stolen, imitated, doubled-up (if you had one legitimate citizen, why not two?—it's not unsanitary to share an identity), forged, secretly printed, altered, reused, and, every now and then, properly obtained. To the Germans, documentation was a fence; to the Poles, it was a ladder.

And they discovered a curious fact about the German security police: they had a slight aversion to combat soldiers. It wasn't serious, or even particularly conscious, it was just that they felt powerful when elbowing Polish civilians out of their way in a passenger train. Among German soldiers, however, whose enemies tended to be armed, they experienced some contraction of self-esteem, so avoided, in a general way, those situations.

The lowly *untermenschen* caught on to that little quirk in their masters right away: the new ZWZ intelligence officer for France reached the port of Gdynia by using *Sonderzuge*—special night trains taking Wehrmacht soldiers home to leave in Germany. These "specials" were also used by railway workers, who rode them to and from trains making up in stations and railyards all over Poland. De Milja was one of them—according to his papers and permits a brakeman—headed to an assignment in Gdansk. Taken under the care of escape-route operators, he moved slowly north over a period of three nights.

Three April nights. Suddenly warm, then showery, crickets

loud in the fields, apple trees in clouds of white blossom. It meant to de Milja that he would not see this country again—it was that strange habit of a thing to show you its loveliest face just before you lost it.

The trains clanked along slowly under the stars in the countryside. Across the river on the rebuilt bridge at Novy Dvor, back to the other side at Wyszogrod, then tracking the curves and bends of the Vistula as it headed for the sea. The railwaymen gathered in a few seats in the rear of the last car on the *Sonderzuge* trains, and the tired Wehrmacht soldiers left them alone. They were just working people, doing their jobs, not interested in politics. A heel of bread or a boiled potato wrapped in a piece of newspaper, a cigarette, a little quiet conversation with fellow workers—that was the disguise of the Polish train crews.

Captain de Milja rarely spoke, simply faded into the background. The escape-route operators were young—the boy who brought him to the town of Torun was sixteen. But the Germans had helped him to grow up quickly, and had sharpened his conspirative instincts to a fine edge. He'd never been an angel, but he should have been lying to some schoolteacher about homework, or bullshitting his girlfriend's father about going to a dance. Instead, he was saying "Nice evening, Sergeant," to the *shkopy* police Kontroll at the Wloclawek railroad station.

"New man?" the sergeant said.

"Unh-huh," said the teenager.

Polite, but pointless to seek anything further. The sergeant had had a teaspoon of human warmth in this godforsaken country, he'd have to make do with that. Stamped de Milja's papers, met his eyes for an instant, end of discussion.

In the daytime, he was hidden in apartments, and he'd grab a few hours sleep on a couch while young people talked quietly around him. The escape-route safe house in Torun was run by a girl no more than seventeen, snub-nosed, with cornsilk hair. De Milja felt tenderness and desire all mixed up together. Tough as a stick, this one. Made sure he had a place to sleep, a threadbare blanket, and a glass of beer. Christ, his heart ached for her, for them all because they wouldn't live the year.

Germans too thought in numbers, and their counter-espionage array was massive: Abwehr, KRIPO—criminal police, SIPO—security police, including the Gestapo—the SD intelligence units, Ukrainian gestapo, railway police, special detachments for roads, bridges, forests, river traffic, and factories. In Poland, it *rained* crossed leather belts and side arms. People got caught.

"There is soup for you," Snub-nose said when he woke up.

"Thank you," de Milja said.

"Are those glasses false?"

"Yes." Because they had his photograph, he had grown a little mustache and wore clear glasses.

"You must not wear them in Torun. The Germans here know the trick—they stop people on the street and if their lenses are clear they arrest them."

People came in and out all day; whispered, argued, left messages, envelopes, intelligence collection. Young as she was, Snub-nose had the local authority and nobody challenged her. That night, another railwayman arrived, this one eighteen, and de Milja's journey continued.

Late in the evening, they left the train at Grudziaz. De Milja, wearing a railroadman's blue shirt and trousers, metal lunchbox in hand, walked through the rain down a street in front of the station. A whore in a doorway blew him a kiss, a half-peeled German poster on a wall showed a Polish soldier in tattered uniform, Warsaw in flames in the background. The soldier shook his fist in anger at a picture of Neville Chamberlin, the British prime minister. "England, this is your work!" said the caption. Along with their propaganda, the Germans had put up endless proclamations, "strictly forbidden" and "pain of death" in every sentence.

They were stopped briefly by the police, but nothing serious. They played their part, eternally patient Poles. The Germans knew that Russia had owned the country for a hundred and twenty-three years, until 1918. They certainly meant to do better than that. The policeman said in slow German, "Let's see your papers, boys." Hell, who cared what the politicians did. Weren't they all just working folks, looking for a little peace in this life?

After midnight, the leave train slowly wound through the flat fields toward the coast, toward Gdynia and Gdansk. It kept on raining, the soldiers slept and smoked and stared out the windows of the darkened railcar.

The escape-route way station in Gdynia was an office over a bar down by the docks, run by the woman who owned the bar. Tough exterior—black, curly hair like wire, blood-red lipstick—but a heart like steel. "Something's wrong here," she grumbled. "*Shkopy*'s got a flea up his ass."

In a room lit blue by a sign outside the window that said BAR, the couriers ran in and out. Most carried information on German naval activity in the port.

"Look out the window," said the woman. "What do you see?"

"Nothing."

"Right. Eight German ships due in this week—two destroyers and the rest merchantmen. Where are they?"

"Where do you think?"

"Something's up. Troops or war supplies—ammunition and so forth. That's what they're moving. Maybe to Norway, or Denmark. It means invasion, my friend."

"I have to get to Stockholm," de Milja said.

"Oh, you'll be all right," she said. An ironic little smile meant that he wouldn't be, not in the long run, and neither would she. "The Swedes are neutral. And it's no technicality— they're making money hand over fist selling iron ore to the Germans, so they'll keep Hitler sweet. And he's not going to annoy them—no panzer tanks without Swedish iron."

They were getting very rich indeed—de Milja had seen a report. Meanwhile they were righteous as parsons; issued ringing indictments at every opportunity and sat in judgment on the world. Pious hypocrites, he thought, yet they managed to get away with it.

"When do I go out?" de Milja asked.

"Tomorrow," she said. "On the *Enköping*."

Two men in working clothes arrived before dawn. They handed de Milja an old greasy shirt, overalls, and cap. De Milja shivered when he put them on. One of the men took coal dust from a paper bag, mixed it with water, and rubbed it into de Milja's face and hands. Then they gave him a shovel to carry and walked him through the wire gates to the dock area. A German customs official, glancing at de Milja's pass to the port, held himself as far away as possible, his lip curled with distaste.

They joined other Polish stevedores working at two cranes loading coal into the hold of the *Enköping*. The Swedish seamen ignored them, smoking pipes and leaning on the rail. De Milja had a bag on a leather string around his neck, it held microfilm, a watch, some chocolate, and a small bottle of water. Casually, one of the workers climbed down a rope ladder into the hold. De Milja followed him. "We're not going to fill this all the way up—we'll leave you a little space," said the man. "Just be sure you stay well to one side. All right?"

"Yes."

Above them, a crane engine chugged and whined. "Good luck," the man said. "Give the Swedish girls a kiss for me." They shook hands and the man climbed back up the rope ladder. An avalanche of coal followed. De Milja pressed his back against the iron plates of the hold as it cascaded through the hatch and grew into a mountain. When it stopped, there were only three feet between de Milja and the decking above him as he lay on the lumpy coal. The hatch cover was fitted on, the screws squeaked as it was tightened down. Darkness was complete. Later in the

morning he heard commands shouted in German and the barking of dogs as the ship was searched. Then the engines rumbled
to life, and the freighter wallowed out into the Baltic.

It was seventy hours to Stockholm.

The deck plates sweated with condensation and acid coal-
water dripped steadily and soaked him to the skin. At first, discomfort kept him alert—he turned and twisted, wet, miserable,
and mad. But that didn't last. With the steady motion of the ship
and the beat of the engines, the black darkness and the cold,
dead air, de Milja fell into a kind of stupor. It was not unpleas-
ant. Rather the reverse. He drifted down through his life,
watched certain moments as they floated by. He saw dead leaves
on a path in the forest in the Volhynia, his feet kicking them as
he walked along, a little girl who'd come to stay with a neighbor
that summer, a kiss, more than that. It made them giggle. This
silly stuff—what did adults see in it? He had no idea he was
dying, not for the longest time. Heavy snow fell past a window
in Warsaw, Madame Kuester looked over her shoulder into a
mirror, a red mark where he'd held her too tightly. He said he
was sorry, she shrugged, her expression reflective, bittersweet.
It must be time to sleep, he thought, because at last he did not feel
the cold. He was relieved. His wife jammed her hands in the
pockets of her coat, stood at the shore of the lake as evening
came on. She looked a little rueful, that was all. It you stood far
enough back, the world wasn't frightening. It wasn't anything.
In the end, you were a little sad at what went on. Really, it
ought to be better. Casement window at the manor house, the
first gleam of the sun at the rim of a hill, two dogs trotting out of
the forest onto the wet grass of the lawn. Finally, he became
aware, for a moment, of what was happening. He did what he
could—took long, deep breaths. *Coal,* he thought. *Sulfur, carbon
monoxide, confined space, red blood cells.* It was all very confusing.
One painful stab of regret: a crumpled body, Polish stowaway
found on a mound of coal in a Swedish freighter. Captain Alex-

ander de Milja hated that idea, simply one more senseless, muted death in time of war. He lay on his back at the foot of a poplar tree and looked up as the wind rattled the little leaves.

Every summer had one perfect day.

The green sea rose under the ship, held a moment, then fell away. Sometime later, the engines slowed, the iron walls shuddered, a tug tied on and nudged the *Enköping* against its pier. The rusty bolts squeaked as they were backed off, the hatch cover swung into the air, and a crane began to scoop the coal away. Later, under the dock lights, too bright against the pale evening sky of Sweden, a booming voice shouted recognition signals down into the echoing hold.

LEZHEV'S
LAST
DAY

W as the third of June, 1940.

A springtime day in Paris and, last days being tricky this way, especially breezy and soft. No, Lezhev told himself, don't be seduced. *Le printemps,* like every other spectacle of the French theater of life, was an illusion, a fraud. That was absurd, of course, and Lezhev knew it; spring was spring. But he chose to indulge himself in a little unjust spite, then smiled acidly at his intransigence. On this day above all he could say whatever he wanted— nobody contradicts a man writing a suicide note.

Stationed at the window of the smelly little garret room, he had watched spring come to the Parisian slums: to the tiny, dark street covered in horseshit and dire juices, to the fat women who stood with folded arms in doorways waiting to be insulted, and to the girls. Such girls. It would take the words of a Blok, a Bely, a Lezhev, to do them justice. "In *Lights of a Lost Evening,* the tenth volume from Boris Lezhev, this fierce apostle of Yesenin reveals a more tender, more lyric voice than usual. In the title work, for instance, Lezhev . . ."

Now, *there* you had girls. Lithe, momentary, a flash in the corner of your eye, then gone. Nothing good lasted in the world, Lezhev thought, that's why you needed poets to grab it as it went flying by.

Well, now and then there was something good. For example, Genya Beilis. Genya. Yes, he thought, Genya. Lithe and momentary? Hah! You could never call her a girl. Girls had no such secret valleys and mysterious creases, girls did not contrive to occupy the nether mind quite as Genya did. He would miss her, up on his cloud or wherever he was going. Miss her terribly. She'd been his salvation—good thing in a bad life—the last few years of exile. Sometimes his lover, sometimes not, indomitable friend always, his brilliant bitch of a hundred breeds.

It was true, she was an extraordinary mixture. Her father, the publisher Max Beilis, was Russian, Jewish, and French. Her mother was Spanish, with some ancient Arab blood from Cordoba. Also an Irish grandmother on the maternal side. Lord, he thought, what wasn't she? You could feel the racial rivers that flowed through her. She had strange skin; sallow, olive, smooth and taut. Hair thick, dark, with reddish tints in full sunlight, and long enough so that she twined and wound it in complicated ways. Strong eyebrows, supple waist, sexy hands, eyes sharp with intelligence, eyes that saw through people.——You were right to be a little afraid of Genya Beilis. The idea of some great, naked, flabby whale of a German hovering above her made Lezhev sick with rage, he would rise up and—

No, he wouldn't. The German panzer divisions were racing south from Belgium, French troops surrendering or running away as they advanced, the police were on the verge of arresting him—the closer the Germans got, the worse for all the Lezhevs of Paris. So he wasn't going to be anybody's protector, not even his own.

Fact was, they had finally hounded him to the edge of the grave. The Bolsheviks had chased him out of St. Petersburg in 1922. He fled to Odessa. They ran him out of there in 1925. So he'd gone to Germany. Written for the émigré magazines, played some émigré politics. 1933, in came Hitler, out went Lezhev. So, off to sad Brussels; earnest, neutral Belgium. He hadn't much left by then—every time he ran, things flew away: clothes, money, poems, friends. 1936, off to fight in Spain—the NKVD almost got him there, he had to walk over the Pyrenees at night, in snow up to his knees. He barely made it into Liberté-Egalité-and-Fraternité, where they threw him in prison.

Amazing, Lezhev thought, the things he'd done. As a St. Petersburg teenager in 1917, he'd torn a czarist policeman's club from his hands and cracked him on the nose. Stayed up all night, haunting the dark alleyways of the city and its women: talking to the whores, screwing the intellectuals. He saw a man executed with a leather cord as he sat in a kitchen chair at a busy intersection. He was a worker of the world. For a year or two, anyhow. Worked with a pen, which was mightier than the sword, he discovered, only when approximately the same size. He'd run from raging fires, crazed mobs, brawling Nazis, rumbling tanks, and the security police of at least six nations.

> My valise, dark-eyes. Quick.
> It's under your bed.
> There's nothing in there,
> and nothing to pack,
> but I take it along.

So, at last, after all that, who got him? The *ronds-de-cuir*. French bureaucrats, laboring all day on wooden chairs, were prone to a shine on the seat of the pants. The antidote was a chair-sized round of leather—*rond de cuir*—carried daily to work, placed ever so precisely beneath the clerical behind. The makers of Parisian slang were not slow to see the possibilities in this. To Lezhev, the *ronds-de-cuir* seemed, at first, a doleful but inevitable feature of French life but, in time, he came to understand them in a different way. Fussy, niggling, insatiable, they had some kinship with the infamous winds of Catalonia, which will not blow out a candle but will put a man in his grave. And now, he realized, they were going to do what all the Okhrana agents and Chekists and Nazis and pimps and machine gunners and Spanish cooks had failed to do.

They were going to kill him.

· · ·

But maybe not.

On his rounds that night, in Le Chasseur Vert and the Jean Bart out in the Russian seventeenth arrondissement and Petrukhov's place up in Pigalle, he felt the life force surge inside him. He laid some little glovemaker's assistant among the mops and brooms in Petrukhov's storeroom. Tossed his last francs out on the zinc bars as a rich slice of émigré Paris got drunk on his money and told him what a fine fellow he was. Sometime near dawn he was with the acmeist playwright Yushin, too plastered to walk any farther, propped on a wall and staring down into the Seine by the Alexandre III bridge.

"Don't give up now," Yushin said. "You've been through too much. We all have."

Lezhev belched, and nodded vigorously. Yushin was right.

"Remember the Cossacks chased you?"

"Mm," Lezhev said. Cossacks had never chased him, Yushin had him confused with some other émigré poet from St. Petersburg.

"How you ran!"

"Mm!"

"Still, they didn't catch you."

"No."

"Well, there it is."

"You're right."

"Don't weaken, Boris Ivanovich. Don't let these sanctimonious prigs stab your heart with their little quills."

"Well said!"

"You think so?"

"Yes."

"You're kind to say that."

"Not at all." Lezhev saw that the compliment had put Yushin to sleep, still standing, propped against the stone wall.

· · ·

But then, on the morning of 4 June, he had to report to the Prefecture of Police and slid, like a man who cannot get a grip on an icy hillside, down into a black depression. The Parisian police, responsible for immigration, had placed him on what they called a Régime des Sursis. *Sursis* meant reprieves, but *régime* was a little harder to define. The authorities would have said system, but the word was used for a diet, implying control, and some discomfort. Lezhev would describe it as "a very refined cruelty."

In March, the French had declared Lezhev an undesirable alien, subject to deportation back to Germany—his last country of legal residence, since he'd entered Belgium, Spain, and France illegally. Of course all sorts of judicial nightmares awaited him in Berlin; he could expect concentration camp, beating, and probably execution. The French perfectly understood his predicament. You may, they told him, appeal the order of deportation.

This he did, and was granted a stay—for twenty-four hours. Since the stay would lapse at 5:00 P.M. the following afternoon, he had to go to the Prefecture at 1:00 P.M. to stand on the lines. At 4:20, they stamped his papers—this enabled him to stay in France an additional twenty-four hours. And so forth, and so on. For four months.

The lines at the Prefecture—across from Notre-Dame cathedral on the Île de la Cité—had a life of their own, and Lezhev grimly joined in. He'd been hit on the head in his life, missed plenty of meals, been tumbled about by fate. Standing in line every day held no terrors for him. He couldn't earn any money, but Genya Beilis had a little and she helped him out; so did others. He'd written behind barbed wire, on a sandbag, under a bridge, now he'd write while standing on line.

This defiance held for March and April, but in May he began to slip. The *ronds-de-cuir,* on the other side of their wire-grille partitions, did not become friendly over time—that astonished, then horrified, finally sickened Lezhev. What sort of human, he wondered, behaved this way? What sort of reptilian heart remained so cold to somebody in trouble? The sort that, evidently, lived in the hollow chest of the little man with the little man's mustache. That lived within the mountainous bosom of the woman with the lacquer hairdo and scarlet lips, or behind the three-point handkerchief of Coquelet the Rooster, with his cockscomb of wild hair and the triumphant crow of the dunghill. "Tomorrow, then, Monsieur Lezhev. Bright and early, eh?" Stamp—*kachuck*—sign, blot, admire, hand over, and smile.

The line itself, snaking around the building, then heading up the quay, was a madhouse: Jews, Republican Spaniards, Gypsies, Hungarian artists, the lost and the dispossessed, criminals who hadn't yet gotten around to committing crimes, the full riptide of unwanted humanity—spring of 1940. They whispered and argued and bartered and conspired, laughed and cried, stole and shared, extemporized life from one hour to the next.

But slowly, inevitably, the Régime de Sursis gnawed away until it ate a life, took one victim, then another. Zoltan in the river, Petra with cyanide, Sygelbohm under a train.

Boris Lezhev, papers stamped for one more day of existence, returned to his room late at night on the fourth of June. He'd stopped at a café, listened to a report on the radio of the British Expeditionary Force's departure, in small boats, from the beaches of Dunkirk. But the population was to remain calm at all costs—Prime Minister Reynaud had demanded that President Roosevelt send "clouds of warplanes." Victory was a certainty.

Lezhev was temporarily distracted from writing by a drunken altercation in the tiny street below his window. One old man wanted to defend Paris, the other favored the declaration of an open city—the treasures of the capital, its bridges, arcades, and museums, would be spared. Trading arguments, then insults, the old men worked themselves up into a fulminous rage. They slapped each other in the face—which made them both wildly indignant—they swore complicated oaths, threatened to kick each other, snarled and turned red, then strode off in opposite directions, threatening vengeance and shaking their fists.

When this was over, Lezhev sat on a broken chair in front of an upturned crate and wrote, on paper torn from a notebook, a long letter to Genya Beilis. He wanted her to be the custodian of his poetry. Over the years, he'd tinkered endlessly with his work, back and forth, this way and that. Now, tonight, he had to decide, so: here a birch was a poplar. The sea shattered, it didn't melt. Tania did not smell of cows or spring earth—she simply walked along the path where the ivy had pulled down the stake fence.

"I don't exactly thank you, Genya—my feelings for you are warmer than courtesy. I will say that I remember you. That I have spent considerable time and remembered you very carefully. It is a compliment, my love, the way you live in my imagination. The world should be that perfect."

7 June 1940. Boulogne-Billancourt cemetery.

A few mourners for Lezhev: he'd made the enemies émigré poets make, some of the regulars had already fled south, and it was a warm, humid evening with the threat of a thunderstorm in the air. Those who did attend were those who, if they kept nothing else, kept faith with community: a dozen men with military posture, in dark suits, medals pinned to their breast pockets. There was a scattering of beards—Lezhev's colleagues, gloomy men with too much character in their faces. And the old women, well practiced at standing before open graves, you could not be buried without them. The priest was, as always, Father Ilarion, forced once again to pray over some agnostic/atheist/anarchist—who really knew?—by the exigencies of expatriate life.

Doz'vidanya, Boris Ivanovich.

There wasn't much in the way of flowers, but a generous spread awaited the funeral party in an upstairs room at the Bala-laika—Efrimov's restaurant in St. Petersburg had also been steps away from the cemetery—vodka, little sandwiches of sturgeon or cucumber, cookies decorated with half a candied cherry. Genya Beilis, lover, muse, nurse, editor, and practical goddess to the deceased, had, once again, been generous and openhanded. "God bless you," an old woman said to her as they walked down the gravel path toward the restaurant.

Genya acknowledged the blessing with a smile, and the old woman limped ahead to catch up with a friend.

"Madame Beilis, my sympathies."

He crunched along the path beside her, and her first view of him was blurred by the black veil she wore. His French wasn't native, yet he did not speak to her in Russian.

"A friend of Monsieur Lezhev?" she asked.

"Unfortunately, no."

Polite, she thought. Through the veil, she could see a strong, pale forehead. He was in his late thirties, hair expensively cut, faintly military bearing. *Aristocrat,* she thought. But not from here.

"An associate of Monsieur Pavel," he said.

Oh.

She was, just for a moment, very angry. Boris was gone, she would never hear his voice again. For all his drinking and brawl-ing he'd been a tender soul, accidentally caught up in flags and blood and honor and history, now dead of it. And here by her side was a man whose work lay in such things. *I am sick of coun-tries,* she wanted to say to him. But she did not say it. They walked together on the gravel path as the first thunder of the storm grumbled in the distance.

"The help you've provided is very much appreciated," he said quietly. She sensed he knew what she'd been thinking.

"The government has to leave Paris—but we wanted to set up a contact protocol for the future, if that is acceptable to you."

She hesitated a moment, then said, "Yes, it's acceptable." Suddenly she was dizzy, thought she might faint. She stopped walking and put a hand on the man's forearm to steady herself. The thunder rumbled again and she pressed her lips together hard—she did not want to cry.

"There's a bench—" the man said.

She shook her head no, fumbled in her purse for a handkerchief. The other mourners circled around them. Yushin the playwright tipped his hat. "So sorry, Genya Maximova, so sorry. Just the other night, he . . . my regrets." He walked backward for a step or two, tipped his hat again, then turned around and scurried away.

The man at her side handed her a clean white handkerchief and she held it to her eyes. It smelled faintly of bay rum cologne. "Thank you," she said.

"You're welcome." They started walking again. "The protocol will mention the church of Saint-Etienne-du-Mont, and the view from the rue de la Montagne. Can you remember it?"

"Yes. I like that church."

"The contact may come by mail, or in person. But it will come—sooner or later. As I said, we are grateful."

His voice trailed away. She nodded yes, she understood; yes, she'd help; yes, it had to be done; whatever yes they needed to hear that day. He understood immediately. "Again, our sympathies," he said. Then: "I'll leave you here—there are French security agents in a car at the bottom of the hill."

He moved ahead of her, down the path. He wasn't so bad, she thought. It just happened that information flowed to her like waves on a beach, and he was an intelligence officer in time of war. Big drops of rain began to fall on the gravel path and one of the men in dark suits with medals on the breast pocket appeared at her side and opened a black umbrella above her head.

. . .

It was a long way from the Russian neighborhoods in Boulogne to Neuilly—where he was staying in the villa of an industrialist who'd fled to Canada—and a storm was coming, but
Captain Alexander de Milja decided to walk, and spent the evening headed north along the curve of the Seine, past factories
and docks and rail sidings, past workers' neighborhoods and little cafés where bargemen came in to drink at night.

They had dragged him, black with coal dust and more dead
than alive, from the hold of the freighter *Enköping,* laid him on
the back seat of a Polish diplomatic car and sped off to the em-
bassy. A strange time. Not connected with the real world at all,
drifting among dim lights and hollow sounds, a sort of mystic's
paradise, and when people said "Stockholm" he could only
wonder what they meant. Wherever he'd been, it hadn't been
Stockholm.

And where was he now? A place called *poor Paris,* he thought.
In *poor France.* He saw the posters on his walk, half torn, flapping
aimlessly on the brick factory walls: NOUS VAINCRONS CAR
NOUS SOMMES LES PLUS FORTS. Signed by the new prime minister, Paul Reynaud. "We will win because we are the strongest." *Yes, well,* was all de Milja could think. What could you
say, even to yourself, about such empty huffing and puffing?
Paris had been bombed twice, not heavily. But, while the Wehrmacht was still north of the Belgian border, France had quit. He
knew it—it was what he and Colonel Broza had fought against in
Warsaw—and he'd felt it happen here.

De Milja had arrived in Paris in late April and gone to work
for Colonel Vyborg, the "Baltic knight" who had recruited him
into the ZWZ as the Germans began the siege of Warsaw. At
first it was as though he'd returned to his old job—staff work in
military intelligence. There were meetings, dinners, papers
written and read, serious and urgent business but essentially the

life of the military attaché. He had assisted in some of the intelligence collection, developed assets, liaised with French officers.

They were sympathetic—*poor Poland*. Clandestine flights with money and explosives for the underground would be starting any day now, any day now. There were technical problems, you needed a full moon, calm weather, extra gas tanks on the airplanes. That was true, de Milja knew, yet somehow he sensed it wouldn't happen even when conditions were right. "Steady pressure," Vyborg said. "Representatives of governments-in-exile are patient, courteous men who do not lose their tempers." De Milja understood, and smiled.

His counterpart, a Major Kercheval of the SR—Service des renseignements, the foreign intelligence operation that supplied data to the Deuxième Bureau of the French General Staff—invited him to tour the Maginot Line. "Be impressed," Vyborg told him. Well, he was, truly he was. A long drive through spring rains, past the Meuse, the Marne, the battlefields of the 1914 war. Then barbed wire, and an iron gate with a grille, opening into a tunnel dug deep in the side of a hill. Over the entrance, a sign: ILS NE PASSERONT PAS—They shall not pass. Three hundred feet down by elevator, then a cage of mice hung by the door as a warning—they'd keel over if gas were present—and a brilliantly lit tunnel traversed by a little train that rang a bell. In vast, concrete chambers there were offices, blackboards, and telephones—a huge fire-control center staffed by sharp young soldiers dressed in white coveralls. A general officiated, demanding that de Milja choose a German target from a selection of black-and-white photographs. All he could see were trees and brush, but his cartographer's eye turned up a woodcutter's hut by a stream and he pinned it with his finger. "*Voilá,*" said the general, and great activity ensued—bells rang, soliders talked on telephones, maps were unrolled, numbers written hurriedly on blackboards. At last, a dial in the wall was turned and the deep gong of a bell sounded again and again.

"The target has received full artillery fire. It is completely destroyed." De Milja was impressed. He did wonder, briefly, why, since the French were officially at war with the Germans, they rang a bell instead of firing an actual gun, but that was, he supposed, a detail. In fact, the series of fortresses could direct enormous firepower at an enemy from underground bunkers. The Maginot Line went as far as the Belgian border. And there it stopped.

So on 10 May, when Hitler felt the time was ripe, the Wehrmacht went through Belgium. A French officer said to de Milja, "But don't you see? They have violated Belgian neutrality! They have played into our hands!"

Just where the river rounded the Isle of Puteaux, de Milja came to a *tabac,* a *boulangerie,* and a cluster of cheap cafés: a little village. Because of the blackout the streetlamps of Paris had been painted blue, and now the city was suffused with strange, cold light. It made the street cinematic, surreal. Friday night, the cafés should have been jammed with Parisians—*to hell with the world, have a glass of wine! Can I see you home?* Now they were triste, half-empty. But these were workers. Out in Passy, in Neuilly, in Saint-Germain and Palais-Royal there wasn't anybody. They had all discovered a sudden need to go to the country; to Tante Giselle or their adored *grandmère* or their little house on the river whatever-it-was. Where they'd gone in 1914. Where they'd gone, for that matter, in 1789.

Meanwhile, in Poland, they were committing suicide. Vyborg had told him that, white lines of anger at the corners of his mouth. France was a kind of special heaven to the Poles, with its great depths of culture, its adept wit, and ancient, forgiving intelligence. To the Poles, it was simple: don't give in, fight on, when Hitler tangles with the French that'll be the end of him. But that wasn't what happened and now they knew it—they risked their lives listening to the BBC and they heard what the announcer tried not to say. The French ran. They didn't, wouldn't, fight. A wave of suicides washed over Warsaw, Cracow, the manor houses in the mountains.

A girl at a café table looked at de Milja. Beret and raincoat, curly, copper-colored hair with a lock tumbled onto the forehead, a dark mole setting off the white skin on her cheek, lips a deep, solemn red. With her eyes she asked him some sort of question that could not quite be put into words. De Milja wanted her—he wanted all of them—but he kept walking and she turned back to her glass of wine. What was she after, he wondered. A little money? A husband for a little problem in her belly? A man to beat up the landlord? Something, something. Nothing was free here—he'd learned that in the 1920s when he was studying at Saint-Cyr. He turned and looked back at her; sad now, staring into her glass. She had a heavy upper lip with a soft curve to it, and he could imagine the weight of her breasts against her cotton blouse. Jesus, she was beautiful; they all were. They couldn't help it, it wasn't their fault. He stopped, half turned, then continued on his way. Probably she was a whore, and he didn't want to pay to make love.

Yes, well.

The industrialist who'd fled to Canada had not had time, apparently, to clean out his things in Neuilly. He'd left behind mounds of women's clothing, much of it still folded in soft tissue paper, a crate of twenty telephones, a stack of chic little boxes covered in slick gold paper, and dozens of etchings—animals of every sort; lions, zebras, camels—signed *Dovoz* in a fluid hand. De Milja had simply made a neat pile on the dining-room table and ignored it. The toothbrush left in the sink, the paste dried on it, he'd thrown away.

Hard to sleep in a city waiting for invaders. De Milja stared out the window into the garden of the neighboring villa. So, the barbarians were due to arrive; plans were being made, the angles of survival calculated. He read for a time, a little Joseph Roth, a book he'd found on the night table—*The Radetzky*

March. Roth had been an émigré who'd killed himself in Paris a year earlier. It was slow going in German, but de Milja was patient and dawn was long hours away.

> The Trottas were not an old family. Their founder's title had been conferred on him after the battle of Solferino. He was a Slovene and chose the name of his native village, Sipolje. Though fate elected him to perform an outstanding deed, he himself saw to it that his memory became obscured to posterity.
>
> An infantry lieutenant, he was in command of a platoon at Solferino. The fighting had been in progress for half an hour. He watched the white backs of his men three paces in front of him. The front line was kneeling, the rear standing. They were all cheerful and confident of victory. They had . . .

Now it rained. Hard. De Milja had been lying on a long red-and-gold couch with a brocade pillow under his head. He got to his feet, walked to the French doors, index finger holding his place in the book, and stared out into the night. Someone had stored pieces of old statuary behind the villa, water glistened on the stone when the lightning flickered. The wind grew stronger, rain blew in sheets over the garden, then the air cooled suddenly and the sound of thunder rolled and echoed down the deserted streets.

9 June 1940. 2, avenue de Tourville, Hôtel des Invalides.

De Milja was prompt for his eleven o'clock meeting with Major Kercheval of the SR. The streets around the walled military complex at the center of the seventh arrondissement were quiet—the residents were away—but in the courtyard they were busy loading filing cabinets onto military trucks. It was hot, no air moved, the soldiers had their jackets off, sleeves rolled up, suspenders dangling, making them look like cannoneers from the Franco-Prussian war of 1870.

A fifteen-minute wait, then an elderly sergeant with plentiful decorations led him up long flights of stairs to Kercheval's office. The major's greeting was friendly but correct. They sat opposite each other in upholstered chairs. The office was impressive, a wall of leatherbound volumes, historic maps in elaborate frames were hung on the walnut boiserie.

"Not a happy moment," Kercheval said, watching the trucks being loaded in the courtyard below.

"No," de Milja agreed. "We went through it in Warsaw."

Kercheval's eyebrow twitched—*this is not Warsaw.* "We're thinking," he said, "it won't be quite so difficult here. Some of our files are being shifted for temporary safekeeping."

De Milja made a polite sound of agreement. "How is it up north?" he asked.

Kercheval steepled his fingers. "The Tenth Army's situation on the Somme appears to have stabilized. At the river Oise we have a few problems still—mostly logistics, supply and whatnot. But we expect to clear that up in seventy-two hours. Our current appreciation of the position is this: we've got hell to pay for two or three days yet, we then achieve a static situation—*une situation statique.* We can maintain that indefinitely, of course, but I'd say give us two weeks of hard work and then, in the first heat of summer, look for us to be going the other way. Germans are Nordic—they don't like hot weather."

He shifted to the particular concerns they shared—the flow of information from open and clandestine sources, how much of it the Poles got to see. He spoke easily, at length, in confidential tones. The meaning of what he said, as far as de Milja could make out, was that the people above them, the diplomats and senior officers in the rarefied atmosphere of binational relations, had yet to complete work on a format of cooperation but they would soon do so, and at that time de Milja and his colleagues could look forward to a substantive increase of shared intelligence.

Kercheval was in his late forties, with dry skin, a corded underside to his jaw, and smooth, glossy hair combed flat. A turtle's head, de Milja thought. The small, mobile mouth, whether talking or eating, strengthened that impression. The exterior was flawless: courteous, confident, polished and hard as a diamond. If Kercheval lied, he lied, regrettably, for reasons of state—*raisons d'état*—and if you listened carefully you would hear a faint and deeply subtle signal inviting you to agree that deception was simply a part of life, as all very old cultures had learned, sadder but wiser, to acknowledge. *Come now, you must admit it's so.*

"It's an ordeal, and takes forever," he went on, "but experience has shown that relations go much more smoothly, indeed much more productively, when the initial understandings are thoroughly formulated."

He smiled warmly at de Milja, perhaps a hint of apology in his face—*our friendship will surely survive all the nonsense I'm forced to tell you, you certainly won't hold it against me. Life's too short for resentment, my dear fellow.*

De Milja tried to nod agreement as enthusiastically as he could, an importunate smile nailed to his mouth. The *situation statique* on the Somme was that the Tenth Army had been encircled and destroyed, and de Milja knew it. To Kercheval, however, the fate of an army was of secondary importance to the conversation he was having with de Milja. Of primary concern was that adverse and humiliating information could not be stated in front of a foreigner, of lesser rank and lower social position. As for "some of our files are being shifted," de Milja passed through the sentry gates, turned right toward the métro, and passed sixty trucks lined up and waiting to enter the courtyard.

On the train he read *The Daily Telegraph* to see what the British were thinking about that morning. Asked if Paris would be declared an open city, a French spokesman replied, "Never. We are confident that Hitler's mechanized hordes will never get to Paris. But should they come so far, you may tell your countrymen we shall defend every stone, every clod of earth, every lamppost, every building, for we would rather have our city razed to the ground than fall into the hands of the Germans.''

Emerging at the Pont de Neuilly métro stop, de Milja saw a group of white-haired garbagemen—veterans, wearing their decorations—working on a line of twelve garbage trucks. They were engrossed in mounting machine guns on the trucks and, by that afternoon, the Paris police were wearing tin-pot helmets and carrying rifles.

''The government's going to Tours,'' Vyborg said.

''From what I saw this morning they were certainly going *somewhere*,'' de Milja said.

Late afternoon, an anonymous café on the rue Blanche. Amber walls tinted brown with Gauloises smoke, etched glass panels between booths. An old lady with a small dog sat at the bar, the bored owner scowled as he read one of the single-sheet newspapers that had replaced the usual editions.

Vyborg and de Milja sat facing each other in a booth and sipped at glasses of beer. The afternoon was hot and still, a fly buzzing around a motionless fan in the ceiling. Sometimes, from the refugee columns trudging down the boulevards a block away, the sound of an auto horn. Vyborg wore an old gray suit, with no tie and shirt collar open. He looked, de Milja thought, like a lawyer with unpaid office rent and no clients.

''Hard to believe that it's over here. That the French army lasted one month,'' Vyborg said.

''It is over, then.''

''Yes. Paris will be declared an open city today or tomorrow. The Germans will be in here in a week or less.''

''But France will fight on.''

''No, it won't. Reynaud cabled Roosevelt and demanded American intervention, Roosevelt's response was a speech that dithered and said nothing. Pétain appeared before the cabinet in Tours and said that an armistice is, in his view, 'the necessary condition for the survival of eternal France.' That's that.''

De Milja was incredulous. France remained powerful, had a formidable navy, had army units in Morocco, Syria, Algeria, could have fought on for years. ''In Warsaw—''

''This isn't Warsaw,'' Vyborg said. ''In Tours, they lost a top-secret cable, turned the whole chateau upside down looking for it. Finally a maid found it, crumpled up in Reynaud's mistress's bed. Now, that's not the first time in the history of the world that such a thing has happened, but you get the feeling it's the way things are. It's as though they've woken from a dream, discovered the house on fire, then shrugged and walked away rather than calling the fire department or looking for a bucket. If you read history, you know there are times when nations fail, that's what happened here.''

Vyborg took a pack of Gitanes from his pocket, offered it to de Milja, took one for himself, then lit both with a silver lighter. In the rue Blanche, a refugee family had become separated from the stream moving south across Paris. A man pulled a cart with quilts tied over the top of a mound of furniture; here and there a chair leg poked through. His wife led two goats on a rope. The farm dog, panting hard in the afternoon heat, walked in the shadow of the cart. Behind the cart were three small children, the oldest girl holding the hands of two little boys. The family had been on the road a long time; their eyes, glazed with fatigue, saw nothing of their surroundings.

The proprietor put his paper down for a moment and stared at the family as they labored past. A tough Parisian, his only comment was to turn his head and make a spitting sound before going back to his newspaper with an almost imperceptible shake of the head. The old woman's lapdog barked fiercely at the goats. The farm dog glanced up, then ignored it—*some little woolly thing in Paris that thought it was a dog; the things you see when you travel*. The old woman shushed her dog, muttering something about "unfortunates" that de Milja could barely make out.

"Fucking German pigs," Vyborg said quietly, with resignation. "The local bully-boys—come Friday night and they beat up the neighbors. Which is why, I guess, the French and the Poles have always been friends; they share the problem."

"I suppose," de Milja said, "we're going to London. Unless there's a miracle."

"There will be no miracle," Vyborg said. "And, yes, it is London. We've got a destroyer berthed at the mouth of the Loire, in Nantes, not too far from the government in Tours. I'm going down there tomorrow, we have to be where official France is. You're going to stay here—the last man out. Work on the reactivation program, whatever you can manage to get done. Just don't stray too far from base, meaning Neuilly. That villa is now the French station of the Polish army's intelligence service. As for a time of departure, it's hard to predict exactly. It will be at the final hour—Polish honor demands at least that, with shells falling on in the harbor and our fantail on fire. You'll be contacted when we know a little more, by telephone or courier. Given a cipher, probably. The BBC has agreed to broadcast signals for us—we're likely to do it that way, in the *Messages Personnels,* so get yourself a working radio and listen to it—ten, four, and midnight. Myself, I like the garden programs. Did you know that periwinkle can be used as a ground cover on a shady hillside?"

It was dark when de Milja returned to Neuilly. He carried with him a battered briefcase stuffed with French francs and a new list, in code, of Polish agents in Paris. People on the Genya Beilis level had been contacted, now there remained the small-fry, a surprisingly long list. But Poland had always had an aggressive, busy intelligence service—a characteristic of small countries with big enemies.

De Milja made a successful contact at 11:20 that night at a

dance hall in Clichy—an aging, embittered clerk in the French department of the Admiralty who was paid a small monthly stipend. Then he hurried to the Notre-Dame-de-Lorette métro stop, but the woman he expected, an ethnic Pole running a group of engineers in the Hungarian armament industry, did not appear.

The following morning he awoke to find the air dark, the leaves of the tree outside his window covered in oily grime, and the spring birds fled. Later that day a taxi driver confirmed his suspicion: the Germans had bombed the gasoline storage tanks at Levallois-Perret, the black cloud of soot had drifted down on the city.

At the fall-back meeting of 2:25 P.M.—Notre-Dame-de-Lorette station replaced by Abbesses—the ethnic Pole appeared: Chanel scarf, clouds of perfume, and a refusal to meet his eyes when he handed her a payment of five thousand francs. She was gone, he thought. But he was doubly gracious, thanked her profusely, and passed her the Saint-Etienne-du-Mont protocol anyhow. The best he could do was to try to leave a positive impression—the world changed, luck went sour, he wanted her to feel that working for the Polish service was a life preserver in a stormy sea.

Paris dying.

Refugees streaming past, among them disarmed French soldiers, still in uniform. The city now silent, seemingly empty but for the shuffle of the refugee columns. The abandoned government offices had caused consternation—even the one-page newspapers were gone now, the kiosks were shut tight, and the garbage was no longer collected.

De Milja could not escape the sadness. Even when it rained death and fire, Warsaw had fought desperately to survive; improvising and improvising, ingenuity and courage set against iron and explosives. They'd had no chance, but they fought anyhow; brave, deluded, stubborn. Closing his eyes, he saw the passengers on the Pilava local, clothing dirty, here and there bloody, walking into Romania with the heavy little crates of bullion.

He tried to keep his spirits up. The fight against despair was, he told himself, just another way of fighting Germany. But as the life of the streets faded away, he began to wonder why anybody cared so much about flags and nations. An old, old city, everything had happened here, people loved and people died and none of it mattered very much. Or maybe it was just him— maybe he was just tired of life. Sometimes that happened.

He'd scheduled a dawn contact out in the nineteenth arrondissement, at the Canal de l'Ourcq, the home dock of a Dutch barge captain with knowledge of the production capacities of petroleum refining centers along the upper Seine. Not much point at the moment—every ounce of French gasoline was either in flames or pumped into government cars in full flight. But in the future it might be a useful thing to know.

At 2:00 A.M. he tossed and turned, unable to sleep. The silence of the little street was oppressive. He moved to an armchair, read The Radetzky March, dozed off, then woke suddenly—not knowing why until the fist hammered on the door a second time. He ran down the hall and looked out the judas hole. A Breton, he thought. Reddish hair clipped high on the sides, fair skin, a cold face, a silk tie, and a certain practiced patience in the way he stood. De Milja left him and walked silently to the back door. The one waiting there had his hands in his pockets, was looking aimlessly up at the stars.

He returned to the bedroom, struggled into pants, shirt, and shoes as the one in front knocked again. "Are you in there?" If a voice could be good at calling through doors, this one was: *I'm being polite—don't test my patience.* "*Allons,* eh!" Let's go! *Last warning.* De Milja opened the door.

The man made a soft grunt of satisfaction—at least we got that much done. "Captain de Milja," he said, polite in an official way. "I am sorry to trouble you, but . . ."

But what? The Germans at the gates? The times we live in?

"Yes?" de Milja said.

"Perhaps you would get dressed, we're ordered to escort you to our office."

"Where is that, please?"

"At the Prefecture of Police."

"Could you identify yourself?"

"Of course. Forgive me." He produced a small leather case with an identity card of the DST—*Direction de la Surveillance de la Territoire,* the French FBI—and held it up for de Milja to see. "All right?" the man said.

"Come in," de Milja said.

The man entered, whistling tunelessly, strolled through the villa and opened the back door. The one who'd waited there had a little mustache trimmed to the line of his upper lip. He looked around the villa curiously. "It's quite a place here. Belong to you?"

"I'm just a tenant," de Milja said.

"Ah." A professional skeptic, it amused him to seem easily satisfied.

De Milja went into the bedroom; the man he thought of as the Breton stood in the doorway as he put on a tie, smoothed his hair to one side, put on a jacket. He had a weapon, he intended to use it, it was just a question of timing. "Now I'm ready," he said to the Breton.

In the blue shadow of the street, de Milja could make out a blocky Citroen, black and well polished. The Breton opened the back door, then went around the car while the other waited by de Milja's side. *Now,* he thought. The weaker one first.

"This is going to cause very serious difficulties," de Milja said. The man looked at him sharply. Was he mad? "In scheduling," he hastened to add. "I'm expected someplace else."

"Well . . ." said the man, not unkindly. So the world went.

"The problem is, I'm supposed to deliver certain funds," de Milja said. The Breton started the car, which rumbled to life, sputtering and missing. "It's forty thousand francs—I'm reluctant to leave it here."

The man was likely proud of his opacity—policemen don't react if they don't choose to—but de Milja saw it hit. At least two years' salary. "I wonder," he continued, "if you could keep that money for me, at the Prefecture. Then I'll be along, later tonight, after my meeting."

The man with the mustache opened the back door and said something to the driver. Then, to de Milja, "Where is it?"

"Inside."

"Let's go."

He was on the streets for the rest of the night. They went out one door with a briefcase, he went out the other ten minutes later. He moved to cover, checked from a vantage point at 3:15, saw a car at each end of his street with silhouette of driver and passenger.

Au revoir.

He walked miles, headed east into Paris proper, and tried two hotels, but they were locked up tight, doors chained, windows shuttered. On the main thoroughfares, the stream of refugees flowed on; at the intersection of the boulevards Saint-Germain and Saint-Michel humanity collided and struggled as one column moved west, another south. On the north–south métro lines—Porte d'Orléans–Clignancourt—people fought their way onto trains that would never move. De Milja walked and walked, hiding in chaos.

At least they hadn't killed him. But he had calculated they wouldn't go that far. He was nothing to them, probably just somebody to lock up until the Germans arrived. Welcome to Paris—we couldn't find any flowers but here's a Polish spy. The Breton and Pencil-Mustache had gone back wherever they came from and reported, simply enough, that he wasn't home, so the next shift came on and parked cars at either end of his street.

Dawn was warm, a little strange beneath a disordered sky of

scudding purplish cloud. He saw a line of Flemish monks, faces bright red above their woolen robes, toiling along on women's bicycles. A city bus from Lille packed with families, a fire truck from Caen, a tank—a few pathetic twigs tied to its turret in attempted camouflage—an ambulance, a chauffeured Daimler; all of it moving one mile an hour along the choked boulevard. Past an abandoned parrot in a cage, a barrel organ, a hearse with smoke drifting from its blown engine and a featherbed tied to its roof.

He was tired; sat at the base of a plane tree by a bench somewhere and held his head in his hands. Deep instinct, survival, got him on his feet and headed north, toward Clichy and Pigalle, toward whores, who had hotel rooms where nobody asked questions.

Then, a better idea. The neighborhood around the Gare Saint-Lazare railway station, deep in the ninth arrondissement, was a commercial stew of small, unrespectable enterprises of all kinds. A world of its own where the buildings, the streets, and the people were all a little crooked. You could get insurance from the Agence ABC at the top of the wooden stairway—who didn't need every sort of official documentation in this complex, modern age?—but had you asked them to actually pay a claim they would have fainted with surprise and fallen over onto the packed suitcases that stood by the door. The leather in the Frères Brugger company's chic belts and purses came, unquestionably, from an animal, and, frankly, who were you to demand that it be a cow? And probably you had no business being out in the rain in the first place. There was an agency for singing waiters, an import company for green bamboo, a union office for the drivers of wagons that hauled butchers' bones.

Even a publisher of books—Parthenon Press. There, see the little drawing with the broken columns? That's the Parthenon. They were proud, at the little suite of offices at 39 rue de Rome, to issue an extraordinarily wide and diverse list of books. The poetry of Fedyakov, Vainshtok, Sygelbohm, and Lezhev. The plays of Yushin and Var. And all sorts of novels, all sorts. *October Wheat,* which told of the nobility of peasant life in the Ukraine. *The Sea,* a saga which, through the lives of a family of fisherfolk in the eastern Crimea, suggested the ebb and flow of both oceanic and human tides. *The Baronsky Pearls*—a noble family loses its money and survives on love; *Letter from Smolensk*—experimental fiction about the machines in a tractor factory—no human character appears; *Natasha*—a girl of the streets rises to fame and fortune. There was *Private Chamber,* in English, by Henry Thomas; *The Schoolmistress of Lausanne,* about the need for discipline at a school for wealthy young women, by Thomas Henry; and *Slender Birch,* not, as you might imagine, about the romance of the Russian steppe, by Martin Payne. These novels in English had found an appreciative audience first among British and American soldiers after the Great War, then among tourists from those nations, pleased to find, during their trip to Paris, books in their own language about their own personal interests and hobbies.

The huge pair of ancient, ironbound doors at 39 rue de Rome was firmly locked, but de Milja knocked and refused to go away when nothing happened. Finally, in the first watery light of morning, a panel in the concierge's station by the doorway slid open and a large eye peered out. Clearly he wasn't the German army—just a man with his tie pulled down and sleepless eyes who'd been walking all night—and the door creaked open. The concierge, not a day under eighty, a Lebel rifle held in his trembling hands, said, "We're closed. What do you want here?"

"Please tell Madame Beilis that a friend has come to call."

"What friend?"

"A friend from the church of Saint-Etienne-du-Mont, tell her."

"A priest? You?"

"No," de Milja said. "Just an old friend."

. . .

14 June 1940. Dawn. It rained. But then, it would. Not a human soul to be seen in Paris. Out at the Porte d'Auteuil, untended cattle had broken through the fence at the stockyard pens and were wandering about the empty streets mooing and looking for something to eat.

At the northern edge of the city, the sound of a German motorcycle, engine perfectly tuned, approached from the suburbs. A young Wehrmacht soldier sped across the place Voltaire, downshifted, revved the engine a little—*here I am, girls*—put the gear back where it belonged, and disappeared, in a rising whine, up the rue Grenoble.

From the northeast, from the direction of Belgium and Luxembourg and Germany, a series of canvas-covered trucks drove through the Porte de la Villette. One broke off from the file and moved slowly down the rue de Flandre, headed toward the railroad stations: the Gare de l'Est and the Gare du Nord and the Gare Saint-Lazare. The truck stopped every few blocks and a single German soldier jumped from the back. Like all the others, the one on the rue de Rome wore white gloves and a crossed white belt. A traffic policeman. When the armored cars and the troop transports rolled past an hour later, he waved them on.

At seven-thirty in the morning, the German army occupied the Hôtel Crillon and set up an office for local administration in the lobby. Two officers showed up at the military complex just abandoned by Major Kercheval and his colleagues at Invalides and demanded the return of German battle flags captured in 1918. France had lost a war but it was still France. The battle flags, an officer explained, had been mislaid. Of course the gentlemen were more than welcome to look for them.

The Germans hung a swastika flag from the Eiffel Tower, and one from the Arc de Triomphe.

. . .

Over on the rue de Rome, Genya Beilis pushed a sheer curtain aside and watched the Wehrmacht traffic policeman at the corner. She lit a Lucky Strike and blew long plumes of smoke from her nostrils. "What happens now?" she asked.

De Milja came and stood by her, gently pulled the fabric of the curtain from her fingers and let it fall closed. "The fighting changes," he said. "And people hide. Hide in themselves, or hide from the war in enemy beds, or hide in the mountains. Sooner or later, they hide in the sewers. We learn, under occupation, that there's more rat in us than we knew."

"They'll get rid of us, won't they," she said.

"Us?"

"All the—what? The little bits and pieces that always seem to wash up in Paris: Russians, Jews, the Spaniards on the run from Franco, Poles and whatnot. Castaways. People who dance naked in ateliers and wave scarfs, people who paste feathers and seashells on a board."

"That 'us,' " de Milja said. "The French, the real French, they'll be safe if they mind their manners. But the others, better for them to disappear."

She left the window, settled herself in a chair at the dining-room table. It was never clear where the office stopped and the residence began. The mahogany table was piled high with stacks of a slim volume in a pale-blue dustjacket—*The Golden Shell*. "You aren't supposed to be here, are you?" she said.

"Why do you say that?"

"Monsieur Pavel, your, ah, predecessor. One saw him for just a moment. Here or there, in a museum or a big brasserie, someplace public."

"That's the recommended way."

"But you don't care."

"I care," he said. He started to qualify that, then shrugged.

She got up and went into a pantry off the dining room and started to make coffee, cigarette hanging from her lips. Her blouse was a very flat red and she wore little gold-hoop earrings. In profile, she spooned out coffee, liberally, then fiddled with a nickel-plated coffee urn. Smoke rose around her face and hung in drifts below the brass ceiling lamp. He couldn't stop looking at her; the texture of her hair didn't go with the color, he thought, so black it should have been coarse. But it hung loose and soft and moved as she did things with her hands.

He couldn't stop looking at her. He had been in the apartment since the previous day, had slept in a spare room, had wanted her so badly it hurt. Anyone would, he thought; man, woman, or tree. It wasn't that she was beautiful. More than that. Dark, and supple, with fingers that lingered on everything she touched for just a moment longer than they should. He wanted to carry her to the bed, put his hands in the waistbands of everything she was wearing and pull down. But then, at the same time, he was afraid to touch her.

On a wall above a desk hung a portrait of the publisher Max Beilis, her father, a small, handsome man with a sneer and angry, brilliant eyes. She would, of course, be his single weakness—*anything she wanted*.

She turned on the radio, let it warm up and tuned in the BBC. He moved closer, could smell a hint of perfume in the cigarette smoke. *People who dance naked in ateliers,* she'd said. Part of her world—the held breath of the audience, the brush of bare feet on cold floorboards. Her Parisian heart could not, of course, be shocked by such things.

On the BBC, modern music, atonal and discordant. Music for the fall of a city. It faded and returned, disappeared into the static, then came in strong. Not jammed, though, not yet—jamming came in rising and falling waves, they'd find that out soon enough. When the announcer came on, Genya leaned forward in concentration, lit a new cigarette, ran her hair back behind one ear.

"And now the news . . ."

The French government had left Tours and had set up shop in

Bordeaux. Reynaud had stated that "France can continue the struggle only if American intervention reverses the situation by making Allied victory certain." In the USA, the chairman of the Senate Foreign Relations Committee suggested that, since it was hopeless for the British to fight on alone, they should surrender to Germany. Fighting continued sporadically in France, the Maginot Line was now being abandoned. German troops had crossed the Marne. German forces in Norway this, in Denmark that, in Belgium and Holland the other thing. This morning, German troops had entered Paris and occupied the city.

When it was over, another symphony.

16 July 1940. Banque Nationale de Commerce, Orléans. 11:30 A.M.

Was he French?

Monsieur LeBlanc had a second, covert, look at the man waiting behind the railing that separated bank officers from the cashiers' windows. He was rather clever about people—who was who and what was what, as they said. Now this one had been, in his day, quite the fellow. An athlete or a soldier—a certain pride in the carriage of the shoulders indicated that. But lately, perhaps things weren't going so well. Inexpensive glasses, hat held in both hands—an unconscious gesture of submission—scuffed shoes. A drinker? No, some wine, like all the world, but no more than his share. Death of a loved one? A strong possibility. By now, most of the refugees who'd taken the road south had found their way home, but many had died—the delicate ones, some of the strong as well.

Not French.

Monsieur LeBlanc didn't know how he knew that, but he did. The set of the mouth or the angle of the head, a subtle gesture, revealed the foreigner, *the stranger.* Could he be a German? Hah! What an idea! No German would wait on the pleasure of Monsieur LeBlanc, he'd be served now, ahead of everyone else, and rightly so. Yes, you had to admire that. A shame about the war, a swastika flew over the Lycée where he'd gone to school, and German officers filled the better restaurants. On the other hand, one didn't say so out loud but this might not turn out to be the worst possible thing for France. Hard work, discipline—the German virtues, coupled with the traditional French flair. A triumphant combination for both countries, Monsieur LeBlanc thought, in the New Europe.

"Monsieur." He gestured toward a chair by the side of his desk.

"*Bonjour, Monsieur,*" said the man.

Not French.

"And you are Monsieur—?"

"Lezhev. Boris Lezhev."

"Very well, and you will require?"

"A safe-deposit box, Monsieur."

"You've moved recently to Orléans?"

"Yes, sir."

Was that all? He waited. Evidently that was all. "And what size did you have in mind? We have three."

"The least thick, would be best."

Ignoramus. He meant the least *large,* but used the word *gros,* which meant thick, or heavy. Oh well, what could one do. He was tired of this shabby Russian. He reached in a drawer and took out a long sheet of yellow paper. He dipped his pen in the inkwell and began taking down Lezhev's particulars; birth and parentage and police card number and residence and work permits and all the rest of it. When he was done, he scratched his initials on the page and went off to retrieve the list of available boxes.

At the assistant cashier's office, a shock awaited him. This was a culturally interesting city but not a major one—Jeanne d'Arc was long gone from sleepy Orléans, now a regional business center for the farming community. But when Monsieur LeBlanc obtained the list of available boxes, there was exactly one that remained unrented. A number of local residents evidently expected good fortune to be coming their way.

As Lezhev signed forms and accepted the keys, Monsieur LeBlanc took a discreet look at his watch. Only a few minutes until noon. Excellent. What was today? Wednesday. At Tante Marie that meant, uh, blanquette de veau and baby carrots.

"Thank you, Monsieur," said the Russian.

"You are very welcome, we're pleased to have you, Monsieur, as our customer."

Barbarian.

And Mildred Green wasn't much better—Monsieur LeBlanc, had he ever encountered her, likely would have clapped his hat on his head and run the other way.

She was squat, homely, and Texan, with sparse hair, a pursed mouth, and a short temper. Her redeeming qualities were, on the other hand, only narrowly known—to American soldiers wounded in the Great War, when she'd been an army nurse, and to the American military attaché in France, for whom she now worked as secretary, administrative assistant, and bull terrier.

The military attaché's office had moved down to Vichy on 5 July, panting hot on the tail of the mobile French government, which had pulled stakes in Bordeaux on the first of July and moved to Vichy on the river Allier, a stuffy old spa town with copious hotels and private houses to absorb the bureaucracy and those privileged souls allowed to kneel at its feet.

Life had not been easy for Mildred Green. The people running France now loathed the British and hated their American cousins. Better Germans, better *anything,* than Brits or Yanks. The assignment of housing space in Vichy rather reflected that point of view, so the villa would take, at least, some fixing up. Water bubbled from the pipes, the windows had last been opened in the heat wave of 1904, mice lived in one closet, squir-

rels in another, and God only knew what in the third because
they could hear it in there but nobody could open the door.

Mildred Green did not lose her temper, staunch amid the
hammering and banging, fits of artistic temperament and huge
bills courteously presented for no known service or product.
She had worked in France since 1937, she knew what to expect,
how to deal with it, and how to maintain her own equilibrium in
the process—some of the time, anyhow. She knew, for example, that all laborers stopped work around ten in the morning
for *casse-croûte,* a piece of bread and some red wine to keep them
going until lunchtime.

Thus she was surprised, sitting at her typewriter, when a man
carrying a toolbox and wearing *bleu de travail* knocked at the
door and asked if he could work on the wiring in her ceiling. She
said yes, but had no intention of leaving the office—fearing not
so much for the codebooks as for the typewriters. The electrician made a grand show of it, tapped on the wall with a screwdriver handle, then moved to her desk and handed her an
envelope. Inside she could feel the outline of a key.

"I'm not an electrician," the man said in French. "I'm a
Polish army officer and I need to get this letter to the Polish
government-in-exile in London."

Mildred Green did not react, simply tapped a corner of the
envelope thoughtfully against her desk. She knew that the
French counterespionage services were aggressive, and fully
versed in the uses of *agents provocateurs.* "I'm not sure I can help
you," she said in correct, one-word-at-a-time French.

"Please," he said. "Please help me. Help *us.*"

She took a breath, let it out, face without expression. "Can't
promise you a thing, sir. I will speak to somebody, a decision
will be made. If this isn't right, in the garbage it goes. That's the
best I can do for you."

"Read it," he said. "It just says that they should contact me,
and tells them how to go about it, through a safe-deposit box in
Orléans. It can't hurt you to give that information to the Poles

in London. On the other hand if you give it to the French I'm probably finished.''

Mildred Green had a mean Texas eye, which now bored into the false electrician in *bleu de travail*. This was, perhaps, monkey business, but likely not. What the Pole didn't know was that when she returned home that night, the hotel desk would have a fistful of messages for her, all of them delivered quietly. From Jews, intellectuals, all sorts of people on the run from Hitler. A few left names, others left instructions—for ads in personal columns, for notes hidden in abandoned workshops, for contact through third parties. Every single one of them was urgent, sometimes desperate. Europe had festered for a long time, now the wound was open and running, and suddenly it seemed as if everybody in the neighborhood wanted her to clean the damn thing up.

"We'll just have to see," she said. "Can't promise anything." She said that for whatever little ears might be listening. Her real response was to slide the envelope into her big leather shoulder bag—a gesture her lost Pole immediately understood. He inclined his head to thank her—almost a bow—then saluted. Then vanished.

The nights of July were especially soft that Paris summer. All cars, taxis, and buses had been requisitioned by the Germans, and with curfew at 11:00 P.M., windows masked by blackout curtains, and the streetlamps painted over, the city glowed a deep, luminous blue, like Hollywood moonlight, while the steps of a lone policeman echoed for blocks in the empty streets. Nightingales returned and sang in the shrubbery, and the nighttime breeze carried great clouds of scent from the flowers in the parks. Paris, like a princess in a folk tale, found itself ancient, enchanted, and chained.

Hidden away on a side street in the seventh arrondissement—the richest, and most aloof, of all Parisian neighborhoods—the Brasserie Heininger was an oasis of life on these silent evenings. Started by competing beer breweries at the turn of the century, the brasseries of Paris had never abandoned their fin-de-siècle glitter. At Heininger, a white marble staircase climbed to a room of red-plush banquettes, mirrors trimmed in gold, painted cupids, and lamps lowered to a soft glow. Waiters with muttonchop whiskers ran across the carpet carrying silver trays of langouste with mayonnaise, sausage grilled black, and whole poached salmon in golden aspic. The brasserie spirit was refined madness; you opened your heart, you laughed and shouted and told your best secrets—tonight was the last night on earth and here was the best place to spend it.

And if the Heininger cuisine was rich and aromatic, the history of the place was even more so. In 1937, as storm clouds gathered over Europe, the Bulgarian headwaiter Omaraeff had been shot to death in the ladies' room by an NKVD assassin while two accomplices raked the mirrored walls with tommy-gun fire. A single mirror had survived the evening, its one bullet hole a monument, the table beneath it—number fourteen, seating ten—becoming almost immediately the favored venue of the restaurant's preferred clientele. Lady Angela Hope, later exposed in *Le Matin* as an operative of the British Secret Intelligence Service, was said to have recruited the agent known as *Curate*—a Russian foreign correspondent—at that table. Ginger Pudakis, wife of the Chicago meat baron, had made it her evening headquarters, with Winnie and Dicky Beale, the American stove-pipe millionaires, the Polish Countess K——— and her deerhound, and the mysterious LaReine Haric-Overt. Fum, the beloved clown of the Cirque Dujardin was often seen there, with the tenor Mario Thoeni, the impresario Adelstein, and the dissolute British captain-of-the-night Roddy Fitzware. What times were had at table fourteen! Astonishing revelations, brilliant seductions, lost fortunes, found pleasures.

Then war came. And from the fourth of June to the twenty-eighth of June, the great brasserie slumbered in darkness behind its locked shutters.

But such a place could not die any more than the city of Paris could; it had come alive again, and table fourteen once again took center stage at its nightly theater. Some of the regulars returned; Mario Thoeni was often there—though his friend Adelstein had not been seen lately—Count Iava still came by, as did Kiko Bettendorf, the race-car driver and Olympic fencer for Germany, now serving in the local administration.

Kiko's stylish friends, on arriving in Paris from Hamburg or Munich, had made the Brasserie Heininger a second home. On this particular summer night, Freddi Schoen was there, just turned twenty-eight, wearing a handsomely tailored naval officer's uniform that set off his angular frame and pretty hazel eyes. Next to him sat his cousin, Traudl von Behr, quite scarlet with excitement, and her close friend, the Wehrmacht staff officer Paul Jünger. They had been joined at table fourteen by the White Russian general Vassily Fedin, who'd given the Red Army such a bad time outside Odessa in 1919; the general's longtime fellow-émigré, the world-wandering poet Boris Lezhev; and the lovely Genya Beilis, of the Parthenon Press publishing family. Completing the party were M. Pertot—whose Boucheries Pertot provided beef to all German installations in the Lower Normandy region—tonight accompanied by his beautiful niece; and the Baron Baillot de Coutry, whose company provided cement for German construction projects along the northern coasts of France and Belgium; tonight accompanied by his beautiful niece.

Just after midnight—the Brasserie Heininger was untroubled by the curfew, the occupation authorities had quickly seen to that—Freddi Schoen tapped a crystal vase with his knife, and held a glass of Pétrus up to the light. "A toast," he said. "A toast."

The group took a moment to subside—not everybody spoke quite the same language, but enough people spoke enough of them—French, German, English—so that everybody more or less understood, with occasional help from a neighbor, most of what was going on. In this milieu one soon learned that a vague smile was appropriate to more than ninety percent of what went on in the world.

"To this night," Freddi said, turning the glass back and forth in front of the light. "To these times." There was more, everybody waited. M. Pertot, all silver hair and pink skin, smiled encouragement. "To," Freddi said. The niece of Baron Baillot de Coutry blinked twice.

"Wine and friendship?" the poet Lezhev offered.

Freddi Schoen stared at him a moment. This was *his* toast. But then, Lezhev was a man of words. "Yes," Freddi said, just the bare edge of a sulk in his voice. "Wine and friendship."

"Hear, hear," said M. Pertot, raising his glass in approval. "One must drink to such a wine." He paused, then said, "And friendship. Well, these days, that means something."

Freddi Schoen smiled. That's what he'd been getting at—unities, harmonies.

"One Europe," General Fedin said. "We've had too many wars, too much squabbling. We must go forward together." He had a hard face, the bones sharply evident beneath the skin, and smoked a cigarette in an ivory holder clenched between his teeth.

Jünger excused himself from the table, M. Pertot spoke confidentially to his niece, the waiter poured wine in Mademoiselle Beilis's glass.

"Is that what you meant, Herr Lezhev?" Freddi said quietly.

"Yes. We'll have one Europe now, with strong leadership. And strength is the only thing we Europeans understand."

Freddi Schoen nodded agreement. He was fairly drunk, and seemed preoccupied with some interior dialogue. "I envy you your craft," he said after a moment.

"Mine?" Lezhev's smile was tart.

"Yes, yours. It is difficult." Freddi said.

"It cannot be 'easy' to be a naval officer, Lieutenant Schoen."

"Pfft." Freddi Schoen laughed to himself. "Sign a paper, give an order. The petty officers, clerks, you know, tell me what to do. It can be technical. But people like yourself, who can see a thing, and can make it come alive." He shook his head.

Lezhev squinted one eye. "You write, Lieutenant." A good-humored accusation.

A pink flush spread along Freddi Schoen's jawline, and he shook his head.

"No? Then what?"

"I, ah, put some things on canvas."

"You paint."

"I try, sometimes . . ."

"Portraits? Nudes?"

"Country scenes."

"Now that *is* difficult."

"I try to take the countryside, and to express an emotion. To feel what emotion it has, and to bring that out. The melancholy of autumn. In spring, abandon."

Lezhev smiled, and nodded as though confirming something to himself—*now this fellow makes sense, all night I wondered, but I couldn't quite put my finger on it.*

"Here is . . . guess who!" The wild shout came from Lieutenant Jünger, who had returned to the table with a tall, striking Frenchwoman in captivity. She was a redhead, fortyish, with a Cupid's-bow mouth, carmine lipstick, and a pair of enormous breasts corseted to sharp points in a black silk evening dress. Jünger held her tightly above the elbow.

"Please forgive the intrusion," she said.

"Tell them!" Jünger shouted. "You must!" He was a small-boned man with narrow shoulders and tortoiseshell eyeglasses. Very drunk and sweaty and pale at the moment, and swaying back and forth.

"My name is Fifi," she said. "My baptismal name is Françoise, but Fifi I am called."

Jünger doubled over and howled with laughter. Pertot and

Baillot de Coutry and the two nieces wore the taut smiles of people who just know the punchline of the joke will be hilarious when it comes.

Freddi Schoen said, "Paul?" but Jünger gasped for breath and, shaking the woman by jerking on her elbow, managed to whisper, "Say what you do! Say what you do!"

Her smile was now perhaps just a degree forced. "I work in the cloakroom—take the customers' coats and hats."

"The hatcheck girl! Fifi the French hatcheck girl!" Jünger whooped with laughter and grabbed at the table to steady himself; the cloth began to slide but Pertot—the cheerful, expectant smile on his face remaining absolutely fixed in place—shot out a hand and grabbed the bottle of Pétrus. A balloon glass of melon balls in kirsch tumbled off the edge of the table and several waiters came rushing over to clean up.

"Bad Paul, bad Paul." Traudl von Behr's eyes glowed with admiration. She had square shoulders and straw hair and very white skin that had turned even redder at Lieutenant Jünger's performance. "Well, sit *down*," she said to the tall Frenchwoman. "You must tell us all about those hats, and how you check them."

Jünger shrieked with laughter. The corner of Fifi's mouth trembled and a man with gray hair materialized at her side and led her away. "A problem in the cloakroom!" he called back over his shoulder, joining the mood just enough to make good their escape.

"Those two! They were like that in school," Freddi Schoen said to Lezhev. "We all were." He smiled with amused recollection. "Such a sweet madness," he added. "Such a special time. Do you know the University of Göttingen?"

"I don't," Lezhev said.

"If only I had your gift—it is not like other places, and the students are not like other students. Their world has," he thought a moment, "a glow!" he said triumphantly.

Lezhev understood. Freddi Schoen could see that he did.

Strange to find such sympathy in a Russian, usually blunt and thick-skinned. A pea hit him in the temple. He covered his eyes with his hand—what could you *do* with such friends? He glanced over to see Traudl von Behr using a page torn from the *carte des vins,* rolled up into a blowpipe. She was bombarding a couple at another table, who pretended not to notice.

"It's hopeless," Freddi Schoen said to Lezhev. "But I would like to continue this conversation some other time."

"This week, perhaps?"

Freddi Schoen started to answer, then Jünger yelled his name so he shrugged and nodded yes and turned to see what his friend wanted.

Lezhev excused himself and went to the palatial men's room, all sage-colored marble and polished brass fixtures. He stared at his face in the mirror and took a deep breath. He seemed to be ten thousand miles away from everything. From one of the stalls came the voice of General Fedin, a rough-edged voice speaking Russian. "We're alone?"

"Yes."

"Careful with him, Alexander."

Noontime, the late July day hot and still. The German naval staff had chosen for its offices a financier's mansion near the Hotel Bristol, just a few steps off the elegant Faubourg St.-Honoré. Lezhev waited in a park across the street as naval officers in twos and threes trotted briskly down the steps of the building and walked around the cobbled carriage path on their way to lunch. When Freddi Schoen appeared outside the door of the mansion and peered around, Lezhev waved.

"You're certain this will be acceptable?" Freddi Schoen asked, as they walked toward the river.

"I'm sure," Lezhev said. "Everything's going well?"

"Ach yes, I suppose it is."

"Every day something new?" Lezhev said.

"No. You'd have to be in the military to understand. Sometimes a superior officer will really tell off a subordinate. It mustn't be taken to heart—it's just the way these things have always been done.''

"Well then, tomorrow it's your turn.''

"Of course. You're absolutely right to see it that way.''

They walked through the summer streets, crossed the Seine at the place de la Concorde. Parisians now rode about on bicycle-cart affairs, taxi-bicycles that advertised themselves as offering "Speed, comfort, safety!" The operators—only yesterday Parisian cabdrivers—had changed neither their manners nor their style; now they simply pedaled madly instead of stomping on the accelerator.

"Are you hard at work writing?" Schoen asked.

"Yes, when I can. I have a small job at Parthenon, it takes up most of my time.''

"We all face that.'' They admired a pair of French girls in frocks so light they floated even on a windless day. "Good afternoon, ladies,'' Schoen said with a charming smile, tipping his officer's cap. They ignored him with tosses of the head, but not the really serious kind. It seemed to make him feel a little better. "May I ask what you are writing about these days?"

"Oh, all that old Russian stuff—passion for the land, Slavic melancholy, life and fate. You know.''

Schoen chuckled. "You keep a good perspective, that's important, I think.''

They reached the Saint-Germain-des-Prés quarter, one of the centers of Parisian arts, and Parisian artiness as well. The cafés were busy; the customers played chess, read the collaborationist newspapers, argued, flirted, and conspired in a haze of pipe smoke. Freddi Schoen and Lezhev turned up a narrow street with three German staff cars parked half on the sidewalk. Schoen was nervous. "It won't be crowded, will it?"

"You won't notice.''

They climbed five flights of stairs to an unmarked door that stood open a few inches. Inside they found nine or ten German officers, hands clasped behind their backs or insouciantly thrust into pockets, very intent on what they were watching. One of them, a Wehrmacht colonel, turned briefly to see who'd come in. The message on his face was clear: do not make your presence evident here, no coughing or boot scraping or whispering or, God forbid, conversation.

At the far end of the room, lit by a vast skylight, Pablo Picasso, wearing wide trousers and rope-soled Basque espadrilles, was sketching with a charcoal stick on a large sheet of newsprint pinned to the wall. At first the shape seemed a pure abstraction, but then a horse emerged. One leg bent up, head turned sideways and pressed forward and down—it was not natural, not the way a horse's body worked. Lezhev understood it as tension: an animal form forced into an alien position. Understood it all too well.

"My God," Freddi Schoen whispered in awe.

The colonel's head swiveled round, his ferocious eye turning them both to stone as Picasso's charcoal scratched across the rough paper.

2 August. Occupation or no occupation, Parisians left Paris in August: streets empty, heat flowing in waves from the stone city. A telephone call from Freddi Schoen canceled lunch near the Parthenon Press office. Too busy.

4 August. Late-afternoon coffee. But not on the Faubourg St.-Honoré. The addition of extra staff, he apologized, had forced his department to find new, likely temporary, quarters: a former college of pharmacy not far from the wine warehouses at the eastern end of the city.

7 August. A soirée to celebrate Freddi Schoen's new painting studio in the Latin Quarter. Cocktails at seven, supper to follow. Invitations had been sent out in late July, but now the arrival time was changed. Telephone calls from a German

secretary set it for eight. Then nine-thirty. Freddi Schoen did not appear until eleven-fifteen, pale and sweaty and out of breath.

The paintings, hung around the room and displayed on three easels, weren't so bad. They were muddy, and dense. The landscapes themselves, almost exclusively scenes of canals, might have been, probably were, luminous. But light and shadow were unknown to Freddi Schoen. Here you had woods. So. There you had water. So. The former was green. The latter was blue. So.

After a few glasses of wine, Freddi shook his head sadly. He could see. "In the countryside it is right there before you, right there," he said to Lezhev. "But then you try to make it on the canvas, and look what happens."

"Oh," said Lezhev, "don't carry on so. We've all been down this road."

It was, Lezhev could tell, the *we* that thrilled Freddi Schoen—he was one of them. "It's time that helps," he added, the kindly poet.

"Time!" Freddi said. "I tell you I don't have it—some of these I did when everybody else was eating lunch."

"Let me fill your glass," Genya said. Her kindness was practiced—she'd been soothing frantic writers since girlhood, by now it was second nature. She well knew the world where nothing was ever good enough. So, nothing was. So what?

Freddi Schoen smiled gratefully at her, then some German friends demanded his attention. Genya leaned close to Lezhev and said, "Can you take me home when this is over?"

Clothes off, laid on a chair along with Lezhev's personality. A relief after a day that seemed a hundred hours long. De Milja stared at the ceiling above Genya's bed, picked over the evening, decided that he hadn't done all that well. I'm a *mapmaker*, he thought. I can't do these other things, these deceptions. All he'd ever wanted was to show people the way home—now look what he'd become, the world's most completely lost man.

Not his fault that he was cut off from the Sixth Bureau in London—he was improvising, doing the best he could, doing what he supposed they would have wanted done and waiting for them to reestablish contact. *Yes, but even so,* he said to himself. This wasn't an operation, it was an, an *adventure*. And he suspected it wasn't going to end well for anybody.

But, otherwise, what?

"Share this with me," Genya said. He inhaled her breath and perfume mixed in the smoke. She had a dark shadow on her upper lip, and a dark line that ran from her naval to her triangle. Or at least that's where it disappeared, like a seam. He traced it gently with his fingernail.

She put the cigarette out delicately, took the ashtray off the bed and put it on the night table. Then she settled back, took his hand and put it between her legs and held it there. Then she sighed. It wasn't a passionate sigh, it simply meant she liked his hand between her legs, and not much else in the world made her happy, and the sigh was more for the second part of the thought than the first. "Yes," she said, referring to the state of affairs down below, "that's for you."

Of course in a few hours she would spy for him, if that was what he wanted. The *schleuh*—the Germans—couldn't just be allowed to, well, they couldn't just be allowed. This was France, she was French, she'd sung the national anthem in school with her little hand on her little breast—excuse her, her little heart. If the world demanded fighting, she'd fight. Just the instant they got out of bed. What? Not quite yet?

"France spreads her legs" he'd once said in a moment of frustration. Yes, she supposed it rather did, everybody had always said so. They'd said so in *Latin,* for God's sake, so it must be true. Did he not, after all, approve of spread legs? Did he not wish to spread her legs? Oh, pardon her, *évidemment* a mistake on her part. And did he also find France, like her, duck-assed? What did that mean? It meant this.

There was an English pilot, shot out of the sky in the early raids over France, they had heard about him. He'd been taken in by farmers up in Picardy, where they'd lost everything to the Germans in the last war. They knew that trained pilots were weapons, just like rifles or tanks. Not innocent up there. So they passed him along, from the curé to the schoolmistress to the countess to the postman, and he went to ground in Paris in late June, just after the surrender. Certainly he would be heading back to England, there to fight once more. How else could he arrange to be shot down and killed—a fate which had danced maddeningly out of reach on the previous try.

Only, he didn't want to be put on the escape route down to the Pyrenees, guided across to freedom by patriots, or sold to the Spanish police by realists—it all depended these days on whom one happened to meet. Then he met Sylvie or Monique or Francette or whoever it was, and he decided that Paris might be, even hidden out, just the very place to spend the war. Because he'd learned a terrible truth about the Germans: unless you were a Jew they wouldn't bother you if you didn't bother them. The French understood that right away.

So the pilot stayed hidden, and he chanced to gamble, and he chanced to win a racehorse. And, the second week in July, the racetracks opened. Goebbels had ordered that France return to merriment and gaiety or he'd have them all hanged, so the racetracks joined the whorehouses and the movie theaters, which had closed for twenty-four long hours the day the Germans arrived. The pilot's horse won. And won again. It ran like the wind—a good idea for a horse in a city with horsemeat butchers and rationed beef. And the English pilot was in no hurry at all to go home.

That was one answer to the question *what should we do about the Germans*. Genya Beilis stood naked at the window and pulled the blackout curtain aside so she could see the sky. "My God, the stars," she said.

He rolled off the damp sheet and stood by her, their bare skin touching. He bent his knees in order to see above the roof across the street, a medieval clutter of chimneys and broken slates and flowerpots, and there was the sky. There was no city light, the summer heavens were satin black with a sweep of white stars. "Look," she said.

15 August. Ninety-five degrees in the street. They had no idea what it was in the attic under the copper-sheeted roof, amid trunks and piles of gauze curtains, stacks of picture frames and a dressmaker's dummy, all of it the color of dust. The BBC had a particular, very identifiable, sound to it, and they worried about neighbors, or people passing in the street. Some Parisians had seen right away that Germans should be treated like other visitors; groomed and fed and milked. The characteristic British voice, amid the static and hiss, meant there was a "terrorist" or a "Bolshevik" in the neighborhood, and you could get a damn good price for one of those if you knew who to talk to down at the local police station.

It was too hot and dirty for clothes, so they stripped at the foot of the narrow staircase and climbed up in their underwear. They sat on a sprung old sofa that somebody had covered with a sheet, and put the radio on the floor, with picture wire run up into the eaves as an aerial. In the evening, when reception was marginally better, Genya would stare into space as she concentrated on the radio voice; bare brown arms clasping her knees, hair limp in the humid summer air, sweat glistening between her breasts.

Midnight in the century, someone called that time, and she was the perfect companion for it. He was lucky, he thought, that at the end he had a woman to be with. Because the end had pretty clearly come. First Czechoslovakia, then Poland, then Norway, Denmark, Belgium, and Holland. Then France. Now England. It wasn't a question of if, only how. And then a matter—not uncomplicated—of working out your personal arrangements with what was called the New Europe.

On the subject of the immediate future, two French generals

had recently been heard from. Weygand, who'd helped the Poles beat the Russians in 1920, had said that the Germans would "wring England's neck like a chicken." De Gaulle, a former defense minister, had surfaced in London and was trying to sell the French the idea of resistance, while *L'Humanité,* the communist newspaper, called him a British agent, and advised French workers to welcome German soldiers and to make them feel at home.

On the sweltering evening of 15 August, the BBC had "music for dancing, with the Harry Thorndyke Society Orchestra from Brighton," then the news: "In the skies over Britain today, more than one thousand five hundred sorties were flown against various targets, met by hundreds of RAF fighter planes and turned back."

Then, Harry Thorndyke himself: "Good evening, everybody. Good evening, good evening. Tonight, we thought it might be just the thing to pay a call on Mr. Cole Porter—thank you, thank you—and so now, without further ado, why don't we just . . . 'Begin the Beguine'?"

Genya flopped over on her stomach, hands beneath her chin. They listened to the music in silence for a while, then she said, "How long will it take?"

"A few weeks."

"Perhaps the English planes can win."

"Perhaps. But the German planes are probably better."

"We French had fighter planes, you know. Made by a certain Monsieur Bloch—and very rich he got, too. They were known as '*cerceuils volants*,' flying coffins, but nobody thought it mattered. An opportunity for the French pilots to show how much more skillful and courageous they were than their German opponents, who had superior machines."

There was no answering that.

"It's hot," she said. "I smell."

There was no answering that either. The music played, through the crackling night air, and they listened, preoccupied and silent. He unhooked her bra, and she pushed herself up so he could get it free of her. He rubbed his finger across the welt it had made on the skin of her back.

"Why does it do that?"

"Too tight," she said. "And cheap. I buy them from the Arab carts up on the boulevard Clichy."

"What about these?"

"Silk."

He slid her panties down.

"You like that?" she said.

"Yes."

"French girls have the most beautiful asses in Europe."

"Well, this French girl."

"No, Alexander, I am serious. Women are cold on this point, there's no illusion. And we are just built the way we are. What I wonder is, do you suppose that it's why they always come here?"

"You mean this is what the conquerors are after?"

"Yes."

"Perhaps they are. And the gold. Steel mills, castles. Blood-stock and paintings. Your watch." He traced his finger along her curves.

"Alexander?"

"Yes?"

"Should we go to Switzerland?"

He thought for a time. "They'd just kick us out. And everybody in Europe can't go to Switzerland."

"Yes, but *we* can, I think. There's time to do that, for the moment. And if we stay here, I feel in my heart that they will kill us. We don't matter to anybody, my sweet boy, not to anybody at all."

"I don't think," he said slowly, "that it's time to run."

She closed her eyes, moved her hips a little, took a deep breath and exhaled slowly, a sorrowful sound. "You know what it is, Alexander? I like to fuck. It's that simple. To drink a glass of wine. Just to watch the day go by in the most pointless way.''

''Really? You like those sorts of things?''

''All right, I give up. Go ahead and get me killed. But you know what will be my revenge? I'll leave a will and have a statue built in a public square: it will be you and I, just exactly as we are now, in polished stone. *Patriots in 1940* it will be called. A true-life monument for the tourists to visit. Ow! Yes, good, that's exactly what you'll be doing on the statue.''

''Lezhev, you must help me.''

It was just a manner of speaking, but when Freddi Schoen used the expression, even over the noisy line of a French telephone, the *must* had a way of lingering in the air.

''Of course. What is it?''

''First of all, please understand that I am in love.''

''Bravo.''

''No, Lezhev, I beg you, don't make light of it. She is, it is, just don't, all right?''

''You are smitten.''

''Yes. It's true. Cupid's arrow—it was an ambush, completely a surprise. A dinner in Passy, I didn't want to go. The man's in textiles, a vicomte he says, some sort of complicated business connection with my family. Expecting the worst, I went. And then . . .''

''She is French?''

''Very. And of the most elevated family—that's the problem.''

''Problem?''

''Well, here is what happened. I arrived late, and very excited. I had just taken a country estate; a lovely place and, great good luck for me, an open lease, so I can have it as long as I like. The owner was most accommodating. So naturally I talked about it at the dinner—where it was, and how old, and the river—and she was delighted. *'Ah, les collines d'Artois, mais qu'elles sont belles!'* she said. So I said, 'But you must come and see it.' And I could tell she wanted to but there was, how to say, a momentary sense of frost in the air. Then I realized! For me to ask her there alone would be most awkward, but with friends . . . So quickly I added that a couple I knew was coming on Sunday, wouldn't she join us for lunch? And Mama and Papa too, I insist! But no, as soon as they heard there was another couple, they were occupied. So, now . . .''

"We're the couple."

"You must say yes!"

"Yes. And with pleasure."

"Thank heaven. I'll have Fauchon do the picnic, in wicker hampers, with Dom Pérignon, and monogrammed champagne flutes, and lobsters, and the napkins they have that fit in the little leather loops in the hamper. What do you think?"

"Perfect."

"Now, here is my scheme. My driver will take the two of us up there—it's a good morning's drive from Paris—and that way we'll be alone, but, of course, by happenstance, so all will be quite correct."

"A natural situation."

"Who could object? Meanwhile, you and Mademoiselle Beilis will take the train up to Boulogne—it gets in there from Paris about noon. And we'll pick you up. Did I mention the day? Sunday."

"*Boulogne?*"

Genya, paying bills in the Parthenon office, looked up in surprise. "Nobody's been there since 1890. Deauville, yes. Cabourg, well, maybe. But Boulogne?"

"What's it like?"

"It's all those *sur-la-plage* paintings—the French flag fluttering in the breeze, miles of sand because the tide's always out, little dogs, ladies with hats."

"Actually, the way he spoke, it sounded as though the house was inland—'the hills of Artois.' ''

"Well I hope he doesn't dig in his garden—because what he'll find is bones and unexploded shells. That's *Flanders,* is what that is."

The goddess was, as advertised, a goddess. Fine porcelain, with china-blue eyes and spots of color in the cheeks, thick auburn hair with a flip that just touched the collar, and a porcelain heart. Freddi Schoen was lost—if he'd cantered about on his hands and knees and bayed it might, *might,* have been more obvious.

As for Lezhev and Genya, the porcelain doll wasted no time. She couldn't have been sweeter *but:* one could understand that a foreign gentleman might not have the knack of social relations in a new country; however, if she took possession of this particular spaniel, they could be sure that he'd seen the last of émigré poets and publishers' daughters. Rue de Rome publishers' daughters especially.

Lezhev found it damned hard to be Lezhev. The toasts, the snippets of poems, and all that whooping and carrying-on—his version of a Russian poet *loved and lived life to the hilt.* Sometimes he silently apologized to poor Lezhev's shade; clearly he hadn't loved life all that much, but Freddi Schoen seemed responsive to the performance so that's where he pitched it, with Genya loving life to the hilt right beside him.

De Milja, on the other hand, had an unforeseen reaction to the porcelain doll. To his considerable surprise, she offended the aristocrat in him, put him in mind of the Ostrow uncles, who would have made short work of such snobbery.

Still, whatever his taste in French aristocrats, Freddi Schoen had been right about the estate. A very old Norman farmhouse—how it had survived the unending wars in that part of the world God only knew, but there it was. Ancient timber and cracked plaster, leaning left and right at once, with tiny windows to keep the arrows out and thick walls to keep the dampness in. It sat in a valley just over a low hill from the river

Authie, which just there was quite pretty, winding its course past a network of canals. Naturally August would be its most sumptuous month, the woods a thousand shades of gold and green in the tender light of the French countryside, the banks of the canals cut back to stands of willow, leaves dancing in the little sea breeze. For they were only a few miles from La Manche, the French name for what was called, on the opposite shore some thirty miles away, the English Channel.

After lunch they went for a ride, Freddi Schoen's driver dressed up in a chauffeur's uniform for the day. The road ran through breathtaking countryside, forest to the left, meadow to the right. Surprising how the land had healed since 1918, but it had. The grass grew lush and deep green, and there was a cloud of orange butterflies at the edge of a canal where even the barges—some two hundred and forty of them at Lezhev's count, it took several minutes to drive past—seemed part of the natural beauty of the place. Or, at least, not alien to it; big, square hulls, dark and tarry from a thousand journeys, with only the painted names, Dutch, Belgian, German, or French, to disrupt the harmony of the handsome old wood.

Freddi Schoen, holding court on the leather seat of the big Mercedes, was at his best, charming and voluble and witty as only he could be; the porcelain doll smiled with delight and it was all Lezhev and Genya could do to keep up. Sitting next to the driver, Freddi hung his elbow over the seat and entertained them. "Of course the admiral was a *Prussian,* with a big, red face like, oh, like . . . a ball!"

Ha ha, but was it eighteen tugboats tied in a row after the intersection of the Route Departmentale 34? No, twenty, Genya told him later.

"A deer!" Freddi Schoen cried out. Then, when the women turned to look at the forest side of the road, he winked at Lezhev. Wasn't this fine? These two French lovelies riding with them along a road in a Pissarro painting? From Lezhev, a poet's smile of vast sagacity, confirmed by a wise little shake of the head. No, life wasn't all bad, it had its moments of great purity, say on a summer day near the sea, rolling past a particularly charming little canal, where some good old soul a generation ago had planted borders of Lombardy poplar, where thirty-one seagoing tugs, tied up to cleats, bobbed lazily when the wind ruffled the surface of the still water.

"I saw it!" Genya Beilis cried out.

Freddi Schoen's eyes grew wide with amazement—his little joke had grown wings. Fate had put a real deer in the forest; even the gods of Chance were with them today.

19 August, Banque Nationale de Commerce, Orléans.

An old woman wearing a funeral hat had preceded him into one of the little rooms where one communed with one's safe-deposit box. He could hear her through the wall, mumbling to herself, then counting, each number articulated with whispered ferocity. "*Quatorze. Quinze. Seize. Dix-sept. Dix-huit.*"

Lezhev had less to whisper about. Only a small slip of paper: "Hôtel Bretagne. 38, rue Lepic. Room 608. You are Monsieur Gris, from Lille."

To hell and gone up an endless hill in the back streets of Montmartre, a hotel two windows wide and six floors tall, the smell of the toilet in the hall good and strong on the fiery August day.

He knocked.

"Yes?"

"Monsieur Gris. From Lille."

She was five feet tall, blond hair cut back to a boyish cap above a round face and a snub nose. Scared to death, intrepid, Polish.

"How old are you?" he asked in French. She just stood there. He tried again in Polish.

"Seventeen," she said.

She went to the peeling armoire and opened the door. The

suitcase radio was open and ready to transmit. "You are not to be here when I send," she explained. "An order."

He indicated that he understood.

She went on, a carefully memorized speech. "Colonel Vyborg sends his regards. You are to occupy yourself with information pertinent to the German plan to attack Great Britain. Where, how, and when. He tells you that the English are the only hope now—airplane drops of ammunition and money and specialists are planned for Poland. For their part, they ask our help in France, in any way we are able. I am to transmit for you, whenever you like, as much as you like."

"How did you come?"

"Fishing boat to the Brittany coast, from Scotland. Then on a train."

"With the suitcase in hand."

She shrugged. "There is no control on the trains. It's very different here."

"Where were you in Poland?"

"Lodz. I came to France as a courier, then we fled on the ship *Batory,* from Bordeaux. On the twenty-second of June, after the surrender. We were the last ship to leave France."

"What name do I call you?" he asked.

"Janina," she said. Her smile was radiant, they were comrades in arms, she was proud to serve at his side. She returned to the armoire, brought out a thick packet of French francs. "We will beat them, Monsieur Gris. We will certainly beat them."

The two brothers owned a garage in Saclay, in the poor southern suburbs of Paris. This was Wednesday, another three days until the Saturday shave, the white bristle on their cheeks was shiny with motor oil and dark with grime. Hidden somewhere in the complex of fallen-down sheds was a pig they were fattening for market; de Milja and Fedin could hear it grunting and snuffling in the mud.

"When will the pig be ready?" de Milja said.

"October," one of the brothers said. " 'Cannibal,' we call him."

"We need a little Citroen truck, a delivery truck."

"Expensive, such things."

"We know."

"Could be fifteen thousand francs."

"Maybe nine."

"Fifteen, I think I said."

"Eleven, then."

"What money?"

"French francs."

"We like those American dollars."

"Francs is what we have."

"Fourteen five—don't say we didn't give you a break. Have it with you?"

De Milja showed a packet of notes, the man nodded and grunted with satisfaction. When he leaned close, de Milja could smell the wine in his sweat. "What country do you come from?" he asked. "I want to hear about it." The second brother had left the shack abruptly after the money was shown—de Milja had barely noticed that he'd gone. Now Fedin stood at the door, shaking his head in mock disillusion and pointing a Lüger out into the yard. "Put that down," he said.

The response was a whine. "I was just going to cut up some firewood. To cook the lunch."

They used what they had:

Whatever remained of the old Polish networks, sturdy White Russian operatives who'd put in their time for a variety of services, friends, friends of friends. They were not so concerned about being betrayed to the Germans. That would happen—it was just a question of when, and whether or not they would be surprised when they figured out who'd done it.

"As you get older, you accept venality. Then you learn to like it—a certainty in an uncertain world." Fedin the skull, the

Lüger under his worker's apron, cigarette holder clenched in his teeth as though he were a Chinese warlord in a Fu Manchu film.

Wearing workmen's smocks, they drove their little delivery van slowly through what remained of the streets of Dunkirk. Two hundred thousand weapons had been left on the oil-stained beaches, abandoned by the British Expeditionary Force and several French divisions making their escape across the Channel. All along the shore, German soldiers were trying to deal with the mess, stripping tires from shot-up trucks, emptying ammunition from machine-gun belts.

In the back streets they found a heavy woman who walked with a cane and kept a dollmaker's shop not far from the canals that ran out into the countryside. She painted eyebrows on tiny doll heads with a cat's whisker, and counted barges when she walked her elderly poodle. She was a Frenchwoman; her Polish coal-miner husband had gone off to fight in Spain in the Dabrowsky Brigade, and that was the last she'd heard of him. De Milja's predecessor had found her through a relief organization, and now the Polish service was her *petit boulot,* her little job. Before the Germans had come she'd been a postbox on a secret mail route, a courier, the owner of a discreet upstairs bedroom where one could get away from the world for a night or two without hotel—and therefore police—registration.

"A hard week, Monsieur," she said as de Milja counted out francs.

"You're confident of your numbers?"

"Oh yes, Monsieur. One hundred and seven of the beastly things. It took four expeditions to find them all."

"Well then, keep up the good work. This may go on for months."

"Mmm? Poor Roquette." The poodle's tail managed a single listless thump against the floorboards when she heard her name. Perhaps, de Milja thought, Rocket had been the right name for her at one time, but that was long ago. "Having to walk all those miles on that cinder path," the woman added.

"Buy her a lamb chop," de Milja said, counting out some extra francs into the attentive hand.

Fedin was exactly right, de Milja thought, as a German sentry waved them away from a turnoff for the coastal road—the pleasure of venality was that Madame would be faithful as long as the francs held out.

The van rolled to a stop. De Milja climbed out and approached the sentry. "Excuse, kind sir. This place?" He showed the soldier, who smiled involuntarily at de Milja's eccentric German, a commissary form. On the bottom, an inventory of Vienna sausage and tinned sardines; on top, an address.

"The airfield," the sentry said. "You must go down this road, but mind your own business."

The Germans were of two minds, it seemed to him. Down the beach road, all preparations were defensive. Engineered—concrete—positions with heavy machine guns pointing out into the Channel. Rows of concrete teeth sunk into the sand at the low-tide mark, strung with generous coils of barbed wire. French POWs were digging trenches and building antiaircraft gun emplacements, and clusters of artillery had been positioned just behind the sand dunes. This was nothing to do with an invasion of England: this was somebody worried that the British were coming back, unlikely as that seemed. But then somebody, *somebody* had screamed "We will invade!" and so Freddi Schoen and all the rest of the Kriegsmarine, the German navy, had started moving barges up and down the canals of Europe. They must have stripped every river in northern Europe, de Milja thought. Stopped commerce dead. On the Danube and the Rhine, the Weser and the Mosel, the Yser, Escaut, Canche, and Somme, nothing moved.

Fedin laid it out for him. Quite a number of the Russian generals in Paris had never been in anyone's army, but Fedin was a real general who'd commanded real troops in battle and done well at it. De Milja watched with admiration as he planned the invasion of Britain on a café napkin.

"Twelve divisions," he said. "Hand-picked. With a hundred thousand men in the first wave, all along the English coastline for, say, two hundred miles. That's the Wehrmacht thinking— spread the invasion, thin down the British defense forces, dissipate energy, resources, everything. Lots of refugees moving on the roads, miles and miles for the ammunition trucks to cover, honking all the time to get Mrs. Jones and her baby carriage out of the way.

"For the German navy, on the other hand, the two-hundred-mile spread is a nightmare, precisely what they don't want. They need a concentrated beachhead, ships hurrying back and forth across the Channel, multiplying their load capabilities by the hour, with airplanes overhead to keep the British bombers away."

"That's the key."

"Yes, that's the key. If they can keep the RAF out of their business, the Germans can secure the beaches. That will do it. They hold out seventy-two hours, twenty-five divisions make the crossing, with the tanks, the big guns, all the stuff that wins wars. Churchill will demand that Roosevelt send clouds of warplanes, Roosevelt will give an uplifting speech and do nothing, the governments-in-exile will make a run for Canada, and that will be that. The New Europe will be in place; a sort of hardheaded trade association with German consultants making sure it all goes the way they want."

"What will it take to get across the Channel?"

The café was on the seafront in Veulettes. General Fedin stared out at the calm sea for a moment, then started a new napkin. "Well, let's say . . . about two thousand barges should do it. With their bows refitted with ramps that can be raised and lowered. They'll want motor launches, for speed, to get the beach-masters and the medical people and staff officers moved around. About twelve hundred of those. To move the barges back and forth—five hundred tugboats, seagoing or adapted for it. And two hundred transport ships. That's for the big stuff, tanks and heavy guns and repair shops—and for the horses, which still do eighty percent of the army's haulage.''

''Four thousand ships. That's it?''

Fedin shrugged. War was logistics. You got your infantry extra socks, they marched another thirty miles.

''They'll need decent weather. They can't afford to wait for autumn, the Channel will swamp the barges. So, end of summer is the time.''

''And the date?''

Fedin smiled to himself. Flipped the pages of a French newspaper someone had left on a chair, then ran his finger down a column. ''Seventeen September,'' he announced. ''Full moon.''

They drove into Belgium, into Holland. German occupation made it easier—northern Europe was more or less under a single government. In the Belgian ports, Ostend and Blankenberge and Knokke-Le-Zoute, and up as far as Rotterdam, they talked to the dockyard workers, because the dockyard workers were the ones who knew what went on. The ordinary civilian saw ''invasion fleet'' as something tied up on a beach, stretched out for miles, all in a row. But ports didn't work that way.

Ports wandered inland from the sea; secondary harbors and river docks, canals dug out a hundred years ago for something supremely important that nobody remembered anymore. Waterways for this or that, rank weeds and dead, black water, where cats came for courtship in the moonlight and men got laid standing up. You could hide an invasion fleet in such places, in Zeebrugge and Breskens, and that's what the Germans had tried to do.

''Four tugboats,'' said a Dutchman with a little pipe. ''Well fitted out and ready for the sea.''

''How do you know?'' Fedin asked.

''We built them, is how.''

. . .

Back to Paris. Back to Janina.

In the sweltering room on the top floor of the Hôtel Bretagne, she enciphered the data, then settled in to wait for the night, the best time for radio waves. When it was dark, she climbed up on a chair and fed the aerial through a hole in the top of the armoire to a pipe that crossed the ceiling on its way from the roof to the toilet.

She stopped for a moment and, as they'd trained her to do, ran through a mental checklist, a kind of catechism, until she was satisfied that everything was right. Then she plugged the radio into the wall, turned it on, and settled the heavy earphones on her head. Using a delicate thumb and forefinger, she explored the width of her frequency. Her neighbor to the left was very far away, very faint, and keyed at a slower and more deliberate pace than she did. But always there, this neighbor, and still transmitting when she signed off. On her right, a deep bass hum, unchanging, some piece of equipment that ran all night long. A radio beam, she thought, used by the Germans or the English for some esoteric purpose—not her destiny to know about it. An electronic strategem; a beacon that guided, or a beacon that deceived. She wondered if whoever depended on it, to their triumph or their sorrow, listened to her transmission. Submariners, perhaps. Or pilots. All of them moving around in the dark ocean or the night sky.

119 675 she began. Her call sign. Janina in Paris.

In London, at the Sixth Bureau headquarters in the Rubens Hotel on Buckingham Palace Road, four officers and a radio operator waited in a dark room, cigarette smoke hanging thick in the air. They looked at their watches long before the minute hand advanced. 8:22 P.M. Paris time was one hour later; by now the August dusk had faded away into darkness. 8:24. One minute after the scheduled time of transmission. Of course, life was uncertain, they told themselves. Watches ran slow or fast, even Wireless/Telegraph operators missed trains or heard suspicious sounds, and sometimes equipment failed. 8:27. The operator wearing the headset had an annoying habit of biting his lower lip when he concentrated. 8:28. He fussed with his dial, eyes blank with concentration. Colonel Vyborg took the deep breath that steadied him for bad news. So soon? How could they have her this soon?

Then the operator's face relaxed, and they knew what had happened before he got around to saying "Here she is." He said it as though the worrying were beside the point—he had trained her, she could do no wrong.

The Sixth Bureau operator sent 202 855. *I know you have important things to say, my darling, let's go someplace where we can be alone.* He moved his dial from 43 meters down to 39 meters.

Sent 807 449.

Hello, Janina.

But not here. In the Hôtel Bretagne, the dial moved up to 49 meters.

Sent 264 962—sent it several times, the way operators transmitted call signs until their base acknowledged. A false call sign, in essence, that actually said: *now we can talk.*

551 223. London agreed.

It wasn't a perfect night, the wet August evening brewed thunderstorms and the interference crackled as the Sixth Bureau operator bit his lip. The Germans didn't jam her frequency, but that might mean they were listening silently. That might mean a thousand things.

Meanwhile Janina, dependable, stolid Janina, sent her groups. The sweat ran down her sides and darkened the back of her shirt, the boards creaked as a large man walked down the hall to the toilet, a woman cried out. But for Janina there were only the numbers.

So many numbers. Canals, barges, towns, roads. Three freighters at anchor in Boulogne harbor with no cargo, ammunition train into Middlekerke, Wehrmacht Pioneer insignia seen at Point Gris Nez, phrase *Operation Sealion* reported by prostitute in Antwerp.

Fifteen minutes, Janina. Remember, I told you that.

But then: what to leave out? Which rivers, for example, did the RAF not really care to know about? No, Captain Alexander de Milja's improvised information machine shuddered and clanked, steam whistled from a rag knotted around a broken pipe, but somehow it worked, and it needed far more than fifteen minutes to report what it had found out.

The Funkabwehr—the signals intelligence unit of the Gestapo—maintained offices in the army barracks on the boulevard Suchet. They too had darkened rooms, and operators with headsets wandering among the nighttime frequencies.

"What's this up at 49?" one of them said, making a note of the time, 9:42 P.M., in his log.

"They were there last night," his colleague said.

They listened for thirty seconds. "Same one," he continued. "Slow and steady—refuses to make a mistake, nothing bothers him."

The first operator threw a switch that played the telegraphy through a speaker, listened a moment, then he picked up a telephone and dialed a single digit. A moment later, Sturmbannführer Grahnweis came through the door.

Grahnweis was a legend, and he didn't mind that. He was enormously fat—the shape of a renaissance cherub grotesquely overblown—and moved with heavy dignity. He had been at dinner when the call came, a white damask napkin still tucked into the collar of his black Gestapo uniform, and a waiter followed him into the office carrying a plate of venison sausages and a half stein of beer. Grahnweis nodded to his operators and smiled benevolently. He forgave them the interrupted dinner.

Then he listened.

Perhaps he made a little more of it than necessary, but who was going to blame him for a touch of theater? As the numbers tapped out, in the foreground of the atmospheric sighs and crackles, Grahnweis tilted his head to one side and puckered his mouth, then, slowly, nodded in confirmation. Yes, yes. No question about it. The diagnosis is as you suspected, gentlemen. Herr Doktor Grahnweis will take the case.

"Be so good as to serve the dinner in my office," he said to the waiter.

The desk was vast, and contained his weapons.

There were five: a very good radio receiver, a street map of Paris, two celluloid discs calibrated zero to 360°, with silk threads attached to their precise centers, and a telephone.

Grahnweis had spent his life in radio: as a childhood ham operator in Munich, he'd built his own crystal sets. He had worked for the Marconi company, then enlisted in the army in 1914 and served as a signals NCO on the eastern front. That was followed by unemployment, then the Nazi party—which made great use of radio—in 1927, and finally the Gestapo as a major. "Send the trucks, please," he said into the phone, cut a piece of venison sausage, swirled it in the chestnut puree, used his knife to top it with a dab of gooseberry jelly. As he chewed, his eyes closed with pleasure, a sigh rumbled deep in his chest, beads of sweat stood on his forehead.

Casually, without putting down his fork, he flicked on his radio receiver, then turned the dial with the side of his hand until he found the transmission on 49 meters.

236 775 109 805 429

"Take your time, my friend," he said under his breath. "No reason to rush on this warm summer night."

The trucks drove out of the boulevard Suchet garage within seconds of Grahnweis' call. They were RDF—radio direction finding—vans built by the Loewe-Opta Radio Company for the practice of what was technically known as goniometry. They sped through the empty streets to their prearranged positions: one at place de la Concorde, the other in front of the Gare de l'Est railroad station. Almost as soon as they arrived, they were on the radio to Grahnweis' office:

Place de la Concorde reports a radio beam at 66 degrees.

Gare de l'Est reports a radio beam at 131 degrees.

Grahnweis put down his fork, rubbed his hands on the napkin, took a sip of beer. He placed the celluloid discs on the street map of Paris, one at each of the truck locations. Then he ran the two silk threads along the reported angles. They crossed at Montmartre.

4 September, 6:30 P.M., Calais railroad station.

De Milja and Genya Beilis said good-bye on the platform. She had been drafted as a courier, from the Channel ports to the Hôtel Bretagne, because de Milja and Fedin could no longer go back and forth. The full moon in September was too close, the fuel for the van took so many black-market ration coupons it potentially exposed the operation to the French police, and, as the German invasion plan gathered momentum, information began to flow so fast they could barely deal with it.

Genya's summery print dress stirred as the locomotive chugged into the station; she moved toward de Milja so that her breasts touched him. "Do you know," she said, her voice just above the noise of the train, "you can ride with me to Amiens, and then come back here."

"It's direct," de Milja said. "Express to Paris."

"No, no," Genya said. "This train stops in Amiens. I'm certain of it."

De Milja smiled ruefully.

Genya studied him. "On second thought," she said, looking down.

He stared at her, at first took what she said for a lover's joke. But she wasn't smiling. Her eyes shone in the dim light of the station platform, and her lips seemed swollen. He took her by the shoulders, gripped her hard for a moment. To tell her, without trying to have a conversation while a train waited to leave a station, that he had to do what he was doing, that he was exhausted and scared, that he loved her.

But she shrugged. "Oh well," she said. Picked up a string-tied bundle as the loudspeakers announced the departure of the train. The way Parisians survived the rationing system was to get food in the countryside—everybody on the crowded platform had a large suitcase or a package.

"A few days," de Milja said.

She pushed him away and fled to the step of the coach just before it began to move. When she turned to him, her face had changed to a brainless, bourgeois mask, and she waved at him—the dumb ox, her poor excuse for a husband—and called out, "*Au revoir! Au revoir! À bientôt, chéri!*"

In silence Fedin and de Milja drove out of Calais on a little country road, the E2, headed for the village of Aire, where the Lys River met the Calais canal. They were to meet with a man called Martagne—formerly the director of the port of Calais, now an assistant to a German naval officer—at his grandfather's house in the village.

A few miles down the E2, a camouflage-painted Wehrmacht armored car blocked the road. A soldier with a machine pistol slung over his shoulder held up a hand. "Out of the car," he said.

As Fedin moved to open the door he asked quietly, "Who are they?"

"*Feldengendarmerie,*" de Milja said. "Field police units. It means they're starting to secure the staging areas for the invasion." He wondered where Fedin's Lüger was. Normally he hid it in the springs beneath the driver's seat.

"Papers, please."

They handed them over.

"Ruzicki," he said to de Milja. "You're Polish?"

"French citizen."

"Your work pass runs only to November, you know."

"Yes. I know. I'm getting it renewed."

He glanced at Fedin's papers, then gestured for them to open the back of the truck. He studied the crates of Vienna sausage and sardines, the name of the distributor stenciled on the rough wood. "Unload it," he said.

"All of it?"

"You heard me."

He lit a cigarette as they worked, and another soldier joined him, watching them haul the crates out and stack them on the warm tarred gravel of the road. "Did I see this truck up in Le Touquet last week?" the second soldier asked.

"Might have," de Milja said. "Sometimes we go up there."

"Where do you go there?"

"Oh, Sainte Cecile's—you know, the orphanage."

"French orphans eat Vienna sausage?"

"For the sisters, I think. The nuns."

When they were done they stood aside. The first soldier slid a bayonet out of a case on his belt and neatly popped a slat loose from a crate of sardines. He speared one of the tins, held it away from his uniform to avoid the dripping oil, sniffed it, then flung it away, cleaning his bayonet on the weeds beside the road.

"Load it up," he said.

While they worked, the soldier wandered around the van. Something displeased him, something wasn't right. He opened the passenger-side door, squatted on the road, stared into the cab. De Milja sensed he was a moment away from putting his hand beneath the front seat and finding Fedin's pistol.

"Do you know, sir, we took an extra crate of sausage from the storeroom? There's one more than we're supposed to have."

The soldier stood and walked to the back of the truck. His face was dark with anger. "What does that mean? Why do you tell me that?"

De Milja was completely flustered. "Why, ah, I don't know, I didn't mean . . ."

His voice hung in the air, the soldier leaned close, saw the fear in his eyes. "You do not offer bribes to German soldiers," he said very softly. "It is something you do not do."

"Of course, I know, I didn't—" de Milja sputtered.

The soldier jerked his head toward the road: it meant *get moving.* Fedin grabbed the last two crates, carried them into the front seat with him. When he tried to start the car it stalled. The engine caught, Fedin made a grinding shift, the car lurched forward, almost stalled again. The soldier turned away from them, clasped his hands behind his back and stared down the road in the direction they'd come from.

4 September, 9:26 P.M.

In the Funkabwehr bureau on the boulevard Suchet, at the end of the hall where Sturmbannführer Grahnweis' personal office was located, there was a mood of great anticipation. Grahnweis was cool and businesslike in the summer heat. He could be seen through the open door doing a little late paperwork; studying reports, sometimes writing a comment in the margin. Work went on, he seemed to suggest, the glory and the drudge in turn, such was life.

A few senior officers had found it necessary to be in the Funkabwehr office that night, chatting in low voices with attentive junior staff, who busied themselves with the thousand little jobs that must be done every day in a military office. *The devil is in the details,* the Germans say.

Klaus was hunting for the CARNET file, Helmut needed a look at the July pay vouchers for the Strasbourg station, Walter asked Helmut if the Lyons relay tower plan was still locked up in committee in Berlin. Heinrich, at 9:27, nodded sharply to himself, held the headphones tightly to his ears for a moment to make absolutely sure, then dialed a single digit on his telephone. The crowd in the Funkabwehr office knew immediately that what had been a strong possibility was now confirmed: Grahnweis had caught a spy.

But the Sturmbannführer let the receiver rest on its cradle. He finished the final paragraph of his report, initialed the lower corner, and then answered the phone. The frequency was the same as last night, Heinrich reported. Grahnweis thanked him, turned on his receiver, fiddled with the dial until the transmitted numbers came through crisp and clear. Several of the senior officers and a few people on his own staff drifted into the large office, close enough to Grahnweis' desk to hear what went on.

The two Loewe-Opta radio trucks had been in position since early evening, strategically placed on either side of the Montmartre hill. Grahnweis gave them a few minutes to get a fix on the transmission, then called Truck Number One to come in on his communications radio.

"I can confirm the forty-nine meters—are you getting it?"

"We hear him, but the direction is a little blurred. The way we're receiving, he's bouncing between eighteen and twenty-three degrees."

"I see." Grahnweis studied his city map for a moment. "Then go up to the rue Caulaincourt, try for a reading there and call me back."

From the second truck, on the boulevard Barbès side of Montmartre, the news was better. Their signal was clear, just about precisely on 178.4 degrees. Grahnweis made certain the celluloid disc was perfectly centered, then ran the silk thread out along the degree line. "Could be in Sacré-Coeur," he said. "Perhaps in the belfry. I wonder—have they also a hunchback, like Notre-Dame?"

The first RDF truck came over the radio a few minutes later. "Not much better, Herr Sturmbannführer. Maybe it's the elevation—but something's deflecting here, something's hurting the reception."

"But not in London, we hope."

There was a pause as the radio technician tried to decide how to answer this. Grahnweis saved him the trouble. "We're doing just fine. Stay where you are, I'll be back in a moment."

The technician said *Yes sir* briskly and signed off in a hurry. This working for a legend required a steady nerve.

Grahnweis reached into his desk drawer and retrieved a spe-

cial map of Paris, in book form, printed on heavy paper, showing every street, every alley, the number of every building. He
then dialed his intercom and instructed his chief clerk to telephone the northern electrical power substation. Moments later
he was talking to the French night supervisor, asking to be connected with the office of Leftenant Schillich.

As he waited, he could hear the deep hum of the station's
giant turbines. Leftenant Schillich, he thought to himself, you
had best be available for this call, and don't make a fool of
Grahnweis.

"Leftenant Schillich," said a youthful voice.

Grahnweis explained what he needed, starting at the rue
Caulaincourt side of Montmartre and working along a certain
line toward the east, street by street. Then he turned up the volume on his receiver and silently begged the W/T operator to
keep on transmitting.

"Starting at Caulaincourt, *now,*" Schillich announced.

From the speaker: 562 511

"Next on the list is the avenue Junot, from number thirty to
the end." Grahnweis' audience was hushed and anticipatory,
sensing that the moment of the kill was near. At the leftenant's
direction, the substation engineers worked their way east,
across the grid of steep, crooked streets that made up the old
village high above Paris.

"Next we have," said Schillich, following his own edition of
Grahnweis' map, "the rue Lepic."

Grahnweis found the street and marked it with his index
finger.

From the receiver: 335.

Then 428.

Then silence.

In the Hôtel Bretagne, the room went dark. Janina's hand
froze on the dead key and she tore the earphones from her head.

But there was nothing, other than the evening hush of an occupied city, for her to hear. For a few seconds she sat there, then, before she could do anything, the lights came on, the red filaments in her radio tubes glowed back to life.

It was just a brief outage, she realized, some problem with the electricity.

A few miles south of the roadblock, Fedin pulled off the E2 and drove a little way down a farmer's dirt path. There was no need to discuss what had to be done—he simply took the weapon from beneath the seat and walked out into the strip of forest that separated two fields. Theoretically they would note where it had been dumped and, some day, return to collect it.

De Milja smoked pensively and stared out over the countryside. The peasants, working in the last light of the late summer dusk, were harvesting wheat with horse-drawn mowing machines. There was a haze of dust in the air, cicadas whirred madly, the mowing machines swayed as they cut through the ripe grain. He got out of the truck to stretch his legs and felt a slight vibration in the ground. For a moment, there was no sound. Then there was just the beginning of it, thunder in the distance. Fedin returned, stood by the side of the truck, and squinted up into the darkening sky.

The ground trembled, then shook. The sound swelled, then seemed to explode the air, growing louder and louder until de Milja could feel the waves of it hammering against his heart. In self-defense he knelt down, then tried to count the dark shapes that moved slowly across the sky, returning from London, or Liverpool. Perhaps fifty Heinkel-IIIs and maybe the same number of Ju-88s, the best of the German bombers, and their escort, possibly thirty Messerschmitt-110s.

He had seen it in Warsaw, how the fronts of the buildings slid into the street in a cloud of dust, the silhouette of a fireman on a roof—arms and legs thrown wide like a gingerbread man by the blast, white fire and blue fire, the young woman a block away from harm who sits down and dies without a mark on her. He knew the Germans for the fine engineers they were.

Above him, one of the bombers trailed a delicate strand of white smoke from beneath its wing. Another flew very low and far behind the formation, De Milja could hear its engine; ignition, then silence, ignition, silence. It seemed restless; a wing dipped, the nose of the plane lowered, then righted itself. Perhaps the plane and the pilot were both damaged, de Milja thought. But, two planes among a hundred—only two planes. Others in the sea, maybe. One in poor Mrs. Brown's kitchen. But most of the bombers would be back at it the following day. Even fire hoses wore out eventually, de Milja knew, the white, frayed threads visible through the broken rubber.

The sound faded slowly to the south, toward the Luftwaffe base near Merville. The cicadas started up again, the huge horses plodded along and the mowers creaked as they rolled through the wheat. A Norman peasant walked beside his plow horse—walked slowly, head down, like an old man—one hand riding on the horse's shoulder.

It worked. Once you determined the street by turning off the electricity until the transmission stopped, your sound trucks could identify the building by strength of signal. They radioed back to Grahnweis: *Hôtel Bretagne*. The hunting party was hastily organized; two Gestapo detectives—thick-bodied types—a few senior officers with their side arms, and Walter and Helmut, who squeezed into the second car, encouraged by Grahnweis' wink. The two cars sped through the Paris night, arriving at the rue Lepic in good time—the W/T operator was still at it, according to the technicians in the Loewe-Opta trucks.

The actual entry into the hotel was restricted to the two detectives, along with two of the senior officers who could not be told no, as well as Walter—representing Grahnweis' faithful staff—and Grahnweis himself.

The night clerk, an old man with a white eye, trembled with fear when the Gestapo uniforms swept through the door. He showed them the registration book; they picked out, immediately, the woman "Marie Ladoux," who for ten days had occupied a top-floor room. Rented for her by a cousin, the man said, a week before she arrived. "She doesn't sleep here at night," he confided to one of the detectives. "God only knows where she goes."

They acknowledged later, quietly, among themselves, that she had been very brave. The young French girl or English girl or whoever she was—really very brave. When they kicked the door open she simply turned and stared at them as though they'd been impolite, her hand poised on the telegraph key. "Strange she had no watchers," Walter said later to the others in the Funkabwehr office on the boulevard Suchet.

"A patched-together business, I think," Helmut said. "Extemporized." A sad little smile, and the shrug that went with it: the British were losing now, knocked silly by German bombs, waiting for the blow to fall as a tough, predatory army waited on the chalk cliffs at Boulogne. The same cliffs where Napoleon's Grande Armée had waited. And waited. But this wasn't Napoleon. And the junior officers quite properly read desperation in the girl's mission—one could say *sacrifice*. Clearly nobody had expected her to survive for very long.

She shocked them, though. The rules of the game specified that the W/T operator give up, accept interrogation, accept the consequences of spying, which hadn't changed in a hundred years—the courtyard, the blindfold. But though she did not struggle when they took her, they got her only as far as the back seat of the Gestapo Mercedes, securely handcuffed, with a detective on either side. Yet she managed to do what she had to do; they heard the crunch of bitten glass and a few seconds later her head fell over like a broken doll and that was the end of "Marie Ladoux."

Grahnweis stayed behind with one of the senior officers to

examine the real prize—the clandestine radio. Which turned out to be the good old Mark XV transceiver—actually its first cousin, the Paraset—but, Grahnweis thought, standard MI-6 equipment. He nodded to himself with satisfaction and relief. The British scientists made him nervous—sometimes great bumblers, sometimes not. He feared that under pressure of war they might outperform themselves and conjure up some diabolical apparatus that would make his life a hell. But, so far, nothing like that, as far as he could tell, in the Hôtel Bretagne.

Standard stuff. Two transmission frequencies—from 3.3 to 4.5 megacycles and from 4.5 to 7.6 megacycles. Four to five watts of power—enough to get to London. Three American metal tubes, a 6V6 crystal-controlled pilot, cadmium steel box, silver finish. A calibration curve, to assist the operator, was mounted in the upper-left-hand corner, essentially a graph chart with a diagonal line. Grahnweis took a soft leather tool pouch from the pocket of his uniform jacket and selected a screwdriver for the task of getting behind the control panel. To the senior officer looking over his shoulder he said, "Maybe something new inside."

There was.

Grahnweis left the hotel by the Saint-Rustique side of the building; meanwhile, the senior officer exited on the rue Lepic—this parting company a mysterious event that nobody ever really explained. For a time it wasn't clear that Grahnweis was ever going to be found, but, with persistence and painstaking attention to detail, he was. Crown on the second bicuspid molar, fillings in upper and lower canines, a chipped incisor. Yes, that was Grahnweis, if a tattered charcoal log under a jumble of brick and tile could be called any name at all.

The junior officers of the Funkabwehr were extremely put out by this turn of events. It was, at its heart, rude. And rudeness of this sort they would never have ascribed to the British character. Had they known, of course, that it was the Poles who'd sent their leader from the room they would have thrown up their hands in angry recognition. *What could you expect?* But the British were different: Aryan, northern, civilized, and blessed with certain German virtues—honor in friendship, and love of learning.

The British were, in fact, perhaps a little worse than the Poles, but the Germans wouldn't come to understand that for some time. "Personally," said Heinrich, "it is the very sort of thing I find I cannot forgive."

7 September, 2:30 P.M.

Genya Beilis seated herself by a window in the Café Trois Reines, next to the St. Pierre cemetery in Montmartre. She was a vision, even in the end-of-summer heat. A little white hat with a bow, set just to one side of her head, a little white suit, three dashes of Guerlain. Not the usual for this neighborhood, but who knew what business royalty might have up here—maybe a call on a poor relative, or a bouquet for a former lover, who somehow wound up in the local boneyard. Whatever the truth, she shone, and her tea was served with every courtesy, and every drop still in the cup.

Very damn inspiring, the way she walked. Maybe you didn't believe in heaven but you certainly could believe in that. Chin and shoulders elevated, back like fine steel, the emphatic ring of high heels on the tile floor of a café. In the *cabinet de toilette,* Madame whipped off a lambskin glove and slipped a brown envelope behind a radiator. Then she returned to her tea.

A few blocks away, a number of Gestapo gentlemen read newspapers in cars and doorways all the livelong day as the mess in the rue Lepic was cleaned up, but that was hopeless and they knew it. Nobody was going to be coming around to see what happened to X. The abrupt halt in transmission, the absence of coded start-up signals—missent call sign, incorrect date—and the London people would know their network communication had been cut. One sent the newspaper readers out to the cars and doorways, but one knew better.

The lovely lady in white returned to the *quartier* of the Café Trois Reines on two occasions, but she found no chalk mark on M. Laval's gravestone and the letter in the toilette mailbox went uncollected, so that, in the end, the latest news on canals and barges in the Channel ports went unread.

Though she had never seen her correspondent she felt sad, enough a veteran of the business to know what uncollected mail implied. Then too, she had walked past the spontaneous renovation at the Hôtel Bretagne, noted newspaper readers in the vicinity, noted the absolute silence of the Parisian press on the subject of local explosions, and wondered if it all might not somehow fit together.

But hers not to reason why. Hers to travel down to the Banque de Commerce Nationale in Orléans, humiliate the most vulgar, oily little bank man that God ever made, and collect a new set of procedures.

Now it was the sixteenth arrondissement.

Now it was the Café du Jardin.

Now the adjacent cemetery was in Passy.

Ghouls, she thought.

Starry night in the village of Aire. In 1430, the Roman bridge over the river Lys had been replaced and the Martagne family had built a fine house at the end of it, so the cool air that hung above the water made the stone rooms pleasant on summer evenings.

Martagne, the port supervisor from Calais, had a red face and black hair, a big cleft nose and a big mustache. He sat in the dark kitchen with de Milja—Fedin was waiting at the edge of the village—drinking farmer-made Calvados from a stone crock. "Take another Calva," he said. "Uncle made that in 1903." Martagne liked to spend his time in the bars with the Polish dockyard workers, and they put him on to Fedin and de Milja when he got frustrated with the Germans and threatened *to talk to somebody.*

Now he was drunk. He stared down at the scarred old table and brooded. Finally he said, "You a spy?"

"Yes."

Martagne made a face. "I'm a Norman," he said. "Not French—whatever that means. But we fight their damn battles. They're good at insults, not so good at fighting. Bad combination, you'll agree."

"Yes."

"It's fighting—you'll find a Martagne. Crècy, Agincourt, Sedan, Poitiers, the Marne, Jena, Marengo. Probably went over the Channel with William the Conqueror—last time anybody managed to do that, by the way. Probably somebody looked like me, with my ugly face." Martagne laughed at the idea. "Can't stand the English," he said. "You care?"

"No," de Milja said.

"They care?"

"No."

Martagne laughed again. "Me neither," he said. He stood, swayed a moment, then left the room. Through a crack in the closed shutter de Milja could see that moon and starlight lit the old village and he could hear splashing water where the Lys ran over a small weir. Somewhere in the house Martagne was banging drawers open and shut. Finally he reappeared and handed de Milja three sheets of used carbon paper.

"Sorry I didn't bring the originals," he said. "We'll take one more Calva." He poured generously, the fragrance of distant apples drifted up to de Milja. "Now, Monsieur Spy, one little story before you go."

De Milja sipped the Calvados.

"The last week in June, on the day of the surrender, when Pétain got on the radio about how he was preserving the honor of France, my grandfather put on a nightshirt he'd never worn in his life and got into his bed. He was a healthy old bird, pissed like a fountain. But now he stayed in bed, he didn't speak, he didn't smile, he just stared at the wall. The doctor came, a childhood friend. Didn't help. He made the old jokes, said the old things, left a tonic on the nightstand. But a week later, my grandfather was gone. 'He has died of shame,' the doctor said. So now, what you have in your hand, that is his revenge—and mine. Do you understand?''

"Yes, I understand," de Milja said. He proved it by standing up to leave. Martagne looked away; angry at what he'd done, angry at the world for having made him do it. De Milja said good night and slipped out the door.

Gold in hand, it turned out.

12 September. In Nieuwpoort, just across the Belgian border, dust from the wheat harvest hung in the warm air and the fields shimmered in golden light; the docks were burning, the harbor smelled of dead fish, an RAF Blenheim-IVF came tearing over the jetty at fifty feet with its gunports twinkling. The windows of the Café Nieuwpoort fell in on a dead fisherman and a dead waiter and a German corporal came running out of the toilet with his pants around his ankles. A mackerel boat caught fire and the cook jumped into the harbor. Eight rounds from the .303 guns, including an incendiary tracer, stitched up the side of the harbor gasoline tank, thirty feet high, and absolutely nothing happened. The cook yelled he couldn't swim; a couple of taxi drivers ran to the edge of the pier, but when the Blenheim screamed around the town in a banked turn they threw themselves on their bellies and by the time they looked out at the water again there was nobody there.

The Germans had an antiaircraft gun at the top of the hill, in the little garden behind the town hall, and red fireballs went whizzing through the port as they tried to hit the Blenheim. Flown by some species of madman—in fact a Rhodesian bush pilot—the Blenheim seemed enraged by the attack, tore out over the sea and came skimming back into Nieuwpoort, blazing away at the gun position and hitting two of the gunners and the mayor's secretary.

On the top floor of the dockside Hotel Vlaanderen, de Milja and a whore wearing a slip and a Turkish seaman wearing underpants watched the fight together through a cracked window. De Milja had come running in here when the attack started, but the whore and the sailor hardly seemed to notice him. The room quivered and a blast wave rang the window glass—high explosive going off on the other side of town. De Milja looked out the window to see, just over the town horizon, thick, curling smoke, black and ponderous, tumbling slowly upward, implying the death of an industrial something or other that had lived on heavy oil. Then the hotel was hit, the sailor squawked and grabbed the whore in terror, knocking her blond wig askew and revealing clipped dark hair beneath. "Shh," she said, and stroked the man's hair.

De Milja pressed his palm against the worn linoleum, testing for heat in case the floor below them was on fire. For the moment, he decided, he was about as safe as he was going to get. The bombers seemed to be working north of Nieuwpoort, near the railroad yards. Puffs of dark smoke from spent ack-ack bursts drifted back over the town from that direction. Fedin should have been halfway down to Abbeville—de Milja could only hope he hadn't been killed in the raid.

The mackerel boat was fully ablaze now; a man ran up to it, threw a completely pointless bucket of water on the roof of the crackling wheelhouse, then ran away. "My poor town," the whore said under her breath. The sailor said something in Turkish and the whore, responding to the tone of his voice, said, "Yes, that's right."

As de Milja turned back to the window, the Blenheim flashed by, the wing tip no more than ten feet away, engines howling, rattling the window in its frame. The pilot circled low over the town and headed back out to sea, toward the Dover cliffs and home. The Germans had now gotten their antiaircraft gun working again and sent him on his way with a volley that may have nicked the tail of the airplane. The pilot responded; put his plane in a violent climb, foot on the floor, then a steep bank at the top of the climb, where he vanished into the low cloud. A little bell rang in the street: the Nieuwpoort fire truck, stopped for a moment while two firemen struggled with a large chunk of concrete, dragging it to the edge of the dock by the bent rods sticking out at odd angles.

The men jumped back on the truck and it drove around the harbor to where the burning mackerel boat had now set the pier on fire. A *Feldengendarmerie* open car pulled up behind the truck and a soldier ran over to the driver's window and pointed back the other way. The soldier climbed into his car and both vehicles began the long process of getting themselves turned around without dropping a wheel over the edge of the pier.

Good, de Milja thought. Something's really gone up somewhere and the Germans are very unhappy about it. But even so, de Milja the realist had been watching German equipment go up in flames since September of 1939 and he had to admit that it didn't seem to slow them down. They patched and fixed and improvised and did without. *War's own children,* he thought. They find a way to get the job done and go on to the next town.

Another plane came tearing past the hotel, the clatter of gunfire echoing in the little room. No—the same Blenheim, de Milja realized. He'd been hiding out over the sea somewhere or a little way down the coast and this time, like magic, the huge gasoline storage tank erupted in a great whuff of orange flame and boiling black smoke. The pilot circled the town, getting a good eyeful for his gun cameras and obviously very proud of what he'd done. He then waggled his wings—the AA gunners did everything but throw their lunch at him—and sped out over the sea toward the English coast.

A little rain that night. The Turkish seaman went off to sail away—if he still had a boat to sail away on—and de Milja paid the whore to stay with her in the room. Bernette, she was called. No longer young, short and sturdy, fiercely proud in the face of all the pranks that life had played her. She hung her blond wig on the post at the foot of the bed and fussed over it and combed it out, calling it her *poor beaver,* entirely unselfconscious in her slip and half-inch salt-and-pepper hair.

De Milja gave her some money and she wriggled into a skirt and went off to a café she knew where they cooked on a wood-fired stove—the electricity in Nieuwpoort was out—and returned carrying a big plate of lentils and bacon with vinegar, still warm and covered with yesterday's newspaper, and two bottles of dark beer. Excuse them for not sending the lady and gentleman a glass, but their glassware had not survived the afternoon.

The rain pattered on the wharfside streets, cooling everything a little. In the distance the bells of the fire trucks never stopped. It smelled like Warsaw; charred plaster, burning oil, and cordite. Bernette wrinkled her nose and splashed herself with White Ginger perfume, so that the room smelled like bombs and gardenias. Would the gentleman, she wanted to know, care for a half-and-half when he'd finished his lentils? The money he'd given her entitled him to at least that. No, de Milja said. Somehow the events of the day had left him not much in the mood for such things. Strange, he thought, how much I like you. Like me a wanderer, somehow never home.

That was, it happened, true. She'd had a home, a child, a family, but, well, what did it all matter? God meant her not to have them and now she didn't. It wasn't much of a story anyhow.

Well the hell with everybody, he said. And he was getting tired of the four walls—could they go out for a walk? She agreed to go. Scared as she was, she agreed. Strange, he thought, how you stumble on the world's secret nobility when you're not even looking for them.

When she went down the hall to the toilet de Milja poured half a bottle of beer down his shirt. She made a sour face about that when she returned—she could wash it out in the sink. No, he said, turned away from her so she wouldn't smell that he'd washed his mouth with the rest of the beer and splashed some on his hair.

Outside it was quiet at first, the rain hissing on a few small fires here and there. Some of the townspeople were poking through the burnt-out café, lifting a blackened timber then dropping it quickly when they saw what was under it. The *patron*, the toughest man in Nieuwpoort, was sitting on the curb and weeping into a dirty handkerchief, his shoulders shaking. "Ach," Bernette said, fought back the tears, then steadied. Soot drifted down on them as they walked, walked carefully because the sea fog hung over the town. Quiet water that night, just lapping at the foot of the quai as the tide went out. Walking away from the center of Nieuwpoort they were stopped by a pair of Wehrmacht sentries. Nervy and angry now that they'd been on the wrong end of the war for a moment—they hadn't liked that at all.

But what could they do with a beer-smelling slob and a whore headed down the beach for a blow job? He was now Rosny, Belgian of Czech descent, a long story. In the end the Germans waved them along, but for half a pfennig they would have run a rifle butt under his chin just to see his heels fly up in the air. Because they had dead friends and half-dead friends and would-have-been-better-off-dead friends—de Milja knew what bombing did to people—and they were full of rage, and quite dangerous. Bernette, good Bernette, looked at them a certain way, and maybe that bled out the fury just enough to keep de Milja's jaw from getting broken, but it was a close thing.

The sirens went off about an hour past midnight, and de Milja and Bernette moved off the beach and back into the dunes. They were in the town's shame pit—broken glass, old rags, a dead shoe—a hidden place for those Nieuwpoort citizens who had to do something private and couldn't afford to do it indoors. De Milja moved into the lee of a dune, they sat down on the damp sand, he put an arm around her shoulders and she clung to him, her protector.

Not much more than a gesture, with what came down on Nieuwpoort that night.

The Blenheim, it turned out, was merely an opening act, a juggler on roller skates. Now the full troupe of comedians came running out of the wings. Lancaster bombers, de Milja guessed. The beach shuddered as the bombs hit, to long rolls of thunder and flashes of orange fire in the darkness. Once or twice it was close, sand showered down on them and Bernette whimpered like a poodle and burrowed into him. The antiaircraft people up at the mayor's office got on the scoreboard just as the raid began, hit a Lancaster with a full bomb load a little way out to sea from the harbor and de Milja swore he could see the night cloud for twenty miles around by the light of the explosion. But most of the rest got through, hitting the town and the sea and the villages nearby and God only knew what else. Pretty soon Nieuwpoort was truly on fire, the Hotel Vlaanderen no more than a pile of smoking brick.

The second British attack came at 3:30 in the morning. It seemed very quiet when they left. De Milja and Bernette dozed, then woke up at dawn, stiff and chilled and miserable. The sea had come alive in first light; white combers rolling in a long way, crying gulls hanging in the air above the breaking surf. De Milja walked down to the tideline to splash his face and there, riding to and fro in a foot of water, a thin trail of yellow foam traced up the back of his uniform, was the first German. Face-down, arms above his head. As de Milja watched, a wave a little more powerful than the ones before picked him up, rushed him in a few extra feet, and dumped him on the wet sand.

It wasn't clear how he had died—he hadn't burned, hadn't been hit by shellfire. Probably he had drowned. He wore a field-gray combat uniform, waist encircled by a belt with ammunition pouches and a commando knife, prepared to fight. *One of mine,* de Milja thought. But it wasn't one, it was three, no, a dozen. Hundreds. At first the gray of their uniforms blended with the color of the sea, but as the light changed he could see more and more of them. Most wearing heavy packs, bobbing silently in the surf. Now and then the sea would leave another one on the beach, then, so it seemed to de Milja, go back out in order to bring in a few more.

Dependable port official reports security staff alerting coastal defense units to a landing exercise, to be carried out at division strength, using barges and seagoing tugs, at Westende on the Belgian coast on the night of 12 September.

So this was his kill.

It would have been suicide to try for Westende, so he'd settled for Nieuwpoort, to see what he could see. And here it was. Some of the dead were burned—perhaps a ship had been hit. Perhaps several ships. Invasion troops, from the packs and all the other equipment—the Germans had put on a dress rehearsal for a landing on the beaches of Britain.

And the British had put on a dress rehearsal of their own.

It was much too dangerous to stay where he was, there would be hell to pay on this beach once the Germans discovered what the tide was bringing in. But when he turned to look for Bernette he discovered she'd been standing by his side, bare feet splayed in the sand, arms crossed beneath her breasts.

He put a hand on her shoulder, but she did not respond so he let it drop. Then he knelt down, took a little slip of paper and a stub of pencil from his pocket and sketched the shoulder-patch insignia of one of the dead soldiers: a knight raised a sword above his head, his shield a crusader's cross. The legend above the knight: *Grenadierregiment 46*. Legend below: *21 Infanteriedivision Dresden*.

He tucked the slip of paper into his pants cuff, then stood up. "I know you are a patriot," he said.

She had seen, and certainly understood, what he had just done. It was an act of war to learn who the dead were. "Yes," she said. "I am." Just one more secret, she thought. She kept them all.

15 September.

Martagne had stolen three carbons from the Port of Calais office; the German landing exercise was one of them.

De Milja made his way south to the village of Sangatte, on the road that ran by the sea from Boulogne to Calais. Fedin was waiting for him in a closed-up villa owned by a Russian baron—lately a toy manufacturer, formerly one of the czar's riding masters—in Paris. De Milja arrived a little after one in the afternoon, Genya Beilis came by taxi from the resort town of Le Touquet an hour later. All trains from Paris to Boulogne and Calais had been suspended, she said. Military traffic only. Railroad guns. Field hospitals.

The time had come.

The roads were jammed with panzer tanks and 88 artillery pieces on carriers and fuel tankers with red crosses painted on them to fool the British attack aircraft. Wehrmacht invasion planners were playing chess now—big guns at Calais had engaged British artillery across the Channel, communications frequencies were being jammed, radio towers and radars attacked. *We're coming,* it meant.

"The enemy's ports are our first line of defense." Lord Nelson, in 1805, and nothing had changed. Britain had its little piece of water that it hid behind. The princes of Europe could field huge land armies. But when they reached the coast of France, they stopped.

A Russian general, a publisher's daughter, a Polish cartographer. At the villa they sat on sheets that covered the furniture, in a dark room behind closed shutters. Finished, and they knew it. Fedin, at sixty, perhaps the strongest of them, de Milja thought. To survive Russia you had to fight for life—fight the cold, fight the sadness and its vodka. Those who lived were like iron. Genya, de Milja saw, had covered the dark circles beneath her eyes with powder. He thought the shadows decadent, sexy, but the attempted disguise made her look old, a woman attempting to deceive the world. As for himself, he felt numb, as though a nerve, pounded on by the hour, had gone dead.

The three of them smoked. It made up for food, for sleep.

"They've arrested Rijndal," Fedin said. "The Dutch barge captain. His wife let another friend of ours know about it."

"Do they know why?" de Milja asked.

"No."

"What can he tell them?"

"That he talked to émigrés—Russians, Poles, Czechs— working against the Germans."

"I'm going to sleep," Genya said. She assumed there was a bedroom on the second floor, so climbed the stairs. Fedin and de Milja could hear her up there, walking around in different rooms.

Fedin and de Milja left the house, walked to a café, telephoned another café. In silence, they drank coffee for an hour, then an ambulance pulled up outside. The driver joined them, ordered a marc, opened a newspaper. GERMAN STRENGTH AND FRENCH CULTURE TO INSPIRE NEW EUROPE, read the headline, quoting a French minister.

"How can you read that garbage?" Fedin asked.

The ambulance driver shrugged. "I used to prefer PIG BORN WITH TWO HEADS, but this is all you get now." He looked at his watch. "I can let you have two hours, so if you're going you better go."

Fedin handed over a stack of franc notes.

"What are you moving?" the driver asked.

"Hams," Fedin said.

The driver raised his eyebrows in a way which meant *I wouldn't mind having one.* Fedin smiled a knave's smile and patted him on the arm. *Business is business,* he meant.

Fedin drove the ambulance, de Milja lay down on the

stretcher in the back. The days when they could use the van were now over, only French emergency vehicles were allowed on the roads in the coastal region. Keeping to the farm routes, they reached the village of Colombert, on the D6. In the main square, a military policeman wearing white gloves was directing traffic. Fedin pointed at the road he wanted, the policeman waved him violently in that direction—*yes, go on, hurry!* An army truck in the square had a flat tire; soldiers were standing around waiting for the driver to fix it. They wore the same uniform as the soldiers on the beach at Nieuwpoort, but their shoulder insignia was different. "Commandos," Fedin said, squinting to see the patches. "To climb ropes up cliffs."

"If they can get to the cliffs," de Milja said.

Fedin nosed the wheel over gingerly and drove down a lane between two rows of linden trees. The trunks had grown for too many years, there was barely room for a vehicle. The road divided at a canal. Fedin turned off the ignition. Another lost, exquisite little place—still water, soft sky, leaves barely moving in the breeze. De Milja clambered out of the back of the ambulance. "I hope nobody asks us what we're doing down here."

Fedin shrugged. "We'll say Van Gogh had a fainting spell."

They walked along the canal for a time. Around a curve, fourteen barges were tied up end to end, roped to iron rings set at the edge of what had been, a century earlier, a towpath. By the water there were three blackened, splintered trunks of linden trees; several others had had their leaves blown off. A single sunken barge was lying halfway on its side in the still water. Fedin tapped a cigarette out of his pack, screwed it into his ivory holder, and lit it with a small silver lighter. "Well," he said, "we did try."

The villa at Sangatte, late afternoon. De Milja climbed the stairs, found the bedroom and opened the door quietly. Genya was sleeping in her underwear, hands beneath her head instead of a pillow, on top of a mattress covered with a sheet. He watched her for a time; she was dreaming. What she showed the world was hard and polished. But in her dream she was frightened, her breathing caught. Carefully, he lay down next to her, but she woke up. "You're here," she said.

"Yes."

"How was it?"

"Not so good."

"Really?"

"We managed to see three different places. There was one barge sunk, one transport damaged—the Germans had French shipfitters working on it. In Calais, an old man who fishes off the jetty said that a motor launch blew up the other night when the British came."

Genya didn't answer. De Milja was tired. It was hot and airless on the upper floor, dark behind the shutters. Yet he could feel, just at that moment, summer slipping away. He could hear the ocean breaking on the rocky beach. Two girls on bicycles, talking as they pedaled side by side. Some kind of bird that sang a single, low note in a tree outside. He moved closer to Genya, her skin brown against the white sheet, touched her shoulder with his lips. She moved a little away from him. "I'm asleep," she said.

16 September. The invasion fleet began to assemble. It had been planned for Genya to make a courier run to the Passy W/T operator on the evening of the fifteenth. But the French police had blocked all the roads and the railroad stations were off-limits to civilians. The region had been closed.

The Calais waterfront was a maze of dark, cobbled streets winding among brick warehouses and cargo sheds, small tenements where the dockworkers lived, a few cafés where they drank, and a crumbling hotel with a blue neon sign—HÔTEL NEPTUNE—a whorehouse for foreign sailors.

De Milja and Fedin went into one of the bars, ordered *ballons de rouge*, glasses of red wine, and spent an hour gossiping with the owner and his fat blond wife. The owner wore a tweed cap, had his shirtsleeves rolled up above the elbows. Business was no good, he said, at this rate they wouldn't last much longer. The English dropped bombs on their customers, the Germans paid like drunkards on a spree or they didn't pay at all. One thought one had it tough before May of '40, *et alors,* what one didn't know! The wife had a rich laugh and red cheeks.

And what was that warehouse across the street?

Labard et Labard? Boarded up, now. They used to see the workers all day—first for an eye-opener, then lunch—a very nice plat du jour for a few francs and a coffee. Finally a little something at the end of the day when they gathered to get up their courage to go home and face their wives. So, life wasn't perfect but it went along. But then, the war. The young Monsieur Labard an officer, now a prisoner of war in Germany. The elder Labard was eighty-seven. He'd tried, but it hadn't worked out. *Tant pis,* too bad, oh well, that was life, what could one do, so it went. The owner shook his head grimly at the sorrow of it all while the wife winked at de Milja and rolled her hips when she walked down to the other end of the bar to refill their glasses.

They broke in to the Labard warehouse just after dark. Used an old piece of iron to pry a padlock off a side entry, groped their way up an ancient wooden staircase to the top floor. Found a window with a space between the board and the frame, kicked it a little wider, and got a view of the Calais harbor.

Fedin had been right about the date—full moon on the seventeenth. They counted forty troop transports anchored out in the harbor, six more in position for boarding on the wharf. Trucks pulled in, piled high with wooden ammunition boxes. The first invasion wave would be loaded the following morning, then, that night, they would sail for England.

"This is it," Fedin said, staring intently at the activity in the harbor. "I hope they have something ready on the other side."

"The English abandoned a lot of weapons on the beach at Dunkirk," de Milja said. "That was three months ago—I wonder how much of it they've been able to replace. Some, not all. Every farmer has his shotgun, of course. Which is just what they thought would happen in France, but farmers with shotguns can't do much about artillery."

A broad-beamed tugboat came chugging into the harbor from the direction of the Calais canals. It was pushing three barges from a position on the port side and almost to the stern of the last barge. The tug, built for moving bargeloads of coal among the Rhine ports, made rapid way into the harbor.

"They're going across in that?" Fedin said.

"If the water stays calm."

"What about the Royal Navy?"

"The Germans must feel they can neutralize it for forty-eight hours—after that it doesn't matter. And if the Luftwaffe can get the advantage in the air over the Channel, the Royal Navy can't do a thing."

De Milja watched the harbor in silence. The activity wasn't frantic, but there were thirty operations going on at once, ships moving about, trucks arriving and departing—all of it steady and certain, nobody was smoking or standing around. All non-military ships had been tied up in the small pleasure-boat harbor that adjoined the main dock areas of the city. The name of one of the ships was familiar—he had to think for a moment before he realized why. The rusty freighter with flaking black paint was, according to the letters fading away on her hull, the *Malacca Princess*. Grand name for an old tramp, de Milja thought. It had appeared on one of the carbons Martagne had given them—a schedule of commercial shipping traffic expected to enter or depart the port of Calais over the period 9/14/40 to 9/21/40, with a brief description of each cargo manifest.

The first British attack came at 10:15.

Assault aircraft—built to work near the ground—engines

screaming as they flashed across the harbor. Beauforts, de Milja thought. Perhaps a dozen. One flew into the side of a warehouse, and by the yellow flash of that impact de Milja saw another, cartwheeling twice over the surface of the water. The Germans were waiting for this attack—the stutter of heavy machine guns and the deeper, two-stroke drumming of the antiaircraft cannon rang in de Milja's ears, then deafened him. The Beauforts attacked at one hundred feet, carrying four five hundred-pound bombs apiece, four dives each if they lasted that long.

There were ME-109s above them, nightfighters, one of them followed a Beaufort right down the chute, guns blazing, in such hot pursuit it chased its quarry through a cloud of machine-gun tracer. Moments later, a pair of green flares came floating down, illuminating an airman hanging limp from a parachute, which settled gently on the calm sea then disappeared as the flares hit the water.

Two minutes, no more. The sound faded away, de Milja's hearing came back in time to make out the low wail of an all-clear siren. In the moonlight a single barge settled slowly into the water, a single transport steamer burned, firefighters with hoses silhouetted in its flames.

"Do you have a gun?" de Milja said to Fedin.

"This," Fedin said. A Walther P-38, a German officer's side arm. De Milja extended his hand. Fedin, after a puzzled moment, gave him the pistol.

"What . . . ?"

De Milja didn't answer.

The second British attack came at 11:16.

A chess game somewhere, in offices below ground, linked to radio towers, British air controllers moving a castle here, a knight there. Blind chess. With command-and-control sometimes functioning, sometimes not. Now and then everybody simply had to improvise, to do whatever seemed best. De Milja had seen plenty of that in Poland, where it hadn't worked. A lot of dead, brave people is what you got from that.

The RAF pilots—British and South African, Canadian, Czech, and Polish—were something beyond brave. They flew into the firestorm a second time, and a number of them paid for it. Perhaps, this time out, the controllers had shifted a flight of Spitfires to keep the 109s away from the assault aircraft. Which left the docks in London unprotected when the Junkers and Heinkels flew over, and that was the chess game. The Calais docks on fire—the London docks on fire in exchange. As de Milja watched the raid play itself out, two searchlights nailed a wounded Beaufort trying to sneak home a few feet above the water. De Milja didn't see the 109 that did the job; the Beaufort simply grew a blossom of white fire behind the cockpit, then hit the water in a cloud of steam and spray.

De Milja's hands ached, he had to pull them free of the windowsill he'd been holding. Only a single siren now, a fire truck somewhere in Calais. Not needed at the docks because nothing was on fire. The transport had been saved—though the barge hit in the 10:15 attack had now apparently sunk into the harbor ooze. Probably it would be salvaged, raised and repaired, used to run ammunition across the Channel to the British beaches. Maybe in a week or so, de Milja thought, as London held out valiantly—as had Warsaw—while around the world people gathered close to their radios to hear, through the static and the sirens, the British pleading for help in their last hours.

De Milja stepped back from the window. "One last thing to try," he said.

General Fedin understood him perfectly—he'd been at war, one way or another, for forty years. "I would be honored to accompany you," he said.

"Better if you stay here," de Milja said.

Fedin nodded stiffly. He might have saluted, but how—the salute of which country, which army? De Milja moved toward the door, for a moment a dim shape in the darkness of the warehouse, then gone. The last Fedin heard of him was footsteps descending the old wooden staircase.

Not long, maybe fifteen minutes, from the Labard warehouse to the docks. He moved quickly, low and tight to the buildings, a strange elation in his heart. He circled a burning garage, avoided a street where flames rolled black and orange from the upper windows of a workers' tenement. Faded into a doorway when a German vehicle—a sinister armored car, some kind of SS troop in black uniforms hanging off it—came rumbling slowly around a corner.

In the distance, a low, muttering thunder. Weather or bombs. Probably the latter. The RAF hammering away at Boulogne, or Ostende, or Dunkirk. Staggering its attacks, in and out like a boxer. They would be at it all night on this coast, as long as the planes and pilots held out.

The port was a maze —a jumble of streets, then harbors with rock jetties, miles of them, drydocks and spillways, sagging wood fence and high, stone walls. At the main entry, under the PORT DE CALAIS sign, the security people had cut through their own barbed wire and shoved the stanchions back against the brick walls of the guardhouse. It wasn't security they wanted that night, they wanted speed, fire trucks and ambulances in and out. Then, at first light, after the bomb damage was cleaned up, there were troops and ammunition and equipment to load up. As de Milja watched from cover, a truck sped through the gate, bouncing on the cobbles, never slowing down. Nonetheless, he waited. Saw the glint of a helmet through the window of the guardhouse. Moved off to try somewhere else.

He used the little streets, worked parallel to the harbor. A whore hissed at him from a doorway, swung her trench coat aside when she got his attention He might need an assistant, he thought, and studied her for a moment. "So," she said, a little uncomfortable with the sort of attention he was paying her, "something unusual we have in mind tonight?" De Milja grinned despite himself, *let her live,* just for a moment the choice was his. As he walked away she called after him, a sweet, husky French voice like a café singer—"You never know if you don't ask, my love."

Down the next street, he had what he needed. A Beaufort had opened the way for him. Arriving in France in flames and out of control, it had chosen to set up housekeeping on a street that bordered the harbor, had rolled up a hundred feet of wire fence, collected an empty bus and a little watchman's hut that happened to be lying around, then piled it all up against an ancient stone wall and set it on fire. A few French firemen had attempted to interfere with the project, but, as the Beaufort burned, it cooked off several belts of ammunition and chased them away. Water foamed white from the hoses they'd dropped in the street and they called out to one another from the doorways where they'd taken cover. Somebody yelled at de Milja as he ran through the opening torn in the fence, that was the only challenge. That, and something that sputtered and whizzed past his ear, as though to say *move along there.*

An area of open workshops, stone bays as big as barns—they'd likely worked on Napoleon's fleet here. "Give me six hours' control of the Strait of Dover, and I will gain mastery of the world." Napoleon had said that—de Milja had had to learn it when he'd studied at Saint-Cyr. The workshops were full of small engines, propeller shafts. De Milja's eye fell on a tank of acetylene and he smiled as he trotted past.

It seemed to take a long time—after midnight on his watch—but he finally stood on the old jetty that protected the pleasure-boat harbor; massive slabs of granite piled up a century earlier against the seas of the Pas de Calais—angry North Sea water trapped between the cliffs of England and France. Now it was calm in the September moonlight, just a quiet swell running diagonally to the shore; a slow, lazy ocean like a cat waking up. De Milja trotted past staunch little sailboats—*Atlantic Queen, Domino*—until the hulls of the commercial ships came into view.

Banished here to be kept out of the way of the invasion fleet, allowed to sail into Calais on schedule so as not to give away the date and location of the invasion.

He stopped, looked anxiously into the sky. *Not yet.* No, it was only a flight of German bombers, at high altitude, droning toward England. Perhaps two hundred of them, he thought, they seemed to take forever to pass above him. It was too exposed on the skyline so he half-ran, half-slid to the foot of the jetty where the water lapped at the rocks. The green seaweed reeked in the summer heat and clouds of flies hung above it. He knelt, took the Walther from the back of his waistband, and had a look. The 7.65 mm version, a heavy, dependable weapon, for use, not for show. Eight rounds in the magazine, one in the chamber. He worked the safety, noted the film of oil that glistened on the slide. *Trust Fedin,* he thought, *to keep things in good order.*

The foot of the jetty lay in moon-shadow, so de Milja, invisible, used it as a pathway. Past a pair of Greek tankers, empty from the way they rode high in the water, and a flaking hulk called the *Nicaea,* a sheen of leaked oil coating the water at its stern. Then, last in line, as far away as the harbormaster could berth it, the *Malacca Princess.* The smell! De Milja blinked and shook his head. How did the crew survive it, all the way from the port of Batavia?

He gripped the Walther firmly and thought *no surprises, please.* No stubborn captain who took the care and protection of his cargo as a sacred trust—no fanatics, no heroes. De Milja moved quickly, from the shadows of the jetty to the first step of an iron gangway covered with tattered canvas that climbed ten feet to the deck. On deck, he went down on one knee. *Deserted,* he thought. Only the creak of old iron plates as the ship rose and fell, and the grating of the hawser cable as it strained against its post on the jetty below. The smell was even stronger here, his eyes were tearing. De Milja listened intently, heard, no, didn't hear. Yes, did. Bare feet on iron decking. Then a voice—a native of the Dutch East Indies speaking British English—very frightened and very determined. "Who is there?" A pause. "Please?"

De Milja ran, low to the deck, and flattened himself against the base of a cargo crane. From here he could see a silhouette, standing hunched over, a few feet from the open door of the deck cabin, peering about, head moving left, then right. In one hand, a long shape. What? A rifle? It occurred to de Milja to point the Walther at the man and blaze away but he knew two things—he wouldn't hit him, and somebody, even in the tense, hushed interlude between bombing attacks, would hear a pistol shot and just have to stir up French or German security to go and see what it was all about.

De Milja stepped out where the man could see him, extended the pistol, and called, "Stand still."

The silhouette froze. De Milja worked out the next phrase in his uncertain English. "Let fall." He waggled the pistol once or twice, there followed the clatter of an object dropped on the iron deck. Whatever it was, it didn't sound like a rifle. He approached the man. He was young, wearing only a pair of cotton pants cut off below the knee and a cloth tied around his forehead. De Milja stooped cautiously, retrieved what the man had dropped: a wooden club. "Others?" he said.

"There are none, sir. No others," the man said. "Just me. To keep the watch."

De Milja lowered the pistol. The watchman smiled, then made a certain motion with his hands and shoulders. *Whatever you want,* it meant, *to me it's not worth dying for.*

De Milja nodded that he understood. The young man had a family, in Sumatra or Java somewhere, and if circumstance carried him to the ends of the earth where people had gone mad, well, it was their war, not his.

At first, he didn't know how to do what de Milja needed but he knew where to look, and from there the solution to the problem was evident. Raise the large, metal arm beside the box to its *up* position, then move around the *Malacca Princess,* find its various equipment, for loading and anchorage and warning and identifying other ships and just about anything you could think of, and throw all those switches to the *on* position.

Then wait.

"Your things," de Milja said.

"Sir?"

De Milja pointed to his own pants, shirt, wallet, pistol. The man nodded vigorously and together they went below while he collected a small bundle, then moved back to the main deck.

Where they waited. The ship rocked gently and creaked, the nearby harbor felt deserted. In the dock area, activity continued; trucks, visible even with taped headlights, moving invasion matériel to be loaded onto barges. By 1:30, de Milja began to worry. What if the British had taken too many losses and decided to halt operations for the night? No, it wasn't possible.

It wasn't. At 1:50, the air-raid sirens began to wail, all along the wharf and from the city of Calais. De Milja smiled at the watchman, and pointed at the sky. The man nodded, returned the smile, tight and conciliatory. He understood fighting very well, he understood that de Milja was in the act of fighting; a sort of noble privilege. He just wasn't all that pleased to have been drawn into it—no insult intended, sir.

Poor Charles Grahame, not much success in life. Still young, but the pattern was set. Public school with a name that made people say "Where?" A year at the University of Edinburgh, a year at the Scottish Widows Assurance Society in the City of London. Then, war on the way, an attempt to join the RAF. Well, yes, of course, what they needed just then were meteorologists.

So he joined the Royal Navy, and with grit and determination worked his way into the naval aviator school. He got through it, assigned to the aircraft carrier HMS *Avenger.*

Not to fly fighter-bombers, oh no, not Charley. Tall and

gangly, curly hair that wouldn't stay, ears like jug handles, freckles everywhere, and a silly grin. The headmaster of his school used to say that God didn't quite get around to finishing Charles.

The Royal Navy assigned him to fly the Swordfish torpedo plane.

The Swordfish was a biplane—top and bottom wing and a fixed wheel—that looked like a refugee from World War I. It carried a single torpedo, slung beneath the cockpit. "Quite serviceable, though," the flight instructor said. Its airspeed was 150 miles an hour. "But it *will* get you there, eventually," the flight instructor said. Saying to himself immediately thereafter *now whether or not it will get you home is entirely another matter.*

Not much talent as a pilot. Charles's method of achievement was to learn the rules and follow them to the letter. Do this, then do this, then do that. A different age might have found this approach greatly to its liking but, bad luck, Charles lived at a moment when spontaneity, the daring solution, and the flash of genius were particularly in fashion.

The carrier HMS *Avenger* was steaming in circles in Aldeburgh Bay in the first hours of 17 September, just after midnight. Charles Grahame climbed into the open cockpit beneath the top wing and his gunner/torpedo-man, Sublieutenant Higbee, sat in the gunner's cockpit behind him. They took off, then turned south, in a formation of six Swordfish assigned to attack Calais harbor.

The formation hugged the coastline, protected by coastal antiaircraft defenses. A single ME-109 might have done for all of them, so hiding, down at six thousand feet, was their best—in fact their only—defense. The night was warm and still, moonlight turned the clouds to silver and sparkled on the water below the planes. They flew past navigation beams at Shoeburyness and Sheerness, then turned east at Herne Bay, headed for Margate.

At Margate, a rendezvous with a flight of Hurricanes, well

above them somewhere, godlike, lords of the high cloud. The Hurricane squadron leader came on his radio moments later. "Hullo Hector, hullo Hector. This is Jupiter, we're above you right now, and we're going to keep you company on the way to destination. Radio silence from here on, but we did want to wish you good hunting. Roger and out."

Charles Grahame knew that voice, it had a mustache and it drove a Morgan and its friends called it Tony and it got the girl and, really, worst of all, it knew it. Oh well, he told himself. just get on with it. Not everybody could be lord of the manor.

Coming into the Strait of Dover, the Germans started shooting at them. Puffs of antiaircraft burst that hung in the air like painted smoke. Something tossed the Swordfish's port-side wings in the air, and something else flicked the plane's tail. Charles worked the controls to see if they still responded, and they did, as much as they ever did.

The Swordfish flight attacked in a three-and-three configuration, Charles the wingman on the left in the first wave. Higbee yelled "Good luck, Charley," above the singing of the wind in the struts, his voice at nineteen a high tenor. Then all hell broke loose—*somebody* down there took Charley Grahame pretty damn seriously after all because they tried to kill him. Tracer streamed past the cockpit, flak burst everywhere, a bullet hit the fuselage with an awful tinny rattle. "Easy does it," Charles said to himself. Now he concentrated on doing what he'd been taught. Step One, the approach. Well, they'd managed that well enough. Step Two, acquire the target. By now Higbee should be ready to fire. But Charles couldn't see a thing. Not a bloody thing. He was whipping along, three hundred feet above the water, below him, theoretically, the harbor at Calais. But what he could see was a dark, confused blur, the moon lit up water here and there, but it meant nothing to Charles. He'd been instructed to attack a troop transport, or, almost as good, a tugboat. A barge, which could carry eight hundred tons of supplies, was a very desirable third choice. But Charles couldn't find a harbor, a city, or indeed anything at all. Probably it was France, *probably* . . .

Good heavens!

Right in the middle of the torpedo run, somewhere over on his left, a ship had lit up like a Christmas tree; cabin lights, searchlights, docking lights, navigation lights—and in the muddy darkness of the blacked-out coast it looked, somehow, *celestial.* Higbee and Charles both gasped. "Hold fire!" Charles yelled and threw the Swordfish into a tight left bank that made the plane shudder. Higbee had, just at that moment, been about to fire, a shot that would have sent a torpedo on its way to harrowing a mighty groove in the Protestant cemetery of Calais.

"Is it a trick?" Higbee's voice was dangerously close to soprano now but Charles never noticed. A trick! No, damn it, it wasn't a trick. That was a *ship* and he'd been reliably informed that this was *Calais* and his job was to shoot a ship in Calais and now that was exactly what he meant to do. To which end, he traversed the city of Calais, drawing the fire of every antiaircraft gun in the place but, somehow, the Swordfish was too big and slow to hit.

Charles did it right—one-two-three right. Got enough distance away from the target before circling back, and adjusting his altitude to one hundred feet. The ship grew, bigger and bigger as they plunged toward it, its lights twinkled, then glared brightly. At the end it seemed enormous, a vast, glowing city. "Torpedo away!" Higbee screamed, his voice wobbly with excitement. The plane bucked, then, freed of weight, accelerated. Charles pulled back on the stick, his training calling out *climb, climb.*

Emerging from a blizzard of lights and tracer and cannon fire, the clumsy Swordfish worked its way upward through the thin night air. Then, suddenly, Charles felt the plane quiver and he was, for an instant, blinded. A flash, so intense and white it lit the clouds, and seemed to flicker, like lightning. Now you're shot, he thought. But he was wrong. The plane had been hammered, not by a shell but by a concussive blast.

Higbee had actually hit something.

He had hit the *Malacca Princess,* in its final moments a shining beacon in the harbor at Calais. The torpedo had done what it was supposed to do—run straight through the water, found its target, penetrated the rusty old plate amidships and, there, detonated. Causing the explosion, almost simultaneously, of the *Malacca Princess's* cargo: a hundred thousand gallons of volatile naptha.

Now you could see Calais.

The *Malacca Princess* burned to the waterline in a half-hour—actually it melted—burned like a dazzling white Roman candle, burned so bright it lit up every troop transport and tugboat and barge in the harbor.

25 October 1940.

Only one couple at the auberge by the sea at Cayeux. They used to come up here from Paris in the autumn, the secret couples, park their cars so the license plates couldn't be seen from the road, register as Monsieur and Madame Duval.

But, with the war, only one couple this year. They didn't seem to mind the barbed wire, and they didn't try to walk on the cliffs—where the German sentries would have chased them away. This couple apparently didn't care. They stayed in the room—though that quite often happened at the auberge at Cayeux—and what with all that staying in the room, they brought sharp appetites to the dinner table in the evening, and enough ration coupons so that no awkward explanations had to be made.

They made love, they ate dinner at the table in the bow window, they watched the sea, they paid cash. It made the owner feel sentimental. How nice life used to be, he thought.

. . .

The flan was made with fresh eggs from a nearby farm, and de Milja and Genya cleaned the plate quite shamelessly, then lit cigarettes. The waiter—also the owner and the cook; his wife did the accounts and made the beds—came to the table and said, "Will Monsieur and Madame take a coffee?"

De Milja said they would.

While it was being made they looked out the window at the sea. Long, slow rollers ran into the shore, white spray flying off the crests in the driving wind. The dark water exploded as it hit the rocks at the base of the cliff, a pleasant thunder if you were warm and dry and having dinner.

"One wouldn't want to be out there now," Genya said. She was in a sadder-but-wiser mood that evening, and it made her voice melancholy. What she'd said was normal dinner conversation, but the reference was deeper; to German invasion fleets, to the victory won by the British.

"No," de Milja said. "It's no time of year for boating."

She smiled at that. *Canotage,* he'd said. A word that summoned up the man in straw hat and woman in frock, her hand trailing idly in the river as they floated past a lily pad.

Genya's cigarette glowed as she inhaled. She let the smoke drift from her nostrils. "Probably," she said, "you haven't heard about Freddi Schoen."

"Freddi." De Milja smiled.

"His friend Jünger was leaving Paris and he took me to lunch. Freddi won an Iron Cross. To do with a naval exercise off the Belgian coast somewhere. There was disaster and he took command and, and—did all sorts of things, Jünger's French didn't really last through the whole story. But he was very brave, and they gave him a medal. Posthumously."

"I always wondered," de Milja said, "why the Freddi Schoens of Germany didn't do something about Hitler before he maneuvered them into war."

"Honor," Genya said. "If I'm allowed only one word."

The waiter came with coffee, real coffee, very hard to get in Paris these days unless you bought on the black markets.

"We're not serving sugar tonight," the waiter explained.

"Oh, but we don't take sugar," Genya said.

The waiter nodded appreciatively—a gracious and dignified lie, well told, was a work of art to a man who understood life.

The coffee was very good. They closed their eyes when they drank it. "I've learned to like small things now," de Milja said. "War did that, at least."

When he looked up from his coffee the light of the candles caught the ocean color in his eyes and she took his hand on top of the table and held it tight.

"You are to be loved," she said with a sigh. "No doubt of that."

"And you," he said.

She shook her head; he'd got it wrong there.

Late that night it rained hard, water streamed down the windows and the sound of the sea was muffled as it broke against the cliff. It was cold and damp in the room. De Milja opened an armoire and found an extra blanket, then they wrapped themselves up and began to make love. "We're on a boat," she whispered. "Just us. In the middle of the sea. And now it's a storm."

"Then we better hang on to what's valuable," he said.

She laughed. "I've got what I want."

Some time later he woke up and saw that her eyes were shining. She caught him staring and said, "See what you did?" He got himself untangled from the coarse sheet and moved next to her. Her skin was very hot. Then she wiped at her eyes with her fingers. "I hope you love me, whatever happens," she said.

The letter came a week later. He was sitting at a table in a tiny apartment. She had gone to Switzerland, she would be married when she got there. Please forgive her, she would love him forever.

He read the letter again, it didn't say anything new the second time. He was changing his identity—once again—that week. Becoming someone else in order to do whatever they wanted him to do next, and papers were always a part of that. Still, poor old Lezhev might have lasted out another month if he'd been careful with him. But de Milja ached inside, so the passport and the work permit and all the rest of it went into the blackened little stove that sat in the corner of the room. There was no heat, it was snowing out, the papers burned in a few minutes, and that was the end of it.

PARIS
NIGHTS

N ow he was valuable.

And when they brought him out, to neutral Spain, he was handled very carefully. De Milja knew what it took—people and money and time—and stood off and marveled a little at what they thought him worth. The finest papers, delivered by courier. An invitation to dinner at the chateau of Chenonceaux, a castle that spanned the river Cher, which happened to be the boundary between German-occupied France and Vichy France. He arrived at eight, had a glass of champagne, strolled to the back of the grand house, and found a fisherman and a small boat on the other side of the river. Then a truck, then a car, then a silent, empty hotel in the hills above Marseilles, then a fishing boat after midnight.

No improvisation now.

Now he was *the Poles have someone in Paris,* also known as *I can't tell you how I know this,* or *forgive me, Colonel, but I must ask you to leave the room.* Or maybe he was *Proteus* or whatever code name they'd stuck on him—he was not to know. This kind of attention made him uncomfortable. First of all it was dangerous—he had learned, since 1939, how not to be noticed, so it had become second nature with him to fade away from attention, and he'd gotten so he could sense it *feeling* for him.

Second of all, he didn't like to be managed, or controlled, and that, with some delicacy, was exactly what they were doing. And third, all this was based on the assumption that he was good, and that wasn't quite the word for it. He was, perhaps, two things: unafraid to die, and lucky so far—if they had an unafraid-to-die-and-lucky-so-far medal, he would take it.

He and the watchman, for instance, sprinting for their lives down the slippery jetty, had survived by sheer, eccentric chance. Burning planes zooming over their heads, antiaircraft fallback, then a shattering explosion that cut the *Malacca Princess*'s neighbor, the *Nicaea,* in half and showered down burning metal. They jumped into the harbor, like reasonable men anywhere, where bits and pieces of tramp freighter steamed as they hit the water. When German and French police ran by, cursing and with guns drawn, they ducked below the water. Who wouldn't? Later, in the jumble of streets around the docks, he and the watchman knew it was time for them to go their separate ways. De Milja shook his hand, and the man smiled, then ran like the wind. All this wasn't, to de Milja's way of thinking, definable by the word *good.*

The fishing boat that took de Milja from Marseilles landed on the coast of Spain at night, aided by Sixth Bureau operatives who signaled with flashlights from the beach. Yes, Spain was neutral, but not all *that* neutral. He was hustled into a shiny black sedan and driven at speed to the outskirts of Barcelona. There, in a bedroom on the third floor of a villa with heavy drapes drawn across the window, he was served a chicken and a bottle of wine. His keepers were young Poles—fresh-faced, earnest, well conditioned, and cheerfully homicidal. There was a pile of books on the table—*put a pile of books on his table, damn it.* He read one of them for an hour; *In spring, the Alpine lakes of Slovenia are a miracle of red sunsets and leaping trout*—then fell asleep.

Various terrors he had avoided feeling now returned in force, and he woke up eighteen hours later having sweated through a wool blanket. He remembered only a few fragments of those dreams and forgot them as soon as he could. He staggered into the bathroom, shaved, showered, had a good long look at himself in the mirror. So, this was who he was now, well, that was interesting to know. Older, leaner, marked with fatigue, rather remote, and very watchful. On a chair he found clean slacks, a shirt, and a sweater. He put them on. Shifted the drape an inch aside from the window and stared out at the brown autumn hills. Just the motion of the drape apparently caused a restless footstep or two on the gravel path below his room, so he let it fall back into place. Why didn't they just bar the window and put him in stripes and stop all the pretense?

Vyborg showed up that morning. In a good brown suit and a striped British tie. Had there always been a gentleman under that uniform, or was it just a trick that London tailors did? They could do nothing, however, about the face: the Baltic knight, squinting into a blizzard and ready to cut down a company of Russian pikemen, was still very much in evidence. He suggested a walk in the hills and they did that, with guards following a little way down the path. November, de Milja thought, was a strange time in dry countries; faded colors, sky gray and listless. Vyborg told de Milja that his wife had died. They walked in silence for a long time after that. Finally de Milja was able to say, "Where is she?"

"A small cemetery in the town where the spa is. A mass was said for her. It had to be done quietly, but it was done." They walked for a moment, through a stand of low pines. "My sympathies, Alexander," Vyborg said softly. "It comes from all of us, from everyone who knows you."

"How, please."

"Influenza."

De Milja was again unable to speak.

"She was working in the kitchen," Vyborg went on. "Some of us do best in bad times, and that was true of her. She had a high fever for three days, and then she died in her sleep."

"I think I would like to go back to the house," de Milja said.

He visited Barcelona once or twice, but it was just another conquered city. It had the silence that passed for peace, the courtesy of fear. The police state was in place, people in the street avoided his eyes. There were still bullet chips and shell holes in the buildings, but the masons were at work, and there were glaziers, their glass sheets balanced on the sides of their mules, shouting up the sides of apartment houses to announce their presence.

He spent a lot of time walking in the hills, sometimes with two men from the Sixth Bureau; one clerkish, a man who sat behind a desk, the other with a hard, bald head, a well-groomed mustache, and small, angry eyes. They needed to know about various things in France and de Milja told them what he could. The bald-headed man, though he did not come out and say it, was clearly concerned with the construction of new and better wireless/telegraphy sets, and de Milja didn't feel he was able to help much. The other man asked questions about French political life under the Germans and de Milja helped him, if possible, even less. But they were decent men who tried to make things easy for him—*as long as we all happen to find ourselves in Spain, why not spend a moment chatting about the views of the French communist party*—and de Milja did the best he could for them.

Again and again, he thought about his wife. He had, in October of 1939, said good-bye to her, left her in charge of her destiny, as she'd asked. Maybe he shouldn't have done that. But then he had never once been able to make her, crazy or sane, do anything she did not want to do.

Down the road from the villa was a tiny café in the garden of an old woman's house. She had a granddaughter who said *gracias* when she served coffee, and when it wasn't raining de Milja and Vyborg would sit at a rusty iron table and talk about the war.

"Operation Sealion has failed," Vyborg said. "The first time Hitler's been beaten."

"Do we know what actually happened?" de Milja asked.

"We know some of it. It wasn't a total victory, of course, nothing like that. The RAF sank 21 out of 170 troop transports.

That's a loss, but not a crippling loss for people contemplating an invasion from the sea. Out of 1,900 barges, 214 were destroyed. Only five tugboats out of 368; only three motorboats out of more than a thousand.''

"Three, did you say?"

"Yes."

"Then what made them quit?"

Vyborg shrugged. "An invasion is more than ships. A five-hundred-ton ammunition dump was blown up at Den Helder, in Holland. On the sixth of September, a rations depot was burned out. In Belgium, an ammunition train was destroyed. Then down at Le Havre, where a number of German divisions were based, the waterworks were put out of commission. There was also the training exercise—you saw some of the results at Nieuwpoort, and German hospital trains crossed Belgium all that night. Therefore, if the RAF could hit a practice run through that hard, what would they do once the real thing got started? Funny thing about the German character, they're very brave, not at all afraid to die, but they are afraid to fail. In some ways, our best hope for Germany is the Wehrmacht—the generals. If Germany loses again, and then again, perhaps they can be persuaded that honor lies in a change of government.''

"Can that really happen?"

Vyborg thought about it. "Maybe," he said. "With time."

It drizzled, then stopped. The little girl came and put up a faded umbrella and wiped the table with a cloth and said, "*Gracias*." She smiled at de Milja, then ran away.

"One last time, the people who knew you as Lezhev?" Vyborg said.

"Freddi Schoen."

"Dead."

"Jünger, the Wehrmacht staff officer."

"Transferred. In Germany at the OKW headquarters."

"Traudl von Behr."

"She's in Lille, at the moment. Aide to a staff major running transports from northern France to Germany."

"There were more Germans, but they didn't know who I was. Somebody they saw here and there, perhaps Russian."

"Be absolutely certain," Vyborg said.

De Milja nodded that he was.

12 January 1941.

In the cold, still air of the Paris winter, smoke spilled from the chimneys and hung lifeless above the tiled rooftops.

Stein crunched along the snow-covered rue du Château-d'Eau, head down, hands jammed deep in the pockets of his overcoat. Cold in the 5:00 P.M. darkness, colder with the snow turned blue by the lamplight, colder with the wind that blew all the way from the Russian steppe. You can feel it, Parisians said, you can feel the bite. Eighteen degrees, the newspaper said that morning.

Stein walked fast, breath visible. Here was 26, rue du Château-d'Eau. Was that right? He reached into an inside pocket, drew out the typewritten letter with the exquisite signature. Office of the notary LeGros, yes, this was the building. Notaries and lawyers and *huissiers*—officers of the court—all through this quarter. It wasn't that it was pleasant, because it wasn't. It was simply where they gathered. Probably, as usual, something to do with a Napoleonic decree—a patent, a license, a dispensation. A special privilege.

The concierge was sweeping snow from the courtyard entry with a twig broom, two mufflers tied around her face, her hands wound in flannel cloths. "Notaire LeGros? Third floor, take the stairs to your left, Monsieur."

LeGros opened the door immediately. He was an old man with a finely made face and snow-white hair. He wore a cardigan sweater beneath his jacket and his hand was like ice when Stein shook it.

The business was done in the dining room, at an enormous chestnut table covered with official papers. Huysmanns, a Belgian with broad shoulders and a thick neck, was waiting for him, stood and grunted in guttural French when they shook hands. Stein sat down, kept his coat on—the apartment was freezing and he could still see his breath. "Hard winter," Huysmanns said.

"Yes, that's true," Stein said.

"Gentlemen," said the notary.

He gathered papers from the table, which he seemed to understand by geology: the Stein-Huysmanns matter buried just below the Duval matter. The two men signed and signed, writing *read and approved,* then dating each signature, their pens scratching over the paper, their breathing audible. Finally LeGros said, "I believe the agreed payment is forty thousand francs?"

Stein reached into the inner pocket of his overcoat and withdrew a sheaf of five-hundred-franc notes. He counted out eighty, passed them to the notary, who counted and gave them to Huysmanns, who wet his thumb in order to count and said the numbers in a whisper. LeGros then coughed—a cough of delicacy—and said, "A call of nature, gentlemen. You will excuse me for a moment."

He left the room, as notaries had been leaving rooms, Stein imagined, since the days of Richelieu. The remainder of the money would now be paid, theoretically out of sight of the honest notary, theoretically out of sight of the tax authorities. Stein counted out an additional hundred and twenty-five thousand francs. Huysmanns wet his thumb and made sure.

The notary returned, efficiently, just as Huysmanns stuffed the money in his pocket. "Shall we continue?" he chirped. They signed more papers, the notary produced his official stamp, made an impression in wax, then certified the documents with his magnificent signature.

"I would like," Stein said, "to make certain of the provision

that specifies the name of the business is to continue as Huysmanns. To assure that the goodwill of established customers is
not lost to me.''

As the notary rattled papers, Huysmanns stared at him.
Goodwill? He had an opaque face, spots of bright color in his
cheeks, a face from a Flemish military painting. LeGros found
the relevant paragraph and pointed it out; the two men read it
with their index fingers and grunted to confirm their understanding.

Then the notary said, ''Congratulations, gentlemen.'' And
wished them success and good fortune. In other times, they
might have adjourned to a café, but those days were gone.

Stein walked back to the métro, paid his fourteen centimes
for a ticket, and rode the train back to the avenue Hoche, where
he had a grand apartment, just around the corner from Gestapo
headquarters on the rue de Courcelles. He was now the owner
of a business, a *dépôt de charbon*—coal yard—out by the freight
tracks near the Porte de la Chapelle. The train was crowded
with Parisians, their expressions empty, eyes blank as their
minds turned away from the world.

It was seven; Stein had an appointment in an hour. He took
off the disguise: the dark overcoat, the black suit, the olive silk
tie, the white shirt, the diamond ring, the gold watch. De Milja
sighed with exhaustion and put the Stein costume on a chair. Except for the Clark Gable mustache, he was rid of the disguise.
He lay down on a big featherbed in a pale-blue bedstead flecked
with gold. The walls were covered in silk fabric, somber red,
burgundy, with a raised pattern. Facing the bed, a marble fireplace. On the wall by the doorway, a large oil painting in the
manner of Watteau—*school of Watteau*. An eighteenth-century
swain in a white wig, a lady with gown lowered to reveal pow-
dered bosoms and pink nipples, a King Charles spaniel playing
on the couch between them. The swain has in hand a little ball;
when he tosses it, the dog will leap off the couch, the space be-

tween the lovers will be clear. Both are at that instant when the strategem has occurred to them; they are delighted with the idea of it, and with what will inevitably follow. Below the painting, a Louis XVI chiffonier in pale blue flecked with gold, its drawers lined with silk, its top drawer holding mother-of-pearl tuxedo studs in a leather box and a French army 7.65 automatic—in fact a Colt .45 rechambered for French military ammunition. De Milja didn't expect to last out the winter.

He hated Anton Stein, but Anton Stein made for a useful disguise in the winter of 1941. A *Volksdeutsch,* ethnic German, from Czechoslovakia, the Slovakian capital of Bratislava. So he spoke, in the natural way of things, de Milja's rough German and de Milja's bad but effective French. He had even, according to Vyborg, existed. The records were there in case anybody looked— the tack on the teacher's chair and the punch on the policeman's nose lived on, in filing cabinets somewhere in Bratislava. But that was all, that was the legacy of Stein. "He's no longer with us," Vyborg had said.

Anton Stein came to Paris in the wake of the German occupation. A minor predator, he knew an opportunity when he saw one. The Nazis had a sweet way with the Anton Steins of the world, they'd had it since 1925: *too bad nobody ever gave you a chance.* A kind of ferocious, law-of-the-jungle loyalty was, once that took hold, theirs to command.

De Milja slept. The apartment was warm, the quilt soft against his skin. There was, in his dreams, no war. An Ostrow uncle carved a boat in a soft piece of wood, Alexander's eyes followed every move. Then he woke up. What was, was. Every Thursday, Madame Roubier made love at twilight.

"Take a mistress," Vyborg had said. After he'd rented the apartment on the avenue Hoche, the woman at the rental agency had suggested one Madame Roubier to see to the decoration and furnishing. The money made de Milja's heart ache—in Warsaw they were starving and freezing, heating apartments with sticks of wood torn from crates, working all day, then spending the night making explosives or loading bullets. And here he was, amid pale blue flecked with gold.

"Pale blue, flecked with gold."

Madame Roubier was a redhead, with thin lips, pale skin, a savage temper, and a daintily obscure history that changed with her mood. She was that indeterminate age where French women pause for many years—between virginal girlhood (about thirty-five) and wicked-old-ladyhood—a good long run of life. Yes, she was a natural redhead, but she was most certainly *not* a Breton, that impossibly rude class of people. She was, at times, from Mâcon. Or perhaps Angers.

To supervise the furnishings, she had visited the apartment. Made little notes with a little gold pen on a little gold pad. "And this window will take a jabot and festoon," she said.

Suddenly, their eyes met. And met.

". . . a jabot . . . and . . . festoon . . ."

Her voice faded away to a long Hollywood silence—*they suddenly understand they are fated to become lovers*. They stood close to each other by the window, snow falling softly on the gray stone of the avenue Hoche. Madame Roubier looked deep into his eyes, a strange magnetism drawing her to him as the consultation slowly quivered to a halt: ". . . jabot . . . and . . . festoon . . ."

She had a soft, creamy body that flowed into its natural contours as her corsets were removed. "Oh, oh," she cried. She was exquisitely tended, the skin of her ample behind kept smooth by spinning sessions on a chamois-covered stool, the light of her apartment never more than a pink bulb in a little lamp. "I know what you like," she would say. "You are a dirty-minded little boy." Well, he thought, if nothing else I know what dirty-minded little boys like.

They would make love through the long Paris dusk—*l'heure bleu*—then Stein would be banished from the chamber, replaced by Maria, the maid. Sometime later, Madame Roubier would appear, in emerald-green taffeta, for example—whatever made her red hair blaze redder and her skin whiter, and Stein would say *Oh, mais c'est Hedy Lamarr!* and she would shush him and pooh-pooh him as he helped her wrestle into a white ermine coat.

Then dinner. Then a tour of the night. Then business.

Thursday night. Chez Tolo.

All the black-market restaurants were in obscure streets, down alleys, you had to know somebody in order to find them. Chez Tolo was at the end of a narrow lane—nineteenth-century France—reached through fourteen-foot-high wooden doors that appeared to lead into the courtyard of a large building. The lane had been home to tanneries in an earlier age, but the workshops had long since been converted to workers' housing and now, thanks to war and scarcity, and the vibrant new life that bobbed to the surface in such times, it found itself at the dawn of a new age.

Wood-burning taxicabs pulled up to the door, then a De Bouton with its tulipwood body, a Citroen *traction-avant*—the favored car of the Gestapo a Lagonda, a black Daimler. Madame Roubier took note of the last. "The Comte de Rieu," she said.

Inside it was dark and crowded. Stein and Madame Roubier moved among the diners; a wave, a nod, a smile, acknowledging the new aristocracy—the ones who, like Anton Stein, had never been given a chance. A fistful of francs to the headwaiter—formerly a city clerk—and they were seated at a good table.

Madame Roubier ate prodigiously. Stein could never quite catch her doing it, but somehow she made the food disappear. Oysters on shaved ice, veal chops in the shape of a crown, sauced with Madeira and heavy cream and served with walnut puree, a salad of baby cabbage, red and green, with raisins and vinegar and honey. Then a cascade of Spanish orange sections soaked in Cointreau and glistening in the candlelight. Stein se-

lected a vintage Moët & Chandon champagne to accompany the
dinner.

With the cognac, came visitors. The Comte de Rieu, and his
seventeen-year-old Romanian mistress, Isia, fragile and lovely,
who peered out at the world through curtains of long black hair.
The count, said to be staggeringly rich, dealt in morphine, dia-
monds, and milk.

"You must take a cognac with us," Stein said.

A waiter brought small gilt chairs. Jammed together at the
table they were pleasantly crowded, breathing an atmosphere of
cigarette smoke and perfume and body heat and breaths of
oranges and mints and wine. The count's white-and-black hair
was combed back smoothly and rested lightly atop his ears.

"A celebration tonight," Stein said.

"Oh?" said the count.

"I became, today, a *charbonnier.*"

"You did?"

"Yes."

"A coal merchant, eh? Well, you must permit us to be your
customers. Shall you haul the sacks down the cellar stairs?"

"Absolutely, you may depend on it."

"A Polack!"

"Exactly!"

"Stein?"

"Yes?"

"You're an amusing fellow."

They sipped at their balloon glasses of cognac. "What year?"
said the count.

"Nineteen ten."

"Alas, before your time," the count said to Madame
Roubier.

"Yes? It's your guess?"

"My certain knowledge!"

"Dear me, how is one to repay such a compliment?"

The taxi that served as limousine took them home from a

nightclub at dawn, the snow turned gray in the January light. Madame Roubier snored by his side in the backseat. She slept snuggled up to him, the ermine warm against his cheek.

Success purchased investment.

Perhaps you fought, with luck you won, then came the little men with the money. Vyborg had made a point of telling him that, because Vyborg knew exactly who de Milja really was. Vyborg knew how happy he'd been fussing over his maps, knew about his academic papers, worked over endlessly, on the signalization of braiding, or aggrading, rivers. He'd spent his daily life occupied with the Lehman system of hachuring, the way in which the angle of slope is shown on military surveys—important knowledge for artillery people—contour intervals, hydrographic symbolism. He was, in Vyborg's words to Sixth Bureau staff meetings, "his father's very own son." He was, in fact, a man whose physical presence to some degree betrayed his personality. He wanted to be a mole who lived in libraries, but he didn't look like that, and the world didn't take him that way.

His mother, de Milja thought, would have made a good spy. She was deceptive, manipulative, attractive—people wanted to talk to her. The world she lived in was a corrupt and cynical place where one had to keep one's guard up at all times, and the probable truth of her opinions had often been the subject of a sort of communal sigh privately shared by de Milja and his father.

But the chief resident intelligence officer for France had to be an executive, not a cartographer. De Milja's quarterly budget was 600,000 francs; rental of safe houses, agents' pay, railroad tickets, hotels, endless expenses. Bribes were extra. The money for Huysmanns was extra—and it had been made clear to de Milja that the company had to succeed and profit.

Instinctively, de Milja knew what he would find at Huysmanns Coal. He knew Huysmanns—phlegmatic, northern, Belgian. Profit earned a franc at a time, dogged patience, do we really need all these lights on? Would such a man employ a troupe of merry philosophers?

Never. Thus the man de Milja needed was already in place, right there in Huysmanns's office overlooking the coal yard by the railroad tracks. Monsieur Zim-*maire* it was said. Zimmer, an Alsatian, fifty or so, who wore a clean, gray dustcoat every day, buttoned all the way to the knees. At one time or another he'd taken a hand in everything the company did. He'd driven the trucks, hauled sacks of coal, a job that turned the deliveryman black by the second or third call. He talked to the suppliers, the mines in northern France, and he knew the important customers: hospitals and office buildings and workshops. There were two secretaries who kept the books and sent out the bills, Helene and Cybeline. At Zimmer's suggestion, they fired Cybeline. She was a distant relation of Huysmanns—that didn't matter to Zimmer or de Milja but she insisted it meant she didn't have to work. She filed her nails, sipped coffee, gossiped on the phone and flirted with the drivers. As for Helene, who actually did the work, she got a raise.

Zimmer, too, got a raise. He would, in fact, be running the company. "I'll be seeking out new customers," was the way de Milja put it. "So I expect to be traveling a good part of the time."

That was true. The Sixth Bureau had directed him to assist in certain British operations against Luftwaffe units based in France. The nightly bombing was relentless. Something had to be done.

8 March 1941.

West of Bourges, de Milja pedaled a bicycle down a cow path. Early spring morning, raw and chilly, the ground mist lying thick on the fields. Leading the way, a Frenchman called Bonneau. Perhaps thirty, a tank officer wounded and captured in late May of 1940. Sent to a POW camp, a munitions factory near Aachen. Escaped. Recaptured. Escaped again, this time reached France and made it stick.

Riding just ahead of de Milja, Bonneau's sister Jeanne-Marie, perhaps twenty, thin and intense and avid to fight the Germans. Through a prewar association—something commercial, Bonneau had sold British agricultural equipment in central France— he'd gotten in touch with somebody in London, and his name had been passed to the special services.

De Milja liked him. Forthright, handsome, with a scrupulous sense of honor. The best of the French, de Milja thought, were the incarnations of heroes in boys' books. Or girls' books—because the principle was twice as true for the French women. De Milja had seen them face down the Germans more than once; iron-willed idealists, proud and free, and quite prepared to die to keep it that way.

"*Bonjour,* Monsieur Gache," Bonneau called out, coasting on his bicycle. Jeanne-Marie echoed the greeting.

Monsieur Gache was a fourteenth-century peasant. He'd loomed up through the milky-gray mist holding a long switch, surrounded by a half-dozen cows, their breaths steaming, bells clanking. He squinted at de Milja from beneath a heavy brow, his glance suspicious and hostile. He knew every pebble and cowpie in these fields—perhaps this stranger was aiming to help himself to a few. Well, he'd know about it soon enough.

It's spring, start of the war season in Europe, de Milja thought. And Monsieur Gache knew, in some ancient, intuitive sense, exactly who he was and what his appearance meant. Nothing good, certainly. Caesar likely sent somebody up here in the spring of 56 B.C. to take a look at the Gauls—and there was Monsieur Gache and his six cows.

"That's old Gache," Bonneau called back to him. "It's his uncle's land we'll be using."

De Milja grunted assent, implying that it seemed a good idea. He hoped it was. This was something worked out between people in the countryside, such rural arrangements being typically far too complicated to be successfully explained to outsiders.

They pedaled on for fifteen minutes, threading their way among great expanses of plowed black earth separated by patches of old-growth forest, oak and beech, left standing as windbreak. The cow path ended at a small stream and Bonneau dismounted like a ten-year-old, riding a little way on one pedal, then hopping off.

"Oop-la!" he said with a laugh. He grinned cheerfully, a man who meant to like whatever life brought him that day. Wounded during the German attack, he had fought on for twelve hours with only a gunner left alive in his tank.

"Now, sir, we shall have to walk," Jeanne-Marie said. "For, perhaps, twenty-five minutes."

"Exactly?" de Milja said.

"In good weather, close to it."

"If she says it, it's probably true," Bonneau said wearily, admiring his sister and teasing her in the same breath.

"Here is the Creuse," she said, pointing across a field.

They could see it from the hill, a ribbon of quiet water that flowed through brush-lined banks and joined, a few miles downstream near the town of Tournon, the Gartempe. This in turn became part of the Loire, and all of it eventually emptied into the Atlantic at the port of Saint-Nazaire.

What mattered was the confluence of the rivers—a geographical feature visible from an airplane flying on a moonlit night. They walked on in silence. The field was a good distance from any road, and therefore a good distance from German motorized transport. If the Germans saw parachutes floating from the sky, they were going to have to organize an overland expedition to go see about the problem.

The field itself had been chosen, de Milja thought, with great care. "It's Jeanne-Marie's choice," Bonneau explained. "She is a serious naturalist—turns up everywhere in the countryside, so nobody notices what she does."

"I've paced it more than once," Jeanne-Marie said. "It is as suggested, about 650 by 250 yards."

They walked its perimeter. "There were stumps, but I had our workmen haul them out with the plow horses." Silently, on behalf of a descending parachutist, de Milja was grateful for her forethought. He saw also that somebody had moved big stones to one side of the field.

"How many people will you have?" de Milja asked.

"Four, perhaps. Six altogether."

"You'll need brushwood for your fires. It's best to store it under canvas to keep it dry. Then the fires should be set in the shape of an arrow, giving wind direction."

"Yes," Jeanne-Marie said. "We know that."

De Milja smiled at her. The mysterious foreigner who came from nowhere and told them things they already knew. She stood, holding her bicycle by the handlebars, in front of a huge French spring sky; a few strands of hair had escaped from the front of her kerchief and she brushed them back impatiently.

"Shall we have something before we go back?" Bonneau said.

Jeanne-Marie grinned to herself and nodded yes. She untied a cloth-wrapped packet from the back of her bicycle. They sat on the rim of the field—true to the suggested standard, Jeanne-Marie had located a slightly concave area—and ate bread and crumbly farm cheese and last fall's apples, dried-out and sweet.

"Something must be done, and we hope it is soon," Bonneau said. "The people here don't like the Germans, but they are drifting. Pétain speaks on the radio and says that all this has happened to us because France was immoral and self-indulgent. A number of people believe that, others will do whatever makes them comfortable at that moment. One lately hears the word *attentisme*—the philosophy of waiting. Do nothing, we'll see what happens next. This is dangerous for France, because here we don't really live in a country, you know. We live in our houses with our families, that's our true nationality, and what's best is determined from that point of view."

It was Jeanne-Marie who answered her brother. "The English will do what they can," she said, a snap in her voice. "But not from any tender feeling for the French. We're allies, not friends."

"Again she's right," de Milja said.

A local train west, then to Nantes, then north on a series of locals. *Very, very careful now,* he told himself. Where he was going the Germans were sensitive, because they had a secret.

As the train rolled to a stop at each little town, de Milja could see he was in the country of Madame Roubier. Brittany. Tall redheads with fair, freckled skin. Sharp-eyed—not easily fooled. Often venal, because it was them against the world, had always been so, and this unending war was fought with wealth.

It was late afternoon when he reached the town of Vannes, down the coast of Brittany from L'Orient, one of the bomber fields used in the Luftwaffe campaign against Britain. North from Vannes was Brest—on the south shore of the widening English Channel, across from Plymouth, on the Cornish coast. No doubt about the bomber field, Vannes railroad station was full of German airmen, returning from leave or heading off to sinful Paris for ten days.

De Milja kept his eyes down. Cheap leather briefcase in hand, felt hat with brim turned down, well-worn blue suit. A provincial lawyer, perhaps, snuffling out a living from feuding heirs and stubborn property owners and the tax indiscretions of *petits commerçants.* He walked for a long time, toward the edge of town. No more Germans. Sidewalks that narrowed, then vanished. Old women with string bags, a few cats. The neighborhood darkened—buildings crumbling softly into genteel poverty, a grocery store with a sign on the boarded window: FERMÉ.

Finally, a *confiserie*—a candy shop, the miniature gold-foil packets of chocolates in the window covered with a layer of fine dust. A bell jangled above the door as he entered and a young girl stood to attention behind the counter. She was very plain, skin and hair the same washed-out color, and wore a tight sweater that was more hopeful than seductive. The smell of candied violets and burnt sugar was intense in the dark interior of the shop. It made de Milja feel slightly queasy.

"Mademoiselle Herault?" he asked the clerk.

"In back, Monsieur." Her voice was tiny.

Mademoiselle Herault sat at a desk in the office. She was in her forties, he guessed. But older than her years. A hard face, lined and severe. As though she dealt in candy from contempt for human appetite, not a desire to sell the world something sweet. Or maybe it was the silent store, the trays of stale orange drops, a small business failing by slow, agonizing degrees.

He identified himself—*Guillaume* for this meeting, and her eyes searched his, to see if he could be trusted. She was, he thought, not a particularly attractive woman, but she had probably never lacked for lovers, being one of those women who understands that attraction hasn't much to do with it.

"May I take a minute of your time?" he asked.

She looked at him a little sideways—minutes, hours, she had nothing but time. Very slowly she worked a Gauloise free of its pack, tapped one end against her thumbnail, held it in her mouth with thumb and forefinger, handed de Milja a box of matches and leaned toward him so he could light it. "Thank you," she said.

She opened a drawer in the desk, searched through papers, found an unsealed envelope and handed it to him. "Here it is," she said.

He took out what looked like a polite note, written in purple ink on bordered paper sold in stationary stores. His eyes ran along the lines, trying to decipher the penmanship. Then, when he realized what he had, he read it through again.

"This is—this is extremely important," he said.

She nodded in a sort of vague agreement—*yes, so it seemed to her*. She drew on her Gauloise and blew a plume of smoke at the ceiling.

"Was there a reason you did so much? The occupation?"

"No," she said. "I am not French," she added.

"What then?"

"I'm a Pole, though I've lived here a long time."

De Milja came close to responding in Polish. He wanted to— then raged at himself for being so stupid. Guillaume was Guillaume—nobody. "Herault?" he said.

She shrugged. "That was my father's attempt to fit in."

"Did he fit in?"

"No," she said. They were silent for a moment. "I don't think I'll tell you any reasons," she said. "For what I've done, that is. I don't especially believe in reasons."

De Milja ran his eyes back over the paper. *Kampfgeschwader 100, Pathfinder, Knickbein beam*. De Milja was stunned at the quality of what he had in hand. He'd gotten the woman's name from Fedin—an old contact from the late '30s, nothing very productive, but an address that placed her, quite by accident, on the front line of the German offensive against Britain. Fedin had made the initial contact, then a signal from Vannes reached Paris that meant *I have something for you*. But this was well beyond anything de Milja had expected.

"Please, Mademoiselle. I must ask you to tell me how you managed this."

A ghost of a smile passed over the woman's face. She found his urgency a little bit pleasing. She nodded her head toward the front of the shop. "Veronique," she said.

"Who?"

"My little clerk."

She almost laughed out loud, so stupid and lost did he look. Then, when she saw the mist clear, she said, "Yes, that."

"By design?"

She made a face: *who could say?* Paused a moment, leaned

closer, lowered her voice. "Ugly as sin, poor thing. But for everyone there is someone, and for poor Veronique there is poor Kurt. Eighteen, away from home for the first time, short, homely, with bad teeth and bad eyes. In his unit the lowest of the low: he helps the mechanics who fix the aircraft. I believe engine parts are washed in gasoline. Is that so?"

"Yes."

"He does mostly that. Red hands the result. But he is a *conqueror*, Monsieur Whatever-you-call-yourself. And he has discovered, in this shapeless lump of a child, *le vrai passion*. He drives her, I assure you, to the very edge of sanity. No, beyond."

"And in bed, he tells her things?"

"No, Monsieur. Men don't tell women things in bed. Men tell women things when they are trying to get them into bed. To let women know how important they are. Once in bed, the time for telling things is over."

"But Veronique continues."

"Yes. She loves Kurt. He is her man, hers alone. National borders are here transcended. You understand?"

"Yes."

"Of course they do chatter, in the way people do, and she tells me things—just to gossip, just to have something to say. They are innocent, Monsieur."

De Milja nodded sympathetically.

"Someday, you might be asked to do something for Veronique."

"What is that?"

"Well, national borders are never transcended. Love doesn't conquer all. In Veronique's mind, the Germans will be here for forty years. Should she wait until she's fifty-nine to go on with life? Of course not. Unfortunately for her, I suspect the end of this war may come sooner than forty years. And then, the women who have made love with the enemy will not fare well. The people here who have collaborated silently, *skillfully*, the ones who talk but do nothing, they will take it out on the poor Veroniques of the world. And they can be very cruel. When this happens, perhaps I will find you, or somebody like you, and you will try to do something for poor Veronique.''

''How do you know these things?''

''I know. I'm a Pole—it came to me in my mother's milk. Will you help?''

''If I can, I will,'' he said. ''In the meantime, *stop*. Don't do anything—and don't permit her to do anything—that could lead to exposure. The most important thing now is that nobody finds out what was discovered.''

It rained in Paris. Slowly, endlessly. The bare branches of the chestnut trees dripped water in the gray light. At five in the afternoon, Anton Stein stared out the window above his coal yard. A freight train moved slowly along the track. Its couplings rattled and banged as it maneuvered—stopped, jerked ahead a few feet, stopped, backed up. The board siding of the freight cars and the cast-iron wheels glistened in the rain.

On his desk, March earnings. They were doing well—Zimmer was implacable. All day long, in his clean gray smock, he tended the business. Spillage. Theft. Truck fuel. Suppliers' invoices with added charges. Defaulting customers. Margin of profit, date of delivery. Anton Stein made money.

And Captain Alexander de Milja spent it.

Rental of the apartment on the rue A, where a W/T operator enciphered and transmitted, moving like a butterfly among a hundred different bands to elude the Funkabwehr technicians. Rental of the apartment on the rue B, where an alternate W/T operator was based. Rental of the villa in the suburb of C, where a wounded British pilot was in hiding. Not to mention the apartment on the avenue Hoche, each window dressed with jabot and festoon.

He was tired now. Spirit worn away by the tide. Clandestine

war since September of 1939—it had gone on too long, there'd been too much of it.

He forced his eyes away from the freight cars, back to a sheet of cheap paper on the desk. Huysmanns's desk. Scarred oak, burns on the edge where somebody had rested a cigarette, little drawers full of used rubber bands and thumbtacks and dried-out inkpads for stamps.

On the paper, in his own informal code, the first draft of a report to London: at the Luftwaffe base at Vannes was *Kampfgeschwader 100,* a unit of Pathfinders—pilots who flew along a radio beam, called a *Knickbein beam* because it had the shape of a dog leg. The job of these Pathfinders was to lead flights of bombers to the target, then drop incendiaries, to light fires for the guidance of the planes behind them.

What Veronique the shop clerk had found out was this: the pilots of *Kampfgeschwader 100* did not live on the base in barracks, they lived in various billets in the town of Vannes, and on the afternoon before a mission they traveled to the field by bus. All together, maybe thirty of them, slated to lead various night attacks against British targets. De Milja knew what happened next. He went to the movie theaters on the Champs-Élysées where they showed German newsreels—always with the lights on, because in darkness the French audience made rude noises—of the bombing raids. So he had seen the burning factories, and the bridges down in the rivers, and the firemen weeping with exhaustion.

All together, maybe thirty of them, traveled to the field by bus.

On the Route Nationale—the RN18—that traced the coast of Brittany: from Brest south to Quimper, L'Orient, then Vannes. The airfield was twelve miles from the outskirts of Vannes, and there were several points of interest along the way. A curve with a rock outcropping to the east, a grove of stunted beach pine to the west, between the road and the sea. Or perhaps the old fish cannery, abandoned in '38, with rows of dark windows, the glass long ago broken out.

Block the road. A coal truck—somebody else's coal truck— would do that nicely. You'd want six—no eight—operatives. Take the driver and the tires. Then you had leisure for the pilots. Fragmentation grenades in the windows, then someone with a carbine in the bus. Short range, multiple rounds.

Thirty Pathfinder pilots. All that training, experience, talent. Hard to replace. The ratio of bravado to skill was nearly one to one. Flying an aeroplane along a transmitted beam meant constant correction as you drifted and the signal tone faded. Flying at the apex of the attack meant searchlights and flak—you had to have a real demon in you to want to do that.

"Monsieur Stein?"

He looked up from the wood-flecked paper, initials and numbers, a curving line for a road, a rectangle for a blocking truck. Helene was holding a large leatherbound book. "Monsieur Zimmer asked that these be sent out today, Monsieur." She left the book on Stein's desk and returned to work.

Inside the leather cover were checks for him to sign—a typical practice in a French office. He made sure his pen had ink and went to work—*Anton Stein, Anton Stein.* The payees were coal mines up in Metz, mostly. He was permitted to buy what was left over after the Germans, paying with absurdly inflated currency, took what they wanted and shipped it east. Just after the New Year the Germans had returned the ashes of Napoleon's son, L'Aiglon, to France. Thus the joke of the week: they take our coal and send us back ashes.

Two more to sign. One a *donation,* to the Comité France-Allemagne, in business since 1933 to foster Franco-German harmony and understanding. Well, they'd fostered it all right—now the French had just about all the harmony and understanding anybody could want. The other check was made out to Anton Stein for ten thousand francs. His night money.

. . .

At the avenue Matignon, the evening performance with Madame Roubier. "Oh, oh," she cried out. Under the guise of nuzzling her pale neck he got a view of his watch. 8:25. Outside, the air-raid sirens began. Gently, he unwound himself from her, stood by the bed and turned off the pink bed-table lamp that made her skin glow. Opened the window, then the shutter, just a crack.

Circles of light against the clouds, then arching yellow flames and golden fire that seemed to drip back down toward the dark earth. Kids would be in the parks tomorrow, he thought, adding to their shrapnel collections. A sharp fingernail traveled across his bare backside.

"*Bonjour, Monsieur,*" Madame Roubier said. It amused her to pretend to be his language teacher. "*Comment allez-vous?*" The fingernail headed back in the other direction.

He turned away from the fiery lights, looked over his shoulder. She was sprawled on her stomach, reaching out to touch him. "He ignores me," she pouted like a little girl. "Yes he does." He turned back to the sky. A sudden stutter, bright yellow. Then a slow, red trail, curving down toward the earth. It made his heart sick to see that. "Yes he *does.*"

Brasserie Heininger. 11:30.

At table, a party of seven: the Comte de Rieu and his little friend Isia. Isia had paid a visit that afternoon to the milliner Karachine, who had fashioned, for her exclusively, a hat of bright cherries and pears with a red veil that just brushed the cheekbones.

At her left, the coal dealer Stein, his mood heavy and quiet, his cigar omnipresent. His companion, the fashionable Lisette Roubier, wore emerald silk. Next to her, the art dealer Labarthe, hair shiny with brilliantine, who specialized in Dutch and Flemish masters and jailed relatives. He could, for a price, produce any loved one from any prison in France. His companion was called Bella, a circus acrobat of Balkan origins.

At her side, the amusing Willy—*w* pronounced *v*—Kappler. The silliest-looking man: a fringe of colorless hair, a long, pointed nose like a comic witch, ears to catch the wind; a face lit up by a huge melon slice of a smile, as though to say *well then what can I do about it?*

"Coal!" he said to Stein. "Well, that's a lucky job these days." Then he laughed—melodious, infectious. You couldn't resist joining in; if you didn't get the joke, maybe you would later.

"I can sell as much as they'll let me have," Stein admitted. "But," he added, "the stocks are often low."

"Yes, it's true. This ridiculous war drags on—but go talk sense to the English. Then too, Herr Stein, those rascals up there in the mines don't like to work." With fist and extended thumb he imitated a bottle, tilted it up to his mouth and made glug-glug sounds. Stein laughed. "Oh but it's true, you know," Kappler said.

"And you, Herr Kappler," Stein said. "What is it that keeps you in Paris?"

"Hah! What a way to put it. I hardly need anything to keep me *here*."

"In business?"

"Jah, jah. Business, all right."

Across the table, the Comte de Rieu could barely suppress a laugh—he knew what Kappler did.

"The truth is," Kappler said, "I'm just an old cop from Hamburg—like my poppa was before me. I was born to it. A cop under the kaiser, a cop during the Weimar time. So now I work for Heini and Reini, but believe me, Herr Stein, it's the same old thing."

Heini and Reini meant Heinrich Himmler and Reinhard Heydrich. Which put Kappler somewhere in the RSHA empire—most likely the Gestapo or one of the SD intelligence units. Stein puffed at his cigar but it had gone out.

"Here, let me," Kappler said. He snapped a silver lighter and Stein turned the cigar in the flame before inhaling.

"Tell them what you heard today, darling," Labarthe said to his friend Bella.

She looked confused. "In beauty salon?"

"Yes, that's right."

She nodded and smiled—now she knew what was wanted. She wore a military-style soft cap with a black feather arching back from one side, and theatrical circles of rouge on her cheeks.

"It was, it was . . ." She turned to Labarthe for help, whispered in his ear, he spoke a phrase or two behind his hand and she nodded with relief. "Hairdresser was telling me about *death ray,*" she said brightly.

"Death ray?" Madame Roubier said.

"Yes. Was made by man who invented telegraph."

"Marconi," Labarthe prompted.

"Yes, Marconi. Now for Mussolini he build death ray. So, war is over." She smiled enthusiastically.

Willy Kappler shook with silent laughter, then pressed a hand against the side of his face. "People love a rumor," he said. "The stranger it is, the better they like it. Did you hear last week? How de Gaulle was killed in an air raid in London and British spies smuggled his ashes into Paris and buried them in Napoleon's tomb?"

"I did hear that," said the comte. "From my dentist. And on the last visit he'd told me the British had invented a powder that set water on fire. Told me in strictest confidence, mind you."

"Mesdames . . . et . . . monsieurs!"

The waiter made sure he had their attention, then, with a flourish, he presented a *foie gras blond en bloc,* at least two pounds of it. In a basket, a mountain of toast triangles, crusts trimmed off. For each person at the table a tiny chilled dish of Charentais butter. The champagne-colored aspic quivered as the waiter

carved slabs off the block and slid them deftly onto monogrammed plates. *"Et alors!"* said the comte, when the first cut
was made and the size of the black truffle within revealed. Then
the table was quiet as knives worked foie gras on toast and little
sips of Beaune were taken to wash it down. "I tell you," said
Willy Kappler, eyes glazed with rapture, "the best is really very
good."

The headwaiter appeared at Stein's chair.

"Yes?" Stein said.

"A telephone call for you, Monsieur."

The phone was on a marble table in an alcove by the men's
toilet. "Stein," he said into the receiver. But the line just
hissed, there was nobody on the other end.

The men's room attendant opened the door a few inches and
said, "Monsieur Stein?" Stein went into the small tiled foyer
that led to the urinals. The attendant's table held a stack of
white towels, scented soaps, and combs. A little dish of coins
stood to one side. The white-jacketed attendant was called
Voyschinkowsky, a man in his sixties, with the red-rimmed,
pouchy eyes and hollow cheeks of the lifelong insomniac.
Rumor had it that he had, at one time, been one of the richest
men in Paris, a brilliant speculator, known as the Lion of the
Bourse. But now, with his gravel-voiced Hungarian accent and
white jacket, he was just an amusing character.

"I have your message, Monsieur Stein," Voyschinkowsky
said. "A young man is waiting downstairs, looking at newspapers at the stand just east of the restaurant. He needs to see you
urgently."

De Milja peeled a hundred-franc note from a roll in his
pocket and laid it in Voyschinkowsky's dish. "What next, I
wonder," he grumbled under his breath.

Voyschinkowsky's face remained opaque. "Thank you, Monsieur," he said. De Milja went downstairs. It was a warmish
April night, the street smelled like fish—a waiter in a rubber
apron was shucking oysters over a hill of chipped ice. The young

man reading the headlines at the newspaper stand wore a thin jacket and a scarf. "Yes? You're waiting for me?" de Milja said.

The young man looked him over. "Fedin needs to see you right away," he said.

"Where?"

"Up at Boulogne-Billancourt." Boulogne meant the factory district at the edge of Paris, not the seaside town.

De Milja stared at the young man. It could be anything—an emergency, a trap. There was nothing he could do about it. "All right," he said. "I'll be back."

The young man looked at his watch. "Twenty minutes to curfew."

"I'll hurry," de Milja said. He had a pass that allowed him to be out any time he wished, but he didn't want to go into that now.

Back at the table he said, "An emergency."

"What happened?" Madame Roubier said.

"An accident at the yard. A man is injured." He turned to the comte. "Would you see Madame home?"

"Yes, of course."

"May I help?" said Willy Kappler, very concerned. "Not much I can't do in this city." De Milja seemed to consider. "Thank you," he said. "I think the best thing is for me to go, but I appreciate the offer."

Kappler nodded sympathetically. "Another time," he said.

They rode the métro to the Quai d'Issy station. The train stopped there because the tunnel up ahead had flooded but the police wouldn't let anybody exit to the street. So they crossed over, took a train back one stop, and walked. The quarter was a snarl of freight tracks and old factories surrounding the Renault plant and the large docks on the Seine. On the other side of the river was a Russian neighborhood—émigrés packed into brick tenements and working on the automobile assembly lines.

Under German occupation, Renault manufactured military

vehicles for the Wehrmacht, so the British bombed the plant. De Milja and Fedin's messenger crunched broken glass underfoot as they walked. Water flooded from broken mains, black smoke that smelled like burning rubber made de Milja's eyes run and he kept wiping at them with his hand. An ambulance drove by, siren wailing. Where a building had collapsed into the street, de Milja stepped over a smoldering mattress, picking his way among scattered pans and shoes and sheet music.

At the Eastern Orthodox Church of Saint Basil, the young man stood back. Tears ran from his eyes and cut tracks in the soot on his face. "He's in there," he said to de Milja.

"The church?"

The young man nodded and walked away quickly.

The church was being used as an emergency room. General Fedin was lying on a blanket on the stone floor, a second blanket was drawn up to his chin. When de Milja stood over him he opened his eyes. "Good," he said. "I hoped they'd find you."

De Milja knelt by his side. Fedin's face, once fierce and skull-like, had collapsed, and his skin was the color of wax. Suddenly, an old man. He lowered the blanket a little—gauze bandage was taped across his chest—and made a sour face that meant *no good*.

"Better for you to be in the hospital," de Milja said. "Fastest way is a taxi, you'll lie on the backseat."

"Let's not be stupid," Fedin said gently. "I know this wound very well, I've seen it many times."

"Vassily Alexandrovich . . ."

Fedin gripped his arm, he meant to grip it hard, but he couldn't. "Stop it," he said.

De Milja was silent for a time. "How did this happen?"

"I was at the Double Eagle, a Russian club, people playing chess and drinking tea. The sirens went off, like always. We shrugged and ignored them, like always. The next thing, somebody pulled me out from under some boards. Then I woke up here."

He paused a moment, lips pressed tight. "I'm sixty-three years old," he said.

It was dark in the church, a few candles the only light. People were talking in low voices, taking care to walk quietly on the stone floors. Like actors in a play, de Milja thought. Some still wore the costumes—cabdrivers, cleaning women—that exile had assigned them, but in this church they were themselves, and spoke and gestured like the people they had once been. Outside, the last sirens of police cars and ambulances faded away and it was quiet again.

"I always thought I'd die on a horse, on a battlefield," Fedin said. "Not in a chess club in Paris. You know I fought at Tannenberg, in 1914? Then with Brusilov, in Galicia. Against the Japanese, in 1905. In the Balkans, 1912 that was, I was on the staff of the Russian military attaché to Serbia. 1912. I was in love."

He smiled at that. Thought for a time, with his eyes closed. Then looked directly at de Milja and said "Jesus, the world's a slaughterhouse. Really it is. If you're weak they're going to cut your throat—ask the Armenians, ask the Jews. The bad people want it their way, my friend. And how badly they want it is the study of a lifetime."

He shook his head with sorrow. "So," he said, "so then what. You step into it, if you're a certain sort. But then you're taking sides, and you've written yourself down for an appointment with the butchers. There's a waiting list—but they'll get around to you, never fear. Christ, look at me, killed by my own side." He paused a moment, then said, "Damn fine bomb, though, even so. Made in Birmingham or somewhere. Didn't hit any factories, this one didn't. But it settled with the Double Eagle club once and for all. And it settled with General Fedin."

Fedin laughed, then his mood changed. "Listen, I know all about what you did on the docks that night. Running off to die because you couldn't stand to live in a bad world. What the hell did you think you were doing? You can't do that, you can't *resign.*" He thought a moment, then said sternly, "That's not for you, boy. Not for you."

He sighed, wandered a little, said something, but too quietly for de Milja to hear. De Milja leaned closer. "What did you say?"

"I want to rest for a minute, but don't let me go yet," Fedin said.

De Milja sat back, hands on knees, in the gloom of the darkened church. He looked at his watch: just after one in the morning. Now the night was very quiet. He sensed somebody nearby, turned to see a woman standing next to him. She had gray hair, hastily pinned up, wore a dark, ill-fitting suit, had a stethoscope around her neck. She stared at Fedin for a long moment, knelt by his side and drew the blanket up over his face.

"Wait," de Milja said. "What are you doing?" She stood, then put a hand on his shoulder. He felt warmth enter him, as though the woman had done this so often she had contrived a single gesture to say everything that could be said. Then, after a moment, she took her hand off and walked away.

17 April. 3:20 A.M. West of Bourges.

Bonneau drove the rattletrap farm truck, Jeanne-Marie sat in the middle, de Milja by the window. They drove with the headlights off, no more than twenty miles an hour over the dirt farm roads. The truck bounced and bucked so hard de Milja shut his mouth tight to keep from cracking a tooth.

Three-quarter moon, the fields visible once the eyes adjusted. With airplanes on clandestine missions, you fought the war by the phases of the moon. "The Soulier farm," Jeanne-Marie said in a whisper. Bonneau hauled the wheel over and the old truck shuddered and swayed into a farmyard. The dogs were on them immediately, barking and yelping and jumping up to leave muddy paw marks on the windows.

A huge silhouette appeared in the yard, the shadows of dogs dancing away from its kicking feet as the barking turned to whining. A shutter banged open and a kerosene lamp was lit in the window of the farmhouse. The silhouette approached the truck. "Bonneau?"

"Yes."

"We're all ready to go, here. Come and take a coffee."

"Perhaps later. The rendezvous is in forty minutes and we've got to walk across the fields."

The silhouette sighed. "Don't offend my wife, Bonneau. If you do, I can reasonably well guarantee you that the Germans will be here for generations."

Jeanne-Marie whispered a curse beneath her breath.

"What? Who is that? Jeanne-Marie? *Ma biche*—my jewel! Are you going to war?" The silhouette laughed, Bonneau put his forehead on his hands holding the steering wheel. To de Milja he said, "Soulier was my sergeant in the tank corps." Then, to the silhouette at the truck window, "You're right, of course, a coffee will be just the thing."

They entered the farmhouse. The stove had been lit to drive off the night chill. On a plank table there was a loaf of bread and a sawtooth knife on a board, butter wrapped in a damp cloth, and a bottle of red wine. Madame Soulier stood at the stove and heated milk in a black iron pot. "We just got this from Violet," she said.

De Milja teetered dangerously on the edge of asking who Violet was—then from the corner of his eye caught Jeanne-Marie's discreet signal, a two-handed teat-pulling gesture.

Madame Soulier gathered the skin off the top of the milk with a wooden spoon, then whacked the spoon on the rim of the zinc-lined kitchen sink to send it flying. "That's for the devil," she muttered to herself.

De Milja knew this coffee—it was the same coffee, black, bitter, searing hot, he'd drunk in the Volhynia before going hunting on autumn mornings. He held the chipped cup in both hands. The cities were different in Europe; the countryside was very much the same.

"And the Clarais cousins? They're coming?" Bonneau said.

Soulier shrugged. It scared de Milja a little, the quality of that shrug. He understood it, he feared, all too well—the Clarais cousins hadn't shown up where they'd promised to be since the spring of 1285, likely tonight would be no different. Jeanne-Marie's face remained immobile, perhaps the Clarais cousins were not crucial to the enterprise but had been asked for other reasons.

"Townspeople," Soulier said to him, a confidential aside that explained everything.

"Better without them?" de Milja asked.

"Oh yes, no question of that."

Soulier sucked up the last of his coffee and emitted a steamy sigh of pleasure. He rose from the table, pushing with his hands on the plank surface, then said, "Must have a word with the pig."

When he returned, the aroma came with him. He stopped at the open door, wiped the muck off his boots, then entered, his arms full of rifles. He laid them out on the kitchen table and proceeded to strip off the oiled paper that had protected them. He dumped an old tin can on the table, moving bullets with a thick forefinger, and counted to eighteen. "Souvenirs of the war," he said to de Milja.

There were four rifles, Soulier and Bonneau each took one. Jeanne-Marie wasn't expected to use such things, and de Milja declined. He carried a 9 mm Italian automatic that had found its way to him, part of the Anton Stein persona, but he had no intention of shooting at anybody.

Soulier examined one of the rifles. "We kept these with us in the tank just in case," he said.

Just in case, de Milja thought, the 1914 war started up again. They were bolt-action rifles, with five-round magazines, and far too many soldiers in the French infantry had carried them in 1940.

De Milja looked meaningfully at his watch. Soulier said fondly, "Ah my friend, do not concern yourself too much. We're not in the city now, you know. Life here happens in its own time."

"We'll have to explain that to the pilot," de Milja said.

Soulier laughed heartily—sarcasm was of absolutely no use with him. "There's no point in worrying about that," he said. "These contraptions have never yet been on time."

The BBC *Message Personnel*—delivered in a cluster of meaningless phrases to deny the Germans analysis of traffic volume—had been broadcast forty-eight hours earlier. *In the afternoon, visit the cathedral at Rouen.* Then confirmed, a day later, by the BBC's playing Django Reinhardt's "In a Sentimental Mood" at a specified time.

They had avoided offending the hospitality of Madame Soulier, but the Bonneau reception committee was now behind schedule. They tried riding their bicycles across the countryside, but it was too dark, and most of the time they had to walk, following cattle paths that wound around the low hills, soaking their feet when the land turned to marsh, sweating with effort in the cold night air.

De Milja had been right, they were late getting to the field Jeanne-Marie had chosen. But Soulier was right too—the contraption had not been on time. A triumph of what was called *System D, D* for the verb *débrouiller*, to muddle through, to manage somehow. First used to describe the French railway system's response to supply obligations in the war of 1914, it explained, in a few syllables, the French method of managing life.

They got to the field late, four instead of the expected six, and had to hurry to arrange the brush piles. Somehow they managed, although the head of the arrow that indicated wind direction was missing one side. Then Bonneau stopped dead, looked up, signaled for quiet. A low, distant hum. Getting louder, a drone. Then, clearly, the sound of airplane engines. *"Les flambeaux!"* Soulier cried.

It was Jeanne-Marie who actually had matches. The torches were lit. Rags, smeared thickly with pitch-pine resin and knotted at the ends of branches, they crackled and sputtered and threw wild shadows across the meadow as the reception party ran from brush pile to brush pile. Jeanne-Marie and de Milja raced past each other on the dead run—by firelight he saw her face, close to tears with anger and pride, with fierce joy.

In the clouds above them, a Whitley bomber, slow and cumbersome.

The pilot banked gently to get a better view of the land below him. He had sifted through the air defenses on the Brittany coast—a few desultory rounds of ack-ack, nothing more, the gunners not sorry to hear him droning off to somebody else's sector. Then he'd followed the Loire, just about due east, the shadow of his plane cast by moonlight running next to the river. He picked up the Vienne—he hoped—branching south, then found the confluence of the Creuse and the Gartempe. Here he adjusted his bearing, a few degrees south of east, and watched the seconds tick away. *Now,* he thought.

Nothing there, dark and peaceful fields. Then came the voice of his navigator, "Here we are. Just a little north of us, sir."

An orange fire appeared below—then another and another as the pilot watched. He pushed a button, a green light went on in the cargo hold but the drop-master could see as well as he could. First the crates, shoved out the door, white parachutes flaring off into the darkness before they caught the wind and jerked upright, swaying down toward the fires in the field below.

"Best of luck to you, gentlemen," said the drop-master and the four French paratroopers jumped in rapid succession. They had been given little paper French flags to take down with them and one of them, Lucien, the leader, actually managed to hold one aloft as he floated to earth. He had left France from the port of Dunkirk, not quite a year earlier, by swimming toward a British fishing boat. His pants and shirt and officer's cap were left on the beach, his pistol was at the bottom of the Channel. He thought, as the wind rushed past him, he heard someone cry out down below.

That was Soulier, crazed with excitement. "It worked! By God it worked!" He might have said *Vive la France*—the paratroopers would certainly have appreciated the sentiment—but, for the moment, surprise had exceeded patriotism. The paratroopers wrestled free of their harness, then menaced the night with their Sten guns, but there was only the reception committee in the field, so they greeted each other formally, embraced, and talked in whispers. Then the officer excused himself to Jeanne-Marie, turned away, undid his fly, watered a rock, and mumbled something relieved and grateful under his breath—thus, at last, was *Vive la France* said on that occasion.

As the fires burned themselves out, they took Soulier's pry bar and tore open the crates. Unpacked two dozen Sten guns—rapid-firing carbines of no particular range but brutal effect up close, the British solution to the problem of a weapon for clandestine war. There were W/T sets, maps printed on silk, cans of a nasty green jelly that British scientists had concocted to burn down Europe.

Everything took longer than they'd calculated. With dawn came a cold, dirty drizzle, the wind blowing the smell of raw spring earth off the fields. Using the bicycles as carts they hauled the shipment off to Soulier's farm. Were suitably impressed when Soulier reached down through the pig shit and opened a trapdoor in the earth, as the tenant of the sty looked on, slit-eyed and suspicious, from the fence where he'd been tied up.

Once again, on local trains to Vannes.

De Milja had appointed Jeanne-Marie liaison officer for the Kampfgeschwader 100 attack. Bonneau and Soulier to handle logistics and supply, the paratroopers to do the actual shooting.

They rode together in the first-class compartment. Jeanne-Marie, with open shirt collar spread across the lapels of a dark suit and mannish hat with feather, looked exactly like what she was—a part of the high bourgeois or petit nobility—the French landowning class. De Milja, briefcase in hand, hat with brim snapped down—her provincial lawyer.

Two German officers entered their compartment at Poitiers, very polite and correct. From their insignia, they were involved with engineering—perhaps construction. Essentially they were German businessmen, on leave from daily life in Frankfurt or Düsseldorf or wherever it was in order to fight a war. Still, a great deal of silence in the compartment. Jeanne-Marie, living just below the Vichy line, had not seen many Germans and wasn't really used to moving around among them. For their part, the Germans found French women irresistible, and Jeanne-Marie, pale and reserved with small, fine features and aristocratic bearing, was of a type particularly attractive to the officer class.

"Would Madame care to have the window open?" one of them said, using vacation French.

"No, thank you."

"Not too warm for you, in here?"

"Quite comfortable, thank you."

"Well then . . ."

The train chugged along, the fields of the Poitou plain falling away slowly behind them.

"I wonder, sir, if you can tell me what time we arrive in Nantes?"

"I'm not really certain," de Milja said.

"Just after two, perhaps?"

"I believe that's right."

The man smiled at Jeanne-Marie: isn't it satisfying, in some deliciously mysterious way, for us all to be rolling through the French countryside together? Not actually an *adventure*, not quite that. But, surely, not the usual thing either. Wouldn't you agree?

In this rising tide of banality, de Milja sensed danger. Just such moments, he knew, could turn fatal. You did not see it coming.

With a sigh, a sigh of apology, he set to unbuckling the briefcase that lay across his knees. Providently, he had fitted it out with its own false identity in case it was searched: mostly land deeds, obtained from clerks in an office of registry just outside Paris.

"What have you there, Duval?" Jeanne-Marie said.

De Milja found a name on the deed. "The Bredon papers. I'm afraid we'll have to go over them together sometime before tomorrow."

Jeanne-Marie took the deed and began to read it.

The German folded his hands across his middle and turned toward the window—an admission of defeat.

In Vannes, Jeanne-Marie was checked in at the better hotel by the railroad station. De Milja set off toward the street where Mademoiselle Herault kept a *confiserie*. The mood of the neighborhood hadn't changed, perhaps it had grown darker, quieter. Five o'clock on a spring afternoon, it should have been hopeful. Paris, hungry and cold and beginning to fray badly after a year of occupation, somehow kept its hopes up. But not here.

Then he came around the corner, saw what had happened, and just kept walking. There wasn't much to see—a lowered shutter, a chain, and a padlock.

It was what he would have seen at eight that evening, when mademoiselle herself had locked up the money and locked up the office and sent her clerk home. Her final act of the day would have been to lower the shutter and chain it to a ring set in the sill. But she had not done this.

De Milja couldn't defend his intuition. Perhaps the padlock

was slightly better, slightly newer than the one she had used, but otherwise there was nothing. Absence. Five on a spring afternoon, even in a sad little town, even in a shadowy street, somebody buys candy. But Mademoiselle Herault was closed. And she wouldn't, de Milja knew in his heart, be reopening.

He didn't stop walking, he didn't slow down. Just glanced at the rolled-down shutter, then made certain he was in the right street. That was all. Somebody might be watching the street, but he thought not. There wouldn't be anything here for them now, they would simply lock it up and think about it for a time—*here a spy worked*. That was an instinct of policemen. Perhaps evidence could be retrieved, perhaps something had been forgotten.

So de Milja knew what had happened—but of course that kind of knowing wasn't acceptable. He could not return to Paris and have his operator cipher up some bedtime story for the Sixth Bureau: *Officer instinctively sensed* . . . He returned to the hotel, made sure Jeanne-Marie was where he'd left her. Normally he would not have said anything to her, would have kept her where she belonged, with a high brick wall between her and Mademoiselle Herault. In one of the first French attempts at an underground network, earlier that year, a single arrested individual had compromised a hundred and sixty-five people. So, you compartmentalized. And if they didn't know about that over here, they sure as hell knew it in the eastern part of Europe, where nobody had any illusions about what went on in the basements of police stations. What people knew, they told.

No, that was wrong. Some people never told. Some people, only the bravest, or perhaps the angriest, let the interrogation run its course, and died in silence. He suspected, again an intuition, that Mademoiselle Herault had not given the operation away. What she was, she was—a soured sort of life, he believed. Ignoring the spiteful neighbors, squeezing every sou, hating the world, but strong. Stronger than the people who would try to dominate her. That was it, he realized, that was what he knew about her. She would not be dominated, no matter how they made her suffer.

He went to the not-so-good hotel at the railroad station, across the square from Jeanne-Marie, and checked in. The lawyer Benoit from Nantes, a boring little man on a boring little errand—please God let them believe that. Below his window, freight cars rolled past all night. The Germans were building here: massive defenses to repel an invasion, and submarine pens to attack British shipping.

De Milja couldn't sleep. He smoked, sat in a chair by the window, and stared out into the darkened square. Some nights he could travel like a ghost, skimming over the landmass of Europe, the bloody cellars and the silent streets, the castles and the princes and the assassins who waited for them. Wolves in the snow—at the edge of town, where the butchers made sausage.

At seven he stood in front of the sink, bare-chested, suspenders dangling from the waistband of his trousers. He washed himself with cold water, then rubbed his skin with a towel.

In the lobby of the hotel, an old man was sweeping the tile floor, moving slowly among the ancient velvet chairs and sofas. De Milja went out in the street. Better there—the sun just up, the cobblestones of the square sluiced down with water. Around the corner he found an open café, ordered a coffee, stood at the bar and chatted with the *patron*.

The *patron* had a friend called Henri, who could get him anything he wanted. A pair of bicycles? No problem. An arching eyebrow indicated that the resources available to Henri went much deeper than that. Henri himself appeared an hour later, pushing the bicycles. De Milja paid him handsomely, then mentioned *truck tires,* price no object, perhaps at the end of the week? No problem! Henri nodded, gestured, winked. What de Milja really wanted was seventy-two hours during which Henri would refrain from selling him to the police, and he thought he'd accomplished that. First tires, then betrayal, so read the heart of Henri.

The following day, at five in the morning, in a patter of spring rain, they were on the road. They pedaled out of Vannes with some forty other cyclists, all headed to work at the fish-oil plant, at the small machine shops and boat-repair yards found in every port, some of them no doubt going the twelve miles to the air base, where the pilots of the Kampfgeschwader 100 also worked. The riders were silent—it was too early in the morning to be among strangers. Now and then a bicycle bell rang, two or three times an automobile, no doubt carrying somebody important and German, went roaring past.

De Milja let the crowd get ahead of them so they could talk. "Now this curve," he said, "is a possibility. To the right, the pine forest provides some cover. To the left, the rock makes it impossible for the bus to swerve, to simply drive away from the attack."

They rode on, Jeanne-Marie making mental notes about the road, the terrain, the time of day—everything that would have to be factored into an assault plan. "Of course," de Milja said, "it will be up to the officer leading the attack to make the decision—exactly where to conceal his firing points and everything else. But there are locations along the route that he ought to at least consider."

Up ahead, a warning bell rang and a railwayman lowered a safety gate. Then a locomotive sounded its whistle and a slow freight came rumbling across the road. De Milja and Jeanne-Marie pulled up to the crowd of cyclists, standing patiently on one foot while the boxcars rolled past. A dark green sports car, its hood secured by a leather strap, stopped next to de Milja. The driver and his companion were young men, wearing good tweed jackets and pigskin gloves. "*Ach du lieber!*" the driver said, his hand clapped over his eyes. What had struck him blind was a girl in a tight skirt astride a bicycle seat. The other man

shook his head in wonder, said in German, "Sweet sugar—
come fly through the clouds with me." The girl ignored them.

The freight train moved off into the distance, the railwayman
raised the gate. The driver of the sports car gunned his engine,
the cyclists scurried out of the way, and the two Germans went
tearing down the road, an echo of speed shifts and screaming engine lingering after them.

5:30 P.M. The first minutes of darkness. Outlines blurred,
faces indistinct. People were out; coming home from work,
going visiting, shopping. A couple, even strangers, moved easily
along the street, unremarkable, nobody really saw them.

De Milja took Jeanne-Marie by the arm for a moment, guided
her into a long alley, a crooked lane no more than three feet
wide with lead-sheathed drain tiles running down both sides and
crumbling stone arches above. It was chaos back here; stake
fences concealing garden plots, leaning sheds and rusty tin roofs,
curved tiles stacked against walls, dripping pipes, sheets hung to
dry on lines spanning the alley—a thousand years of village life
concealed from the public street.

Finding the back entrance to a particular shop should have
been a nightmare, but no, in fact the Germans had done him a
favor. The back door of the *confiserie* was chained and pad-
locked—the same equipment they'd used for the front door.

The chain ran from a rusty cleat in the wall to the iron door
handle. It wasn't a system Mademoiselle Herault had ever used,
and it didn't work now. De Milja took an iron bar from under
his coat, slotted one end next to the chain in the wall cleat, used
a piece of broken brick as a fulcrum, and put his weight against
it. Out came the cleat with a puff of dust, a chunk of old ma-
sonry still attached to it. Next the door lock. He threw a shoulder into the door, but nothing happened. Drew a foot up and
drove his heel against the lock plate—same result. Finally he
worked the sharp end of the bar into the dried-out wood between the door and the jamb, levered it apart until he could get

the end of the bar past the inside edge of the door, used every bit of strength he had. Nothing at first, then it gave a little, finally there was a loud squeak and the sound of ripping wood as the lock tore free. He swung the door open, waited a beat, stepped inside.

What he needed to see he saw immediately—the dusk of closed spaces was broken up by shadowy light from the doorway, and the last two years had taught him to see in the dark. There was no malice or evil in the *confiserie*, just a professional job, cold and thorough.

They had searched: dumped the canisters of flour into the stone sink, then the sugar, the salt, the baking soda, whatever else had been on the shelf, stirring through each new addition. They would have used a thin metal rod, sifting, probing, hunting the spool of microfilm or the miniature camera, the book marked for ciphering or a set of crystals for a radio. De Milja walked into the office, every step a brittle crunch—they'd spilled a bin of hard candies on the floor, and their boots had ground them into powdery shards of red and green.

Mademoiselle Herault's office was torn to pieces. Not a piece of paper to be seen, upholstery fabric sliced from the bottom of an upside-down chair, drawers pulled from the desk, then the desk flipped over, smashing the drawers beneath it. In the store itself, the glass had been kicked out of the counters and the wooden frame torn apart—spies were diabolical when it came to hiding things. The searchers had unwrapped the chocolates and squashed them—ants were at work on the result, tossed atop the shards of glass.

By the cash register, where Veronique the clerk had spent her days, de Milja smelled something strange. Even amid the orange essence and vanilla and peppermint and God knew what else— something strong and particular, like flowers. He knelt, the smell got stronger. A small glass bottle, in pieces, half-hidden by the leg of a counter. Candy clerk's perfume, he thought. They had stood her against a wall, searched through her purse, and it had fallen out, or perhaps they'd thrown it on the floor.

No more than a minute inside the shop, but too long.

Jeanne-Marie called in a whisper, de Milja was up and out in one motion. A flashlight bobbed at the other end of the alley. He kicked the door shut with his foot and embraced Jeanne-Marie in the same instant. Passionately, pressing his mouth against hers. She made a small sound of distaste, stiffened, tried to pull away from him just as the flashlight pinned them both.

The voice was a growl. "What's this?"

It was the eternal voice of the *flic*, the cop, tired and sour beyond redemption. "Romance?" it wondered.

De Milja shielded his eyes from the light, squinting helplessly as he did so, a profoundly virtuous gesture. "We have no place to meet," he said.

A moment while that was considered. "Well, you can't *meet* here."

The light was lowered. De Milja heard the little pop of a holster flap snapped back into place. "Take a walk," the cop said. He sensed something, but he wished not to know about it. He simply made it vanish so it no longer troubled him.

They took local trains out of Vannes that night. Jeanne-Marie back to the country house, de Milja to the avenue Hoche.

It was, inevitably, spring in Paris. The first chestnut trees bloomed at the entrances to the métro, where warm air flowed up the staircases. Greece was taken in April, so was Yugoslavia. Belgrade, pressured by tank columns on three sides, was surrendered to a German captain and nine enlisted men who had bluffed their way through the defense lines. The United States had frozen German and Italian assets held in American banks.

For Parisians, daily existence was a struggle, and people simply tried to stay out of the way of the Germans. There had, in the first year of occupation, been one execution—Jacques Bonsergent, shot for jostling a German officer in the Gare Saint-Lazare.

The mood in the cafés was now resignation, the defeat by the Germans called *the debacle*. De Milja found this a curious expression once he thought about it—just the sort of linguistic trap that the French liked to construct. It meant a complete rout, a total collapse. But somewhere in the spirit of the word was a touch of the absurd, the comic: it wasn't anyone's fault, no point in assigning blame, it was just that everything went wrong all at once—a moment of Divine slapstick and poof, we lost the country.

For de Milja, contacts in the Polish community had finally begun to pay off. He had enlisted a railroad clerk and a miner's daughter from Alsace—both contacts made through Polish clergy at local churches. The value of priests now became particularly apparent. They had political views, strong ones often enough, and were the keepers of community secrets. They knew who drank, who made money, and who lost it. They knew who the collaborators were, and who the patriots were. People, perhaps resisting an urge to gossip over the back fence, told the priest everything. Sometimes in church, more often in the parlor or at the vegetable stall. That couldn't be wrong, could it? Heaven knew all your secrets anyhow.

The Alsatian girl, very studious and shy, in her early twenties, came to live in Paris at de Milja's request. He assigned her the code name *Vera,* then, in a slow and curiously difficult effort, tried to place her in a job in a German bureau. She spoke excellent German, perfect French, it should have been easy. "I have never felt French, exactly," she told her interviewers. "Always we spoke German in my house." She was offered two jobs, both clerical and meaningless, in the office that handled payments flowing from France to Germany—400 million francs a day, the cost of the German military and civilian administration. After all, one couldn't expect one's country to be occupied for free.

With de Milja's coaching, *Vera* extracted herself from those offers, moved to a *pension,* and waited patiently.

. . .

26 April 1941. 3:20 A.M. Le Chabanais.

Paris's finest brothel. Draperies, brocades, velvets, and cut crystal—such weight as to suggest a thick and impenetrable wall of discretion. Waitresses in golden slippers served osetra caviar. In one of the private rooms, the Slovakian coal dealer Anton Stein had invited the Comte de Rieu and the art dealer Labarthe to be his guests for a late supper and whatever other diversions they might enjoy. They had a peaceful, relaxed, gentlemen's evening of it.

The count had been entertained, in one of the upstairs bedrooms, by a "Hungarian countess" and her "Spanish maid"—the glass of wine tipped over, the slipper applied, then forgiveness, at length and in many ways. The count returned, shaking his head in wonder at what the world had to offer him. Lit a Camel cigarette, drank a sip of champagne, rested his head on the back of a chair and blew two seemingly endless plumes of smoke at the chandelier.

No need to talk, a grand silence—a moment to contemplate human desire and the masks it wore. De Milja had seen the countess; hair dark red, Magyar cheekbones, long, delicate fingers. But a temper, as you might expect. Not the one to stand for a maid's clumsy behavior.

The count smiled at his host by way of saying thank you. "The pleasures of excess," he said quietly. Labarthe snored lightly on a settee, head fallen to one side.

Stein raised his glass in a silent toast to the count's words. He drank, then after a moment said, "I was in Alsace recently. Stumbled on treasure."

"Let me guess: a Rhine maiden?"

"Oh no. Completely the opposite."

"Really?"

Stein nodded yes. Opened a tortoiseshell case and selected a small, pale-leafed cigar. He rolled it between his fingers, then snapped a silver lighter until a flame appeared. "Mmm," he said, putting the lighter away. "Spinster type—to look at her you'd never imagine."

"Oh, I can imagine."

"Little more champagne?"

"Not just yet, thanks."

"Anyhow, I have her here. In a *pension*."

"Can't get enough?"

"That's it." He paused a moment. "Thing is, she's bored. Nothing to do all day."

"Why not a job? Coming from there, she must speak German."

"She does, she does. Wants to work for *Jeder Einmal*."

"Why there?"

"I think she worked at Eszterhazy, the travel agency, before the war."

"Well, that shouldn't be a problem. I don't know anyone there, exactly, but Kappler can do it in a minute. I'll call him Monday, if you like."

"Would you? That would certainly help me out."

"Consider it done."

From somewhere in the vast building came the sound of a violin. It was playing a folk melody, slow and melancholy, something eastern, perhaps Russian. Both men listened attentively. Labarthe stopped snoring, mumbled something, then fell back asleep. "Remarkable, the way life is now," the count said. "Untold stories." Then, after a moment, he said, "A spinster?" He meant, in a rather delicate way, that such an appetite in Stein was unexpected.

Stein shrugged. "Quite religious," he said. "She is like a storm."

Transmission of 12 May. 1:25 A.M.

To Director. Source: Albert
Railway Bureau designates departures 21 May/26 May. 3rd

class and livestock cars making up at Reims yards. Route: Reims/Metz/Trier/Würzburg/Prague/Breslau/Cracow/Tarnow. Including: Artillery regiment 181, Fusilier Regiment 202 (Stettin), Grenadier Regiments 80, 107, 253 (Wiesbaden). Grenadier regiments 151, 162, and 176 (Wehrkreis X, Hamburg).

Of 21 Divisions in France as of 4/22/41, total of 9 (135,000 men) now moved east.

De Milja's railroad clerk. Fussy little man, fierce patriot. Dead drop at the Église Sainte Thérèse—Albert to the six o'clock mass, de Milja at ten. The take from Wehrmacht rail scheduling made de Milja's heart lift. Great numbers of troops—and their vehicles, weapons, files, and draft horses—on the move from conquered France and Belgium to conquered Poland. That meant Russia. And that meant the end. There was in Wilno a historical marker, alongside the Moscow road, that read "On 28 June, 1812, Napoleon Bonaparte passed this way with 450,000 men." Then, on the other side, approached from the east, was a different message: "On 9 December, 1812, Napoleon Bonaparte passed this way with 900 men."

Could Adolf Hitler—shrewd, cunning—do such a foolish thing? Maybe not. De Milja had observed that the failed Operation Sealion had been undertaken without a feint, without deception. If the Germans were going to try again, June would be the time to lay a false trail, such as the shipment of men and arms to the east.

To find out, de Milja had Albert on the one hand, Vera on the other. The Comte de Rieu had been true to his word, Vera was hired as a clerk—"But in six months, we'll see about something better"—by the *Jeder Einmal in Paris* organization. This was Goebbels at work, the phrase meant *Paris for Everybody Once*. A morale builder for the military, and a spy's dream. *Everybody* meant just that—from privates to generals, two weeks' leave in romantic, naughty Paris. The brothels and the nightclubs were fully staffed, the inflated Occupation Reichsmark would buy an astonishing mound of gifts for Momma and Poppa and the ever-faithful Helga.

The German empire now ran from Norway to North Africa, from Brest, France, to Brest Litovsk in Poland. Getting all those people in and out of Paris was a logistical nightmare, but not for the efficient *Jeder* organization, a vast travel agency coordinating hotels, barracks, and train reservations. They simply had to know—thus Vera had to know—where everybody was: the location of every unit in the German war machine. Where it was strong, and where it wasn't.

French students still went to university—a privilege not enjoyed in Poland, where by Himmler's order the slave population was to learn to count on its fingers and acknowledge orders with affirmative grunts. De Milja's response was to hide one of his W/T operators in a tiny room in the student quarter of the fifth arrondissement. The agent seemed to belong there, with a beard tracing the outline of his jaw, a piercing student gaze, and hair he cut himself.

It was in the tiny room, with pictures of philosophers pinned to the walls, that de Milja learned, from a Sixth Bureau transmission on 17 May, that the operation in Vannes had to be completely reworked. The Pathfinder pilots of Kampfgeschwader 100 now drove their own cars to the airfield rather than going by bus.

And it was in the tiny room that de Milja learned, from a Sixth Bureau transmission of 19 May, that he'd been fired.

It wasn't put that way—the word *relieved* was not used—but that was what it meant. De Milja's reaction was first shock, then anguished disbelief. Why? How could this happen? What had he done wrong?

"Is this correct?" he asked the operator.

"I believe so," the man said. He was embarrassed, did not meet de Milja's eyes. "Of course I can request retransmission. Or clarification."

But it was already quite clear. The reference to de Milja by his assigned cipher, rendezvous on a certain beach on a certain night, to be transported back to Sixth Bureau London headquarters for reassignment. Prepare all field agents and technical staff for a change of resident officer.

He did that. Vera didn't like it. Albert nodded grimly, war was war. He could say nothing to Lisette Roubier, to Zimmer at the coal company, to the people who were simply there in his life as he was in theirs. The French placed great store by daily encounters, small friendships carried on a few minutes at a time, and he would have liked to have said good-bye.

Lost people, lost money. Huysmanns coal, probably the apartment on the avenue Hoche, gone. Abandoned. Intelligence services had to operate in that fashion, build and walk away, it was in the nature of their existence. But de Milja knew, in a hungry city, what that money would buy.

A certain night in June, sweet and sad, he chased Madame Roubier around the bed with real conviction. "Oh my," she said, and scowled with pleasure. Then it was time to go and he kissed her on the lips and she put her arms around him and squeezed him tight. Pulling back a little to have a look at him, her eyes were shiny in the peach light that made her pretty. She knew, she knew. What, exactly? Could you fool a woman you made love to? Well, of course you could, he thought. Well, of course you couldn't.

The tears never quite came. A French woman understood love. Its beginning, and its ending. "Shall I see you tomorrow?"

"Not quite sure," he said. "I'll telephone in the afternoon."

"If not, then some other time," she said.

"Yes," he said. "*Au revoir.*" *I'll see you again.*

"*Adieu,*" she said. *Not in this life.*

Later he stood at the door of the apartment on the avenue Hoche. Dawn just breaking, the sky in the window a dozen shades of blue.

He had to ride the trains for long days across the springtime fields. He tried, again and again, to find a reason for what had happened, and was shocked at how broken his heart was. Over the months in Paris he had thought he hated what he did. Maybe not. Out the train window: spring earth, flowering apple trees, villages with bakeries and town halls. He had lost a lot of people, he realized. The obvious ones; Janina the telegraphist, Mademoiselle Herault, Veronique. And the not-so-obvious ones; Genya Beilis, and Fedin. Could someone else do better? Is that what the Sixth Bureau thought? You should be happy to be alive, he told himself savagely. But he wasn't.

Four nights on the beach at Saint-Jean-de-Luz, just north of the Spanish border, where the last Polish ship, the *Batory,* had departed in June of 1940, twelve months earlier. He pretended to be a tourist, a specter from another time, strolled down to the beach at night, then uncovered a hidden bicycle and worked his way north, to a deserted stretch of rocky shore miles from a road. There he sat amid the dune grass, waiting, as the ocean crashed against the beach, but no light signaled. He stayed at a boardinghouse run by a Portuguese couple who had lived in France for thirty years and barely acknowledged that a war was in progress. There were other guests, but they averted their eyes, and there were no conversations. Everybody on the run now, he thought, in every possible direction.

Then at last, on 28 May, a light.

A rubber boat gliding over a calm sea. Two sailors with their faces lamp-blacked, and a man he'd never seen before, perhaps his replacement, brought into shore. Older, heavyset, distinguished, with thick eyebrows. They shook hands and wished each other well.

The sailors worked hard, digging their paddles into the water. The land fell away, France disappeared into the darkness. De Milja knelt in the stern of the little boat. Above the sound of the waves lapping against the beach he could hear a dog barking somewhere on the shore. Two barks, deep and urgent, repeated over and over again.

In London, people seemed pale, cold and polite, bright-eyed with fatigue. They spent their days running a war, which meant questions with no answers and ferocious, bureaucratic infighting. Then at night the bombs whistled down and the city burned.

De Milja was quartered in a small hotel just north of Euston Station. He had braced himself for criticism, or chilly disapproval, even accusations, but none of that happened. Some of the British liaison staff seemed not entirely sure why he'd shown up. Colonel Vyborg was "away." The Polish officers he reported to that May and early June he had never met before. The ZWZ, he realized, had grown up. Had become an institution, with a bottom, a middle and a top. Poles had found their way to England by every conceivable means, ordinary and miraculous. And they all wanted to shoot at somebody. But getting them to that point—fed, dressed, assigned, transported—took an extraordinary effort, a price paid in meetings and memoranda.

This was the war they wanted de Milja to fight. In the course of his debriefing he was told, in a very undramatic way, why he'd been relieved. Somebody somewhere, in the infrastructure that had grown up around the government-in-exile, had decided he'd lost too many people. The senior staff had taken his part, particularly Vyborg and his allies, but that battle had eventually been lost and there were others that had to be fought.

De Milja didn't say a word. The people around the table looked down, cleared their throats, squared the papers in front of them. Of course he'd done well, they said, nobody disputed that. Perhaps he'd just been unlucky. Perhaps it had become accepted doctrine in some quarters that his stars were bad. De Milja was silent, his face was still. Somebody lit a cigarette. Somebody else polished his spectacles. Silence, silence. "What we need you to do now," they said, "is help to run things."

He tried. Sat behind a desk, read reports, wrote notes in the margins, and sent them away. Some came back. Others appeared. A very pleasant colonel, formerly a lawyer in Cracow, took him to an English pub and let him know, very politely, that he wasn't doing all that well. Was something wrong? He tried harder. Then, one late afternoon, he looked up from A's analysis of XYZ and there was Vyborg, framed in the doorway.

Now at least he would have the truth, names and faces filled in. But it wasn't so very different from what he'd been told. This was, he came to realize, not the same world he'd lived in. The Kampfgeschwader 100 operation, for instance, had been canceled. The RAF leadership felt that such guerrilla tactics would lead the Germans to brutalize downed and captured British airmen—the game wasn't worth the candle.

"You're lucky to be out of it," Vyborg said one day at lunch. They ate in a military canteen in Bayswater Road. Women in hairnets served potatoes and cauliflower and canned sausage.

De Milja nodded. Yes, lucky.

Vyborg looked at him closely. "It takes time to get used to a new job."

De Milja nodded again. "I hate it," he said quietly.

Vyborg shrugged. *Too bad.* "Two things, Alexander. This is an army—we tell people what to do and they do it the best they know how. The other thing is that the good jobs are taken. You are not going to Madrid or to Geneva."

Vyborg paused a moment, then continued. "The only person who's hiring right now runs the eastern sector. We have four thousand panzer tanks on the border and prevailing opinion in the bureau says they will be leaving for Moscow on 21 June. Certainly there will be work in Russia, a great deal of work. Because those operatives will not survive. They will be replaced, then replaced again."

"I know," de Milja said.

THE
FOREST

On 21 June 1941, by the Koden bridge over the river Bug, Russian guards—of the Main Directorate of Border Troops under the NKVD—were ordered to execute a spy who had infiltrated Soviet territory three days earlier as part of a provocation intended to cause war. The man, a Wehrmacht trooper, had left German lines a few miles to the west, swum the river just after dark, and asked to see the officer in charge. Through an interpreter he explained he was from Munich, a worker and a lifelong communist. He wished to join the Soviet fighting forces, and he had important information: his unit had orders to attack the Soviet Union at 0300 hours on the morning of 22 June.

The Russian officer telephoned superiors, and the information rose quickly to very senior levels of the counterespionage *apparat*. Likely the Kremlin itself was consulted, likely at very high, the highest, levels. Meanwhile, the deserter was kept in a barracks jail on the Soviet side of the river. The guards tried to communicate with him—sign language, a few words of German. He was one of them, he let them know, and they shared their cigarettes with him and made sure he had a bowl of barley and fat at mealtime.

Late in the afternoon of 21 June, an answer came down from the top: the German deserter is a spy and his mission is provocation: shoot him. The officer in charge was surprised but the order was clear, and he'd been told confidentially that the British Secret Service had orchestrated similar incidents all along the

Soviet/German border—formerly eastern Poland—to foster suspicion, and worse, between the two nations.

The sergeant assigned to take care of the business sighed when he came to collect the deserter. He'd felt some sympathy for the man, but, it seemed, he'd been tricked. Well, that was the world for you. *"Podnimaisa zvieshchami,"* he said to the German. This was formula, part of a ritual language that predated the Revolution and went back to czarist times. *Get going, with things,* it meant. You are going to be executed. If he'd said *Get going, with overcoat, without things,* for example, it would have meant the man was going to be deported, and his blanket and plate should be left behind.

The German didn't understand the words, but he could read the sergeant's expression and could easily enough interpret the significance of the Makarov pistol thrust in his belt. *At least I tried,* he thought. He'd known where this all might lead, now it had led there, now he had to make peace with his gods and say good-bye, and that was that.

They walked, with a guard of three soldiers, to the edge of the river. It was a warm evening, very still, thousands of crickets racketing away, flickers of summer lightning on the horizon. The deserter glanced back over his shoulder as they walked— *anything possible?* The sergeant just shook his head and gave him a fraternal little push in the back—*be a man.* The German took a deep breath, headed where the sergeant pointed and the sergeant shot him in the back of the head.

And again, a coup de grâce in the temple. Then the sergeant signaled to the troopers and they came and took the body away. The sergeant found a stub of cigarette deep in his pocket and lit it in cupped hands, staring across the river. What the hell *were* they doing over there? This was the third night in a row they'd fired up the panzer tank engines—a huge roar that drowned out the crickets—then changed positions, treads clanking away as the iron plates rolled over the dirt.

The sergeant finished his cigarette, then headed back to his barracks. Too bad about the German. That was fate, however, and there was no sense trying to get in its way. But the sergeant was in its way anyhow, some instinct—the rumbling of German tanks—may have been telling him that, and he himself had less than seven hours to live.

3:00 A.M. The sergeant asleep. The sound of German boots thumping across the wooden bridge, calls of "Important business! Important business!" in Russian. The Soviet sentry signaled to the German messengers to wait one moment, and shook the sergeant awake. Grumbling, he worked his feet into his boots and, rubbing his eyes, walked onto the bridge. A brief drumming, orange muzzle flares—the force of the bullets took him and the sentry back through a wooden railing and down into the river.

The sergeant didn't die right away. He lay where he'd fallen, on a gravel bank in the slow, warm river. So he heard running on the bridge, heard the explosions as the barracks were blown apart by hand grenades, heard machine-gun fire and shouts in German as the commandos finished up with the border guards. Dim shapes—German combat engineers—swung themselves beneath the bridge and crawled among the struts, pulling wires out of the explosive charges. *Tell headquarters,* the sergeant thought. A soldier's instinct—*I'm finished but command must know what's happened.* It had, in fact, been tried. A young soldier bleeding on the floor of the guardhouse had managed to get hold of the telephone, but the line was dead. Other units of Regiment 800, the Brandenburgers—the Wehrmacht special-action force—some of them Russian-speaking, had been at work for hours, and telegraph and telephone wires had been cut all along the front lines.

The sergeant lost consciousness, then was brought back one last time. By a thousand artillery pieces fired in unison; the riverbed shook with the force of it. Overhead, hundreds of Luftwaffe fighters and bombers streaked east to destroy the Soviet air force on its airfields. Three million German troops crossed the border, thousands of Soviet troops, tens of thousands, would join the sergeant in the river by morning.

Soviet radio transmissions continued. The German Funk-abwehr recorded an exchange near the city of Minsk. To head-quarters: "We are being fired on. What should we do?" The response: "You must be insane. And why is this message not in code?"

The sergeant died sometime after dawn. By then, hundreds of tanks had rolled across the Koden bridge because it was the Schwerpunkt—the spearpoint—of the blitzkrieg in the region of the Brest fortress. Just to the south, the Koden railroad bridge, also secured by the Brandenburgers, was made ready to serve in an immense resupply effort to fighting units advancing at an extraordinary rate. By the following evening young Rus-sian reservists were boarding trains, cardboard suitcases in hand, heading off to report to mobilization centers already occupied by Wehrmacht troops.

Days of glory. The Germans advanced against Soviet armies completely in confusion. Hitler had been right—"Just kick in the door and the whole thing will come tumbling down." Soviet air cover was blown up, ammunition used up, no food, tanks destroyed. Russians attacked into enfilading machine-gun fire and were mown down by the thousands. Nothing stopped the panzer tanks, great engines rumbling across the steppe. Some peasants came out of their huts and stared. Others, Ukrainians, offered bread and salt to the conquerors who had come to free them from the Bolshevik yoke.

Yet, here and there, every now and again, there were strange and troublesome events. Five commissars firing pistols from a schoolhouse until they were killed. A single rifleman holding up an advance for ten minutes. When they found his body, his dog was tied to a nearby tree with a rope, as though he had, some-how, expected to live through the assault. A man came out of a house and threw two hand grenades. Somehow this wasn't like the blitzkriegs in western Europe. They found a note folded into an empty cartridge case and hidden in a tree by the highway to Minsk. "Now there are only three of us left. We shall stand firm as long as there's any life left in us. Now I am alone, wounded in my arm and my head. The number of tanks has increased. There are twenty-three. I shall probably die. Somebody may find my note and remember me: I am a Russian from Frunze. I have no parents. Good-bye, dear friends. Your Alexander Vinogradov."

The German advance continued, nothing could stop it, whole armies were encircled. Yet, still, there was resistance, and something in its nature was deeply disturbing. They had attacked the U.S.S.R. But it was Russia that fought back.

10 October 1941. 11:45 P.M. Near the Koden bridge.

The Wehrmacht was long gone now. They were busy fighting to the east, on the highway to Moscow. Now it was quiet again—quiet as any place where three nations mixed. The Ukraine, Byelorussia, and Poland. "Thank heaven," Razakavia would say, "we are all such good friends." People laughed when he said that—a little tentatively at first until they were sure he meant them to, then a big, loud, flattering laugh. He was tall and bony, with the blowing white hair and white beard of an Old Testament prophet. But the similarity ended there. A pucker scar marked the back of his neck—bullet in 1922—and a rifle was slung across his back. Razakavia was a leader—of outcasts, of free men and women, of bandits. It depended who you asked.

Razakavia pulled his sheepskin jacket tight around him and leaned closer to his horse's neck. "Cold, Miszka. Hurry up a little." The pony obliged, the rhythm of his trot a beat or two faster. It was cold—Razakavia could smell winter hiding in the autumn air, and the moonlight lay hard on the white-frosted fields. He reached into a pocket and pulled out a railroad watch. Getting toward midnight. Up ahead of him he could hear Frantek's pony. Frantek was fourteen, Razakavia's best scout. He carried no rifle, only a pistol buried in his clothing—so he could play the innocent traveler as long as possible, should they chance to meet a stranger on the trails they rode. Somewhere behind Razakavia was Kotior, his second-in-command, a machine gun resting across his saddle.

They had ridden these fields before. This operation had been attempted twice since the end of September. Razakavia didn't like it, but he had no choice. The people who had arrived in the wake of the Wehrmacht—the SS, German administrators, murder squads hunting Jews, all sorts really, were not much to his taste. He was used to fighting the Polish gendarmerie, not themselves so very appealing, frankly, but a fact of life and something he'd got used to. These new lords and masters were worse. They were also temporary. They didn't understand what was going to happen to them, and that made them more dangerous as allies than they were as enemies. So he needed some new allies.

Frantek appeared just ahead of him, his horse standing still with breath steaming from its nose and mouth. The river was visible from here, not frozen yet but very slow and thick. Razakavia pulled his pony up, twenty seconds later Kotior arrived. The three sat in a row but did not speak—voices carried a long way at night. The wind sighed here as it climbed the hillside above the river, and Razakavia listened carefully to it for a time until he could make out the whine of an airplane engine. So, perhaps this time it would work. Frantek pointed: a few degrees west of north, a mile or so from where the river Bug met the Lesna. A triangle of fires suddenly appeared, sparks flying up into the still air. Frantek looked at him expectantly, waiting for orders.

Razakavia didn't move—always he weighed the world around him for a moment before he did anything—then chucked the reins and the three of them trotted off in the direction of the fires.

He had six men in the meadow, where the hay had been cut a month earlier. They stood with rifles slung, warming their hands over the signal fires, faces red in the flickering light. The sound of the plane's engines grew louder and louder, then it faded and moved away into the distance. Above, three white flowers came floating to earth.

At Razakavia's right hand, Frantek watched avidly. Such things intrigued him—airplanes, parachutes. The world had come here along with the war, and Frantek was being educated by both at once. Kotior just glanced up, then scanned the perimeter. He was not quick of mind, but he killed easily and good-naturedly, and he was remorselessly loyal.

The white flowers were just overhead now and Razakavia could see what they were. As he'd been promised, a Polish officer and two crates of explosives. It is a long life, Razakavia thought, one takes the bad with the good.

Captain Alexander de Milja was the last to leave the plane, the other two operatives—an explosives expert and a political courier—had jumped when they got to the outskirts of Warsaw. His body ached from the ride, six and a half hours in a four-engine Halifax, every bolt and screw vibrating, and the cold air ferocious as it flowed through the riveted panels. He hoped this was the right triangle of fires below him—and that the builders of these brush piles had not changed sides while the Halifax droned across Europe. He was, in truth, a rich prize: $18,000 in czarist gold rubles, $50,000 in American paper money. A fortune once converted to zlotys or occupation currency. German cigarettes and German razor blades, warm clothing, two VIS pistols—WZ 35s with the Polish eagle engraved on the slide, and a hundred rounds of ammunition. He might very well do them more good simply murdered and stripped, he thought. No, he *would* do them more good that way, because he was not here to do them good.

He had been forced to wait four months to return to Poland, because the distance from London to Warsaw was 900 miles—

in fact Route One, over Denmark, was 960 miles and de Milja had to go a hundred miles farther east. Route Two, over Göteberg, Sweden, was even longer. The normal range of the Halifax bomber was 1,500 miles, the normal load capacity, 4,180 pounds. With the addition of an extra fuel tank, the range increased to 2,100 miles—the bomber could now fly home after dropping its cargo—but the load capacity decreased to 2,420 pounds; of guns, ammunition, medical supplies, people: and the crew had to be reduced from nine to seven.

The airspeed of the Halifax was 150 miles an hour, thus a trip of 2,000 miles was going to take thirteen hours—discounting the wind as a factor. Those thirteen hours had to be hours of darkness, from 5:00 P.M. in London to 6:00 A.M. the following morning. And that was cutting it close. The flight could only be made when there was enough of a moon to see the confluence of rivers that would mark the drop zone. This period, the second and third phases of the moon, was code-named *Tercet*. So the first Tercet with sufficient darkness was 7 October—in fact it was 10 October before he actually took off. That was the moment when there was just enough autumn darkness and just enough moonlight to give the operation a chance of success.

They'd taken him by car to Newmarket racecourse, where the special services had built a secret airfield to house the 138th Squadron—British and Polish aircrews. A final check of his pockets: no London bus tickets, no matchboxes with English words. He was now Roman Brzeski, a horse breeder from Chelm. As he waited to board the plane, a jeep drove across the tarmac and stopped by his side. Vyborg climbed out, holding on to his uniform cap in the backwash from the Halifax's propellers. The engines were very loud, and Vyborg had to shout as he shook hands. "You'll be careful?"

"I will."

"Need anything?"

"No."

"Well . . . No end to it, is there?"

De Milja gave him a mock salute.

"Good luck," Vyborg said. "Good luck."

De Milja nodded that he understood.

One of the partisans came into the hut well before dawn, nudging de Milja and the others with his boot. "Work today. Work today," he said. De Milja got one eye open. "Move your bones, dear friends. Prove you're not dead." He gave de Milja, the honored guest, an extra little kick in the ankle and left the hut.

De Milja shuddered in the cold as he worked himself free of the blanket. Through the open door he could see black night, a slice of moon. There would be a skim of ice on the water barrel, white mist hanging in the birch trees. Beside him, Kotior rolled over and sat up slowly, held his face in his hands, cursed the cold, the Russians, the Germans, what women had between their legs, the guard, the forest, and life itself. De Milja forced his swollen feet into his boots, sat up, touched his face—two weeks' growth of beard, chapped skin—and scratched his ankles where he'd been bitten the night before.

There was a small iron stove in a hut where food was cooked. A young woman handed him a metal cup of powerful, scalding tea; it warmed him and woke him up when he drank it. The woman was dark, muffled in kerchiefs and layers of clothing. "Another cup, sir?"

Educated, he thought, from the pitch of the voice. Perhaps a Jew. "Please," de Milja said. He held the cup in both hands and let the steam warm his face. Razakavia's band, about forty men and fifteen women, came from everywhere: a few Russian soldiers, escaped from Wehrmacht encirclement; a few Jews, escaped from the German roundups; a few criminals, escaped from Ukrainian and Byelorussian jails; a few Poles, who'd fled from the Russian deportations of 1939; a few Byelorussians—army deserters, nationalists—who'd fled Polish administration before the Russian occupation. To de Milja it seemed as though half the world had nowhere to go but the forest. He finished the tea and handed the cup back to the young woman. "Thank you," he said. "It was very good."

Later he rode beside Razakavia—as always, Kotior somewhere behind them. They had given him, as the honored guest, a Russian *panje* horse to ride. She was small, with a thick mane and shaggy coat. When the band stopped for a moment, she grazed on whatever weeds happened to be there, apparently she could eat anything at all. They had also given him, as the honored guest who brought explosives and gold coins, one of the better weapons in their armory: a Simonov automatic rifle with a ten-shot magazine box forward of the trigger guard, and two hundred rounds of 7.62 ammunition.

As they rode two by two on a forest trail, Razakavia explained that a courier had reached them with intelligence from local railwaymen: a small train was due, late in the day, carrying soldiers being rotated back for leave in Germany, some of them walking wounded. There would also be flatcars of damaged equipment, scheduled for repair at the Pruszkow Tank Works outside Warsaw. The train was from the Sixth Panzer Division, fighting 400 miles east at Smolensk.

"We watched them brought up to the line in late summer," Razakavia told him. "A hundred and sixty trains, we counted. About fifty cars each. Tanks and armored cars and ammunition and horses—and the men. Very splendid, the Germans. Nothing they don't have, makes you wonder what they want from us."

At noon they left the forest, and rode for a time along the open steppe. It was cold and gray and wet; they rode past smashed Russian tanks and trucks abandoned during the June retreat, then moved back into the forest for an hour, watered the horses at a stream, and emerged at a point where the railroad line passed about a hundred yards from the birch groves. The line was a single track that seemed to go from nowhere to nowhere, disappearing into the distance on either end. "This goes northwest to Baranovici," Razakavia told him. "Then to Minsk, Orsha, Smolensk, and Viazma. Eventually to Mozhaisk, and Moscow. It is the lifeline of the Wehrmacht Army Group Center. Our Russians tell us that a German force cannot survive more than sixty miles from a railhead."

A man called Bronstein assembled the bomb for the rails. A Soviet army ammunition box, made of zinc, was filled with cheddite. British, in this case, from the honored guest, though the ZWZ in Poland also manufactured the product. A compression fuse, made of a sulfuric-acid vial and paper impregnated with potassium chloride, was inserted beneath the lid of the box.

De Milja sat by Bronstein as the bomb was put together. "Where did you learn to do that?" he asked.

"I was a teacher of science," Bronstein said, "in Brest Litovsk." He took the cigarette from his mouth and set it on a stone while he packed cheddite into the box. "And this is science."

They dug a hole beneath the rail and inserted the mine, the weight of the locomotive would do the rest. A scout—Frantek—came galloping up to Razakavia just as it began to get dark. "It comes now," he said.

The band settled into positions at the edge of the forest. De Milja lay on his stomach, using a rotten log for cover, feeling the cold from the earth seeping up into his body. The train came slowly, ten miles an hour, in case the track was sabotaged. It was. Bronstein's device worked—a dull bang, a cloud of dirt blown sideways from beneath the creeping locomotive, wheels ripping up the ties, then the locomotive heeling over slowly as a jet of white steam hissed from its boiler. A man screamed. A German machine-gun crew on a platform mounted toward the rear of the train began to traverse the forest.

De Milja sighted down the barrel of the Simonov. From the slats of a cattle car he could see pinpricks of rifle fire. He returned it, squeezing off ten rounds, then changing magazines as

bullets rattled in the branches above his head. One of Razakavia's men leaped from a depression in the earth on the other
side of the track and threw a bomb into the last car on the train.
The walls blew out and the wooden frame started to burn. German riflemen, some wearing white bandages, jumped out of the
train on the side away from the gunfire and began to shoot from
behind the wheels of the cars. De Milja heard a cry from his left,
a bullet smacked into his log. He aimed carefully and fired off his
magazine, then looked up. A figure in field gray had slumped beneath the train, the wind flapping a bandage that had come loose
from his head. De Milja changed magazines again. Some of the
German soldiers were shooting from behind a tank chained to a
flatcar, de Milja could hear the ricochet as gunfire from the forest hit the iron armor.

Another group of Germans began firing from the coal tender,
half on, half off the rails where the locomotive had dragged it,
and the machine gun came back to life. De Milja heard the sharp
whistle that meant it was time to break off the engagement and
head back into the forest.

He ran with the others, his breath coming in harsh gasps, up a
slight rise to where several young women were guarding the
ponies. They left immediately on orders from Kotior, two
wounded men slung sideways across the backs of the horses. A
third man was shot too badly to move, and Razakavia had to finish him off with a pistol. The rest of the band rode off at a fast
trot, vanishing into the forest as the railcar burned brightly in
the gray evening.

"The Germans, they always counterattack," Kotior told
him. "Always." He pointed up at several Fiesler-Storch reconnaissance planes, little two-seater things that buzzed back and
forth above the forest. "This is how partisans die," Kotior
added.

They were up there all night, crisscrossing the dark sky. So
there could be no fires, no smoking outside the huts. De Milja

pulled the blanket tight around his shoulders and loaded box magazines. The cold made his fingers numb, and the springs, like everything Russian, were too strong, tended to snap the feeder bar back into place, ejecting the bullet two feet in the air and producing a snarl of laughter from Kotior. Four hundred miles to the east, on the line Smolensk/Roslavl/Bryansk, the Wehrmacht was fighting. How the hell did they manage in this kind of cold? he wondered. And it was only October. At night the temperature fell and the puddles froze and huge clouds gathered in the sky, but it did not snow. And in the morning it was blue and sunny: *winter isn't coming this year.*

At dawn, an alert. De Milja in position on the camp perimeter, aiming into the forest gloom. Somewhere south, perhaps a mile away, he could hear the faint popping of riflery, then the chatter of a light machine gun. Two scouts arrived at midday—they'd had a brush with a Ukrainian SS unit. "They shot at us," the scout said. "And we shot back. So they fired the machine gun." He was about fifteen, grinned like a kid. "Frantek went around and he got one of them, we think. They were screaming and, yelling 'fucking Bolsheviks' and every kind of thing like that. Calling for God."

"Where is Frantek?" Razakavia said.

The boy shrugged. "He led them away into the marsh. He'll be back."

"*Banderovsty.*" Razakavia spat the word.

He meant Ukrainian nationalists under the command of the leader Bandera, absorbed into an SS regiment called the Nachtigall. Kotior turned to de Milja and explained. "They do what the SS won't."

With Razakavia and Kotior he went to a town on the outskirts of Brest Litovsk. The owner of a bakery sold them milled oats and rye flour for bread. "We pay for this," Razakavia told him as they knocked at the back door. "Not everyone does." There was an ancient relationship in these lands, de Milja knew, between groups of armed men and keepers of granaries. Both sides had to survive, together they defined where honor might lie.

The iron door swung open and a hot wind, heavy with the smell of baking bread, swept over de Milja. "Come in," the baker said. He had a pink face, and a big belly in an undershirt. They sat at a marble-top table, there was flour everywhere. The baker wiped his hands on his shirt and accepted a cigarette from Razakavia. Behind him the brick ovens were at work, with sometimes a lick of flame where the furnace doors didn't quite meet. A black bread was brought over and cut up with a saw-tooth knife.

Razakavia and the baker talked about the weather. The baker shook his head grimly. "All the old *babas* have been reading the signs. Caterpillars and geese and bear scat. Probably nonsense, but even if it is, they're all saying the same thing: it's going to freeze your balls off."

Razakavia nodded and chewed on a piece of bread. He reached into a pocket and counted out zlotys he'd bought with the gold rubles. The money lay in stacks on the marble table.

"It's in the barn in the village of Krymno," the baker said. "You know where I mean? The same as last spring. In wooden bins."

"I remember," Razakavia said.

"You want to take care on the roads, over there."

"What's going on?"

"I don't know. Somebody goes out and doesn't come back. Somebody else has to give up a horse. People moving around in the forest."

"A partisan band?"

"Who knows? These days it could be anything." He nodded at de Milja. "Who's your friend?"

"One of us. He's from down in the Volhynia."

"Polish?"

"Yes," de Milja said.

"One of my grandmothers was Polish," the baker said. "Crazy, she was. All with spells and potions and times of the moon, but good to us. Always jam or a little cake." The baker's face softened as he remembered. He put out a hand and de Milja shook it. "Times change, maybe we can have something to drink," he said.

De Milja smiled. "Better have it now," he said.

The baker laughed. "Well," he said.

The dirt track back to the forest went through a little settlement called Gradh. They smelled smoke a mile away, walked the horses in a wide circle around the village. Near the old Jewish cemetery was a great scar of newly packed earth, they saw a lost shoe and a bloody shirt. Above the village, ravens circled in a haze of dirty gray smoke.

"It was a Jewish town," Razakavia said.

The weather. At first you didn't notice. A leaf fell. You put on a jacket, took it off later. Then suddenly it tried to kill you, you hid from it as best you could but it seemed to search, to seek you out. In the swamps and woodlands there was mist, snow showers, a freeze, a thaw, heavy rain; then impossible, unimaginable mud. Like dull-minded peasants, de Milja and Frantek would stand by the road—the "road," the "Moscow highway"—and stare at the German columns. Some days the equipment could move, some days it ground the lightly frozen earth into the mud below, and sank. At night they could hear the panzer tanks—every four hours the engines had to be run to a hundred and forty degrees Fahrenheit, which took about fifteen minutes. Then they had to move the tanks around, to use the transmissions—because the oil was of too low a viscosity to protect the gears. Razakavia's forest was well behind the front lines, a night attack was unlikely. But the Germans could not be sure, and the Soviet air force sent over a plane to harass them now and then, to stir up the defenses on icy nights.

The partisans attacked a repair train the following week. This time Bronstein's bomb derailed all seven cars, and some of the railway workers tried to surrender, as did a Wehrmacht railroad officer. But every German was shot down, as well as most of the Poles and Ukrainians who worked on the track. The partisans looted the train, taking tools and coal and cigarettes and ammunition. One of the Polish laborers, lightly wounded, pleaded for mercy. Frantek worked the bolt on his rifle, but de Milja stepped between them. "Leave him to me," he said.

The man fell on his knees and tried to wrap his arms around de Milja's legs. "Mercy," he said.

De Milja took him by the shoulder of his jacket and hauled him to his feet. "Stop it," he hissed in Polish. The man wept. "I have children," he said. "Four children, little girls."

De Milja saw Razakavia staring at him coldly: take him as a gift, but don't ask for another. "It's all right," de Milja said. "You can come with us."

All around him, in the smoking wreckage of the repair train—a tangle of coaches with smashed windows, a flatcar with a crane bent at right angles—single shots rang out as the crew was finished off.

The man de Milja had saved was, by trade, a cobbler, and spent his first days in the encampment sewing boots and improvising repairs of all kinds. De Milja took him, late one afternoon, to a village near the forest, where a young widow sold vodka. If you paid a little extra you could drink it in a toolshed behind her house—she would even supply a few sticks of wood for the stove.

"My family is from Rovno, south of the Pripet marsh," the man explained. "Life wasn't so bad. The Poles had to watch it down there, but there was plenty of work, the police protected us, we had everything we needed. Maybe a little more."

He took a pull from the vodka bottle, wiped his mustache with his fingers. Outside it was growing dark, and rain drummed on the roof of the shed. "Then, September of '39.

The Russians came and occupied the town. We were working people, didn't put on airs, and we'd always been decent to the peasants, so when the commissars appointed a council of workers, they spared us, and let us go on with our lives. Very honestly, a lot of them had boots for the first time—it was the deportees who went barefoot—so they needed us and they knew it.

"Still, some of my family didn't fare so well. One of my sisters was a nun, she disappeared. Another sister was married to a clerk in the district administration—they were sent east in freight cars. Gone. Door of the house banging in the wind, dinner rotting on the table. Make your heart sick to see it. My brother was a sergeant in the army. He'd been captured in the first days of the invasion, but maybe that was better for him. At least he wasn't arrested, and he came from a unit that had laid down their guns when the Soviet troops said they'd arrived to fight the Germans.

"So him they sent to a prisoner-of-war camp, an NKVD camp called Ostashkov, not far from Smolensk. They really didn't seem to know what they wanted to do with them. The officers—mostly reserve officers; engineers, teachers, doctors—they took them away, rumor was to a camp in the Katyn forest. Stefan, that's my brother, and the other enlisted men, they just sat there and starved. Finally, they sent him to Moscow."

"*Moscow!* It's true?"

"It's true, I swear it. What happened to Stefan was, the Russians thought he was one of them. Almost by accident—but then, that's how he is. He's not like me, doesn't matter what I try it goes wrong. But Stefan's not like that—if the world had gone on like it always did, he'd be doing very well now."

The cobbler took another pull at the vodka. He looked off into the dusk, watching fondly as his brother did well.

"What happened?" de Milja said. "At the camp."

"Oh. He befriended one of the NKVD men."

"A political officer?"

"No! Nothing like that—a sergeant, just like him. This man had a hunting dog, a spaniel bitch, and his pleasure was to go into the marsh with this dog and perhaps shoot a duck or two and the dog would go into the reeds and bring them back. But the dog got hurt, and it wouldn't eat, and it was dying. Stefan found out about it, and he told the NKVD man what to do, and the dog got better. And that was the end of it—except that it wasn't. One day the man came to where he was kept and said, 'You're going to have a choice. Everybody here is going to a new camp, in the Katyn forest. For you, it's better to tell them that you want to go to school, in Moscow.' And that's what Stefan did."

"And then?"

"Well, he came home."

"Just like that?"

The cobbler shrugged. "Yes."

"A free man?"

"Well, yes. For a time, anyhow."

"What happened?"

"Poor Stefan."

"Another drink? There's a little left."

"Yes, all right, thank you. I owe you my life, you know."

"Oh, anyone would have done what I did. But, ah, what happened to Stefan?"

"Too strong, Stefan. Sometimes it isn't for the best. He went into the town, I don't know why. And some German didn't like his looks, and they asked for his papers, and Stefan hit him."

"In Rovno, this was?"

"Yes. He managed to run away—a friend saw it and told us. But then they caught him. They beat him up and took him off in one of those black trucks, and now he's in Czarny prison." The cobbler looked away, his face angry and bitter. "They are going to hang him."

"He has a family?"

"Oh yes. Just like me."

"Name the same as yours?"

"Yes. Krewinski, just like mine. Why wouldn't it be?"

"Don't get angry."

"Shameful thing. It's the Russians' fault, they won't leave us alone." He paused a moment, took another sip of vodka. "You think there's hope? I mean, we're told to pray for this and for that. We're told there's always hope. Do you think that's true?"

De Milja thought it over. "Well," he said at last, "there's always hope. But I think you ought to pray for his soul. That might be the best thing."

The cobbler shook his head in reluctant agreement. "Poor Stefan," he said, wiping the tears from his eyes.

Kotior commanded the unit sent off to Krymno to retrieve the grain. He was accompanied by Frantek, his fellow scout Pavel, an older man called Korbin, de Milja, and two Ukrainian peasant girls who drove the farm wagons. The rifles were hidden under burlap sacks in the wagons.

They rode all morning, along a track that wound through water meadows, fields of reeds rustling as they swayed in the wind, the air chill and heavy. The village was no more than fifteen miles from Brest but it lay beyond the forest, some distance into the marshland along a tributary of the river Pripet. A few wooden huts, a farm with stone barns, then reeds again, pools of black, still water, and windswept sky to the horizon on every side.

The farm dogs snarled at them as they rode up and the peasant who tended the farm came out of his house with a battered shotgun riding the crook of his arm. The man spoke some form of local dialect de Milja could barely understand but Kotior told him to call the dogs off, dismounted, and explained slowly who they were and what they had come for. Then they all went into the barn—warmed by a cow, smelling of dung and damp straw, the dogs drinking eagerly at pools of water where grain stalks had fermented.

"Where is the rest?" Kotior asked, standing in front of empty wooden bins.

The peasant, agitated now, seemed to be telling Kotior a long and complicated story. Kotior nodded, a reasonable man who would accept whatever he was told, then suddenly barred a forearm across the peasant's throat and forced him back against a wall. A Russian bayonet—four-edged, it made a cross-shaped wound—had appeared in his hand and he held the point under the man's chin. The shotgun dropped to the floor. The dogs went wild, but Frantek kicked one and it ran away with the rest following.

The peasant didn't struggle, his face went passive as he pre-pared to die. Then Kotior let him go. "He says the grain was taken away. By a detachment of partisans. He thinks they intend to come back for the rest of it." After some discussion they de-cided to wait, at least until morning. They pulled the wagons into the barn, posted Frantek and Pavel at the two ends of the settlement, and took turns sleeping.

They came at dawn. Pavel sounded the alarm in time for them to set up an ambush. At Kotior's direction, de Milja was in the hayloft of the barn, the Simonov covering the road below.

The column appeared from the gray mist, silent but for the sound of hooves on the muddy road. There were forty of them, well armed. He saw several automatic rifles, several *pepechas*—Russian submachine guns—a few weapons he could not iden-tify. Otherwise they looked like the Razakavia band. They wore wool jackets and peaked caps and boots, sometimes a military coat or trousers. The leader, de Milja guessed he was the leader, had a pair of binoculars on a strap and a holstered pistol.

The peasant came out of the barn and raised his hand. The column stopped. The leader—de Milja had been right—climbed off his horse and led it forward. De Milja sighted on him. He was perhaps forty, a Slav, clean-shaven, something of the soldier in the way he held his shoulders. He talked with the peasant for a time. Then Kotior came out of the barn and joined the conversation, eventually signaling to de Milja that he should come down.

They were joined by another man, who the leader referred to as *politruk*. The conversation was very tense. "He has told me they are taking the grain," Kotior said evenly. "Requisitioned," the leader said in Russian. "For partisan operations."

"We are also partisans," Kotior said.

"Not bandits, perhaps?"

"Polish partisans."

"Then we are friends," the politruk said. "Poland and the Soviet Union. Allies." He wore a leather coat, had cropped fair hair and albino coloring. His hands were deep in his pockets— de Milja could almost see the NKVD-issue Makarov in there. "This matter of the grain, a misunderstanding," he said.

Kotior and de Milja were silent.

"Best to come back to our camp, we can sit down and talk this out."

"Another time, perhaps," de Milja said.

The politruk was angry. "War doesn't wait," he said.

De Milja saw no signal, but the mounted partisans shifted, some of them moving out of de Milja's line of sight.

"I think it would be best . . ." The politruk stopped in mid-sentence. De Milja watched his eyes, then turned to see what he was looking at. One of the wagons was moving slowly out of the barn, the pair of shaggy horses trudging through the mud. The Ukrainian girl held the reins in the crook of her knee and was pointing a rifle at the two Russians. The leader made a gesture—*enough,* let it go. Frantek rode up, pistol in one hand, face pinched like an angry child. In his other hand, the reins of de Milja's and Kotior's horses. When he spat, meaningfully, down into the dirt, the politruk blinked.

De Milja put a foot in the stirrup and swung up on the pony. The politruk and the leader stared without expression as the unit rode off, walking the horses at wagon speed. The skies over the marsh were alive, broken gray cloud blown west, and a few dry flakes of snow drifting down.

"We'll need a rear guard," de Milja said to Kotior as the settlement fell behind them.

"Yes, I know. You stay, with Frantek." He paused. "I can understand most Russians when they speak, we all can in this place. But what is a *politruk?*"

"It means *political officer.*"

Kotior shrugged—that was to raise life to a level where it only pretended to exist. "We'll need an hour," he said, gesturing at the wagons. "At least that."

"You will have it," de Milja said.

There wasn't much cover. Frantek and de Milja rode at the back of the column until they found a low hill with a grove of pine trees that marked the edge of the forest east of Brest. There they waited, watching the dirt road below them, the cold working its way through their sheepskins.

Frantek seemed, to de Milja, to have been born to the life he lived. His parents had gone to market one Saturday morning and never come home. So, at the age of twelve, he had gone to the forest and found Razakavia. The forest bands always needed scouts, and Frantek and his friends knew it. Now he leaned back against a tree, folded his arms around his rifle and across his chest, and pulled his knees up, completely at rest except for his eyes, slitted against the snow, watching the approaches to the hilltop.

"Do you like the life in the forest?" de Milja asked him, tired of listening to the wind.

Frantek thought it over. "I miss my dog," he said. "Her name was Chaya."

The Russians came thirty minutes later, four scouts riding single file. One of them dismounted, squatted, determined that the horse droppings were fresh, and climbed back on his horse.

They moved slowly, at wagon speed, waiting for the band to leave the steppe and enter the forest.

"Do not fire," de Milja said to Frantek as they flattened out behind the pine trees. "That is an order," he added.

Frantek acknowledged it—barely. To him, de Milja seemed cautious, even hesitant, and he'd killed enough to know how attentive it made people. But he'd also come across many inexplicable things in his short life and he'd decided that de Milja was just one more.

De Milja sighted down the Simonov at four hundred yards. *Ping.* That animated the Russians and drew an appreciative chuckle from Frantek. They leaped off their horses and went flat on the ground. Disciplined, they did not fire their rifles. They waited. Ten long minutes.

"Mine is on the far left," Frantek said, squinting through his gunsight.

"Not yet," de Milja said.

One of the Russian scouts rose to one knee, rifle at his hip swinging back and forth across the axis of the road. Then he stood.

"Now?" said Frantek.

"No."

The scout retrieved his horse. Climbed up in the saddle. *Ping.*

At first, de Milja was afraid he'd miscalculated and killed him, because he seemed to fly off the horse, which shied and galloped a few yards. And the other three scouts returned fire, including a long staccato rattle, at least half a drum of pepecha rounds. Some of it in their direction—a white mark chipped in a tree trunk, the sound of canvas ripping overhead—but not the sort of enthusiastic concentration that would mean the scouts knew where they were. Then the man de Milja had fired at moved, changed positions, scuttling along low to the ground and throwing himself flat.

De Milja's greatest worry was Frantek, an excellent shot with young eyes. But discipline held. De Milja extended his left hand, palm flat, fingers slightly spread: *hold on, do nothing.* Frantek pressed himself against the earth, outraged he had to endure this insulting gunfire but, for the moment, under control.

The wind rose, snowflakes spun through the air, swirling like dust and whitening the dirt road. It saved their lives, Razakavia said later. "Russians read snow like priests read Bibles." Or, perhaps, that day, nobody wanted to die.

The Russians mounted their horses, slow and deliberate under the eyes of the unseen riflemen, and rode back the way they came.

De Milja had been ice inside for a long time—there wasn't any other way for him to do what he had to do—but Rovno scared him. The Germans had it all their own way in Rovno. The SS were everywhere, death's-head insignia and lightning flashes, a certain walk, a certain smile. The Einsatzgruppen came through, on the way to murder Jews in another ghetto somewhere, there were Ukrainian SS, Latvian SS, and German criminals, alley killers the Nazi recruiters had quarried from the prisons since 1927. As well as those ordinary Germans, always liked by their neighbors, who, given the opportunity, turned out to be not so very mild-mannered after all. They were the worst, and one taste of blood was all it took.

De Milja met their eyes in Rovno. He dared not be furtive. So he returned the stares, trudged along in the snow, cold and absentminded and absorbed in his business. And armed. It went against the current wisdom—one street search and you were finished. But he would not be taken alive. The cyanide capsule sewn in the point of his shirt collar was the last resort, but the VIS snugged against the small of his back gave him at least the illusion of survival.

The ZWZ secret mail system operated all over Poland, mostly out of dress shops, with couriers carrying letters from city to city. De Milja had used it to report the Russian contact and that had produced a request—delivered in a park in Brest Litovsk—for a meeting in Rovno. With Major Olenik, his former superior in Warsaw and, now that he was no longer under the direct orders of the Sixth Bureau in London, his superior once again.

Rovno had always been a border city—a Polish possession, claimed by Russia, populated by Ukrainians. Narrow streets, brick buildings darkened by factory smoke, November ice, November fog, Gestapo cars with chains on the tires.

"They will yet take Moscow," Olenik said. "Or maybe not. The Russians have introduced a weapon they call the Katyusha rocket, also known as the Stalin Organ—multiple rockets fired simultaneously from a launcher that can be towed by a truck. The Germans don't like it. They are afraid of it—they ran away from it up in Smolensk. And the Russians have a new tank, the T-34. German shells bounce off. If they can produce enough of them, they'll shut the panzer divisions down. There's that, and the fact that our weather people predict December temperatures outside Moscow of sixty-five degrees below zero. We'll see what *that* does to their *Wehrwille.*"

The word meant *war will,* a cherished German idea: who wants most to win, wins.

De Milja and Olenik sat in the parlor of a safe house in Rovno, a small apartment, old-fashioned, as though a couple had grown old there and never changed anything. It was all curtains and doilies and clocks with loud ticks—a certain musty smell, a certain silence. De Milja wondered what it would be like in the forest at sixty-five degrees below zero. Olenik apparently read his mind. "We expect you'll finish up before then," he said.

Olenik hadn't changed. Narrow shoulders, tousled gray hair and mustache, pockmarked skin—triumphantly seedy in a worn gray cardigan, you'd walk past him and never see him on any street in the world. He rummaged in a briefcase, found a pipe, fussed with it until he got it lit, then searched again until he found a single sheet of yellowish newsprint. "Have a look," he said.

The newspaper was called *Miecz i Mlot—Sword and Hammer*. It was published in Polish by the League of Friends of the Soviet Union and the PPR, the Polska Partia Robotnicza, the Polish Workers' Party.

"It comes from Bialystok," Olenik said. "From Stryj and Brody and Wilno. From Brest and Rovno. All over the eastern districts. Curious, with a hundred and sixty-five newspapers issued by underground presses in Poland, including every prewar party, socialist, and peasant and all the rest of it, we now see this. Reference to a *communist* underground in Poland. If it exists, we don't know about it. If it exists, it does nothing *but* exist, but that may be just precisely to the point. Its existence will make it easier for them to say, later on, that the communist state of Poland was preceded by a communist underground."

De Milja handed the newspaper back and Olenik returned it to his briefcase. "Of course," Olenik said, "we're not spending life and money to find out what the Russians think about us. They enslaved us for a hundred and twenty years. Attacked in 1920. Attacked again in 1939. And they'll be coming back this way, pushing a wave of Wehrmacht gray in front of them. We have to decide what to do then.

"If they go all the way to the Oder, to the Rhine, we're done for—they'll occupy the country. It's that simple. So what we may have to do is, at the right moment, throw the Germans out by ourselves and declare a free Polish state, recognition by the British and the Americans to follow. That means a rising, and a terrible price to pay in blood.

"The alternative: reveal Soviet intentions—stick a knife in Stalin before he can get to the conference table. Britain won't give him Poland, but the Americans are blind to life beyond their oceans." He stopped for a moment and seemed to drift, then spoke again in a softer voice. "If you're a small country and you have a bully for a neighbor, God help you, because nobody else will. You're alone. You'll cry out in the night, but nobody will come.''

He stopped abruptly, had said more of what was in his heart than he'd meant to. He cleared his throat. "What matters now," he went on, "are the particular and demonstrable intentions of the Soviet state. If their partisan units take food without paying for it—and they do. If those partisan units have political officers—and they do. If they are forcing Poles to fight in those units and burning down villages that resist, and we know they are doing that, too, then they are acting, according to their own rules, like people fighting in an enemy country among enemies.''

"It was certainly that way in Krymno," de Milja said. "And we were asked—that's not really the word for the way it was put—to follow them to their camp.''

"Two of our people, in the northern Polesian district, did just that. They believed they were going somewhere to sit down and work out an agreement. One is dead. The other, we're told, is in the Lubianka. So we are both fighting the Germans, but we are not allies.''

He stopped a moment, considered what he would say next. "So," he said. "We, I mean London and Warsaw, we are interested in the story of Sergeant Krewinski, the brother of the man captured in the attack on the repair train.''

"The man in Rovno prison?''

"Yes. What we want you to do now, Captain, is to force Rovno prison. Liberate Krewinski—and two ZWZ officers who are also being held there. All are going to be executed.''

De Milja met the major's eyes, but his look was opaque and distant. There'd been three attempts on German prisons that de Milja knew about, all had failed. Then he understood: this was a committee at work, and if they assigned what was in effect a suicide mission, there was nothing Olenik could do about it.

"It's right away, then?" de Milja said.

Olenik spread his hands: *of course.*

That completed Major Olenik's work and he left the city by train the following evening. As a notional waterworks engineer, his papers allowed him to travel anywhere within German-occupied lands. He handed over to de Milja a group of code and contact procedures: ZWZ officers and operatives in the district were at his disposal. Explosives, weapons, whatever he needed was available.

De Milja returned to the forest, explaining to Razakavia what had to be done. The first step was to move the encampment, from huts in a clearing to an abandoned farm at the edge of a wood about ten miles from Rovno. The farm would serve as a reception base for the freed prisoners and some members of the attack commando. A doctor and nurse would set up an aid station at the farmhouse twenty-four hours before the attack.

Back in Rovno he made contact with a local ZWZ operative known as Vlach, a man in his late twenties, with tipped-up nose, carefully combed blond hair and a wise-guy curl to his lip. The ZWZ ran, in general, to more sober and stable personalities— Vlach had replaced one of those very gentlemen in late July. Had survived, had impressed Major Olenik; those were his credentials. At Vlach's suggestion they met in a tearoom in Rovno's central square, a very proper place, where German officials' wives and girlfriends could drink tea with extended pinkies and nibble at mounds of pale-green petits fours. "Ha ha," Vlach laughed. "Who would look for us here?"

Then he grew serious. "We can get you anything you like," he said. "Cars, trucks, you say what."

"How can you do that?"

"We all do the same thing here, everybody who you-know-what. See, the Luftwaffe and the panzer tanks, they can really do the job. Whatever the Russians had here is flat, gone. I never saw such a mess; staff cars on top of each other, railroad tracks peeled straight up into the air, airfields turned into junkyards. So now it's conquered, so now it all has to be rebuilt.

"So, just about the time the Wehrmacht shot the last sniper and hanged the last commissar, the big German construction companies came in. Ho, ho—Ve gonna make money now, Fritz! The military authority told them what they needed—airfields, barracks, airplane hangars, oil-storage tanks—exactly what they just finished blowing up. Plus, as long as they were at it, roads, which they never had here.

"So, the construction companies get all these contracts, but when they finished rubbing their hands and winking at each other, it begins to dawn on them that they're going to have to find somebody to do the work. Ah, not so easy. Can't bring in people from Germany, either they're building airplanes and submarines back in Essen, or they're shooting more Russians, six hundred miles east of here. See, when you shoot a Russian, somebody puts another one down, but they haven't figured that out yet.

"Anyhow, they're going to have to use local labor. We started by getting one guy hired. Every German's dream of what a Pole should be—cooperative, friendly, religious, trustworthy. A fifty-five-year-old man, a machinist all his life, Henryk. So all the Germans loved Henryk. They could count on him, he never drank, he never stole, he never answered back, and you said be at the job site at five-thirty in the morning, and there he was."

Vlach blew out his cheeks to make a fat German face. "'Henryk, mein friend, maybe you haff a cousin?'" Well, guess what, he does. He has also an uncle, an aunt, a long-lost friend, a nephew—that's me—and about eighteen more, one way and another. We go anywhere we like, we have company trucks, two Opel automobiles. If we want to carry something that's—unusual, you understand, we can request a Wehrmacht driver. When they're behind the wheel, nobody even pretends to look."

. . .

Respectable little man, tortoiseshell spectacles gave him a slight resemblance to the American comedian Harold Lloyd. Except that Harold Lloyd would have bought new glasses if he'd cracked a lens.

"The Russians put him in a camp in '39," Vlach said.

"How did you get out?" de Milja asked.

"I escaped," the man said.

He sat with de Milja and Vlach in the apartment, a map of Rovno unfolded on the kitchen table. "From the central telephone exchange, which is here, there are three lines that leave Rovno." He pointed, his hands cracked and peeling from working as a dishwasher in a restaurant. "The main line goes west, to Lutsk. Then we had a branch north, to Klesow, and one south, to Ostrog. From there a line went to Kiev—but it was often cut, or blocked. The Russians interfered any way they could."

"And the wireless telegraph—is that something you knew about?" The man had been the regional accounting supervisor for the telephone system before the war.

"There were five stations," he said.

"So if we disabled those, and cut the telephone lines—"

"They would use the military wireless. I don't think you can silence them, sir."

The prison guard had never liked his work. They paid him slave wages to sit on the lid of a garbage can, the way he saw it. But it was better than nothing, so he did what he had to do. A mean existence; everything had to be watched, saved, rationed: lightbulbs, soap, coal, meat. He'd never, not once, had a lot of something he liked. His kids were gone, had their own sorry lives. His wife was still with him, mostly the Church to thank for that, but whatever had once been inside her had died years ago. For himself, he sat in a bar after work and soaked up vodka until he was numb enough to go home. He would have liked, once he got older, to go back to the countryside where he'd been raised. Since the war you could buy a small farm, it didn't take much, just more than he'd ever had.

So when the offer came, he didn't say no. They'd probably watched him, the way he looked, the misery in his step. The old man who made the offer wasn't such a bad sort. Polish, with the sharp cheekbones like they had sometimes. And educated, maybe very educated. "You've had enough bad weather," the old man said. "Time to take a walk in the sunshine." Then he mentioned an amount of money, and the guard just nodded.

"You don't have to do anything," the old man said. "Just draw what's inside, the corridors and the offices and the cells, and show me how it's numbered."

"What's going to happen?"

"They don't tell me. It's the Russians gave me this job."

"Bandits. We have some of them locked up."

"Just draw and number."

"I'll take care of it at home," the guard said.

The old man put a sheet of paper and a pencil in front of him. "Why not right now? There's nobody here."

So the guard did it. And when his mind raced as he lay in bed that night—should he tell, could he sell the old man to the Germans, should he have demanded more money?—he realized that his childish drawing was as good as a signed confession. That scared him. So he hid the money under the mattress and kept quiet.

Vlach and de Milja shivered in the cold of the unheated garage. Outside the snow whispered down, the air frozen and still. Henryk was exactly as Vlach had described him, square-jawed and square-shouldered, sleeves and collar buttoned up. An honest man, not a crooked bone in his body. It just happened that he was a patriot, and the construction executives hadn't really thought that through.

Henryk was lying on his back under a large German truck,

working with a wrench. His face reddened as one of the rusty bolts refused to give, then squeaked, and turned. He pulled the muffler, laid it on the floor, and slid from beneath the truck, wiping his hands on a rag. "Start it up," he said.

De Milja climbed into the cab and turned the key. The roar was deafening, it shook the windowpanes in the garage. Vlach appeared at the truck window, hands pressed against his ears, and de Milja had to read his lips even though he appeared to be shouting. "Turn, that, fucking, thing, off."

In the silent apartment with the ticking clock, the sofas had been pushed back to the walls to make room on the floor. The doilies on the backs of the chairs were creased and stained where too many people had rested their heads, and the carpet, pale blue with a pattern of roses and vines, was also ruined, spotted with cosmoline and oil.

The armory was laid out on the rug: three Simonovs, three Russian PPD submachine guns—the pepecha, crude and lethal, named after the rhythm of its fire. Two German machine pistols, all-steel MP34s. Known as the Bergmann, the weapon had been manufactured outside German borders to evade the armament limits of the Treaty of Versailles. There were the two VIS automatics that accompanied de Milja from London, the ones with the Polish eagle on the slide, and four VIS automatics made since the German occupation—no eagle. There were two American Colt .45s. A Hungarian Gepisztoly 39M, a very fast machine pistol that fired Mauser Export cartridges. For hand grenades, they had the variety called Sidolowki—manufactured in clandestine ZWZ workshops and named after the cans of Sidol polish they resembled—logically, since the workshops were hidden in the Sidol factory.

The brothers were nineteen and seventeen, big and broad-shouldered and towheaded. They walked around Rovno all day looking for a candidate. They saw an SS major outside the movie theater—German romantic films and newsreels of the victorious Wehrmacht on the Russian front. An SS sergeant, extremely tall and thin, leaving a restaurant. Two SS corporals, ogling girls on the bridge over the small stream that ran through Rovno.

Then, late in the afternoon, they found another SS sergeant, of medium build, looking at the stills posted on the outside of the movie theater. After some consideration, he paid and went inside. They did too. He wandered down the aisle, they took seats near the back. Not much of an audience, mostly German soldiers on their off-duty hours. On the screen, a man in a tuxedo sitting in an elegant nightclub, speaking rapid German to a blond woman with tight curls and a black dress with a white bib collar. She looked down and bit her lip, he had smooth black hair and a thin mustache. The brothers didn't speak much German but they could tell the man was apologizing.

The woman wasn't really sure how she felt. She kept giving the man shy glances from beneath her dark eyelashes. *I'm supposed to love darling Helmut—what could be the matter with me?* is what she seemed to be saying to herself. Then, a commotion at the entrance to the room, where a maître d' stood guard over a velvet rope. A handsome fellow wearing a yachting cap wanted to go down the steps but the burly waiters wouldn't let him, and they struggled in front of some potted palms.

The SS sergeant came up the aisle and the older brother nudged the younger. They let some time lapse, then went into the men's room. The SS sergeant was buttoning his fly. Up close, he was bigger than they'd thought. He had several medals and ribbons, and a scar on his forehead, but the brothers were practiced and adept and they had him strangled in short order. They stripped off his uniform and left him on the floor with his mouth wide open against the stained tile, still wearing the old green tie they'd used.

. . .

The Czarny prison, on Zamkova Street. Quiet enough in the late afternoon. The weather had warmed up, leaving the cobbles awash in wet, dirty slush. The prison had been built in 1878, a series of courtyards behind a wall, ten feet high, with plaster peeling off the granite block. The neighborhood was deserted. Boarded-up clothing store, a burned-out tenement: people avoided Zamkova Street. De Milja walked along briskly, as though he had business nearby. The windows visible from the street were opaque green glass covered by steel mesh—*dungeon* was the word that came to mind. A sentry box with a big swastika flag stood to one side of the main gate. An old woman in black came through the door in the gate, pulling her shawl up over her head, then folding her arms around herself for warmth. A large brown truck with its canvas top closed in back came rumbling down the street and rolled to a stop in front of the sentry box. The driver joked with the guard. He was German, while the guard, they knew, was part of a Latvian SS unit used for duty outside the cell blocks. Day-to-day supervision inside the prison was managed by local Ukrainian warders.

"Hey, you, what are you staring at?"

De Milja turned to see who it was. Two Germans in black-and-silver uniforms. De Milja smiled hesitantly and started to move away when one of them kicked him in the back of the leg. He fell hard, comically, his feet flying up in the air, into the cold slush. The Germans laughed and walked off. De Milja got to his feet and limped in the opposite direction.

26 November, 4:30 P.M.

The assault commando gathered in the apartment. Group One had four men—de Milja, Vlach, and two he'd never met until that night; one with the nom de guerre *Kolya,* in his twenties, lean and hard-eyed, and the other called *Bron,* the armorer, heavier and older with a deceptively soft face. Group Two, six men, was led by a ZWZ officer who had parachuted into the

Lodz area in late October, formerly an officer in a special reconnaissance unit of the Polish army. He had a full beard and was known as Jan.

They all smoked nervously, looking at their watches, talking in low voices, going over the penciled maps of the prison again and again. Bron said, "I had better get busy," stood up and left the room. One of Jan's men was working the mechanism of a Bergmann machine pistol, the sound of the slide and lock, oiled steel on steel, cutting through the quiet voices. "Hey, Bron," the man called to the armorer.

Bron came out of the kitchen; he was wearing underpants, his bare legs red from the cold, had a cigarette stuck in the corner of his mouth, and was buttoning up an SS sergeant's tunic. "What is it?" he said.

The man worked the Bergmann bolt and said, "Is this right?"

"I had it apart this morning. It works."

The man tried it one last time, then laid the weapon across his knees. De Milja looked at his watch, the minute hand was where it had been the last time he'd looked. His side hurt from where he'd fallen in the street the day before. Strong, that German. They liked to kick, it added insult to injury, the way they saw it, and they were good at it, probably from all the soccer they played.

"So?" Vlach said, and raised his eyebrows. He smiled a wiseguy smile, but his face was very white.

"Eleven of," de Milja said.

Vlach didn't answer. Somebody was tapping his foot rhythmically against the leg of the sofa. Bron came back in the room. Now in SS uniform, he put out the stub of one cigarette and lit another. De Milja stood. "It's time to go," he said. "Good luck to you all." Two of the men crossed themselves. Jan adjusted a fedora in front of the hall mirror. De Milja opened the apartment door and the men flowed out quickly, automatic weapons held beneath overcoats, hats pulled down over their eyes.

One of the men in Jan's unit patted de Milja on the shoulder as he went past and said, "Good luck." A neighbor heard people in the hallway, opened his door a crack, then closed it quickly.

De Milja turned to look back into the dark apartment, then shut the door. On the doorframe was a pen-sized outline with two empty screw holes where something had been removed. De Milja knew that Jews often kept a metal device by their front doors, though he couldn't remember what it was called. The people who had lived in the apartment had apparently taken it off, thinking perhaps that nobody would notice the outline where it had once been fastened.

With Bron driving, they looked like three Gestapo executives with an SS chauffeur. The Opel turned into Zamkova Street, almost dark at 5:00 P.M., an hour before the Rovno curfew, a few people hurrying home with heads down. The second Opel and the truck, Jan's unit, continued on, heading for the entrance that led to the prison offices.

The first Opel pulled up to the sentry box. Bron opened the door, stood half in, half out of the front seat so the guard got a good look at the SS uniform. He started yelling orders in very fast German, angry and impatient and dangerous. The guard had seen such behavior before, and hastened to open the gate. The car shot through, then one of the civilians rolled out of the back and headed for the sentry box on the run. The guard was puzzled. The running man, Kolya, put an automatic pistol against his temple. "Hand over your weapon," he said.

The Latvian guard did as he was told. Kolya emptied the chamber and the magazine and returned the rifle. "Now stand guard, do everything as usual," he said, sitting down in the sentry box below the level of the window. He pressed the VIS against the base of the man's spine. "As usual," he said. The guard nodded.

The second Opel and the truck pulled into the street that ran perpendicular to Zamkova. Two ladders were taken from the truck and placed against the wall. The prison had been built to keep people from getting out—very little thought had been given to keeping them from getting in. As Jan's unit climbed the ladders, the truck was driven fifty yards farther down the street and parked, its engine idling loud enough to cover the sound of gunfire from behind the prison wall.

The street sentry box was visible from the interior guard station, so Bron drove the Opel at normal speed, then stopped and shouted angrily in German. The guard didn't understand what all the fuss was about. "What's the matter?" he asked the SS sergeant. Dimly, he could see two men in civilian suits in the car—that meant important security types. Evidently the poor bastard driving the car had been bullied by his superiors—but why take it out on him? The SS sergeant sputtered and turned red. The guard shrugged and opened the gate. The car sped through, one of the men in civilian clothes got out and ran toward him.

Not right.

He went for his rifle.

De Milja readied himself, his fist tight on the door handle. The Opel jerked to a stop, he shoved the back door open and jumped out. All he could see of the Latvian guard was a pale face in the darkness. The face seemed puzzled, and faintly offended. Three paces from the sentry box their eyes locked, and everyone knew everything. The guard reacted, snatched for a rifle in the sentry box. De Milja brought the VIS up and pulled the trigger as he ran. It bent the guard in two, arms folded across his stomach. De Milja moved around him, took a moment to steady his hand, then shot him four times in the side of the head. The man dropped to his knees, then pitched forward on his face.

De Milja ran back to the car and climbed in. "All right, go to the next gate."

Jan and three of his men climbed over the wall into the administrative courtyard of the prison. A trained commando, Jan had memorized every detail of the guard's sketch. He looked around the courtyard and saw that each doorway and gate was where the map had said it was. A young clerk coming down the stairway from the prison office dropped an armload of files when he saw the machine pistols and the men in the hats with the brims pulled down. He choked off a yell, threw his hands in the air, stood absolutely still.

Jan opened a door at the top of the stairs. There were three more clerks—the German warden and his German assistant had separate offices at the end of the room. "Raise your hands," Jan said. The clerks did as they were told. Two of Jan's men pulled the Germans from their office chairs and stood them against a wall. The warden had been a Nazi streetfighter in the 1930s and the Rovno prison was his reward for faithful service. He'd put on weight since those days, and wore a fine suit, but he met Jan's stare with defiance. "Are you Herr Kruger? The warden?" Jan asked.

"Yes."

"Please give me the keys to blocks four and six."

"I cannot."

Jan raised the machine pistol so Kruger could look down the barrel. Kruger closed his eyes, pressed his lips closed, and drew himself up to his full height. The Hungarian weapon fired a heavy, high-velocity bullet; the warden was thrown back against the wall so hard the plaster cracked, and he left a long red smear as he slid to the floor.

Jan turned the weapon toward the assistant warden. "Please give me the keys to blocks four and six," he said. The assistant trembled with fear but he would not give in. "Is that your answer?" Jan asked.

The man made a sound. Resistance? Assent? Jan shrugged and fired a long burst. The man screamed once before he died. One of the clerks yelled, "Here, here are keys. In this drawer. Take them, please."

In a room down the corridor, a clerk hid behind a bank of

filing cabinets. He heard gunfire, heard the assistant warden cry out, heard several minutes of silence, and carefully lifted the receiver off a telephone and held it to his ear, tapping the disconnect bar impatiently with his finger, but the line was dead.

A darkened courtyard bordered by cell blocks, cobblestones worn smooth by half a century of prisoners' felt slippers. At the center, an iron grating sparkling with frost. De Milja and Vlach ran across the courtyard, bent low to the ground. They reached an entry marked *South* in Cyrillic and used the arched doorway as cover. Czarny prison was silent, the inmates forbidden to talk, so they could hear the jangle of keys as warders moved along the corridors, the idling truck on the other side of the wall, the high-low sirens of German and Ukrainian police in the streets of Rovno. A voice called, another answered, a third laughed—guards on one of the cell blocks. Then footsteps, three or four running men, and Jan and two others came out of the darkness.

"Everybody all right?" de Milja whispered.

Jan nodded. "We shot the wardens."

"Keys?"

"Yes."

Jan was breathing hard, he rummaged through a ring of keys, peering at the stamped markings. He removed two keys and handed them to de Milja. "Block four," he said.

"Good. We go out as planned."

"No change. See you in better times."

"Yes. See you then," de Milja said.

De Milja turned the key and opened the grille that led to Block Four. It creaked when it opened, then clanged shut. A warder came around the corner and said, "Tomek?" Vlach had the machine pistol pressed against his chest before he knew what was happening. He gasped with surprise, dropped a wooden club with a clatter that echoed down the corridor. De Milja pulled the man's arms behind him and wound a piece of wire around his wrists. He'd thought at first that the warder was a fat man, but he wasn't. The muscles in his shoulders and back were massive, and the smell of him, like stale garlic, cut through the prison odor of open drains and crumbling stone.

"Prisoner Krewinski," Vlach whispered.

"Which?"

"Krewinski."

"Yes, wait. It's that corridor. Second to the last, on the left. You see, I don't give you a problem."

"On the floor," de Milja said.

The guard gave a nervous laugh, went to one knee, then both. "Like this? You see, sirs, no trouble from me."

De Milja pushed him over on his side and began wiring his ankles together. "Sirs?" The guard's voice was very high now. "You're going to let men out of these cells, don't leave me tied up here, I beg you."

De Milja didn't answer. He ripped the keys off the warder's belt, held them in front of the man's eyes, and began going through them. "Yes, there," the man said. He was fading now—drifting toward death before anyone touched him, de Milja could see it.

The prisoners, in cells lining the twilit corridor, came to their barred doors and watched with curiosity: two men with weapons, moving quickly. No uniforms, no warder. For the moment, de Milja and Vlach ignored them. In the second cell from the end on the left, a man sat on a bed—a wood frame suspended from the wall by two chains. He was tall and wiry, with a mournful face and hair shaved to a colorless stubble—a hard head and soft eyes. He was clean-shaven, but a cavalry mustache would not have been out of place. *Sergeant* Krewinski, de Milja now saw. The man stared at de Milja and Vlach without much interest, they were only the most recent in a long line of men with guns who'd come for him.

"Are you Sergeant Krewinski?"

"Yes," the man said—meaning *if you like*.

As the three left the cell block, the keys were passed to other prisoners. In Block Six, Jan and his group freed the two ZWZ officers, a group of Russian partisans, all the political prisoners, and the women in the adjoining wing. The pandemonium was just getting started when de Milja and Vlach and the sergeant reached the Opel. Ukrainian guards running for their lives, prisoners running out into the streets of Rovno. Some would escape, and police units would be busy for days. At the Zamkova Street intersection, they saw Jan's truck, rocking from side to side as it sped away from the prison.

The Opel wound through the back alleys of Rovno—there were sirens now, as the attack on Czarny prison began to draw in security elements. They first dropped Kolya at a hideout, a room above a pharmacy. Then Vlach, on the outskirts of the city, at a lumberyard. A few miles down the road, the Opel stopped at the edge of a small village. Bron tapped the horn three times and an ancient farm truck rolled out of a snow-covered lane. The driver of the truck joined Bron in the Opel, they waved good-bye, and drove off in the direction of Rovno. De Milja and the sergeant sat in the cab of the truck, changed into sheepskin jackets, old boots, and new identity papers.

They waited until dawn, then in first light headed for the Razakavia band in the farmhouse at the edge of the forest. De Milja never went more than twenty miles an hour—the tires were old and battered, the road ice over frozen mud, and patches of ground fog turned the windshield white. As they drove along, Krewinski told his story. "The NKVD sergeant, the man whose dog had been sick, he came to the wire one day and told me, 'You go to Moscow, to the training school, because if you stay here, well . . .' I understood what he meant. I never saw him again, but he saved my life. The major who had run my regiment was still in the camp at that time, and he told me how to go about it. He was a reserve officer, a chemist from Lodz, an important man.

"Well, it was just like he said it would be. I asked for a book about communism, and I read it and I discussed it with a guard. A political type called me into his office, and he gave me another book. That went on for a month or two, then they moved me to a separate part of the camp, and they left a gate open." Krewinski laughed. "I'd been told they would do that, and they did. I ignored it. Then, a week later, the provocateur. A little man that worked around the office. Came to me and said, 'I know your game. Let's you and me work together and get ourselves out of here.' "

"What did you do?"

"Went directly to the camp commandant and turned him in. And *that* really seemed to make a difference, that earned their trust. About two weeks later I went east.

"It was a kind of school. On Arbat Street, in an old mansion. And also at the university. A school for guerrilla fighting. Nothing like that in Poland—oh, maybe for officers, but not for an enlisted man like me. They had all kinds of people there, from everywhere in Europe—we could barely talk to one another. Estonians and Lithuanians and Hungarians, Frenchmen and Belgians. All kinds. They taught us how to blow up a train, how to ambush a column. But they also spent time on political matters—putting out a newspaper, and getting it into people's hands; by leaving it on trains, or mailing it to addresses in the phonebook. They taught assassination. How to force peasants to fight for you, how to infiltrate organizations. Then, in August, after the German attack on Russia, they dropped me by parachute into the Tsuman forest. I was to search out a certain band, and work to bring them under the control of the Znamensky Street center—the GRU—in Moscow."

"What happened?"

"I went home," Krewinski said. "It wasn't that simple or easy, and it took time and luck, but that's what I did."

They reached the farm at dusk, were given something to eat, the sergeant spent some time with his brother, then they were given blankets and taken to a hayloft on the second floor of an old stone stable. There they fell into a dead sleep, awakened at 5:00 A.M. when German antipartisan units and Ukrainian militia, acting on a tip from an informer, attacked the farm.

They got very close, killing the sentries silently as they came. Three hundred of them, Ukrainian militia led by a special SS unit—men imprisoned for poaching game in Germany recruited to hunt humans, partisans, in the forests of Poland.

It was a hand grenade that woke Captain de Milja.

It blew a hole in the corner of the stable and set the beams on fire. By the flickering light he saw militia running across a frozen pond. He kicked himself free of his blanket and ran to a window, Simonov in hand. Down below, on the ground floor of the stable, some of the partisans were shouting to one another, trying to organize a defense. But the guards out in the forest were lying in the leaves with their throats cut, and it was too late to organize much of anything.

The Germans had a heavy machine gun in the woods. They traversed window to window across the outbuildings, the main house, then the stable. Only Frantek's final cry alerted de Milja to the gunfire and he dove below the sill just as it reached him. He crawled over to help, but Frantek simply stared at him upside down, eyes wide, a look of indignation frozen on his face.

Sergeant Krewinski knew how to do these things. He waited until the machine gun moved to the next building, then fired a long burst at its muzzle flare with a machine pistol. This occasioned a change of gunners—a few moments of reorganization, but nothing more. By then, the fire in the beams had taken hold and it was getting hard to see, and to breathe, on the upper floor. One of the defenders from down below rushed halfway up the stairway, yelled something, then tumbled, dead weight, back down. A moment later a rifle was poked up from the stairs and fired blind. A partisan reached down and pulled it up, a very surprised Ukrainian hanging on the other end. The sergeant shot him. Then Krewinski and de Milja exchanged a certain look— *the time we always knew would come has come*—and led the others on the second floor in running down the open stairway. Nobody really wanted to burn to death in a stable. Krewinski was shot, but the impulse turned out to have been a good one. There were only five or six militia gathered at the foot of the stairway. Tri- umphant—blood on the walls, dead militia, dead partisans— but undermanned, a successful attack that had spent its strength en route.

Two Ukrainians leaped on de Milja—partisans taken alive were worth gold to the Germans. He fell over backward under the weight but had had the foresight to jump with a VIS in his hand, so he shot each one in the abdomen and they rolled off him in a hurry. He struggled to his feet, saw Krewinski stagger- ing around with blood on his shirt, grabbed him by the collar and pulled him outside.

Into a cloud of hot, black smoke from the burning farmhouse. They both went flat. The smoke made it hard to breathe, but it gave them a moment's camouflage, a moment to think. De Milja, VIS in one hand, Krewinski's collar in the other, decided to crawl into the farmhouse, hoping that Razakavia, or some- body, was holding out there.

It was deserted, except for Kotior. He had been wounded. Badly. He was sitting on a couch holding a light machine gun by its tripod, the feeder belt snaked around his shoulders, the bar- rel pointed at the front door. His face was white, he would not live much longer. "Out the back door," he said. "They have retreated."

"Good-bye, Kotior," de Milja said.

"Good-bye," Kotior said.

He dragged Krewinski toward the back door, was almost there when a shadow flew at him from behind an overturned table. He swung the VIS, then saw it was the Jewish woman who had given him coffee one morning when he'd first arrived in the forest. "I ask you to shoot me," she said formally.

He had no time to think about it. Krewinski's weight was beginning to pull hard, not a good sign. The woman put her hands on his forearm. "Please," she said. "I don't want to be tortured." She was right, the militia liked the screams of women. He pointed the VIS at her forehead, she looked at him, closed her eyes, then lifted her face.

But he couldn't. His hand would not kill her. "No," he said. "Come with me." He dragged Krewinski forward and she followed, holding on to his shirt in the billowing smoke.

The truck.

De Milja had driven it a little way into the forest the night before, now it saved their lives.

The starter failed, four or five times, then he forced himself to a slow and determined effort, pulled the choke out where it belonged, and babied the truck to life. It sputtered and coughed, but it did not die. It took all his strength to ease the big clutch up slowly enough not to stall the engine, his teeth ground with effort and concentration, but he did it. The truck crawled forward, slow but steady, moving down a narrow path into the forest. Branches broke off against the windshield, the wheels climbed over downed logs and rocky outcrops. Occasionally the tires spun on the ice, de Milja let some air out and that enabled them to grip better, somehow finding traction on the frozen earth.

He saw Razakavia once more.

A few miles west of the farmhouse the forest divided—low hills rising from either bank of a small river. De Milja took the right fork, then, an hour after sunrise, found himself on a section of road where foresters had long ago built a corduroy track of cut logs. He stopped the truck to let the engine cool down and there, three hundred yards away, his horse moving at a brisk walk along the bank of the frozen river, was Razakavia.

A scout, riding well in advance of the main party, disappeared into the trees as de Milja watched. The main body of riders was strung out a long way, some of them riding double, many of them slumped over, perhaps wounded, certainly exhausted. Razakavia rode at the front, his white hair and beard stark against the gray-green forest, a rifle slung across his back.

They stopped at midday. There was still gasoline in the truck, and the corduroy track had continued without interruption. Perhaps they had happened on one of the vast estates owned by the Polish nobility in the nineteenth century, the road maintained by the count's foresters for the use of wagons during the hunting season.

The woman he had saved had told him her name was Shura. She had, since they'd fled the burning farmhouse, tried to make Krewinski comfortable as best she could, but at last she said to de Milja, "I think now we must stop for a little time."

He knew what she meant, and turned off the engine. "Thank you," Krewinski whispered, grateful for a few moments of peace. The slow, jolting progress of the truck over the log road had been agony for him, though he had never once complained. When the ignition was turned off, the forest was immediately a very different place. Cold and clean, with a small wind; quiet except for the creak of frozen branches. With Shura's help he settled Krewinski on the matted pine needles beneath a tree and covered him with an old blanket they'd found on the seat of the truck. When Shura tucked the blanket beneath his chin Krewinski closed his eyes and smiled. "Much better," he said.

He went to sleep, and a half-hour later he was gone. There was no question of burial in the frozen ground, so they folded his hands on his chest and scratched his name on a rock and set it by his head as a gravestone.

Contrary to de Milja's fears, the truck started, and moved forward along the corduroy road. The loss of Krewinski hurt—a life that should have continued. And de Milja wondered at the cost of the rescue when he considered the result. Nonetheless, in its own terms, the operation had succeeded. Olenik had been specific: they wanted the sergeant, but, if that proved impossible, they wanted the sergeant's story. Well, that at least they would have, *if* he managed to get back to Warsaw. He was, he calculated, a hundred miles southeast of the town of Biala, and from there it was another hundred and twenty-five miles to Warsaw.

In a leather passport case he had two pairs of railroad tickets—for himself and Krewinski—along with the necessary documents for travel from the Rovno area to Biala, and from there on to Warsaw. His papers were good, and he had money in various forms. But he had no water, no food, and no gasoline. He had a pistol with three rounds, and no idea what he was going to do with the woman sitting next to him. He stared at her a moment. Wrapped in a long black coat and a black shawl, she sat up properly, back straight, bounced around by the motion of the truck.

Even wearing the shawl like a Ukrainian peasant—drawn across the brow so that it hid the hairline—she had a certain look; curved nose, dark eyes, thick eyebrows, and shadowy, somber skin. Someone who could have blended into the Byelorussian or Ukrainian population would not have been a problem, but Shura looked exactly like what she was, a Jew. And in that part of the world, people would see it. The forest bands preyed on Jews, especially on Jewish women. And the only alternative to the forest was a railway system crawling with

SS guards and Gestapo. De Milja knew they would demand papers at every stop.

"Shura," he said.

"Yes?" Her voice seemed resigned, she knew what this was about.

"What am I to do with you?"

"I do not know," she said.

"Do you have identity papers?"

"I burned them. Better to be a phantom than a Jew."

"A family?"

"They were forced into the ghetto, in Tarnopol. After that, I don't know. By accident I wasn't there the day the Germans came, and I fled to the forest with my cousin—he was seventeen. Razakavia agreed to take us in. I cooked, carried water, made myself useful any way I could. My cousin was killed a few weeks later, during an attack on a German train."

"I'm sorry," de Milja said. "And were you married, in Tarnopol?"

"No. And no prospects—though I suppose eventually something would have been arranged. They sent me away to study music when I was twelve years old. They thought I was a prodigy. But I wasn't. So then, I had to do something respectable, and I became a piano teacher. A bad piano teacher, I should add. Children mostly didn't like me, and I mostly didn't like them." They rode in silence for a time. "See?" she said. "I am everything you ever dreamed of."

She let him know, without saying it directly, that he could have her if he liked, she would not resist. But that wasn't what he wanted—a woman taken by some right of sanctuary. Still, by the time it was dark that night it was evident they they would have to sleep holding each other or die. They lay on the seat of the truck in each other's arms, the blanket wrapped around them, the windows closed tight and clouded over with their breath. Outside, the November moon—the hunter's moon—was full, a cold, pale light on the frozen river.

A clear night, the million stars were silver. She was warm to hold, her breath on his temple. When she dreamed, her hands moved. It brought him memories, the embrace with Shura. Long ago. The girls of his twenties. His wife. He missed love, he wondered if war had made it impossible for him. In the drift of his mind he paused on what it would be like to slide her skirt up to her waist. He sighed, shifted his weight, the springs creaked. Where the cold, sharp air touched his skin it actually hurt, and he pressed his face against her shoulder. Sometimes she slept, and sometimes he did.

The road ended.

They let the truck roll down the hill—a foot at a time, it took forever—and out onto the gray ice of the river. They managed five or six miles an hour that way, headed east of north by his calculations. They discovered a tiny settlement on the shore, pole-built docks coated with ice in the morning sun. They bought some black bread and salt from a woman who came down to the river to stare at them. From an old ferryman they bought a jar to melt ice in so they could have water. "Brzesc nad Bugiem" he said, pointing north. Brest Litovsk. He smiled and rubbed his whiskers. They were on, he told them, a tributary of the river Bug.

The gray clouds came in that afternoon and a white fog rose off the ice. Now they drove even slower, because it was hard to see. He worried about fuel, but the truck had a large tank, and a hundred miles wasn't too much to ask of it when they could only go a few miles an hour.

Then there were no more settlements. The rise of the hills above them grew steep, the woods thicker, no trails to be seen. And the river narrowed with every mile. Finally, when it was only ten feet wide, the ice changed. The truck wouldn't go anymore. The tires spun, the engine roared, and the back slid sideways, but that was all. Slipping on the ice, they tried to pile sticks beneath the back wheels. But the truck would not go forward. "So," Shura said. She meant it was finished, but she was glad they had tried it. What awaited them was at least peaceful, no more than going to sleep. He agreed. For him it was enough that somebody was there, that he would not have to be alone.

He turned off the ignition. The sky was fading above the hills, night was an hour away. It was colder now, much colder. They lay down on the seat and held each other beneath the worn blanket. "I am so cold," she said. The wind that night made it even colder, but the fog blew away, and a vast white moon rose above the hillside. A field of reeds sparkled with frost, and they saw a wolf, a gray shadow trotting along the river. It stopped and looked at them, then went on, pads silent on the ice. At last the world has frozen, he thought. A winter that would never end.

They tried in every way not to go to sleep, but they were very tired, and there was nothing more they could do. She fell asleep first, then him.

The truck stood silent on the ice. A few flakes of snow drifted down, then more. The cloud began to gather and the moon faded away until there was hardly any light at all. The snow fell heavier now, hissed down, a white blanket on the river, and the hills, and the truck.

He woke up suddenly. The window of the truck was opaque, and it was not so cold as it had been. He touched her, but she did not move. Then he held his hand against her face, and she stirred, actually managed a smile, putting her hand on top of his.

"We're going," he said.

She opened one eye.

He didn't move his hand. "Shura, look at the window," he said. "Sometimes you can't drive on ice. But you can drive on snow."

. . .

They drove through the war that night, but it didn't want them just then.

They saw panzer tanks and armored cars positioned on a bridge. An SS officer, a dark silhouette leaning on the railing, watched the truck as it passed beneath him, but nothing happened. A few miles north of there a village had been burned down, smoke still rising from the charred beams. And twice they heard gunfire, machine gun answering machine gun, tracer rounds in the darkness like sparks blown across the sky.

Sometimes the snow fell in squalls; swirling, windblown. Then it cleared, the clouds rolling east, the frozen river shimmering in the moonlight. De Milja drove with both hands gripping the wheel, coaxing the truck along the ice, riding the snow that gave them traction. Shura pointed out a small road that led up a hill from the river; perhaps an abandoned ferry crossing. De Milja stopped the truck and climbed the hill. He found a well-used dirt road and an ancient milestone that pointed the way to Biala.

It took a long time to get the truck off the river. De Milja and Shura knelt by the tires and studied the surface like engineers, finally building a track of branches to the edge of the shore. It worked. Engine whining, wheels spinning, the truck lurched, swayed sideways, then climbed.

Once on the upper road, de Milja let the engine idle while he got his breath back. "Where are we?" Shura asked.

"Not far from Biala. A few hours, if nothing goes wrong." He eased the clutch into first gear, moved off slowly on the rutted road.

Midnight passed, then 1:00 A.M. They drove through snow-covered forest, boughs heavy and white bent almost to the ground. Shura fell into an exhausted sleep, then woke suddenly as they bounced over a rock. "I'm sorry," she said. "I didn't mean to abandon you."

"I'm all right," de Milja said.

"I should have helped to keep you awake. I can sing something, if you like."

"You don't have to."

"I can discuss—oh, well certainly music. Chopin. Or Rachmaninoff."

The engine steamed as the truck climbed a long hill. At the crest, de Milja braked gently to a stop. They were on a wooded height above Biala. Directly below, a poor neighborhood at the edge of town. Crooked one-story houses, crooked dirt streets, white with frost. Wisps of wood smoke hung above the chimneys in the still air. De Milja drove the truck to the side of the road and turned off the ignition. "Now we wait for dawn, for the end of the curfew. Then we can go into the open-air market with the produce trucks from the countryside. Once we get there we can make contact with the local ZWZ unit—our luck, it's a good one. Very good. They'll move us the rest of the way, into Warsaw. In a freight train, maybe. Or hidden in a vegetable wagon."

They sat and stared out the window. It seemed very quiet with the engine off.

"Perhaps it would be best if I stayed here," Shura said.

"You know somebody here?"

"No."

"You wouldn't last long."

"No, probably not. But at least . . ."

"You'd have it over with?" De Milja shook his head angrily. "No, no. That isn't right. We'll hide you," he said. "Not in the ghetto—somewhere in Warsaw, one of the working-class neighborhoods. With friends of ours. It won't be easy, but if you're able to stay in the apartment, if you avoid people, in other words if you can live in hiding, you'll survive. You'll need some luck, but you'll see the end of the war."

"And you?"

"Me?" De Milja shrugged. "I have to keep fighting," he

said. "The Germans, the Russians. Perhaps both. Perhaps for years and years. But I might live through it, you never know. Somebody always seems to survive, no matter what happens. Perhaps it will be me."

He was silent for a time, staring at the sleeping town. "There was a moment, about a year ago. Someone I knew in Paris, 'Let's just go to Switzerland,' she said. I could have, maybe I should have, but I didn't. I missed my chance, but I don't really know why. I had a friend, a Russian, he had theories about these things—a world of bad people and good people, a war that never seems to end, you have to take sides. I don't know, maybe that's the way it is."

He paused, then smiled to himself. "Honestly, Shura, right now I will be happy when the sun comes up. The marketplace will be full of people—there'll be a fire in a barrel, a way to get a hot cup of coffee. It's possible!" he laughed.

"Hot coffee," Shura said.

"And some bread. Why not?"

They sat close together in the truck, trying to stay warm. He held her tightly, she pressed against his side. In time the darkness faded and the first sunlight hit the rooftops, a flock of pigeons flew up in the air, a dog barked, another answered.

Dark Star

Alan Furst

In the back alleys and glittering salons of night-time Europe, war is already underway as Soviet intelligence and the Nazi Gestapo confront each other in an intricate duel of espionage. On the front line is André Szara, a born survivor – of the Polish pogroms, the Stalinist purges and the Russian civil wars. His only goal is to keep going in a world where betrayal can come at any time. But slowly, inextricably, he is drawn into the dark intrigues of pre-war Europe where life is a grey uncertainty of cheap hotel rooms, love affairs that cannot last and friends who have ceased to exist. . .

'Outclasses any spy novel I have ever read.'
RICHARD CONDON, author of *The Manchurian Candidate*

'Imagine discovering an unscreened espionage thriller from the late 1930s, a classic black-and-white movie that captures the murky allegiances and moral ambiguity of Europe on the brink of war . . . Nothing can be like watching *Casablanca* for the first time, but Furst comes closer than anyone has in years.'   *Time*

'To call *Dark Star* a classic spy story – which it is – is to do less than justice to Alan Furst's gifts. He writes with restraint, yet brings to life better than most historians the world of fear in which so many human beings felt trapped.'
ALAN BULLOCK, author of *Hitler and Stalin*

'Alan Furst creates moods, nuances and subtleties with the skill of Eric Ambler and John le Carré.'   NELSON DEMILLE

'A jewel – a gripping thriller which is also a novel of quality and a fascinating history lesson.'   *Daily Mail*

'Espionage oozing from every shadow – writing of a high calibre.'
Sunday Express

ISBN 0 586 21318 X

Night Soldiers

Alan Furst

In Bulgaria in 1934 nineteen-year-old Khristo Stoianev sees his brother kicked to death by a gang of strutting thugs. Realising the growing menace of Fascism, he takes a risk on the promise of Communism and flees to Moscow, where he is trained as an agent of the NKVD, precursor of the KGB, and forms a close bond with a group of fellow students. His first mission is to Catalonia, where he is soon caught up in the bloody horrors of the Spanish Civil War. Then he learns that he is about to become the victim of one of Stalin's purges, and is forced to flee once again, this time to Paris. . .

'Furst's intelligent, ambitious, absorbing novel charges along from the rise of Fascism in Bulgaria, to Spain during the Civil War, to France and back to Eastern Europe as World War II draws to an end. The history is deftly incorporated; the viewpoint civilized; the characters and the settings picturesque; the adventures exciting; the writing pungent.'   *New York Times*

'Captures with exceptional fidelity and remarkable descriptive powers the shifting political and national loyalties that marked European life in the decade leading up to and including World War II. The idea of portraying the beginnings of the Cold War in the rubble of 1945 Eastern Europe is ingenious. Best of all is the chilling trail of treachery and betrayal, as the Russian Revolution – in the guise of the NKVD – devours its adherents.'

Washington Post

'*Night Soldiers* has everything the best thrillers offer – excitement, intrigue, romance – plus grown-up writing, characters that matter, and a crisp, carefully researched portrait of the period in which our own postwar world was shaped.'   *USA Today*

'Intelligent and absorbing . . . an unusual viewpoint, solid research and unobtrusively elegant writing make this pure pleasure to read.'   *Kirkus Reviews*

ISBN 0 586 21776 2

Alan Furst

☐ NIGHT SOLDIERS	0 586 21776 2	£5.99
☐ DARK STAR	0 586 21318 X	£4.99
☐ THE POLISH OFFICER	0 00 649356 4	£4.99

All these HarperCollins paperbacks are available from your local book-seller or can be ordered direct from the publishers.
To order direct just tick the titles you want and fill in the form below:

Name: _____

Address: _____

_____

Postcode: _____

Send to HarperCollins Paperbacks Mail Order, Dept 8, HarperCollins
Publishers, Westerhill Road, Bishopbriggs, Glasgow G64 2QT.
Please enclose a cheque or postal order or your authority to debit your
Visa/Access account –

Credit card no: _____

Expiry date: _____

Signature: _____

to the value of the cover price plus:
UK & BFPO: Add £1.00 for the first book and 25p for each additional
book ordered.
Overseas orders including Eire, please add £2.95 service charge.
Books will be sent by surface mail but quotes for airmail despatches will
be given on request.

**24 HOUR TELEPHONE ORDERING SERVICE FOR
ACCESS/VISA CARDHOLDERS –
TEL: GLASGOW 0141 772 2281 or LONDON 0181 307 4052**